PENANCE

by the same author

BOY PARTS

PENANCE

———

ELIZA CLARK

faber

First published in the UK in 2023
by Faber & Faber Limited
The Bindery, 51 Hatton Garden
London EC1N 8HN

Typeset by Faber & Faber Limited
Printed in England by CPI Group (UK) Ltd, Croydon, CR0 4YY

*This book is a work of fiction. Any references to historical events,
real people, or real places are used fictitiously. All other characters,
places, and situations are a product of the author's imagination*

Every effort has been made to trace copyright holders and to obtain permission
for the use of copyright material. The publisher would be pleased to rectify any
omissions that are brought to its attention at the earliest opportunity.

A CIP record for this book
is available from the British Library

ISBN 978-0-571-37176-1

MIX
Paper | Supporting
responsible forestry
FSC
www.fsc.org
FSC® C171272

Printed and bound in the UK on FSC® certified paper in line with our continuing
commitment to ethical business practices, sustainability and the environment.
For further information see faber.co.uk/environmental-policy

4 6 8 10 9 7 5 3

For George,
forever and everywhere.

But mostly they were lies I told; it wasn't my fault,
I couldn't remember, because it was as though I'd been to
one of those supernatural castles visited by characters in
legends: once away, you do not remember, all that is left is
the ghostly echo of haunting wonder.

TRUMAN CAPOTE

This book is an examination of the 2016 murder of teenager Joan Wilson by three girls attending the same high school. It was written by journalist Alec Z. Carelli and first published in March of 2022.

Shortly after publication, several of Carelli's interviewees publicly accused Carelli of misrepresenting and even fabricating some of the content of their interviews.

Following these accusations, it was discovered that therapeutic writing produced by two of the three offenders while incarcerated was illegally acquired by Carelli.

The book was pulled from shelves by the original publisher in September of 2022.

Now republished after the conclusion of relevant litigation, some names have been changed at the request of those involved.

We believe writers (even writers of non-fiction) have a right to express themselves and tell stories in the manner they feel best fits the story in question.

It is our fundamental belief that readers have the freedom and the right to read and judge a text for themselves – that contentious works with artistic merit should not be erased from history simply for causing offence. Despite the controversy attached to this book, we have chosen to republish it in its original form.

Extract: *I Peed On Your Grave*, Episode 341, 01/07/2018

Hosts: Steven Doyle, Andrew Koontz, Lloyd Alan
00:00:31–00:02:46

DOYLE: Hey and welcome to *I Peed on Your Grave*, a true-crime podcast. I'm Stevie Doyle and with me as always is . . .

KOONTZ: Me, big Andy Koontz.

ALAN: And me, Lloyd Alan.

DOYLE: And today we'll be taking a trip to merry old England.

KOONTZ: Oh! [*in a cockney accent*] A little trip to England is it?

ALAN: God not the accents.

KOONTZ: [*in a cockney accent*] What accent, mister, I'm just a lezzy English schoolgirl, aren't I?

DOYLE: [*laughing*] Andy, no.

KOONTZ: [*in a cockney accent*] I'm a lesbian schoolgirl and I'm not wearing any knickers, aren't I?

DOYLE: [*laughing*] Andy, dude.

KOONTZ: [*in a cockney accent*] Don't like my accent, mister? The last girly who made me angry got set on fire, mister, didn't she?

ALAN: Oh, man, is that a spoiler?

DOYLE: No, luckily that's my starting point.

KOONTZ: [*in a cockney accent*] Glad you didn't have to punish me for spoiling the episode, mister . . .

ALAN: Okay, dude, these chicks were like fourteen.

DOYLE: They were more like sixteen, actually.

KOONTZ: Well in England that's kosher, right? I can be as weird and horny as I want.

DOYLE: [*laughing*] I mean, I guess.

KOONTZ: [*in a cockney accent*] Me knickers are staying off, mister . . . [*ceasing accent*] I'll stop. Most of these chicks are not hot.

DOYLE: No, they're pretty fucking gross.

KOONTZ: That Doris chick, though.

ALAN: Doris?

DOYLE: Doris? Doris? What year do you think England is in, dude?

KOONTZ: [*in a cockney accent*] It's 1843, mister! [*laughing, no longer using accent*] Well whatever, Dolly, Doris, she's kind of smoking hot.

ALAN: She's older though, yeah?

KOONTZ: What would you say if I was like, 'No, dude, she's the youngest.'

ALAN: Is she?

DOYLE: No, she's the hot one.

[*all laugh*]

KOONTZ: The hottest chicks are always insane. I'm not saying all hot chicks are crazy because we respect hot chicks on this podcast, but I am saying that the *hottest* chicks are crazy.

DOYLE: The craziness usually makes them extra-hot. We respect crazy chicks too.

KOONTZ: Yeah, really takes them to the next level. It's not sexist – I love crazy hot chicks. I would let Hot Doris set me on fire.

4

[*all laugh*]

ALAN: Oh my God.

DOYLE: Can I please start the episode?

KOONTZ: Go ahead, go ahead, sorry. I'll just be jacking off over here while you read your intro.

[*all laugh*]

DOYLE: Okay, so this is a pretty new case – kind of obscure for us but it's so fucking interesting, dudes. Today we're looking at the murder of Joan Wilson, a sixteen-year-old girl in England who was set on fire by her friends in 2016.

ALAN: What the fuck.

DOYLE: Yep! Other schoolgirls. All like sixteen, seventeen.

ALAN: No way. How the fuck didn't we hear about this?

DOYLE: *Totally* buried by Brexit, man. They literally killed her the night of their fucking Brexit election thing. In fact, I think we're pretty much the first people to cover this. I could not find *anything* about this case.

KOONTZ: Is this an exclusive scoop?

DOYLE: I mean, more or less? There was local coverage, but I basically just heard about this because a wonderful listener – who wanted to remain anonymous – sent us this crazy detailed uh . . . DethJournal post about the case – which included archives of the murderers' blogs, which a bunch of the fucking creepy true-crime Tumblr girls saved. They may or may not be the OP, I don't know, but thank you, anonymous listener!

ALAN: I hate that I know what DethJournal is.

KOONTZ: No fucking way, dude – so this is kinda hot off the press, huh?

5

DOYLE: Totally. I think we've got a flaming-hot potato on
our hands here. Maybe that was a poor choice of words.
[*all laugh*]

Do you know what happened to her already? Did you catch it in the papers? Are you local? Did you know her? Did you see it on the internet? Did some website that trawls local news for the worst details of 'true crimes' bring her to your attention? Did you see the article about her, buried in the chumbox of an already disreputable website? Did you see the red-headed, stock-image model juxtaposed against an edited, charred corpse captioned: 'You Won't Believe What They Did to Her'? Did you listen to a podcast? Did the hosts make jokes? Do you have a dark sense of humour? Did that make it okay? Or were they sensitive about it? Did they coo in the right places? Did they give you a content warning? Did you skip ahead?

Did you see pictures?

Did you look for them?

*

At around 4:30 a.m., on 23 June 2016, sixteen-year-old Joan Wilson was doused in petrol and set on fire after enduring several hours of torture in a small beach chalet. Her assailants were three other teenaged girls – all four girls attended the same high school.

The crime took place in Joan's hometown of Crow-on-Sea in North Yorkshire. The seaside town sits between Scarborough and Whitby, protruding from the east coast of England like a small finger reaching for the continent. It has a beach to the north and a beach to the south.

The North Beach is loud. Brightly coloured amusement arcades, donkey rides, gift shops and a small funfair mean it is favoured by tourists and families. The South Beach is classier. You'll find nice restaurants and little artisan shops overlooked by the ruins of Crow-on-Sea Castle.

Both beaches are rimmed by rainbows of pretty, pastel-coloured beach chalets. The North Beach chalets are council owned and accessibly priced. Most families in Crow could afford to rent a chalet on the North Beach – at least as a treat. The South Beach chalets are modern, privately owned and pricey. Joan died on the South Beach.

During 2015 and 2016 both the northern and southern chalets had been the targets of a spate of arsons and, as a result, the few witnesses who saw the smoke did not inform the authorities. It was a tiny fire, and Crow's emergency services had dubbed the chalet burnings 'a waste of [their] time' in a 2015 local news report.

A beach chalet on fire was nothing to bat an eye at. Neither was a car occupied by three teenaged girls speeding around the empty streets at half past four in the morning. The kids in Crow were bored – minor acts of teen delinquency were a fact of life.

The assailants were dubbed Girls A, B and C until their identities were leaked by the local newspaper. Girl C (the oldest) drove, Girl A sat in the front and Girl B in the back. Their accounts of the mood in the car vary. Their accounts of everything vary. They do not agree whose *idea* it was to hurt Joan, who 'started it' on the night, or who among them set the fire. Girl A blames Girl C and vice versa. Girl B had been waiting in the car. She had not laid a hand on Joan and spent the night walking back and forth from the beach to the car in a state of shock and confusion. She claimed she tried to encourage the other girls to stop their assault. The other girls do not agree on this – Girls A and C say the fire was Girl B's idea.

Some things are clear, at least. The timeline is more or less undisputed. After the girls set the fire, they ran from the South Beach up a concrete staircase to Girl C's vehicle, a Fiat 500 stolen from her older sister. Girl C had been taking driving lessons on and off for a year. She had failed a driving test in January and then again in March. She was due to retake it again in a few weeks. She regularly borrowed her sister's car but had taken it without permission that evening.

The trio drove to the nearest twenty-four-hour McDonald's – a motorway service station a thirty-minute drive west. In the car, Girl A said she hoped Joan would burn up with the chalet, so the police would not see the other injuries. She hoped they might blame Joan for the chalet burnings. It would be a death by misadventure. Joan Wilson would be remembered as a teen arsonist, tragically killed by her own bizarre hobby.

But Joan Wilson did not die.

The small fire the girls set went out very quickly. Damage to the chalet itself was minimal. The petrol they'd poured over Joan was the dregs of a can kept in the car for emergencies. It burned away Joan's clothes, it caught the floor around her. It burned her face beyond recognition, and her body beyond the point she was likely to survive her injuries. But it burned out.

The girls underestimated how difficult it would be to burn a body. Like most things in life, corpse disposal is not as easy as it appears in the movies. I say corpse disposal because they thought Joan was dead. They thought they had already killed her. The fire was not to make Joan's death as painful as possible: it was a panicked bid to cover up a 'prank gone wrong'.

What was the 'prank'?

Hours earlier, Joan had been bundled into the car. Girls A, B and C disposed of her phone and bound her hands. They threw a brick at her when she tried to escape. They locked her in a beach chalet Girl A's father owned. Girl C took a photo of Joan and posted it to Tumblr.

Despite her harrowing night and the numerous head injuries she sustained, Joan was still alive when they set the fire and, at some point, regained consciousness.

It is likely that both Joan and the chalet were still on fire when she crawled onto the beach. She was covered in sand, and doctors speculated she may have rolled around to extinguish the flames.

Bolstered by adrenalin, Joan was able to get to her feet. The human body is capable of miraculous feats in moments like this. She scrambled up a concrete staircase to the street, leaving bloody footprints behind her. She was naked. She staggered down the road looking for help. Barefoot and bare-bodied, she walked. She was caked in sand. She was caught on CCTV weakly banging on the doors of B&Bs and seaside holiday homes with her raw hands before finding an open hotel door. She woke the receptionist.

Then nineteen, asleep at her desk, Lucy Barrow thought she must be having a nightmare. She rang 999, hoping she was dreaming. When asked by the call-taker if Joan's burns were 'larger than the palm of your hand', Lucy replied: 'She's completely burned, she's raw, she's completely raw; I can actually smell her and I'm standing well away from her.'

Lucy told Joan there would be an ambulance there in five minutes, and Joan asked for water. She could speak, but she was hard to understand. Her voice was rough and dry. Her lips had burned away. She asked for water, over and over again.

She could not hold the glass herself, so Lucy fed her a pint of water. She did this against the advice of emergency medical dispatcher Eve Wells, who had told Lucy not to touch Joan – not to go near her. With such severe burns, the risk of infection was high and deadly.

Eve had had a quiet night. She worked at the ambulance service's North Yorkshire control room, just outside of York. A veteran call-taker, Eve says this was one of the most unnerving calls she had ever taken. Eve has talked frantic parents through performing CPR on their babies, she has spoken to spouses immediately following the murder of their partners, she has heard people die on the phone. Spared no exposure to intimate violence, freak accidents and grisly deaths, Eve still counts Lucy's call among the eeriest she has heard. 'I can actually smell her' sent a chill up her spine.

Burns were not something she dealt with often – when she did, they were the products of accidents which were industrial, culinary and recreational. Never deliberate. Eve (placed on speaker) had asked Joan if she'd had an accident. And Joan said no. Her voice was thin. Lucy relayed her answers. Did she do this to herself? *No.* Did someone else do it to her? *Yeah.*

The police arrived before the ambulance. Eve had Lucy pass the phone to an officer. She didn't want them to barge into the small reception area – to bring in germs or touch the patient or try to cover her body with a blanket. If the burns were even a fraction as extensive as Lucy had said, Joan would be extremely vulnerable to infection.

Eve asked that the police keep their distance from Joan – she told them not to enter the room, to follow the ambulance and to save any questions till Joan had arrived at the hospital. They followed some of the instructions they were given. Officers on the scene kept their distance and refrained from touching Joan, but they did enter the hotel and they did ask her questions. *Did someone do this to you? Are they nearby?* Joan nodded to these questions, no longer trying to speak. The ambulance took ten minutes to arrive.

Joan seemed to become more lucid once she was in the ambulance. Paramedic Dave Fisher asked for her name and age (which she gave: Joan Wilson, sixteen) then asked if she'd been in a fire. Did she get in an accident? Sometimes teenagers made bonfires on the beaches – maybe she fell in one, drunk or on drugs. Maybe her friends panicked and scattered and left her. He'd treated a burn victim around her age a few months prior; the girl had been playing a game with friends, drunk on the beach. They were jumping over a small campfire, and this girl's tracksuit bottoms had caught. Dave hoped it was something like that.

Dave asked: *was this an accident?* It wasn't.

She named her attackers. She repeated their names thrice to Dave, who had no paper, and wrote the names on the inside of his arm with a ballpoint pen.

The first girl she named became A, the second B and the third C.

Joan then asked for her mother and lost consciousness. She would never wake back up.

Girls A, B and C arrived too early at McDonald's for the breakfast they'd hoped for. They ordered three large portions of fries, a Diet Coke, a Fanta and a vanilla milkshake. They ordered a plain Hamburger, a twenty-piece Chicken McNugget box, a McChicken Sandwich and a Big Mac.

Girl A put the McChicken Sandwich into the Big Mac, and told the other girls she'd made a 'McGangBang'. Girl B, of the plain Hamburger, talked at length in her police interview about how disgusting it was to watch, to smell, to listen to.

Girl C dipped her fries and Chicken McNuggets into the milkshake.

Girl A said that the half-eaten McGangBang (in its mess of mayo-smothered lettuce, the added ketchup, the chewed-up meat) looked like Joan's body. This was made much of at trial. They had all laughed, hysterically. They were wild, and unrestrained, full of caffeine and sugar and adrenalin. They howled, banging their hands on the table, spraying cola from their noses. Girl B said they were delirious, hysterical, unable to fully comprehend the enormity and permanence of what they had done. Girl A still seemed amused by the joke at trial. Girl C claimed she could not remember any of this.

Joan's mother, Amanda Wilson, arrived at the hospital in a dressing gown and slippers. Freddy Wilson worked on an oil rig; it would take him a further sixteen hours to arrive back home. Amanda was, initially, unable to positively identify her daughter. Her raw, red face was almost featureless. Joan's hair had been cut prior to the fire and what was left had burned away. It was estimated that burns covered 80% of her body. Amanda had to look at Joan's teeth. Joan had a chip in her left incisor, which was usually covered with a temporary plastic cap. The cap had been knocked from Joan's tooth, and Amanda was able to confirm a match. Then Amanda noticed the girl's little fingernail. It was painted blue – the shade matched the blue nail varnish that she had last seen Joan wearing: Blueberry Muffin by Barry M. She positively identified Joan, and vomited in the hallway of the hospital, unable to make it to the bathroom.

Girl B had also vomited, in the bathroom of the service station. Girls A, B and C left the McDonald's around the same time that Joan arrived at the hospital. They left a mess. The staff later described them as loud, disrespectful and in high spirits. Ann Brown, the member of staff who served them, said she thought the girls had been drinking at the beach and possibly taking drugs. They were dishevelled and covered in sand.

Girl C dropped off Girl A then Girl B. Girl A lived slightly outside of Crow, the closest to the service station. Girl B lived around the corner from Girl C.

Girl A fell asleep on the sofa as soon as she arrived home. She was asleep for around twenty minutes before the police arrived. She answered the door while her father slept. At first she was belligerent and calm, but according to officers she 'turned her tears on like a tap' when her father appeared. Her father had only just gotten home himself, still inebriated from celebrating the result of the EU referendum. He threatened to sue them for police brutality when they handcuffed his daughter and led her to the car.

When Girl B made it home, she did not fall asleep. Girl B began to sob and paced the ground floor of the small house she shared with her mother and her mother's partner. She broke a vase. Her mother found her dialling the landline, then hanging it up. Dialling the landline, hanging it up. Girl B and her mother had an extended argument, which eventually led to a half-confession. As officers were knocking on the door of an entirely innocent 'Girl D', Girl B's mother was driving her to the police station.

The erroneously labelled 'Girl D' was an associate of the killers (and the victim) but had absolutely nothing to do with the murder. Girl D was not named by Joan Wilson, but she had the misfortune of being both Girl C's (very recent) ex-girlfriend and from a family known locally to be 'dodgy' ('dodgy' being the word used by police in court when asked to explain their arrest). Girl D herself was not known to the police but her brother was, and so were members of her extended family.

Girl D's mother was very confused when she answered the door to three male police officers. She struggled to contain the small band of rescue greyhounds who had begun barking and panicking at the sight of the police. None of the greyhounds were tolerant of strangers. Mum asked to see 'a warrant' like they were on television. The police pushed past her, and she lost her grip on the collar of her most unpredictable and excitable greyhound. The dogs were especially nervous around men – and were therefore apoplectic at the sight of strange men, shouting and pushing their owner. Most of the dogs were meek by nature, merely barking and howling in bewilderment and distress, but the particularly unpredictable dog bit an officer. The dog was tasered, and later died.

Girl D's mother thought they were here for her son, who she said was asleep and – if they could just give her a minute to shut the dogs up – she would go and get him. But they were after her daughter. She was stunned. She told them her daughter had been in all night – there was CCTV near their house, they could check. But the police ignored this and barged their way upstairs.

Girl D was dragged out of bed. Confused and sobbing, she would be interrogated for almost twenty-four hours before police confirmed that she'd been at home in bed all night and released her. Her photograph was nonetheless taken and later released by the local paper, the *Post-on-Sea*.

After dropping off Girl B, Girl C drove around the estate in circles then headed back to the motorway.

The sister had woken up very early that day for work and was furious to find her car gone. She'd walked to her mother's house 'absolutely fuming' and after her sister's blood. By this point, Girls A and B had already told the police that C was the ringleader. The police were hung up on 'Girl D' – which confused A and B and slowed the progress of the interrogation.

Girl C's mother was making coffee, while the older sister attempted to call C's mobile phone. Her stepfather was calling the police station when officers arrived at their home.

It took several hours for the authorities to locate Girl C. She had pulled over in a lay-by on the motorway and fallen asleep at the wheel.

Confessions were quick, but the story was messy. There was no doubt they were guilty – but the *who*, *what*, *why* and *how* of the attack was complicated. Girls A, B and C gave childish reasons, excuses and bizarre mystical justifications (while a bewildered and distraught Girl D begged to be taken home). They variously painted one another as psychopaths, torturers,

16

violent morons, evil geniuses, weak-minded followers, miniature cult leaders and petty bullies. They gave the officers wild, elaborate backstories which began in primary school.

'It was like having a nightmare about being back in school,' one detective said in court. 'We couldn't follow it.'

Joan died three days after her ordeal. The story of her murder gained little traction in the mainstream media due to its proximity to the UK's EU referendum vote. Brexit dominated the news for weeks, and nothing about Joan Wilson's murder was narratively useful for Britain's majority right-leaning press. All the girls involved were white and British. They were mostly from very average socio-economic backgrounds – though Girl A came from a wealthy family, well known locally. Girl A's father was a right-wing 'politician', a rent-a-gob. It is possible that the papers that had given the father column inches made an intentional effort not to highlight the fact his daughter was a vicious, murdering bully.

Crow voted Leave – and that had nothing to do with the murder. There was nothing to be gained from reporting on this story. There were no grooming gangs or immigrants to blame, no vicious foreign teens. Just four white British girls, in an overwhelmingly white British seaside town in decline.

All three girls (as well as 'Girl D') quickly had their identities revealed by the *Post-on-Sea*. There were, apparently, misunderstandings around some of the girls' ages; it was thought Girl C and Girl D were eighteen, not seventeen. It was assumed that Girl A's marginally famous father made her a public figure. There was no justification for leaking Girl B's name.

I toyed with using pseudonyms for them, but Girls A and

B have now left the detention system and have each received brand-new identities. C has an adult sentence to serve; when (if) she eventually re-enters society, she will certainly require a new identity as well. Their original names are out there – so I've stuck with them. I spoke to Girl D, and she's happy to be named. She wants it to be clear she had nothing to do with this.

Girl D, our innocent collateral damage, is Jayde Spencer. A generation prior, her family were deeply involved in local organised crime. Now, they simply run a bookmakers and carry an unjustified reputation.

Angelica Stirling-Stewart is Girl A. By virtue of her family, her name is baked into the foundations of Crow-on-Sea. It would be hard to paint a full picture of her without using her name. Her father is a local businessman, author, and had recently made an obnoxious foray into right-wing politics. She was a spoiled brat and had been something of a bully in primary school. In high school, the tables turned for her – she was thought to be rather odd and had become the butt of a joke she was not party to. She was part of Joan's friendship group at school though by all reports, the two never got along.

Violet Hubbard is our Girl B. Quiet, and a good student, her mother is a social worker, her father a civil servant living in London. Violet had been Joan's friend throughout primary school. Though they had recently drifted apart they maintained a text correspondence. Most of Violet's life was online. She had no 'IRL' friends before meeting Girl C, was painfully shy, and struggled with anxiety and depression.

Our ringleader, Girl C, is Dorothy 'Dolly' Hart – a girl who moved in with her mother and stepfather around a year and a half before the incident.

Her biological father had died five years prior to the incident, and she had chosen to live with her grandmother following his death, where her half-sister (Heather) had opted to live with their mother. When her behaviour became too erratic for the elderly grandmother to handle, she moved to Crow.

Dolly was, according to teachers, a 'glamorous, charismatic troublemaker'. She was very pretty and initially popular – but she made up rumours, she stole boyfriends and she picked physical fights over nothing. She was unpredictable and cruel, and her name was mud within a month of her arrival at her new school. Dolly struggled to stabilise in her new home and her significant mental health issues were allowed to fester.

Through circumstance the girls found one another. They spent the better part of the year leading up to the murder becoming more and more invested in a bizarre fantasy world – a little religion, fed by each girl's individual obsessions and furies. Joan Wilson became a target for them. For things she had done, and for things the girls imagined she would do.

They were playing pretend. And then they were not.

I came across the case in the 'chumbox' section of a particularly trashy true-crime news website, one which aggregated the most depraved, grotesque stories from all over the world into one place.

Depraved and grotesque was exactly what I was looking for; my last two books had not sold well.

For those of you unfamiliar with my work, I used to be a journalist; I reported on major British crimes for now-defunct tabloid *Polaris*.[1] I was implicated in the News International phone-hacking scandal (despite not being employed by News International) and I was sacked. But I was quite well off and had enough connections that it did not particularly matter. Bigger names went down in that scandal; people are often surprised to hear I was involved at all. At the time my reputation was *tarnished* but this was not the end of the world – it had never been particularly stellar.

So, I decided to write books instead. I wrote two very popular books: *How Could She?*, on the case of killer couple Raymond and Kathleen Skelton, and *Into the Ether*, on the strange disappearance of schoolgirl Molly Lambert – both of which I had covered for *Polaris*.

My latest book, *My Life in Crime*, was published in 2013. The book was part memoir, part true crime. I wrote about the most famous cases I had covered and I wasted a lot of my best material in it. I could've gotten three books out of it, if I'd more liberally stretched some of the material. I also talked about myself far too much, apparently.

1 *Polaris* (1947–2015) was one of Britain's only left-leaning tabloid papers. It printed its last edition in May 2015.

It was called 'self-indulgent' and 'un-insightful' in the press – and I was criticised for reusing material from *How Could She?* and *Into the Ether*, which readers were encouraged to read instead. It did not sell well, but it did not flop as badly as my next book.

The true crime boom began in 2013. And while *Serial* and *Making a Murder* were achieving cultural dominance, I was languishing bitterly in *My Life in Crime*'s relative failure. It felt unfair that I hadn't immediately benefitted from this true-crime explosion – I'd been doing this for decades, hadn't I?

Then my first two books began to experience an uptick in sales after continually being referenced on popular podcasts and appearing on lists like *Twenty Books to Read if You Can't Get Enough of* Serial or *Essential True Crime for Podcast Addicts*. I had earned a second chance and was offered another book by my old publisher in early 2016.

Because I had used my 'best' material in *My Life in Crime*, I had to find something new. I spent the next eighteen months writing a book about a serial rapist. A woman, a teacher, an abuser of boys. It was called *In the Spider's Web* and it was published in late 2017. I thought it was rather good. And, unlike *My Life in Crime*, it reviewed well. But no one read it. The case did not catch the public's attention. I went on a few podcasts, I had a couple of big press interviews, but I was mostly asked about my previous books. It did not launch me as the *true-crime guy* I had hoped it might. Offers were not rolling in. My publishers were not interested in another book from me.

In 2018, I had an embarrassing argument with a popular podcaster on Twitter. I bemoaned how distasteful his podcast was, and he replied with a series of screenshots of old articles about the phone-hacking scandal by way of a counter-argument. It went viral and I was 'dragged' far and wide by self-righteous zoomers, my fellow 'blue ticks' and other people in the true-crime community. In a manner of speaking, I was cancelled. My literary agency dropped me like a hot bag of sick. I was no longer being invited to appear on podcasts, or at conventions. When my books were mentioned by journalists or podcasters, it was always with the caveat that I was 'kind of an asshole' or 'pretty scummy'.

After a year of doing absolutely nothing, you can imagine that I was bored and looking for a new project. I thought I would shoot my shot once again. True crime was still huge – and it wasn't just books and podcasts anymore. Now it was television documentaries, dramatisations of documentaries. True crime was still huge – now beyond the realm of the niche podcast and the one-off Netflix documentary, the genre was ubiquitous and profitable. From Hollywood movies to HBO – A-listers were now clamouring to play Ted Bundy on screen, to executive produce the latest prestige docuseries. I spent my days combing through the trashiest websites the internet had to offer, hoping to find my next big hit.

As a former tabloid journalist, I was no stranger to picking through the rubbish – but even for me, this was beginning to get a bit depressing.

I had been reading about a case in Abilene, Texas: a man kidnapped a young girl and kept her in a dog cage. The man lived on a diet of children's cereals and seemed to be planning to maim the girl and condition her into some sort of doll/slave. Weird, but not weird enough, really. The police found her alive and unharmed, and the kidnapper had no history of this sort of behaviour.

It felt typical of every 'weird' or interesting case I found. It wasn't big enough. We don't have big, messy crimes so much anymore, do we? Not like we used to. Forensics are too developed, and police all over the world seem slightly too wise to their own systemic issues under which serial killers once thrived. There are strange, one-off crimes, but they rarely have the complexities of those long, drawn-out serial cases. Nothing for you to really sink your teeth into – unless the internet was somehow involved. If I could find myself a catfish or a Facebook Svengali – my own Gypsy Rose Blanchard – I would be set.

At the bottom of the article on the case from Abilene, there was the chumbox. 'They called her the most beautiful girl in the world; see what she looks like NOW'; '10 Tips For Losing Fat on Your Belly and gaining it on your ASS'; 'Boyfriend gets LAST LAUGH on cheating ex' – each of these headlines was accompanied, respectively, by images of a heavily edited child model, a woman's backside in tight short-shorts and a busty woman crying. Below the backside, next to the busty cheater:

YOU WON'T BELIEVE WHAT THEY DID TO HER . . .

Below the headline, a split image of a beautiful stock-image model with stark red hair, and a charred corpse, heavily edited to look smooth, uncanny, with strange white eyes, staring into the camera.

Each article seemed tailored to appeal to our basest instincts, calling to the most embarrassing depths of our curiosity. I clicked, I read. I needed to know more.

I googled the name, and I found a few podcasts – you've already read an extract from the first show that covered the case, *I Peed on Your Grave*, a trio of obnoxious American men who shouted over one another to make jokes about teen lesbians and do silly 'British' accents. They'd been handed information by a resident of Crow-on-Sea. *IPOYG* seemed to be the main source from which several copycat podcasts pulled their own episodes. I listened to a pair of white women with white wine who called it 'the best contemporary story' they'd covered in years. They paused in the right places and cooed 'poor girl', 'poor thing', 'poor baby'.

This was all surface-level stuff, of course. They were Americans. They didn't seem terribly interested in the broader socio-economic context of the crime – they didn't talk about the town it took place in (apart from to giggle about its strange name), nor did they dig too deeply into the personal histories of the victim or her killers. The idea that one could talk about this case and gloss over a figure as important as Angelica's father (whom most Brits tapped into politics would have heard of) was absurd to me.

There were a few photographs floating around, and You-Tube videos (again, rehashing the *IPOYG* reporting), and a lot of Reddit threads with screen caps of the killer's social media profiles. One of the best sources I found was a post on 'DethJournal', a clone of LiveJournal used by true-crime fans.

On the 'TCC [true-crime community] Wank'[2] Report board a user had gathered a large archive of Dolly Hart and Violet Hubbard's Tumblr posts prior to their blogs' deletion – as well as posts and chat logs detailing the reactions of Dolly's online acquaintances.

Everywhere I looked people were asking for more info on the case. They wanted sources outside of dodgy local papers, the same handful of podcasts and few DethJournal posts. People were asking for a book.

The story was begging to be told and I appeared to have gotten there first.

I am being flippant. Though my interest was initially self-serving, Joni's case did get to me. The podcasts about her bothered me. In 2014 my only daughter, Frances died. On a snowy January morning she washed up on the south bank of the Thames, apparently having taken her own life. She was twenty. When I first began researching the Joan Wilson case, I imagined how people might talk about Frances. I imagined men laughing about her, strangers making jokes around the circumstances that led to her death and doing her accent.

So, in late 2019, I temporarily moved to Crow-on-Sea. I tried to integrate myself into the community. I wanted to do something worthy. I wanted to write about the town in which this crime had taken place as much as I wanted to write about the crime itself. I got friendly with the locals and

---

2 'Wank' is a colloquial (now somewhat antiquated) term used to describe community infighting within fandoms, or as a catch-all term for bad behaviour. There were communities on LiveJournal and other similar websites which were dedicated to the cataloguing and discussion of 'wank' incidents.

moved into their library – enlisting the help of local historians and journalists. I was privileged enough to interview the friends and loved ones of the victim and the perpetrators, and I was even able to have an extensive correspondence with Violet Hubbard and Angelica Stirling-Stewart. I was unable to contact Dolly Hart, who is still incarcerated as of publication.

Much of what you will read draws from that correspondence, as well as tens of thousands of blog posts and content from interviews. This book represents hundreds of hours of tireless research, in which I hope I have presented the heart of this story. This will not be an abridged version for easy consumption on your commute; there will be no silly accents and no interruptions from mattress adverts.

Joan Margaret Wilson was born on 19 December 1999. Like her death, her birth was overshadowed by a major historical event. Amanda Wilson told me how irritated she was that her daughter's arrival into the world was swallowed by the turn of the millennium.

'It was the millennium-bug stuff that really did my head in,' she said. 'When my friends kept talking to me about how they were going to go to these massive parties or club nights or whatever for New Year's Eve – that was annoying. But the millennium-bug shit was just . . . stupid. Kept bringing it up while I was stressed and knackered. You know, asking daft stuff like: Is that baby monitor millennium-bug proof? Do you have a plan in place in case we lose power? Have you taken all your money out of the bank? That kind of shit.' Amanda was twenty-five when she had Joan. She was 'kind of a hippy' then, and she still is. She wears harem pants and has very long hair. She smokes roll-up cigarettes and eats tofu. She has tattoos, a pierced belly button, and named her daughter after the folk singer Joni Mitchell. Amanda wanted everyone to call the baby Joni.

Amanda's divorce from Joni's father, Freddy, had just been finalised as of my interview with her. Though this is the first interview you will read, Amanda was one of the last people I spoke to. I'd been living in Crow for a few months before she agreed to speak to me in early March of 2020. We were just beginning to understand how much of a threat the COVID-19 virus might be, and I was planning to wrap up my work in Crow and return home to London – just in case things got worse.

Amanda and I chatted about the virus, at first. She was

a little sceptical about it, not seeing how it could be much worse than a flu. At the time, I agreed with her.

She was also sceptical about me. She said she hadn't spoken to anyone in the press about her daughter's death, even though she'd had offers (increasingly so, after the *I Peed on Your Grave* episode was released). She didn't know what to make of it. Four years on, she was still in shock – she probably always would be.

She led me to her conservatory, where she'd stacked some photo albums. There were mandalas on her wall which she drew herself, as well as watercolours of Hindu and Buddhist iconography and lots of animals and plants.

She was thin as a rail. Blue veins crept around the long, delicate bones of her hands and the puffy bags under her eyes. In old photographs her hair is glossy and auburn. In the light of the conservatory, I could see it had become dry, and thin. Grey spilled down from the crown of her skull, as if someone had upended a bucket of silver paint over her head.

Amanda told me she didn't want to discuss finding out about Joni's death, identifying the body or the funeral. She didn't wish to go into detail about the breakdown of her marriage.

She told me she didn't remember much of 2016, beyond June. She spent a lot of it in bed, and Freddy spent a lot of time with his parents. Neither could cope with their own guilt, or the weight of the other's grief. After the funeral, they more or less began living separate lives.

Amanda's parents were both dead and she was an only child. Her friends took care of her. They would bring her meals and tidy her house while Amanda lay in bed or took showers lasting several hours.

'I didn't like leaving my bedroom because I could see her everywhere,' said Amanda. 'Just out of the corner of my eye. Peeking round corners or going back into her room. Just the back of her. And I would get a whiff of her now and again; I'd be able to smell her or . . . I would smell the hospital. And then I'd get in the shower. When I could smell the hospital, I'd shower and try to drown out the smell with this shower gel she used to use. She never used to go into my bedroom, so I . . . If I couldn't cope with it, I'd stay there. But sometimes I would . . . wander around the house, hoping to see her. Just to feel normal for a second.'

I told Amanda I'd felt the same way after my own daughter's death. The circumstances were different, and my daughter hadn't lived with me for a few years – but that I could swear I had seen the end of Frances's ponytail disappearing around a corner, or that I could smell the perfume she wore.

A few months after her death, I was suddenly so worried Frances's perfume would get discontinued that I went to a shop and bought twenty bottles of the stuff. I started spraying it around my flat onto the soft furnishings – but I did it so much I couldn't really smell the perfume anymore. When I realised, I had a complete meltdown and tried to donate all my furniture to the British Heart Foundation in the hope I could replace it all and get the smell back.

Amanda said she'd done something similar with Joni's shower gel – gotten in a bulk order of it one day.

'Whenever I heard a floorboard creaking downstairs, the kettle boiling or the TV turning on – logically I'd know it was just . . . Julie or one of my other friends, but . . . I'd feel like it was her. And that's mostly what I remember. This constant feeling of like . . . knowing she wasn't there but feeling like she was. Logically knowing that she couldn't be there, then feeling like I shouldn't be here either. If she wasn't here, I should be where she was. And that I just wanted her. But I couldn't have her. And when all of this hit me, it made me feel like I'd lost a lung. I couldn't breathe without her.'

She spent that first Christmas with Freddy's family. The day was miserable – bitter, spiteful, alcohol-fuelled arguments which led to their official break-up in early January.

After Christmas, Amanda's friends visited less. She lost a great deal of weight and stopped sleeping.

She began watching a lot of documentaries about murdered children, because they often spoke to the mothers. That was who she was watching for, the mothers. They were dressed and out of the house and speaking about their child's death. Amanda said she started studying them – as if she was hoping to discover a secret. If she watched the other mothers, she might learn how to put her clothes on again. She might learn how to leave the house. She might discover how to continue to function after such a massive loss.

After she ran out of documentaries, she read their blogs and columns and memoirs. She started to feel bitter and jealous of the mothers of victims of school shootings and police violence because they had something to organise around. She couldn't see a cause to attach to Joni's murder; she could not find a purpose in it the way these women had.

'And then I found this woman – Marcia. She's American. And her daughter was fourteen, and she was murdered by two girls she went to school with. And her blog was all about how she'd like . . . forgiven her daughter's murderers and she was

appealing for lighter sentences for them and had even like . . .
One of the killers was training guide dogs in prison, and
Marcia donated a puppy to this girl's training programme.
It boiled my piss. I've never been so infuriated in my life. I
wrote her this mental email, this absolutely insane like five-
page email about everything that'd happened to me and how I
thought she was sick in the head and insane and how I would
never ever forgive the monsters who took away my daughter.'

I asked how Marcia replied.

'Totally magnanimous. *I hear your pain. I feel your pain*,
was what she said. And she . . . I don't want to get into it
but she did end up really helping me,' Amanda said. 'We're
still friends. I probably wouldn't be talking to you without
Marcia, but she said that helping the journalist that did the
book about *her* daughter was really cathartic.'

Plus: Joni's story was already out there. After a few years
of mercifully being ignored by everyone but the local press,
the true-crime industrial complex had found Amanda. And as
much as she did not want people to hear about her daughter's
murder between adverts for mattresses and meal-delivery
kits, it had already begun. And people wanted to speak to
her. There'd be no escaping them now, the true-crime people.
People like me, really.

'The *I Pissed on Your Face* or whatever blokes emailed
me, you know. They got some shit for the episode, for being
disrespectful. And they emailed me to ask if I'd like . . . if I
wanted to come on or something so they could apologise.
How fucking mad is that? How fucking *weird* is that?'

Other journalists had knocked on her door offering interviews and book deals and handfuls of cash. I had the benefit of

being in Crow, of having been vouched for by friends (despite my reputation) and – most of all – I also had a daughter dead under terrible circumstances. Very different – but still terrible.

Even short lives are complex and rich. Even dead children are full of contradictions and flaws and mysteries that will never be fully understood or solved. Even a writer as well versed in this genre as I could never create a perfect photograph of my subject. I could create a beautiful, accurate sketch of Joni, but a sketch from a skilled artist is still a sketch.

Amanda's parents, Jan and John, had owned an amusement arcade on the North Beach. It was called Vegas by the Sea. Amanda showed me photographs of a row of spray-paint showgirls decorating the wall, coin pushers made to look like roulette tables, a photo of her at eight or nine, toothless and grinning, in front of neon lights shaped like giant playing cards. Amanda still finds the sound of arcade machines comforting; she told me when she couldn't sleep, she would often play a ten-hour YouTube video of ambient arcade noises.

Jan and John Black were Crow outsiders. They moved in the late sixties and opened their arcade in 1971 without 'getting in' with the inner circle of business owners and local celebrities who had thoroughly taken over the town. Amanda was born four years after Vegas was.

That inner circle of businessmen's influence grew over the twenty-five years that Vegas was open. They got their hooks into local government and began making it gradually more and more difficult for anyone who wasn't part of their old boys' club to open or run a business. While they began to block the opening of new business owned by anyone besides themselves, prices at the businesses around Vegas by the Sea dropped, and Jan and John were repeatedly and arbitrarily fined (for the placement of their bins, for the number of fire extinguishers on their premises, for failing to produce ancient legal documents), and harassed with constant and decreasing offers of purchase from local businessman Gerald Dowd.[3]

In 1996 Jan and John 'gave up' and sold the arcade to Dowd. They gave Amanda a portion of the money from the sale of Vegas, and Amanda went on holiday with it. She was twenty-one. She had worked at Vegas since she was thirteen and was celebrating her career change with a holiday. She didn't have a new job yet, but knew she'd be able to get one at a hotel or a chippy without much difficulty upon her return. She was going to work part-time and go back to college to do an arts education course.

She went to Corfu because the travel agent had a deal on. Club 18-30. Amanda asks me if I remember travel agents, a little incredulous that they ever existed. She booked it with her best friend, Julie.

She had wanted to go to Ayia Napa, which was more expensive. She'd seen it in the brochures – blue skies, white sand. But Julie told her a mutual friend of theirs had been mugged when she went to Ayia Napa. She refused, point-blank, to go; especially when Corfu was cheaper, and just as beautiful. So they went to Corfu. Amanda had never been on a summer holiday. She couldn't leave Vegas during tourist

3 Dowd was the owner of the amusement arcades *Lucky Lucy's* and *Bowl 'N' Beer* as well as the only cinema in town: *The Red Carpet*. He was co-owner of gentlemen's club *Diamond's*, along with infamous radio DJ and television host Vance Diamond.

season. Her parents would take her out of school, slyly, to the Costa del Sol or Canary Islands at funny times of year. Her childhood holidays were always in February and November.

Amanda, for the first time, bought tiny bikinis and short-shorts. Then she hid them, because she was mortified at the thought of her conservative father finding them. She and Julie waxed each other's legs the evening before their flight.

Amanda saw Freddy the moment she arrived at the hotel. She spotted him at the hotel bar while she and Julie dragged their suitcases through reception. He was her age, and he was tall and blond and tanned. She didn't usually go for blond men – she didn't like their pale eyebrows and lashes. Amanda thought he looked sort of posh, but he wasn't at all. He came over to them and offered to carry their cases. He spoke with a thick, familiar accent. 'Hull?' she'd asked him. He nodded, then asked her if she was from Scarborough. She told him, 'Close enough.' They gave each other their names. She said no to the suitcases, but said she'd catch him later. He smiled at her. He wasn't pushy. He said okay, and he let her go – didn't take it as an insult, or an affront to his masculinity.

Easy-going – Amanda liked the easy-going, *nice* boys her friends occasionally called 'wet'. She had no desire for the jealous, wall-punching thugs that loitered in her arcade all summer, competing with the Test Your Strength cabinets, rattling claw machines, shouting at girls in the street. Perhaps an 18–30 holiday wasn't the best place for her, with that in mind. But they found each other. Mand and Freddy, day one.

He waved at her in the bar later but didn't crowd her. Julie and Amanda sipped sweet drinks with paper umbrellas and plastic pineapple cocktail stirrers. They could hear the ocean from the bar. Amanda joked that they should've gone away from the seaside; they should've gone skiing.

Freddy and Mand bumped into each other on the beach that evening. Julie had gone off with a boy; Mand was just happy sipping her cheap Greek beer and looking up at the moon, with warm sand beneath her toes, in her hair. Freddy plopped down beside her (asking for permission first – 'Hullo! Mind if I sit here?') and recounted how he'd lost each of the four friends he'd come on holiday with this evening. Mand asked if this was a lads' holiday, and Freddy told her he was with two girl friends and two lad friends. This made her like him more. Here was a boy who was fine when you said no to him, *and* had friends who were girls? He was a novelty. She'd lost her friend as well – this was the first thing they had in common.

They chatted for an hour about where they'd grown up, what they did for a living. A jealous squeal of delight came from Freddy when she told him about her parents' arcade – Freddy *loved* arcades. Half his childhood was spent on the Scarborough seafront, with ice-cream-sticky hands that smelt of coppers from two-pence machines, and a hoard of crappy claw-machine toys stuffed into his nana's handbag. He'd broken his front tooth on a stick of Scarborough rock, and never had the little chip fixed – you could see his tongue in the small gap when he smiled.

Years after Mand and Freddy met, their daughter would chip her own front tooth on a stick of rock. The chip was almost exactly the same size and shape as Freddy's. Amanda said all of her memories of Freddy are tied up in Joni, even the ones from before Joni existed. She found that even her own foggy childhood inevitably tangled with her daughter's. Was it Amanda who pulled three of her own baby teeth in one go? Or Joni? Did they both do that at around the same age? The two of them were so similar. The three of them were. Freddy, Mand and Joni. Peas in a pod.

Mand and Julie were absorbed into Freddy's holiday friendship group. Freddy's friends teased him – after just two days, Freddy and Mand were already a pair of gooey-eyed newlyweds; they fussed over each other like little birds. They had everything in common. They ordered pina coladas in sync. They both had dated taste in films and music; Freddy bitterly complained about the superiority of Hendrix and Pink Floyd to the Britpop set, and Mand promised to play him *New Skin for the Old Ceremony* when they got back to Yorkshire and he drove up to visit her. They both liked American grunge. They both loved *Midnight Cowboy, The Deer Hunter, Taxi Driver*.

'It was scary,' Amanda said. 'I almost thought he was winding me up. Like he was just agreeing with me to get my knickers off, and I'd never hear from him again after we got home.'

They exchanged phone numbers and addresses and promised each other they'd stay in touch. Amanda tells me she nearly cried in the taxi to the airport; half the happiest she'd been, half terrified this wouldn't go anywhere. Julie was monumentally hungover and had to stop the cab to vomit out of the door.

They arrived home on a Thursday night, and Freddy rang her at 11 a.m. on Friday morning. Amanda knew he was serious. Her mum answered the phone and gave her a big thumbs up as she passed the receiver over. Freddy drove up the following Saturday.

This was July of 1996. They went to Cyprus together in August of 1997, and Freddy proposed on a beach in Ayia Napa. Amanda showed me her ring, which she still wore – it's vintage, a milky pearl set in a ring of tiny diamonds. She loved it. She loved him. He moved up to Crow.

Mand finished college and started working freelance as an arts educator. She'd go into schools and do art days (printing, tie-dye, painting) with Key Stage 1 children, and children with special educational needs. Freddy worked off-shore on the rigs, in the North Sea; two weeks on, two weeks off, which suited them both well. They liked the money; they liked the space, the intensity of two weeks when he was there, the privacy of his two weeks away.

They were married in September of '98. Freddy and Mand's mothers, Pat and Jan, argued at the wedding. Freddy's parents were the kind of working-class people who made it their business to look down on people who were also working class but more *common* than they were. And nothing screamed common like Mand's parents: her mother's brassy blonde hair and heavy jewellery, her father's gold tooth and red face. Mand's belly ring made Pat's lip curl.

That was what started the argument. Pat made a comment: it was a shame you could see Amanda's belly ring through her wedding dress; two bottles of champagne deep, Jan told Pat to bugger off. Then to fuck off. Then called her a fat, stuck-up cow. It almost ruined the day. Pat cried, melodramatically, and the mothers had to be separated. Mand was relieved they'd done the photos already.

They went to Berlin for their honeymoon, deciding to do something a bit cool and a bit different, because they were too cool and different for beach holidays. Amanda showed me a photo of her flashing a peace sign in front of a chunk of the Berlin Wall. Her hair was bleach-blonde, tied into space buns, and she was wearing a small plastic bindi in the centre of her forehead. She told me she was obsessed with Gwen Stefani. In the next photo of Freddy, his hair had grown into curtains that skimmed his jaw; he wore a ratty Nirvana shirt.

'I was quite cool for about ten minutes there,' Amanda said, smiling. 'Definitely the coolest girl in Crow, but that's saying fuck all. Then I got pregnant. I don't mean that to sound bitter but I just don't think you can be a cool mum. You instantly lose all your street-cred when you get pregnant. I got lippy with my nana once when I was a teenager. Refused to go to my uncle's birthday at the working men's club, told her I wouldn't be caught dead there. She looked at me, and just said something like . . . "You can act like you're royalty now, Mandy, but one day you're going to have shit under your fingernails, and it won't be your own." The first time I changed Joni's nappy I thought about her saying that. I actually thought about that every time I changed her nappy.'

Amanda looked at her thin hands and examined her nails, which were now bitten down to the bed. I asked her if she liked being a mother.

'I did. I really didn't mind the shit under my fingernails. I don't think I come off as very maternal, but I am, in a lot of ways. I love little kids and I love looking after people. It's why I do my job – I just like being around children and I loved having my own.'

We paused to look at baby photos. Joni's tiny hands curled around Amanda's long, skinny fingers. Scratch mittens, bubble baths, dummies, soft blankets. Joni sleeping on Freddy's chest. In one photograph, Joni at around six months is in a cot surrounded by fifteen small teddies. Scrawled under the photo in Amanda's hand: 'The elders have assembled to decide your punishment.'

The *Post-on-Sea* called Amanda 'icy':

> Amanda Wilson (43) was icy with press, refusing to give comments or interviews. Mrs Wilson did not shed a single tear, in contrast to Fredrick Wilson (44), the girl's father, who was inconsolable throughout the proceedings.

I asked her about that – the icy comment. She said she never cries in front of anyone, and that everyone thinks it's weird. But she had been like this since she was a child. She simply found crying in front of others humiliating; she had a real blockage around it. But she had cried a lot at home. She cried in front of her friends, just not at court. And after Christmas of 2016, particularly during the trial, she felt numb.

'After talking to Marcia a lot, she said to me that I might not be able to get *meaning* out of Joni's death. That she certainly hadn't gotten any meaning out of her daughter's death. But that like . . . looking for an outlet and working toward just . . . being more normal again – I was allowed to do that. I didn't have to spend the rest of my life locked in my bedroom, and I wouldn't be forgetting about Joni or being disrespectful because my life wasn't 100% focussed on missing her and thinking about her. And you know . . . people didn't like that. They didn't like it at all.'

As much as friends had begun to pull away from Amanda as she was mired in her grief, they weren't always receptive to her steady attempts to restart her life.

'I had a friend who fell out with me when I went back to work. She said I was stupid to go back now, and I said I needed a distraction and I could just *tell* she thought that was like . . . off. Like there was something wrong about wanting to be distracted. And I fell out with Julie last year because I told her I wanted to foster. I was thinking to foster a disabled kid, because I've got plenty of experience with SEN kids, and it's hardest to place them. I still am, actually. But Julie thought I was replacing Joni. That I was just happy to replace her. But if I can't . . . if I can't do something . . . anything. Something positive. I don't know. I might as well just fucking top myself. Sometimes I think that's what people want from me.

'I've spoken to Marcia about this a lot because she's . . . had similar stuff. Especially with all the steps she's made toward forgiving her daughter's attackers. People have written to her and told her to kill herself. And I'm not as public as Marcia – can't say I'm exactly ready to forgive anyone either, but . . . I really think people want me to kill myself, or something.

'I know I sound mental, but I think that's what people want to see. It's so horrible, what happened to her is so horrible, I reckon they think it's the only appropriate reaction. Nobody understands how anything so awful could happen, so nobody knows how to act, or how I should act, or how I could possibly be coping. They all have their little fucking ideas about what I'm supposed to do, or who I'm supposed to be. So I can't do anything right for anyone. They don't understand how I could go on, and thinking about it makes them sad, so they just want me to go away. To move out of the house, or to just *die*, so they don't have to think about me, or what happened to Joni anymore. Do I sound mental? I sound mental, don't I? I've sounded mental since it happened.'

*

Going forward, an asterisk will indicate any names that have been changed to preserve the anonymity of those who are tangential to the case.

Joni spoke early but walked late. Mand took her to the GP, who examined Joni and said she was fine. He said that some babies were just a bit lazy. Mand and Freddy should try leaving her to sort herself out, to encourage her to get her own toys, her own snacks. Amanda showed me a home video, of a chubby not-quite-two-year-old with red hair. She was in a onesie, lying face down on a rug.

'No, no, no,' she said.
'Go and get teddy, Joni, go get it!'
'She's not a Labrador, Freddy.'
'No, no, no. Mummy Daddy for me.'
'Why not?'
'Can't, Mummy, can't. Need Daddy.'
'Joni, go get it.'
The toddler rolled onto her back, a look of utter contempt on her face. She sighed heavily. Still lying on her back with her knees up, and her feet flat on the floor, she pushed herself across the carpet, like a worm. Freddy and Mand laughed.

41

'At least crawl! Oh my God, Jojo, that looks like so much more effort.'

'No, no, no.'

'No' was her first word. Joni became infamous among her extended family for bluntly refusing cuddles and kisses; for her honest appraisal of meals, and dresses, and other people's children. Did you like your tea at Nana's? *No.* Did you like your Uncle Gavin's present? *No.* Do you want to meet the new baby? *No.*

Mand encouraged it. She hated sickly sweet little girls; she hated watching mothers henpeck their daughters into submission, while their horrid little boys ran around pulling hair and picking noses. She craved balance. She wanted to live in a world where no one pulled hair unpunished, but every child was free to pick their nose at least a little bit.

I was shown a picture of Joni, small and round, on her first day of school. She was grinning; her milk teeth like little white needles. It took her a while to make friends. When the other children asked her to play with them, she said no, because she didn't want to do what they were doing. The other children were wounded by rejection in ways Joni was not. She told them to play other games with her; some said no back, and some bent to her will. The words 'persistent', 'bossy' and 'blunt' would all appear in her school reports. 'Pig-headed' popped up once, in Year 3, and Mand complained to the head teacher.

She didn't really make any close friends until Violet Hubbard joined the school in Year 2. They had a lot in common – they both liked to read and they both liked video games. *Pokémon* was a particular shared favourite. They were fast friends.

Joni got picked on, but Amanda didn't recall it hugely bothering her until she got a bit older. When the other little girls started to grow up, and Joni didn't, her problems began. The small handful of meeker children that Joni had gathered as friends (including Violet) were told by more mature girls that Joni was bossy and they didn't have to do what she said. They could do anything they wanted.

'Aleesha Dowd, Kayleigh Brian,* Angelica Stirling-Stewart,' Amanda told me. 'They always picked on her.'

Aleesha, Kayleigh and Angelica had begun to prepare for secondary school in earnest. From Year 6 onward, they straightened their hair, they rolled up their skirts, they stole their older sisters' body sprays, and laughed at the girls who were yet to put aside their My Little Pony dolls and their *Pokémon* games. Aleesha, Kayleigh and Angelica were shedding their childhoods like old skin, where Joni had begun to cocoon herself in childish things at the first sign of puberty.

'I had the talk with her, but I think it really scared her. Asking her if she wanted a bra, even just a sports bra, freaked her out; she really regressed after that. Got worse when she started her period, I think, 'cause she started it so early. She was quite a bit bigger than most of the other girls by the end of primary school. She was taller and heavier, than the other girls; you had these tiny little things like Angelica and Kayleigh who . . . even with the straightened hair and the lip gloss, you could easily think they were seven or eight years old. And they were ripping into Joni because she was just . . . she didn't want to grow up as quickly as they did.'

There was only so much advice Amanda could give, only so much she could do to help. She'd always been thin, a bit of a late bloomer. Joni's hair and facial features had come from Amanda's side of the family, but her build was all Freddy's. She was a roly-poly baby who grew into a stocky, broad-shouldered girl. She was never self-conscious of her size until the other girls made sure she was.

In early 2010, when Joni was in Year 6, there was an incident involving Joni's Nintendo DS. She brought it to school to play at lunchtimes – to trade Pokémon with Violet. Violet was off sick, so Joni was playing *Pokémon Platinum* by herself. Aleesha began bothering her – she asked Joni why she didn't get some exercise. She told Joni she should go for a run around the playground, that she should try and lose some weight. She snatched the Nintendo DS out of Joni's hands and (allegedly) said, 'If you got off your bum you wouldn't be so fat.'

Aware that smashing the DS itself was a step too far, Aleesha coolly erased Joni's save. Joni, upon realising what Aleesha had done, had a complete meltdown, and ripped a chunk of poker-straight blonde hair from Aleesha's scalp.

This made things far, far worse for Joni. The bullying (which had been mild teasing, up to this point) really started to get to her. Amanda had to call the school on a few occasions, but nothing was done. Angelica Stirling-Stewart and Aleesha Dowd's fathers both had deep ties to local business and government – they knew most of the school governors. Amanda was brushed off every time.

'I don't know why I fucking bothered,' Amanda rolled her eyes. 'Joni had apparently started it. *What* exactly she'd started they never properly explained to me, because I was complaining about *general* bullying, not a specific incident.

44

Joni told me that Aleesha was a complete toerag and had locked Violet in a toilet on her first day. Apparently, all the teachers knew about it, and she wasn't even allowed to go to the toilet unsupervised because she'd locked so many kids in cubicles.

'Joni's actual teacher was sympathetic, but nothing ever got past the head teacher, because everyone with any power was friends with Gerald Dowd or Simon Stirling-Stewart or one of those fucking . . . *inner-circle* wankers who basically run the place.' Amanda leant forward, glowering. 'You know they actually pinned her down and straightened her hair one day? Joni was going to tell on them for bringing straighteners to school, or something. And Aleesha pinned her down to the floor while Angelica straightened her hair. When I rang, apparently Aleesha got put in detention, but Angelica didn't. They asked me if she'd gotten burned and – because Joni hadn't – it was like,' Amanda shrugged, 'no big deal, apparently. *Fuck off.*'

Amanda then told me that the 'lack of consequences' for certain people in Crow-on-Sea was only going to go one way.

Joni retreated further into her childish things. This made the grown-up girls harsher and harsher and harsher. Joni was terrified of going to secondary school – a few of her friends were going to their nearest private school, Amplefield College, rather than Crow-on-Sea Community High School. She wanted to go to Amplefield instead.

'She really went on about it, you know? She didn't seem to quite understand that we just couldn't afford private school. You know, when you're little you just don't realise how much money it costs. I think the fees for Amplefield College are something ridiculous like £15,000 a year. That'd be pretty much all of my salary. We sat down and did the maths, and Freddy's salary is pretty decent on the rigs, and Freddy reckoned we could actually afford it if we just did fuck all else – like no holidays, if we just had one car, if we were careful with clothes and appliances. I'd wanted a new suite as well.

'If we cut all that stuff out, we could probably do it. Oh, and Freddy said it'd be easier if I got a "proper job". I obviously thought I already *did* have a proper job, so we had a huge argument about it. I said her quality of life would be worse overall. If she was getting bullied at a state primary, on what planet was she not getting bullied if she was going to be the poorest kid at the fucking private school. And Violet was going to CCHS, so she wasn't going to be totally by herself. And I assumed Angelica and Aleesha would probably be going to Amplefield, anyway. So we agreed not to send her. Obviously I've never lived that down.'

So off to CCHS Joni would go, after rather a large final hiccup at primary school. The end-of-year trip for Year 6s had been a day at the local waterpark, Poseidon's Kingdom, where (following a series of circumstances I'll explore later) Aleesha Dowd drowned in a freak accident.

'As far as I remember, Aleesha got stuck in one of the slides face-down and drowned,' Amanda sighs. 'Joni didn't see her drown, but she did see the body come out of the slide. Violet tried to go down the same slide, not knowing Aleesha was stuck in there, and knocked the body out, so . . . it was worse for Violet but Joni saw the splash and . . . the body floating in the pool.'

Joni had nightmares that summer. She wouldn't swim. She

was terrified of water. Violet's mother was having her take swimming lessons to help her get over the incident – Joni was invited but refused to go. Amanda wasn't going to make her. In fact, virtually the only time Violet and Joni spent apart during the summer between primary and secondary school was when Violet was at her swimming lessons.

Violet and Joni became even closer than they had been in primary – Violet was always around. They were always playing games together and watching YouTube videos. I asked Amanda if she'd had any concerns about their insular friendship.

'Um . . . no, not really. I mean, I think it's quite normal to just have one best friend when you're that age. I expected them to get into a group together when they were a bit older; I thought they'd find the other sort of . . . alternative, gothy, kind of *different* kids when they were fourteen or fifteen. I think that's the age I remember getting into more of a big friendship group rather than just having one or two girl friends.'

So Mand couldn't believe it when Joni started hanging around with a group of hyper-feminine, athletic and very mainstream girls in Year 9. She was even more surprised when she discovered that Joni's former bullies, Kayleigh and Angelica, were part of this wider friendship group. Joni also stopped speaking to Violet in school. Joni didn't mention this change in any detail to Amanda. She told Amanda she'd made a new friend: a pretty girl called Lauren* who Joni sat next to in English. Joni went over to Lauren's one weekend, and that was that.

'She came back with her hair done properly. My hair's not as curly as hers, so I was always a bit shit with it; it was always a bit dry and frizzy. Lauren – who was actually very nice, she was lovely – Lauren has properly curly hair, and she like . . . sorted it out for her. Joni came back after this sleepover with her new friend with her hair all done, and she was wearing makeup. She'd been shopping, and she'd bought a crop top. I was . . . well, I wasn't *mortified*, I've never . . . I don't know, I don't have a problem with makeup and belly tops, but I was just a bit shocked. I felt like I went from having a little girl to a seventeen-year-old in the space of about two weeks. I think maybe . . . maybe she was getting teased more than she let on and it just got a bit much for her, or she felt like she wanted to do more normal girl stuff. Maybe she felt left out. I really don't know.'

Amanda tried talking to Joni about it. She tried asking why Violet hadn't been over in a while, or why she'd suddenly started wearing makeup. But Joni was evasive – positively breezy.

'Well, with Violet she just shrugged it off. "We're both allowed to have more than one friend" – you know when teenagers speak to you like you're thick for even asking? She was the same with the makeup. I'd say, "About three months ago, you hated makeup," and she'd just make this face, like three months ago was a different lifetime. And I didn't press it because . . . well, when you're a kid a few months *is* a huge chunk of time.'

The first time Amanda's house was invaded en masse by a group of glossy-haired, body-spray-drenched girly-girls – including Kayleigh and Angelica, of all people – Amanda was just bewildered.

'I thought they'd bonded over the trauma of Aleesha Dowd

drowning, or something. I don't know. I just . . . didn't understand it. I tried ringing Violet's mum to see if they'd fallen out but . . . Violet's mum didn't even know they weren't hanging round with each other anymore.'

Amanda was disappointed. She particularly didn't want to see Joni hanging around with Angelica Stirling-Stewart – aside from the historical bullying, Amanda intensely disliked Angelica's father.

'He used to complain about Robin House – the special primary school, the one I work in quite a lot – all the time. It's not actually in Crow – closer to Whitby – and you've got to drive through Moorcock Hill, where he lives, to get to it. So he used to do all these horrible bits on local radio about how the parents' slow driving would make the traffic really bad. And say stuff like, "Just 'cause your kid's slow doesn't mean you have to be." He's a horrible man. Even before the UKIP shit he was just . . . vile.'

Joni assured her mother that she didn't really like Angelica – that no one really did. Angelica was 'the friend we all hate'. But that didn't stop Joni from going to the Stirling-Stewart house for birthday parties or sleepovers.

'I just . . . Honestly most of those girls were fine. They were perfectly nice, they really were. Especially Lauren – I genuinely liked her. I was even prepared to give Angelica a chance. But I didn't want Joni getting *embedded* into Crow. This town is not . . . Like, it's a weird fucking place. It's basically run by this cabal of old gammon Tories – which I know isn't exactly unusual – but it's like they all think they're in *Game of Thrones*. They're all wrapped up in dodgy dealings and local crime and . . . people get sucked into it. I didn't want

49

her to get sucked in. I wanted her to *leave*. I used to defend Crow, but I think it's a shit place to live. I only stayed for my parents. I'm only staying now because I've got nowhere else to go. I hate it here. I didn't want her to get . . . I didn't want her to *identify* with living here, and like . . . the idea of her getting in with Angelica just really bothered me. It felt like a way *in* to Crow for her. I didn't want that.'

A Brief History of Fires in Crow-on-Sea

Ask why the sand is grey in Crow-on-Sea, and any native worth their salt will recount to you the bloody, fiery tale of Hrókr the Crow.

Crow-on-Sea was allegedly first established circa 970 AD as a settlement of Viking raider Hrókr Sigurdsson or Hrókr the Black – more popularly known as Hrókr the Crow, thanks to the fourteenth-century writings of the medieval historian and Benedictine monk Geoffrey of York.

Hrókr means 'crow' in old Norse, and Geoffrey of York's writing is the only work which refers to Sigurdsson as 'The Crow'. No sensible Viking poet would commit a name as silly as 'Crow the Crow' to his saga. Hrókr's existence is corroborated by his appearance (or the appearance of a very similar figure) in the Icelandic Saga *The Tale of Haakon*, compiled by the historian and poet Snorri Sturluson circa the 1220s.

The Tale of Haakon focusses on Hrókr's brother, minor Icelandic jarl and alleged dragon-slayer Haakon the White. An extract from Gunnar Olavsson's 1972 translation of the tale below:

Haakon had a brother by the name of Hrókr who was another son of Sigurd. He had a beard as black as his name and a soul as black as his beard, so they called him Hrókr the Black. He was no friend to Haakon, whose place among the people he coveted. Hrókr plotted against Haakon, but he was caught because Haakon was much beloved to the people and Hrókr could find no confidants or schemers among them.

Hrókr was brought before Haakon, who was merciful and still had love in his heart for his brother. So Hrókr was banished – never to darken the shore of Iceland again. He left in a great black ship, and vowed to make a place as great as Haakon's and return with many warriors and many sons, but he did not.

According to Geoffrey of York, however, he did arrive safely on the shores of England later that year.

From Ellen Mark's 2014 translation of Geoffrey of York's *The Foundation of Northern England*:

Queerly named is the village of Crow-on-Sea which one can find south of Whitby Abbey. It is said that hundreds of years ago (this being shortly before the time of Harold Godwinson) a Northman named Hrókr the Crow landed on the shores of what we know now as the village. It is said he came with a black ship and raped and pillaged what he found there. He raided Whitby Abbey and killed a great many monks. He made many Christian Angle men his slaves and Christian Angle women his concubines. He made those who refused to submit into bloody idols to his false gods and hung them about his dwellings. He burned many homes and built upon their ashes a grand wooden hall. The soil became rich with blood and black with cinders and no good man would walk there for many years.

Then righteous men came and burned down what Hrókr the Crow had made. The sands of Crow-on-Sea, they say, are grey with the ashes of Hrókr's ruination.

The alleged site of Hrókr the Crow's settlement is marked by a statue of a Viking, to be found on Crow's South Beach, opposite shops Viking Antiques and Ethyl's Sweets and Ices. He haunts this spot, apparently, and so it makes an appropriate starting point for Crow's only ghost tour – which always begins with the story of Hrókr's rise and fall.

And did a new, Christian settlement rise from the ashes of Hrókr's plundered land? Not exactly. It seems a small village was built and named Crow-on-Sea at least by the time of Geoffrey of York, but the area was sparsely populated until the advent of the railway in the mid-1800s.

A railway line connected Crow-on-Sea to Scarborough, and Scarborough to York. Another line connected Crow to Whitby, and Whitby to Middlesbrough, and Middlesbrough to Newcastle, but no train stopped at the small village of Crow-on-Sea until significant investment from businessman Horace Stewart pushed the town into the tourist industry in the late nineteenth century.

Stewart had plans to turn the small village into a new rival for Scarborough and Whitby. He invested a great deal of money into this would-be resort town between resort towns, and by 1885, he had begun financing the construction of a small railway station and the town's first hotel: The Empire, intended to rival the luxury establishments found in other seaside resorts.

By 1887 he was dead – but plenty of wannabe hoteliers were sold on Stewart's vision. While The Empire would not be completed for some time (under the less-than-competent stewardship of Stewart's son), Crow-on-Sea was a fully fledged resort town by the early 1900s. It thrived – though never as healthily as Whitby or Scarborough. Even in its earliest days, Crow-on-Sea was a budget destination.

In 1900 the Empire Hotel was finally completed. Once the fifth-largest brick structure in Europe, the foyer had been decorated with a great fresco of a rising sun to reflect the fact that 'the sun never sets on the British Empire'. The entire hotel was a tribute to Queen Victoria and the British Empire; banisters, coving and even curtain poles and carpet runners were decorated with tiny carved crowns. An enormous portrait of Queen Victoria hung in the ballroom.

The Empire was intended as a rival to Scarborough's Grand Hotel, hoping to court some of the larger town's wealthy, upper-class clientele.

Though it never reached the heights of Scarborough's Grand, business was good and consistent through the 1910s and the hotel enjoyed a huge spike in popularity immediately following World War One. This was attributed to the fact that, during the December 1914 German raid of Scarborough, Whitby and Hartlepool, Crow-on-Sea went ignored. While Whitby and Scarborough, Crow's bookends, suffered massive structural damage (the Grand Hotel itself was hit thirty times in a bombardment), Crow went completely untouched. Local legend attributes Crow's safety to a mysterious and remarkably thick fog which descended over its bays as German boats travelled north from Scarborough to Whitby. The more mystical among Crow's citizens say the fog was smoke from Hrókr the Crow's ghost ship, back to protect his plunder from foreign war ships.

Scarborough and Whitby remained scarred by that raid for several years, and holidaymakers avoided them, choosing to stay in Crow instead. Crow-on-Sea enjoyed a period of great prosperity which stretched into the roaring twenties.

Trade began to slow in the 1930s with the advent of the Great Depression, and growing unrest on the continent. On 31 December 1937, The Empire hosted its usual New Year's Eve party in the ballroom. The party was set, for the first time, to include a grand firework display on the beach. At 23:45, guests in thick winter coats over their best outfits were hustled down to the beach where the hotel manager lit the first firework.

The manager had trouble with the small explosive, struggling to light it. Its sudden launch took him off guard and he kicked the firework, inadvertently angling it at the hotel. The firework took off, cutting through the panicked crowd of partygoers, across the road, and into the hotel through a first-floor window, where it exploded. The room caught fire, which spread quickly through the building. The hotel burned to the ground over the course of a few hours, exacerbated by gas lighting, and highly flammable rayon curtains. No guests were harmed, but hotel maid Ellie Miller was trapped and killed.

Throughout the Second World War, the ruins of The Empire stood untouched by all but rain and wind, as its original owner tried (and failed) to raise funds to rebuild it.

In the late 1940s, the lot was purchased by local landowner Leonard Stirling. Stirling came from aristocratic stock and, having aligned himself with the British Union of Fascists before and during the war, was looking to reinvent himself as a philanthropist and 'hotel mogul'. Initially very unpopular in the area (and a frequent flyer in the 'Opinions' pages of the *Post-on-Sea*), his purchase of the land and subsequent promise to rebuild the hotel effectively wiped his slate clean. People were tired of looking at the depressing, burned-out wreck of the building, and were pleased by the prospect of The Empire's revitalisation.

Stirling rebuilt the hotel at a cut price. Locally hewn bricks were replaced by cheap building materials and gas lamps were replaced with slapdash electric lighting. The building was prone to power cuts and guests often reported small power surges and electric shocks from plugs and shaving outlets. The building's piping and paint was largely lead-based. It was a death trap.

Like most seaside towns, Crow-on-Sea slipped into a decline in the 1960s from which it is still yet to recover. With the arrival of commercial airlines and package trips, cheap flights began carrying holidaymakers away from traditional British seaside destinations toward warmer, foreign sands.

Crow (like Blackpool and Skegness and Scarborough and Brighton) saw fewer and fewer tourists – and the tourists it did see became considerably poorer.

Then the railway lines closed: a nail in Crow's coffin. The train that once connected Crow to Whitby was discontinued in 1971, and then the line from Scarborough closed in '72. Crow was now only accessible from Scarborough and Whitby by bus; there was no direct line connecting Crow to its nearest northern cities. The train station was demolished in 1990, squashing any hope that the rail line would reopen.

Since the mid-1970s, Crow-on-Sea has been a tourist town with very few tourists. The lack of visitors to Crow could account for the second Empire Hotel's fifty-year stint without fires, despite its verifiable death-trap status. One can easily delay the inevitable if one rarely has guests to disturb the shoddy electricals or fall asleep with a lit cigarette. When Leonard Stirling sold the hotel to British multinational hospitality company KMP Leisure Holdings in 1979, the hotel was rarely filled beyond 50% capacity, even during the peak of its 'busy' summer season.

KMP Leisure owned the Oasis hotel chain, and The Empire became *The Empire by Oasis*. Prices at the hotel were slashed (as were staff and salaries) and the overall quality of drinks, food and service took a nosedive. The *Post-on-Sea* wondered 'What happened to The Empire?' in 1985, criticising KMP Leisure for destroying the hotel's luxurious identity.

The Empire by Oasis went on sale for a bargain price in 1996, sitting on the market till May of '97, when it made its way back into the hands of its founding families. Local author Simon Stirling-Stewart was the middle-aged son of Leonard Stirling and great-grandson of Horace Stewart and told the *Post-on-Sea* he wanted the hotel back in his family's hands.

He said he was aware that some corners had been cut in The Empire's first reconstruction, and he was hoping to renovate the hotel back to its former glory. In early 1998 Stirling-Stewart took out a massive insurance policy on the building, worth in excess of five million GBP.

Stirling-Stewart used his experience as an author to write a new narrative for his hotel. With its new owner apparently hoping to drum up business from the budding 'ghost tourism' industry, the *Post-on-Sea* ran a story titled: 'HAUNTED EMPIRE . . . Is Crow-on-Sea's most famous hotel host to more than just the living?' Which posited that hotel maid Ellie Miller, who'd died in the 1937 fire, was haunting the new building.

On New Year's Eve of 1937, the Empire hotel famously burned down due to a stray firework. Less famously, however, a young maid named Ellie Miller was trapped in a broom cupboard, and died. Since the hotel was rebuilt in the forties by businessman Leonard Stirling (father of Simon Stirling- Stewart, who recently purchased the hotel back from a major corporation), there have been many reports of supernatural goings-on. We spoke to Simon Stirling-Stewart:

'My father always said that there were some strange goings-on at the hotel. He said there were often power cuts and plugs sparking, particularly on the second floor, where the maid died. People also report a strong smell of cigarettes, or finding cigarettes lit in their rooms when they're non-smokers. We're looking at getting the building exorcised and blessed – we, of course, wouldn't want to get a reputation as one of Britain's most haunted hotels.'

We also spoke to Miller's grand-niece Karen Quinn, who had this to say:

'Well, the family story is basically that she got trapped in the broom cupboard before the fire, and she died of smoke inhalation. I think there were rumours going round that she burned to death, but I've never heard that, and my granddad [Miller's brother] always said she got trapped and died of smoke inhalation, so that's the story I think is true.'

The following week, the *Post-on-Sea* ran a double-page spread on 'the Haunted Hotel', using stories that reported (as

Stirling-Stewart had) electrical surges, cigarette smoke and lit cigarettes discovered in the rooms of non-smokers.

With renovation completed (very quickly) by December of 1998, the building burned down *again* in June of '99. The fire was traced back to a stray cigarette in an unoccupied room. Both cleaners on duty that morning were heavy smokers. They could not remember which of them had dusted the room, and both testified that either of them could've left the cigarette there.

Between the faulty electricals and shoddy building materials, the hotel was ablaze in a matter of minutes and could not be controlled by the fire brigade upon their arrival.

The Empire Hotel's official insurance report made the claim that one of the cleaners' cigarettes had started the fire, but Stirling-Stewart made several wink-nudge comments in the local and national press, referencing the 'haunting' story. When Stirling-Stewart rebuilt the hotel in 2001, it was safer, and a third of the size of its predecessors. No ballroom or function rooms, just seven floors, a small bar and a little French restaurant. It was 'boutiquey', and still is, according to its reviews.

The New Empire still sits on the site of its mother and grandmother, with an elaborate garden in place of a ballroom. A statue of Queen Victoria erupts from an immense rhododendron bush; the garden is a popular wedding spot. The hotel also played host to just about every ghost-hunting television show the English-speaking world had to offer in the mid-2000s. One can learn about the various hauntings of Crow-on-Sea from *Most Haunted*, *6ixth Sense*, *Derek Acorah's Ghost Towns*, *Extreme Ghost Stories*, *Great British Ghosts* and more.

With a combination of insurance money and renewed profits from the UK's ghost-hunting industry, Simon Stirling-Stewart established a new company – Chalet-on-Sea Ltd – in 2005. He bought up the strip of dilapidated council-owned beach chalets along the South Beach, knocked them down and replaced them with modern, rainbow-coloured structures. Stirling-Stewart opened the chalets with an announcement that Crow-on-Sea would now *finally* be able to compete with Scarborough and Whitby. The standard Stirling-Stewart chalets are fitted with kitchenettes, the deluxe models with toilets and small showers. There are even two-storey chalets, with balconies and little dining tables. A standard chalet costs £60 per day to rent, with package deals for weeks and seasons. A strip of ten chalets were put up for individual sale and are privately owned.

Stirling-Stewart made a bid to acquire the town council's North Beach chalets and was refused. The North Beach chalets were in better condition than the pre-renovation South Beach chalets had been. They were cheaper to rent (half the daily price of Stirling-Stewart's chalets) and seemed to be favoured by locals. Several attempts were made to acquire the chalets at increasing prices, and the council said no on every occasion, both for the sake of keeping the income and making sure that some chalets were available at more accessible prices.

In 2006, the first of a spate of chalet arsons began on the North Beach. Vandalism of chalets was a common occurrence: graffiti, littering and minor cosmetic damages to these small structures could be found almost on a weekly basis, particularly during the summer season. But no one had burned one down before.

On the morning of 19 November, Crow-on-Sea Council was alerted to the fire. It had been a damp, rainy evening, and the fire had not spread beyond its intended target. A private fire investigation found that the structure had been doused in petrol – an empty canister had been stuffed with a scarf and lit at the front of the chalet. Stirling-Stewart was investigated by local police, but only very briefly, and no charges were brought against him.

Chalets were subsequently found burned on the North Beach on 8 and 25 December in 2006, then 25 January, 15 February and 11 April (Easter Sunday) in 2007. The *Post-on-Sea* printed a story revealing Stirling-Stewart's attempts to acquire the North Beach chalets, and public suspicion grew immensely. At this point, fires began on the South Beach. Conveniently, two individually owned chalets were burned down on 4 May and 15 June, before one of Stirling-Stewart's standard rentals was targeted on 18 June.

A second police investigation turned up no suspects, and it was suggested the chalet-arsonists were just teenagers messing around. Perhaps chalet burning had become something of a trend at Crow-on-Sea Community High School, the local comprehensive – that it was nothing to do with business, or grievances with the council. Police officers and a fireman were sent to the high school shortly before its summer break in July, to explain the seriousness of the crime of arson. Of course, no police were sent to speak to the student body of independent fee-paying school Amplefield College, which is situated around thirty miles from Crow. This was despite the fact that a reasonable portion of its charges lived in Moorcock Hill, a wealthy satellite village to Crow-on-Sea, and could've easily housed the perpetrator.

Despite the lack of proof, it became generally accepted that teenagers from CCHS were responsible for the chalet burnings. Specifically, some teenaged denizen of Crow's large council estate: Warren's Place (known locally as 'the Warrens'). No one was caught, no individual child was suspected, but ask any resident of Crow-on-Sea 'Who burned down the beach chalets in the mid-2000s?' and they'll likely reply, 'Wasn't it some kid from down the Warrens?'

Because if one lives on Warren's Place, one is 'down the Warrens', and if one is down the Warrens they are, by default, liable to have committed any variety of crimes.

Simon Stirling-Stewart did not kick up much of a fuss; after all, the chalets were insured. His were rebuilt quickly and the council's were not. It took a 2008 fundraising effort by students at CCHS to repair the chalets – it was a project for a Year 10 PCHE class. Few remember that some kids from down the Warrens were responsible for this.

And then, in 2015, the chalet burnings began again.

Locals and crime enthusiasts say this points to only one possibility: that one of the girls involved in Joni's murder (or even Joni herself) was responsible. I think it is more likely that the chalet burnings were politically motivated.

Only Stirling-Stewart's chalets were targeted during the 2015–16 arsons, the first taking place shortly after his campaign for UKIP during the general election; these earlier arsons all seemed to coincide with a particularly obnoxious public appearance from him.

Simon Stirling-Stewart's UKIP candidacy (and his father's

fascist past) had made him a controversial figure nationally as well as locally, winning him spots on *Question Time* and *Newsnight*. He was banned from Twitter for calling an aggressive 'Follow Back, Pro EU' account holder a 'dirty little pikey'. One of the fantasy novels he'd written was torn apart on the popular feminist literature podcast *The Cliterati*, for its transparently pro-eugenics messaging and 'extremely horny' treatment of its Aryan elf and halfling races. His setting was silly and nostalgic – clearly his preferred, imagined version of England. People were talking about him; people hated him. He was a joke, but he was everywhere.

The last chalet burning took place on 23 June, the night of the EU referendum vote, with Joan Wilson inside of it. A few people saw the smoke, but no one called the police, or the fire brigade. It was just another (likely politically motivated) chalet burning. Someone was upset about the Leave result, and taking it out on the business interests of one of Crow's most obnoxious Leaver residents.

One anonymous witness (an early-morning jogger) told me: had the chalet been on the North Beach, she would have contacted emergency services. She saw that it was a Stirling-Stewart chalet, and let it burn.

GIRL A

Extract: *Thrilla Killaz*, Episode 107

Hosts: Kelly Robinson, Hannah Harris

ROBINSON: I fucking hate this Angelica girl, you know.

HARRIS: Yeah?

ROBINSON: Yeah, I think she might be the worst one.

HARRIS: [*Laughing*] Yeah, like the bar is pretty fucking low.

ROBINSON: But she's gone lower.

HARRIS: Do you know much about her dad?

ROBINSON: I remember him on *Question Time* and stuff, yeah. Weird Nazi vibes.

HARRIS: Fashy energy, yeah. I'm not defending her here, I was just going to say – not like she had much of a chance of turning out decent, is it?

ROBINSON: No, that's true, that's true. But yeah, I don't know, don't you think she's like . . .

HARRIS: A massive cringelord?

ROBINSON: [*Laughing*] Yeah, there's no other way to put it is there, she's just cringe. The musical stuff . . .

HARRIS: I know, what the fuck is that.

ROBINSON: Proof every Andrew Lloyd Webber stan is a fucking serial killer.

HARRIS: Can you imagine getting murdered by someone who's just that cringe? It'd make your murder feel cringey by extension, like, wouldn't it? Fucking hell, I don't want to get murdered obviously, but if you were getting killed and the murderer was like . . .

ROBINSON: FYI I'm super into *Cats*.

HARRIS: Yeah it's like . . . you'd rather get done by someone a bit more fucking dignified, wouldn't you?

ROBINSON: Specifically being murdered by someone this into *Cats* is actually my worst nightmare.

HARRIS: She's creeping up on you with a knife like, 'It's me, McStabbity, the murdering cat . . .'

ROBINSON: [*Laughing*] Stabbity stab, that's . . . where it's at?

HARRIS: [*Laughing*] T. S. Eliot found shaking.

ROBINSON: McStabbity found dead.

HARRIS: Stabbed?

ROBINSON: No, he was ironically hit by a car.

I think, to start, I would like to talk about the accusation that I am a bully. I disagree. I think it is unfair to call me a bully. I think adults don't remember what school is like. I feel that there are no 'bullies' and no 'victims' but that school is a place where people both bully and are bullied. So, while I think we can say that I might have 'bullied' Joan Wilson and arguably Violet Hubbard ages ago, I think it is also very fair and important to point out that Joni did actually bully me as well??

Everyone wants to talk about me pinning Joni down and straightening her hair, or when Aleesha messed with her DS, or even when Aleesha and I got the other girls in our class to scream and run away from her for a week. But no one wants to talk about what I went through. It's all about how I was a bully even though that was just in primary school and Joni was much older when she was bullying me. People even call my friend Aleesha a bully because of Joni, even though she DIED TRAGICALLY. We called her names and stuff but that's so like whatever. Like I'm evil or something because I was kind of mean in primary school. We would mostly just make fun and what – occasionally lock people in a bathroom or whatever? It's just stupid kid stuff, it meant nothing.

In primary school she'd always call me and my friends 'Barbies' and call us stupid and 'air heads' even though we were in the same ability sets all the time. And she would act like the way people on American television talked – she would say things like 'normal is just a setting on a washing machine' and was basically extremely cringey. She would shout 'AWKWARD!' in this weird nearly American voice.

69

She thought she was so much better than us, and clearly thought she was this massive underdog, and was like the main character of a TV show, where she was this cool Veronica outsider and we were the bitchy Heathers. So yes, we were mean to her when we were little. I was just calling her as I saw her: she was a freak, she was annoying, so I said it to her face that she was. You would've run away from her as well.

And yeah so she basically decided to ruin my fucking life in high school. But no one ever ever ever wants to talk about that, do they? Like she's the victim here.

*

There was a photo of Angelica on the cover of the *Post-on-Sea* in late 2016, printed the day after the judge waived her right to anonymity. She is staring directly into the lens with her lip curled, as if a persistent aunt has shoved a camera in her face at a family party. She is slim; her face is drawn and pinched-looking; the natural hollowness of her eyes and cheeks are exacerbated by exhaustion, which adds a few years to her. She could be twenty, on her way home from a long shift at a nightclub. Her features are small and symmetrical – she is pretty in a way which is not particularly remarkable. Her blonde highlights have grown out, and a mousy root now ends abruptly at her ears.

Angelica's father, Simon Stirling-Stewart, assured me that it is a particularly unflattering photograph.

'The kids called it "bitchy resting face", or something,' he said, as we sat in the 'drawing room' of his large, strange house.

The Stirling-Stewart home is outside of Crow-on-Sea, sitting in the village of Moorcock Hill. This is where Crow-on-Sea's wealthier pseudo-citizens make their homes; anyone who is anyone in Crow-on-Sea lives in Moorcock Hill.

The Stirling-Stewart house itself is surrounded by a high fence and a huge garden; the fence is adorned with a series of CCTV cameras. Simon had to 'buzz me in' through his grand electric gate. The house – which is massive – is cobbled together in a cacophony of architectural styles and was once featured in the Yorkshire Architectural Society's blog round-up of 'The Ugliest McMansions of North Yorkshire'. Seeing the house's Grecian columns supporting an overly large modern roof, sitting incongruous atop its mock-Tudor-revival visage, I couldn't help but agree with the Yorkshire Architectural Society.

As I arrived, there was both a Range Rover and a racing-green Jaguar convertible in the drive. I decided that the Jaguar had been parked there so that I, specifically, could see it.

Simon welcomed me in himself, and I was genuinely surprised that a member of staff had not seen to me. As if reading my mind, he said 'No butler, I'm afraid.' Then he told me he had a cleaner come twice a week, and a gardener, but he found employing 'a staff' a tad vulgar in this day and age. That surprised me coming from a man who had once written a *Daily Mail* article titled: 'Why Should I Be Embarrassed About Having More Than One Cleaner?'

I was led straight to the drawing room for our interview – not given the tour I had half expected. In the glimpse I got of the hallway, I saw illustrated maps of Yorkshire and a painting of the original Empire Hotel.

The drawing room was decorated like a Victorian library via a Bavarian hunting lodge; there were stuffed deer heads and ornamental shotguns on the walls, peeking out between imposing floor-to-ceiling bookcases. Stirling-Stewart sat me down on a brown Chesterfield couch, then settled in a high-backed leather chair opposite. Between us sat a heavy-looking wooden coffee table with a leather top.

I began with pleasantries (which he did not engage with) then asked if I could begin the interview. He shrugged, as if he hadn't invited me. I took some papers from my bag – mostly photocopies of court transcripts and newspapers – and the photo of Angelica at court was on the top.

He made the 'bitchy resting face' comment then drew my attention away from the newspaper photo and pointed behind me at a photographic portrait of Angelica, printed on a large canvas. 'That's my favourite picture of her. I like that one because she doesn't look at all like her mother,' he chuckled.

The photo was black and white; aged around fourteen, Angelica's long hair and round eyes both looked particularly pale, and her teeth particularly white. I noticed that the photo lacked the awkwardness, the pained expression one often finds in photos of teenagers. Her smile met her eyes; she grinned into the camera with her hand on her cheek. She was positively wholesome: the girl next door. Next to this canvas picture was one of Angelica and her older half-sister from Stirling-Stewart's first marriage. Luciana* takes a more typical teenaged photo, her shoulders hunched almost to her ears, her lips pressed into a tight line and stretched into an uncomfortable smile. Her hair is heavy and dark; her clothes are black.

Simon immediately excused his older daughter's comparative lack of comfort in front of a camera.

'Luciana is on the autism spectrum,' he announced – as if most girls her age wouldn't have loathed to be subject to this type of prissy studio photography. My own daughter at this age was liable to stick her hand in front of the lens if approached with a camera. When I pointed this out, Simon smirked and opened his mouth to say something – then didn't. An awkward silence hung between us for a moment.

I then asked when the canvas portraits were taken. He ignored me, and pointed at the picture of Luciana, commenting: 'That one looks borderline suicidal in every photo I have of her. No offence.' This was his first of many references to suicide, jumping off of bridges and drowning.

'Angelica was always lovely in photos, even if you caught her unawares. So photogenic. Apart from this one, of course.' Stirling-Stewart tapped Angelica's twisted face in the newspaper photo. 'This photo. That's bloody Sandra* all over. The spitting image.' Stirling-Stewart mimicked the sneer. 'That, imagine getting that every time you open your mouth. I got Sandra out of the house then *she* started doing it. That look – you just want to slap it off them, don't you?' Then he clarified that by 'them' he meant teenagers, not women in general. Then he asked me not to print that. Then he told me he doesn't care if I print it or not. He mumbled something about cancelling or being cancelled; not for the last time in this interview.

I found this a little ironic – between the two of us, I had far more experience with being *truly* cancelled than he did. The press were uncharacteristically gentle with him after

Angelica's arrest – probably due to all the clicks he'd earned them over the years. I'd genuinely lost work for controversies I'd been involved in, but, as of late 2019, Simon was practically on a 'I've been cancelled just for siring a murderer' comeback tour. On right-wing news sites and morning television he argued his right to continue his media career – he even threatened to write a book.

'I really do think most teenagers hate having their photograph taken,' I said. He shrugged again.

'Maybe the oddballs do. I never minded it,' he said. 'Angelica always took after me.'

Indeed, the room also contained several framed photos of Simon himself, including a glossy headshot alongside the cover of his first book, *A King Amongst Elves*. The framed images declared him '1997's Fantasy Best-seller'. In the headshot, Stirling-Stewart was looking over his shoulder, wearing a thick flying jacket with one eyebrow raised. The book cover, now dated in style, showed an illustration of a muscular male elf, swishing his long blonde hair as he killed several green goblins with an enormous (and decidedly phallic) sword.

There's also a poster of the book's cinematic adaptation: *Blood Throne*. I was somewhat surprised to see the poster displayed so proudly and prominently, as *Blood Throne* was one of the biggest cinematic flops of 2005. Largely forgotten, the film is occasionally named among 'the worst of all time' but hasn't had the memetic cultural impact of films like *The Room* or *Showgirls*.

'You've got a foot in the entertainment industry,' I tried. 'Angelica was interested in acting, wasn't she?'

'Yes. Taking after me again.'

'How else did she take after you?' I asked.

Simon sighed heavily. He walked over to his desk, past a grand fireplace where three small, framed photos sat on the mantel. I became suddenly aware of how cluttered this room was – a veritable museum of the life and times of Simon Stirling-Stewart. The one which stood out: Stirling-Stewart and disgraced TV and radio personality Vance Diamond, arm in arm, smoking cigars.

On Simon's large oak desk was a cardboard storage box labelled 'Angelica', which I had only just noticed in amongst the visual cacophony of the room. Stirling-Stewart explained that he had taken the time to dig out a few school reports and exercise books for me to look at.

'She takes after me in a lot of ways – you'll see here. In her reports and her schoolwork – I think a lot of her best aspects really shine out,' he said. It's not really the answer I was looking for.

'Does she take after your interest in the occult?' I tried. Simon looked at me, baffled. 'Your haunted hotel, the ghost hunters.'

'No,' said Simon. 'She never believed any of that.'

'No mention of communicating with ghosts, or—'

'No.'

After an awkward silence, I asked why he had now chosen to invite me to his home; to grant me relatively intimate access. He cocked his head, as if I had asked him a stupid question, and I was confused because he had been downright hostile to my prior attempts to contact him.

I had been fobbed off by his publicist, his literary agent and the staff at his hotel. I had a brief phone call with him after several weeks of chasing – he called me a leech and a hack, and while Diana Spencer (Jayde Spencer's mother) might speak to me 'for fifty quid', he was 'too rich to be bought'. Then he hung up on me. Then he called me a week later and invited me to interview him.

When I pointed this out, he seemed nonplussed. He said he thought about it, and he didn't want the book to be biased against Angelica. He was concerned that in a 'post-woke' world, I would attempt to lay the most blame on Angelica. Because she is the most privileged of Joan Wilson's assailants, and because of Simon's own association with UKIP, he wanted to make sure he had input. He wanted to make sure that I did not approach this with a political agenda. He was concerned about my reputation – I am a known 'champagne socialist'.

I changed the subject; I really didn't want to get hung up on our opposing politics. I wanted to get started and start right at the beginning – to talk about Angelica's mother.

Sandra did not wish to speak to me in detail. She asked me to 'take everything Simon says with a huge pinch of salt'. She visited Angelica at the secure unit weekly and feels her ex-husband has neglected their daughter since her conviction.

Sandra is twelve years younger than Simon and was his second wife. Luciana was almost three when Angelica was born, and her own mother had been out of the picture for six months. The revelation of Sandra's pregnancy had, in fact, broken up Stirling-Stewart's first marriage.

Sandra quickly took the place of Luciana's mother. Sandra was younger and from a more stable background than this first wife – a Crow-on-Sea townie who grew up down the infamous Warrens.

Luciana initially lived with her mother, but Stirling-Stewart was granted custody after six months due to the mother's poor mental health and financial difficulties. It was thought this was for the best – Luciana was educated privately, well fed and well dressed. Luciana's mother (who had signed a prenuptial agreement guaranteeing she would receive nothing upon divorce) could not guarantee a comfortable life for both her and her daughter – she left the marriage totally empty-handed. When Luciana clashed with her father (as she often did) Simon was careful to remind her of the life she was granted – and the life from which she had been 'rescued'.

While Simon's first marriage was breaking down, Sandra was being swept off her feet. Her older lover – a glamorous author with his old money and his posh hotel – told her he was already separated from his first wife. She wasn't clear on the details of it all until years into her marriage.

Once the first wife was out of the way, Sandra was moved into the home. They were married in a small ceremony. Her pregnancy was easy – she called it 'blissful'.

Her only worry was discovering that Angelica was in breech position. The baby was delivered early, via Caesarian, and she would be Sandra's only child.

Angelica was a good baby; she slept often and cried little. Simon talked about her infancy only in comparison to Luciana. Angelica was (appropriately) an angel, where Luciana was 'satanic'; a blonde while Luciana was 'a swarthy little thing'; a tiny bundle where Luciana was 'like a sack of potatoes'. He was relieved that with Angelica's birth he hadn't produced 'another one' – another Luciana.

Simon described Angelica as 'singing and dancing before

she could talk and walk'. She played princess games, babied her dolls, and made up dances.

'We took the plunge and paid for dancing and drama lessons as soon as she was old enough to attend. She was just so . . . normal,' Simon told me. 'It was so nice after Lucie, to have a normal one. She was *exactly* what I'd wanted from a little girl.' When I asked what Lucie was like, out of curiosity, he rolled his eyes. '*Pokémon*,' he said. 'I couldn't get her to do anything. All she did was play *Pokémon* and talk about *Pokémon* when she was little.'

I told Simon that Luciana, in what he had told me, reminded me of Violet Hubbard and primary-school-era Joni. I repeated the anecdote I'd heard from Joni's mother – that Joni had pulled a clump of hair from Aleesha Dowd's scalp after Aleesha took her Nintendo DS and erased her *Pokémon* save. Simon's face soured. He asked me why that was relevant and so I moved on.

A report from the nursery Angelica attended described her as 'bubbly', 'talkative' and 'dominant'. She was popular with the staff, who enjoyed her cheerful disposition and made-up dances, despite several incidents with other children.

The report noted that Angelica had 'quite the temper'.

Shortly after joining the nursery, she pushed another girl who had shoved in front of her in the queue for lunch. It had been raining, and their shoes were slippery. The girl fell, and split her chin, requiring stitches. The girl Angelica pushed was Aleesha Dowd. Angelica presented Aleesha with an enormous teddy bear at the weekend by way of apology – Simon not wishing to alienate acquaintance and business associate Gerald Dowd – and the two became fast friends.

'Inseparable, I'd say. I thought they were a little too close at times,' Simon told me. 'One of Angelica's only flaws, particularly at that age – she was more of a follower than a leader. If Aleesha had jumped off a bridge, she'd probably have followed.'

Despite his concerns, Simon chose to send Angelica to Crow-on-Sea Primary with Aleesha. He'd intended to send her to Wicksworth Preparatory School, a private girls' school – and a feeder school for Amplefield College.

'I'd sent Lucie there, obviously – I can't say she thrived there, but they did catch her "symptoms".' Simon made air quotes around the word *symptoms*. 'I did want Angelica to go there. I even tried to convince Gerry to send Aleesha to Wicksworth – God knows he could afford it – but he told me private school robs children of their character. A stance I know he regretted, given what happened. Anyway, I didn't think it'd hurt for her to spend a *bit* of time at a comp – especially just a primary school. She wasn't like Lucie – she was very social; I didn't want to split her up from her little friend. And it'd be easy to pull her out and send her to Wicksworth if anything went wrong.'

At primary school, Angelica's behaviour became worse, according to teachers (though not according to Simon). Angelica's school report from reception stated that she 'must learn to be kinder to other children' and was 'impatient with classmates'. In Year 1, a teacher wrote: *Angelica lacks empathy and patience. If another child annoys her, she will default to name-calling and pushing. I have concerns around several suspected biting incidents I would like to discuss with you. Having attempted to phone your house on several occasions, I would appreciate if you could make time for this.'*

I asked Simon about these 'suspected biting incidents'.

'Oh that woman – the teacher – she had a vendetta against Angelica. That's why I wanted to show you these reports. You can see how unfair they are, how they're obviously biased. They always assumed the worst of her. She could never do anything right.'

I did, however, speak to the teacher, who now works at a different primary school. She wished to remain anonymous. In her words:

'To my memory, which I'm happy to concede is not perfect – this was fifteen years ago after all – Angelica took a reception girl out of sight of teachers on the playground, and bit her very hard on the arm. Then she told the little girl that no one would believe her if she reported what had happened to a teacher. The little girl did end up telling someone, though. At the end of the day, after her own teacher noticed she was upset and coaxed it out of her. It then came out that Angelica had done this several times, to several reception children – and had even bitten a boy twice in two separate incidents. Angelica denied it, and there was no real way to prove it. Her father was very ingrained into the community. I tried to call him into the school to discuss Angelica's behaviour, but he ignored me. When I took the matter to the head teacher, I was advised to drop the matter. When I tried to install the most basic consequence for Angelica's behaviour – I tried to prevent her from attending the Christmas trip to Flamingo Land – her father complained to the head, and I was disciplined.'

By the time Aleesha and Angelica had befriended Kayleigh Brian in Year 2, the trio were firmly established as bullies. They seemed to intentionally style themselves after 'mean girls' they had seen in children's television programmes – and Angelica's penchant for American television, and Americanism in general, is well reported. From my interview with Lauren Everett (a school friend we'll hear more from later):

'It was like she was pretending to be an American high school bitch. Like er . . . have you seen *High School Musical*? She used to really like those films, and she used to act like Sharpay from that. It's like she literally thought she was the Sharpay of the school sometimes.'

The girls would frequently call other children ugly, lock other girls in toilet stalls, and make a show of screaming at and running away from certain children in the playground. When considering if Angelica was happy at home during this period, Simon gave a non-committal and dismissive answer, as if the question had been stupid. He mentioned that Angelica's mother had moved out by the time Angelica was seven but that Angelica was 'fine', and had not been particularly 'bothered about' her mother. Angelica was Daddy's girl – always had been, always would be.

Sandra agreed that the divorce didn't seem to affect Angelica too much – to the point Sandra was a little hurt. According to Sandra, Simon didn't discipline Angelica, leaving Sandra to be the 'bad guy' and constantly undermining her. This put a considerable strain on their relationship.

Regardless of her reaction to the divorce, Angelica's bullying behaviour at school continued. Simon did not agree that Joni Wilson was the focus of much of his daughter's ire. While his daughter may have had a 'mean streak', he viewed her more as a harmless prankster, someone who would play jokes and tricks on other children; that everything she did was 'in good fun' and not particularly targeted at any individual child.

'She only ever talked about her friends and never mentioned Joan or that . . . Violet girl. Violet is the real little psycho here, in my opinion.'

He recalled only one mention of Joni – when they were organising Angelica's eighth birthday party. Simon was making his way down the list of children in her class. Joan Wilson was at the end of the register – Simon remembered thinking Joan was an odd, dated name for an eight-year-old to have. He asked Angelica if she'd like to invite Joan and Angelica tipped her head back and laughed at the idea. It stuck in Simon's head; he remembered thinking Angelica looked like a tiny grown-up.

'I remember Violet better, obviously. From primary school – before she and my Angelica started orbiting that Dolly Hart. There was a bit of an incident. Angelica, Kayleigh and Aleesha locked Violet in a toilet cubicle during her very first week at Crow Primary . . . As much as I'd hate to speak ill of the dead,' Simon told me, 'locking other little girls in the toilet was very much Aleesha's *thing*. I doubt Angelica had much to do with it, beyond being stood there. And even if she did, I honestly don't think locking someone in a loo is the end of the world.'

Aleesha had shoved Violet into the cubicle, and Kayleigh and Angelica had prevented her from opening it again, while Aleesha 'gummed up' the lock with a wad of, as Simon recalls, playdough. Angelica took an equal share of the blame with

Kayleigh and Aleesha – around which there was a sense of injustice in the Stirling-Stewart household.

From Angelica:
It was Aleesha's favourite thing to do – so weird that it gets pinned on me. She would stuff the lock up with blue tack or gum or something, and the teachers wouldn't let her have anything like that after she locked three or four girls in there. I think we got in worse trouble because it was Violet's first week and she was such a baby about it. After that none of us were allowed to go to the toilet without an adult for pretty much all of Year 3 even though all I did was hold the door shut. Even though that's YET another example of how something someone else did get blamed on moi, and it was super unfair? But anyway. Even though I was always getting blamed for things that she did, I really think back with lots of good memories on Aleesha.

I asked Simon how he would describe Angelica as she entered Years 4, 5 and 6.

'Precocious,' he replied.

Years earlier than Simon had expected, Angelica's bedroom became a fog of Impulse body spray, full of sticky pink cosmetics he objected to her wearing. Not enough to make her stop, however. He imagined she might get picked on by the other girls; he didn't want Angelica to feel left out, like she was weird. He remembered the boys he went to school with, how he'd sneer and roll his eyes at the ones who said 'my parents won't let me' about some vaguely dangerous or taboo activity.

'So I let her wear it, basically. I truly didn't think I'd be getting the "your daughter is wearing too much makeup and refuses to wipe her face" phone call till she was in high school. She'd only gone in with some lip gloss and mascara, if I recall correctly. She said Sandra bought it for her.'

Unbeknownst to Simon, Angelica had begun shoplifting makeup.

I was able to speak briefly to Luciana, who told me she was often 'forced' to escort Angelica and friends around the high street. Luciana, by her own admission, was a terrible babysitter and failed to intervene or prevent much of her sister's mischief.

'They tried to steal from Farnham's[4] once, but the staff caught them. We all got pulled into the manager's office, and they tried to tell me off for not watching them and playing on my Nintendo DS instead. Then Angelica told them I'm *intellectually disabled*, and told them who our and Aleesha's dads were, so they just let us go. Put the shits up them about stealing, though. At least for a little bit.'

Simon assured me Angelica wasn't all 'lip gloss and bullying'. Angelica had become extremely serious about following a career as an actress. She wanted to go to drama school in London and move to Los Angeles.

'It seemed like a perfectly decent idea to me. I could use my industry connections to help her. I would've been happy for her to take the plunge.' Simon gestured over his shoulder at the *Blood Throne* poster. 'I've got plenty of contacts.' As

4 A large department store in the middle of Crow which boasts some higher end cosmetic and clothing brands.

if sensing the sarcastic comment about *Most Haunted* et al. that had just popped into my head, he added: 'And not just through the ghost-hunting reality-show scene.' He told me I shouldn't sniff at ghost hunters – everything in this house was either paid for by the business drummed up by ghost television shows or his *Blood Throne* money. He neglected to mention any generational wealth he may have inherited.

Angelica liked to hang around when ghost-hunting shows interviewed her father – she can often be seen in the background of these shows. When she was small, she asked the crews if they would film her singing, or dancing, and occasionally they obliged. One crew even dressed her up as a ghost child and had her run around the gardens of the hotel for B-roll.

'So she *was* interested,' I said.

'In what?'

'The ghosts.'

'She was interested in being on television.'

Simon paid for weekend drama lessons and dancing and singing classes. But she would often only attend in spates. She was sensitive to criticism and would drop out of these classes after just a few weeks. The drama lessons would last longer but would tend to break down over some arcane social drama which Angelica was at the centre of – Simon had no desire to hear about these incidents at the time, never mind recall them for me years later.

Angelica was looking forward to high school, where she could take drama from Year 7 onward. With no grating stage-school children to overshadow her, she felt she'd stand out – she'd really show the other children what she could do.

It seemed that Angelica liked being a big fish in a small pond, and this was perhaps the reason she was so averse to going to private school. She asked Simon once, 'If I go to Amplefield, will everyone still say I'm rich and posh and stuff?' And Simon, thinking she didn't enjoy sticking out, said, 'No, at Amplefield everyone will be like us.'

'And she didn't seem to like that,' he told me. She wanted to follow her friends to the comp. 'I didn't mind. Luciana was doing terribly at Amplefield anyway – I refused to send another penny to them.'

So it was decided (against Sandra's wishes) that Angelica would attend CCHS. In her final year of primary school she tried to act as grown-up as possible – she copied girls from television more and more.

She was so grown-up that she even attempted to lobby teachers to change the location of her class's final school trip. Poseidon's Kingdom, the indoor waterpark – that was for babies. She did not have an alternative suggestion, and the school had a deal with Poseidon's Kingdom. Regardless of her protests, they went.

Poseidon's Kingdom and Other Attractions

Crow-on-Sea was never a jewel in the crown of Britain's coastline – but it served a purpose. An affordable destination sandwiched between two bigger, more popular resort towns – Crow was ready to accept Scarborough and Whitby's run-off, offering cheaper food and leisure activities as well as quieter beaches. But by the 1970s there was an increasing need to draw holidaymakers away from foreign shores – not just Scarborough and Whitby.

But even for destinations more upmarket than Crow-on-Sea, the dream of a booming domestic tourist industry was dying. As fondly as I recall my parents whizzing me over to Hastings or St Leonards as a lad, the idea of staying for longer than a short weekend break seemed absurd even in the 1970s. Particularly when the Riviera, the Amalfi Coast or even the bright lights of New York City were all short plane rides away.

Notable examples of Crow's attempt to elevate itself into one of Britain's best holiday destinations included the construction of Astro Ape's Amusement Park, the Monte-Crow Casino, and later, indoor waterpark Poseidon's Kingdom.

Opened in the early 1980s to much fanfare, the Monte--Crow sits beside the North Beach. It is garish, drenched in neon, and was voted 'Crow-on-Sea's Biggest Eyesore' five years running in the local paper. It is open twenty-four hours a day, and has no windows or natural light sources – on special occasions, it enforces a black-tie dress code. Still hugely popular, the casino is owned by local businessman Colin Collier, and was previously part-owned by Vance Diamond.

Signs hang near the roulette tables and slot machines reading: 'GAMBLING SHOULD BE FUN, NOT A PROBLEM and THIS IS A GAME, NOT AN INVESTMENT.'

Built around the same time as the Monte-Crow, Astro Ape's Amusement Park has been derelict since the late nineties. Owned and run by a rare 'out of town' investor (a large European conglomerate), Astro Ape's is now a favourite haunt of photographers, thrill-seekers and internet people with investment in 'urban exploring' – it was also occasionally featured on the ghost-hunting shows that haunted Crow for much of the 2000s. A search of 'Astro Ape' on YouTube returns hundreds of hours of drone footage, screaming teenagers at night and photograph compilations created by people who have broken into (or flown over) the site of the park, which was closed off by the council for safety reasons.

A particular favourite video of mine is titled 'GHOST MONKEY???? CREEPY ABANDONNED AMUSEMENT PARK AT NIGHT!!' from YouTuber JayPeeMcCafferty. Mr McCafferty's channel features him and his girlfriend Polly as they explore various abandoned places all over the UK. The video has around 100,000 views, and is ten minutes long. Polly (who claims to be psychic) screams every time she encounters one of the many plastic Astro Ape statues dotted around the park, and says they contain 'a weird vibe, a weird energy'.

Despite a forced seriousness to the video, a surprisingly large portion of the footage is dedicated to two pieces of graffiti sprayed on the Space Banana stall,[5] which read,

5 The stand is shaped like a banana, and sold banana-flavoured ice cream from plastic banana-shaped 'cones'.

respectively: *astro ape fingered your dad* and *astro nonce narner in your arse*.

In the early 2000s, a teen climbed the rickety Rumble in the Jungle roller coaster and had to be retrieved by the local fire service. In the mid-2000s, a small group of homeless drug users had taken shelter in the park, and a non-fatal stabbing took place during a dispute over a bag of heroin. Despite these small incidents, constant break-ins and the site's issues with squatters, teenaged drinkers and YouTubers, Astro Ape's Amusement Park is yet to see a death, or any serious injury.

The same cannot be said for Poseidon's Kingdom.

Poseidon's Kingdom was built, quite literally, on a burial ground. This isn't a huge anomaly for the UK, of course. The land is old and as densely packed with corpses as people; you'd be hard pressed to find a structure built with no bones in its foundations. Without incident, the land which had once been known as Old Yard was purchased, its largely worn and unreadable gravestones removed[6] in the mid-1980s. Any skeletons which were inadvertently exhumed during the construction process were reinterred in Crow's largest churchyard, in a mass, unmarked grave.

A search through the *Post-on-Sea*'s archives reveals a few letters sent to the editor around the time of the park's opening, decrying the disturbance of Old Yard, including this gem from April 1986:

6 A handful of intact headstones from Old Yard are still kept by the Yorkshire Heritage Museum just outside Scarborough, and can occasionally be seen on display.

Dear Editor,

I am writing to express my concern, NEIGH, my DISMAY that Old Yard has been dismantled and dare I say RAPED in such a manner. I see not how the owners of this 'Poseidon's Kingdom' expect to go on without retribution from the spirit world! I see your flashy indoors water park and I see it only becoming a cursed place. The spirits will be angry. I am prepared to offer my psychic cleansing services to the owners of Poseidon's Kingdom at an extremely fair price. I will also offer discounted cleansings on anyone who visits Poseidon's Kingdom and feels they have brought home a curse, ghoul or a generally negative psychic residue.

Best regards,

Emmeline Foxx of Crow's Crystal Ball, 112 Seaside Way

In response, editor Tom Carrow wrote:

Dear Emmeline,

Thank you for your concern . . . Generally we charge £20 for a business listing, but I was told this 'warning' could be considered to be in the public interest. So, here it is.

Flabbergasted,

Tom Carrow,

Editor

Rather grand in its heyday, Poseidon's Kingdom was one of the first indoor waterparks to open in the UK. Decked out in a faux neo-classical style, the decor included almost one hundred 'marble' statues, and the walls were printed with mock-frescos of Greek gods, and the Acropolis.

It boasted 'tons of slides and miles of smiles' and contained a small Greek restaurant[7] and bar for the depository of parents and relief of hungry swimmers. Leisure seekers could find small, shallow pools with little slides for very small children, as well as twisting chutes and dramatic body slides.

Two weeks following Poseidon's grand opening, hundreds of children were struck with a gastrointestinal illness caused by the parasitic alveolate cryptosporidium, commonly found in swimming pools. This resulted in bad press, and a brief closure for cleaning. Up and running again by mid-June, the Poseidon saw no issues till December of the next year, when injuries began in earnest after the completed installation of its two most famous slides.

'The Trident' was made up of three tube slides dramatically twisting around one another, spitting riders out into the park's largest swimming pool, Ionia. The end of the slides shot riders out at an ill-considered angle, leading to periodic collisions and injuries.

The slide considered to be the scariest, and the subject of bragging rights for Crow's schoolchildren, was 'The Olympic Drop', almost a sheer thirty-foot plunge into the smaller Aegea pool. Playground boasters could be heard to claim they'd gone down it fifty times, and never even got scared.

Though, perhaps they should have been. Loath as I am to admit some prescience on the part of local psychic Emmeline

7 'Greek-*ish*' I'm told, by a Crow-on-Sea resident who wishes to remain anonymous. A former employee of Poseidon's Kingdom, they tell me that though Greek salads and a northern English approximation of souvlaki were on offer, they largely served hot dogs and pizzas.

Foxx, Poseidon's Kingdom was plagued with problems from its opening in May of 1986 all the way up to its eventual closure in 2012.

The Olympic Drop and the Trident were added to attract older children. Barry Proud, the owner, was aware the park had very quickly gained a reputation as somewhere for babies and little children. Local legend goes that Proud drew the two slides on the back of a beer mat in the pub. The 'designs' were refused by the engineers who'd built Poseidon's original, more pedestrian crop of slides, and Proud had to find a 'rogue engineer' to create the slides for him. Mr Proud, now the area's Conservative MP, refused to comment; but when asked, former employees all came out with the same, slightly strange 'rogue engineer' comment.

A former student of Crow-on-Sea Primary school told me about the first trip the school took there with its Year 5s and 6s, for a Christmas treat. Two students violently crashed into one another as they exited the Trident slide, resulting in a split skull, a broken nose, several missing teeth, and a new rule that only one visitor could ride the Trident at any time (defeating the object of the slide, and causing huge queues).

The Olympic Drop also appeared to see a high number of broken limbs. It was easy to catch a leg or an arm at a funny angle during your plummet, and the pool one landed in was rather shallow, leading to several 'hard landings' (and broken ankles and toes) at the bottom of the pool. Despite calls from parents of injured children to close this slide, complaints went ignored, and the slide stayed open.

Perhaps stoked by Emmeline Foxx's repeated letters to the newspaper, warning of hauntings, negative energies and, at one point, goblins, staff began to report odd sounds at night, missing equipment, and an upswing in accidents around the anniversary of the opening of Poseidon's Kingdom.

In January of 1994, (admittedly, during a slow news week), the *Post-on-Sea* finally took the proverbial bait, and ran a story on the 'haunting'. Tom Carrow having retired from his position as editor-in-chief in 1990, the *Post* was taken over by ex-*Daily Mail* journalist, Isabella Rodney.

The following article was printed alongside a particularly glamorous headshot of Emmeline Foxx.

POSEIDON'S CURSE?

COULD BRITAIN'S FAVOURITE INDOOR WATERPARK BE HAUNTED?

Have a spate of accidents been caused by angry spirits? We spoke to a current member of staff at Poseidon's Kingdom about the terrifying incidents which seem to plague one of Crow-on-Sea's favourite attractions.

Having been provided with the park's accident report book, we can tell you that Poseidon's Kingdom records up to ten accidents a week, and averages one broken limb a month. Many of these breakages are caused by the dramatic 'Olympic Drop' slide, which sees youngsters plummet a sheer thirty feet into the pool below.

What could be causing this glut of injuries? Poor attention paid to safety regulations? Or something supernatural?

We all know Poseidon's Kingdom is built on the former 'Old Yard' gravesite, which housed plague victims, among others.

We spoke to our anonymous source about a particularly spooky incident.

'I was closing the park down with another colleague. We mop and stuff, and add cleaning chemicals to the pool. Some proper cleaners come in once a week on Sundays and do the whole thing over, but we just do the upkeep at night. I was with B, and he was mopping, and I was cleaning up the restaurant area, doing the bins, so I had my back to him. I hear him shout, and then this big splash, and I run over and he's face down in the pool with his head all bleeding and that. I pull him out – we all have lifeguard training – and luckily he's still breathing, but he coughs up loads of water and I have to get an ambulance in and everything. And he says he slipped but he feels like something grabbed his ankle. Because he was literally just stood still mopping, you know, like not running, just stood still. I put my notice in the next day.'

Shocked by this story, and the high number of accidents reported, we asked staunch opponent of the park, local psychic and regular correspondent Emmeline Foxx, for her take on the situation.

'Poseidon's Kingdom has angered the spirit world,' she said, in a husky voice. 'I wouldn't be surprised if there were more incidents. If you've recently been to Poseidon's Kingdom, I will honour my offer of discount cleansings. I'm even happy to offer free cleansings to former employees.'

You can claim your cleansing at Crow's Crystal Ball, 112 Seaside Way.

We reached out to Poseidon's Kingdom for comment, and heard back from owner, Barry Proud:

'Well, for a start, the broken limbs? Not as many as you're

94

claiming, and a lot of those were very minor fractures, anyway. We tell them to keep their legs together, keep their arms folded, and if they ignore the safety guidelines and land a bit funny that's hardly my fault, is it now? Now, your employee there, the one that had the accident. Ex-employee now, because his notice went in. Probably worth noting we give out uniform pool shoes, don't we? Grippy, waterproof shoes for cleaning – basically wellies. It's what we want them wearing unless they're on lifeguard duty. So your man there, he was wearing flipflops wasn't he? Might not have been running round, but it's easy to slip, go over on your ankle in a pair of flipflops. Says he doesn't remember slipping? Feels like something grabbed him? Banged his bloody head, didn't he? And that young lass didn't even see it. Said it herself.'

Have you had a strange experience at Poseidon's Kingdom? Let us know! We pay £50 for stories. Call the news desk on 0405 111-6397 or write to us at News Desk, Post-on-Sea, 23 Crow Road.

And the residents of Crow did indeed call. Next Saturday, the *Post-on-Sea* printed a collection of horror stories, the likes of which made the writers of *Scary Movie* look like Shirley Jackson. Ranging from dull to absurd, to oddly bawdy, I've included a few favourites below:

Zack, 8, Crow-on-Sea
I am eight years old and I went to posidens kingdom for my birthday. I had a lovely time and I ate pizza except for when I went in the big pool I thought I saw a scary face at the bottom and when I tried to get out the pool something grabbed my

ankle!!!! I had a bruise on my ankle but I liked the pizza it was pepperony.

Anonymous, 73, Moorcock Hill

I visited Poseidon's Kingdom in 1991 with my grandson, who is now thirteen years old. I spent much of my time at the restaurant, enjoying the newly released Inspector Rebus novel along with a half price jug of sangria, which is certainly not particularly Greek – but 'when in Rome,' I suppose. Strangely, a saltshaker on the table kept tipping over! I even put it over to the opposite side of the table. I stared at it, and it fell, as if knocked by an invisible hand! I could not believe my eyes. My grandson ran over suddenly, looking panicked. 'Has the salt man gone away nana?' he asked. I was terrified. We left immediately and haven't been back since.

Anonymous

I (23, Female) went to get changed out my swimming costume. I felt something enter the changing room and brush up behind me. I was wet, naked and very vulnerable. I could feel fingers in my long, blonde hair. I thought a man had slipped in behind me! I was very frightened, and immediately covered myself with the tiny towel I had in the changing room. But there was no body there! I swear I felt something touching me, while I was changing, and while I was naked. I wrapped the towel around my still damp body and went to check the area. I only saw other women going into changing cubicles. Perhaps a woman had snuck in with me . . . but I didn't hear the door. I turned to the mirrors, and was terrified to see a pentagram drawn on the mirror in lipstick. 'Who did this?' I asked. But no one answered . . . except that strange feeling of fingers in my hair . . .

For the next two decades, Poseidon's Kingdom carried on like this. Once every couple of years there'd be a few newspaper stories about the accidents, Emmeline Foxx would offer to cleanse its visitors at increasingly discounted prices, and its owner (the park transitioned from the hands of Barry Proud to his son Alfie in 2002) would complain about children ignoring safety instructions, and lazy journalism.

Amusing though this has been, to lay my cards on the table, I do not believe that Poseidon's Kingdom was haunted by anything other than an owner too cheap to refurbish its most popular and dangerous slides. Perhaps it was also haunted by a high-turnover staff of poorly paid teenagers. I certainly do not think 'ghosts' are responsible for the 2012 drowning of eleven-year-old Aleesha Dowd – the final nail in Poseidon's proverbial coffin.

By the late 2000s, the park's reputation had suffered greatly from stories of broken legs, food poisoning and mysterious waterborne illnesses. Emmeline Foxx had moved on from writing to the local paper to ranting on Facebook (both in posts and videos) and attendance to the park had rapidly dwindled.

As of 2012, Crow-on-Sea Primary School had remained one of the park's only loyal customers. The huge discounts given to the school meant that trips to the waterpark occurred almost once per half-term, and with minimal injuries to students on these trips, the school kept going.

As an end-of-year treat, Crow Primary took its Year 5s and 6s, as always, to Poseidon's Kingdom. Staff numbers had shrunk as health and safety issues increased: there were only two lifeguards on duty, both attending to an epileptic Year 5 student's seizure while Aleesha drowned.

Aleesha Dowd had just come back from a holiday with her family in Fuerteventura. The Dowds always went on holiday during term time (to the annoyance of teachers) to catch the better prices. Her hair had been braided while abroad, a small section of it wrapped in colourful thread, fixed into place with a heavy, star-shaped bead.

She went down the left slide of the Trident. The member of staff manning the slide had run to the other pool, where the Year 5 was seizing. Aleesha decided to go down the slide feet first, but lying on her stomach. The left slide of the Trident had developed a tiny gap, over the years. A bolt slackening, ever so slightly. Enough to create space for a star-shaped bead at the end of a hair wrap. The braid was caught and Aleesha was stuck, face down, in a stream of water. Based on best guesses, it took her less than a minute to drown.

The child who'd been waiting to use the slide next (the only child waiting) counted to thirty, then to sixty, then got in and slid down the left slide. That child was Violet Hubbard.

Violet was unable to stop herself from crashing into Aleesha, now limp in the slide. Her weight and sudden impact dislodged the hair wrap from Aleesha's scalp, and they both slid to the bottom of the pool, Violet screaming all the way.

Most children were watching the lifeguards, but Joni Wilson was waiting for Violet. She watched Aleesha's body land in the pool along with a screaming Violet.

Angelica and Kayleigh had been watching the lifeguards deal with the seizure – most of the children had been gathered by teachers, who'd pulled them out of the pool while the lifeguards were busy. When Violet screamed, a number of students ran to see what was happening, followed by teachers. There were more screams as children noticed the body. One teacher pulled Violet from the pool, while another jumped in (fully dressed) for Aleesha. An ambulance was called, and the teenaged lifeguards attempted resuscitation – but it was too late. Aleesha was pronounced dead on the scene.

The children were taken back to school and picked up by their parents. Violet Hubbard was interviewed by the police, along with the lifeguards, teachers and the owner, Alfie Proud. Despite Gerald Dowd's insistence that someone should be charged, the incident was declared a tragic freak accident.

Alfie Proud attempted to reopen Poseidon's Kingdom after a short closure – but Gerald Dowd organised a protest. Concerned parents holding placards outside the park for a week demanded its closure – and after seven days of no business, Proud closed Poseidon's Kingdom.

'CHILD DEATH A LONG TIME COMING, SPIRITS ANGRY' read the headline of Emmeline Foxx's first column for the *Post-on-Sea*; she was even photographed performing an exorcism on the building. After several break-ins, the building was demolished, and the land put up for sale.

Despite the exorcism, the land still has not been sold. There now lies an odd, empty, grassy space behind Crow's North Beach, left curiously alone by day drinkers and picnickers. The council are now in the process of turning the area into a small play park – Gerald Dowd's attempts to have it declared the 'Aleesha Dowd Memorial Park' have so far been denied.

How did Angelica cope with Aleesha's death?

'Well, she was sad,' Simon said. 'But basically fine.' He changed the subject – Gerald, now he was a wreck. 'Drowning is an incredibly painful way to die, isn't it?'

Gerald went mad buying things, and naming them after Aleesha. Vegas by the Sea was briefly renamed 'Aleesha's' – but the name was changed back when business declined. He bought a number of park benches alongside his attempt to have a plaque installed on the empty Poseidon's Kingdom plot. He petitioned Simon to change a name of a hotel suite to 'Aleesha's Room'.

'And then he bought that bloody pub,' Simon told me with a roll of his eyes.

Simon is referring to the Spoiled Princess, which Dowd then gifted to his older daughter, Mia. From Angelica's writing:

Mia Dowd technically owns the pub and there's this memorial wall to Aleesha in there. And it says 'Aleesha – Our Princess Forever'. And Mia always served us there, which was really nice of her. She acted like she owned it even though it was actually her dad's, and he just made it seem like she'd saved up and bought it so it'd make a good story in the paper. I know, because obviously my dad is friends with Gerald Dowd. 'Tragic sister saves money, doesn't go to uni, is a hard grafter and buys pub in sister's honour', or whatever. To be honest I don't think anyone believed the story – like no one thought that Mia actually bought the pub herself. Because everyone actually kind of hates the Dowds, which is saying a lot about them considering them having a dead little kid and everything.

'He let Mia run the Princess from being about eighteen. It became a hub for teen drinkers, I understand,' Simon told me. Then, he became defensive. 'But I'd rather they were drinking there than out in some park, or somewhere I didn't know the owners. Better they're in their little speakeasy – the park in Crow is a rape hotspot, you know. And you don't want them drinking at the beach – not with the tides. One child drowning – that's enough for me. I'd think it'd be enough for you as well.'

I ignored this, and tried to get us back on topic. I asked how often Angelica went to the Spoiled Princess and, disdainfully, he informed me she only really started going when she began 'hanging round' with Dolly Hart. I asked again how Angelica coped with Aleesha's death. How did it affect her as she started high school? Did it contribute to Angelica's psychological state? He stonewalled me, shrugging again like an adolescent and chuckling, insisting his daughter did not have any 'psychological state' that I should concern myself with.

I argued that Angelica's mental state is extremely important to understanding her role in Joni Wilson's death. What about the Vance Diamond scandal? Diamond's death, and the subsequent revelations around it – that wasn't even a year after Aleesha's death. Wasn't that an extremely stressful time for the family? For Angelica, particularly?

Then Simon shut down. He pointed to the photograph of himself with Diamond. He asked me if I would find it stressful if a close friend of mine was 'falsely accused' of serial rape and paedophilia. I told him I would – that was why I asked. I didn't want to argue about Vance Diamond's guilt, and I told him as much. I tried to move on.

'Do you think Aleesha's death might've triggered an interest in the supernatural for Angelica? An interest beyond a sort of . . . peripheral awareness of ghost-hunting shows and so on. She seemed very bought in to some of Dolly Hart's ideas about er . . . hell, and manifesting creatures and so on.'

'I know what you're trying to do here,' snapped Simon. 'Angelica did not believe any of that nonsense. Any of that weird cult stuff the other girls tried to . . . brainwash her with. She wasn't stupid. And I see you're trying to draw some sort of a line between the ghost hunters at my hotel and her being sucked into all of that nasty business. I won't have it.'

Aware I might be pushing it, I asked why he kept referring to Angelica in the past tense. Why was Simon Stirling-Stewart talking about his daughter like she was someone who no longer existed.

'Because she doesn't. Not anymore,' he said. I wanted him to elaborate on that – did he mean the name change she'd have to undergo upon leaving the secure unit? Did he mean Angelica was dead to him? But I didn't get an answer. That was enough for Simon.

He suddenly accused me of having a political agenda, he ranted about 'cancel culture' and then he asked me to leave.

*

When Aleesha died it was really sad I guess?? I don't really remember much about it now, just the funeral and stuff, because I was only like ten or eleven when it happened. Me and Kayleigh just sort of left everyone else alone after it happened. We didn't speak to anyone else and we stopped 'picking on' people because it felt less fun without Aleesha, and everything felt a bit weird and everyone was treating us like we were babies. There wasn't much of primary school left then, only a week or two anyway, so we just went away over the summer and didn't make that much of a big deal of it or anything. The last day of school we just signed each other's shirts and then we both got picked up early. I think I remember being sad that summer but also that my dad took me to see Cats in London, which was really cool. It was the first musical I'd seen in real life. I'd seen Disney musicals on DVDs and I'd seen a DVD of the 1998 recording of Cats (which is the version most people have seen) which I liked, but it was so different to see it live and I loved it. AND we went to Disneyland Paris and Kayleigh was so jealous.

When we got to high school, Violet and Joni were more buddy buddy than I remembered them being. They were always there, like being freaks together in primary school, but they had other weird girls with them then. In high school it was just them on their own because obviously no one would make friends with them. Joni was obviously still really really annoying but I felt I'd grown past doing anything about it, so I just started ignoring her. And that was it for me and her for a year or so.

Me and Kayleigh made friends with the other pretty girls at school like Lauren Everett* and Georgina May* and Annabelle Moore.* Lauren and Georgina both went to this tiny primary school out of town, and got driven in to Crow for school, like me. So obviously we made friends quickly – mine and Georgina's dad even had the same Land Rover. I think we all bonded because it was like, who are these pretty rich girls, and why AREN'T they at Amplefield, you know??

It's obvi why I didn't go to Amplefield (it's so shit there for what you pay fyi!), but to fill you in Lauren didn't go to private school because she wasn't actually that rich because she has like ten siblings or something. I think Georgina was quite rich but my dad says newveaux reesh [sic] people have poor priorities and always piss away their money. Annabelle actually went to Amplefield for like two weeks but her parents got divorced and her dad fucked off to Spain or something so she got moved to CCHS.

And basically we just went around together like looking pretty and being cool and stuff. Then in Year 8, the Year 9 and 10 boys started talking to us. This was socially a pretty big deal, actually. I remember when James Clark from Year 10 came and hung round with us at lunch. James Clark was literally on the Middlesborough under-sixteen squad, and even Year 11s liked him, so that was just proof we were the pretty girls and everyone should try to be like us and be our friends and stuff. James even went out with Georgina AND Annabelle while we were still in Year 9 when he could've literally gone out with a girl in sixth form if he'd wanted to.

And when the boys started talking to us we acquired this like cringey hanger-on group of other girls. They were NOT as pretty as us, but they were sporty and had okay clothes – these were girls like Stephanie and Britney and the two Hannahs, who I wouldn't consider my friends, really, but I invited to birthday parties because I felt sorry for them. They were just there. Like we didn't really talk but they were there and came to stuff. If I was in the A-tier group of girls they were definitely the B-tier.

Joni came back into my life around the time this sub-girl group appeared I suppose . . .

Basically one day, Lauren says to me – did you know Joni Wilson from your primary school? And I was like – yes, and she's a classic FREAK!! But the thing about Lauren is, she really hated bullying because one of her sisters is disabled and got bullied for it.

I remember thinking it was mad Lauren could be related to someone who is properly special needs, because she was SO pretty and smart (I mean obviously I have Luciana but she wasn't properly disabled, she basically just doesn't look you in the eye and it's supposed to be this big deal). Anyway Lauren was pretty and smart and stuff but she was a bit up herself, obviously. Really up on her high horse about this stuff. So I said Joni was a freak and she made this face and said, 'Well I think she's really funny, actually.'

You had to be on Lauren's good side to stay in the group. We lost the Third Hannah we originally had because Violet was running weird in PE and the Third Hannah called her a spazzy retard. Some of us laughed but then Lauren said she was absolutely pathetic and told her to get a life. Then at lunch time, the Third Hannah tried to turn everyone against Lauren, and argued that Violet was actually literally running like a retard and Lauren was just a no-fun bitch, and Lauren overheard and got really angry and pulled Third Hannah's ponytail really hard, and then she just never hung round with us again haha.

Anyway so basically even though I said not to, Lauren started being all like . . . 'Hi Joni!!!' If we passed her in the hallway and at lunch she'd say 'Oh Joni was soooooo

funny in English today' and I tried and tried to tell Lauren
that Joni was annoying and a freak, and then she said I was
being pathetic and I needed to get a life. Whatever!

Then Joni was just . . . there one day. All cuddled up
with Lauren at lunch time. Lauren was fussing over her
hair because they both had curly hair. Lauren was telling
her how to stop it from frizzing up. Lauren invited her
round to her house at the weekend. No one else, just
Joni. And (this was actually quite funny) Violet was just
standing in the corner looking shellshocked – fiddling with
her little Japanese comic book and trying to hide that she
was watching us. Obviously thinking maybe she should
come over, so I scowled at her and she literally ran away! I
couldn't believe it. So funny. Anyway.

The next Monday, Joni turns up to school with her hair
sorted out. Like it's curly but not frizzy – Lauren obviously
showed her how to do it at the weekend, and even the
colour looks much nicer than it did. She was even wearing
fucking makeup. And she never wore makeup. Officially
we weren't actually supposed to wear makeup, but you
wouldn't get told off as long as it wasn't really heavy. But
if you didn't wear any makeup at all, it was like . . . okay,
weird. Do you know what I mean? Like everyone else
is wearing minimum mascara, concealer and matte lips
were really in then, so like a matte nude lip. Sometimes
highlighter, but if you wore too much the teacher would
notice and make you go and wash your face.

She comes in with like this NYX lipstick on (which is
very similar to the shade I wear??) and mascara. She just
looks normal. She used to carry this weird little Spongebob

lunchbox, but she didn't have that. And instead of the stupid backpack with little patches and buttons, the one she used to have, she has like an okay shoulder bag, which looked like it was from Topshop. Like not New Look, but literally a Topshop bag. There isn't even a Topshop in Crow.

Everyone is like 'Oh Joni, you look amazing!' I didn't say anything because big deal, whatever – she's still fat and ugly except with her hair sorted out, it's obvious that she actually isn't fat and ugly anymore if you know what I mean. Like she's still BIG, not as skinny as me, obviously, but her face just looked more normal. Like her whole head looked less blocky and square and she just looked a bit more like prettier generally.

And Lauren was like 'We went shopping and did makeovers at the weekend!' And everyone told Lauren she was so nice, and that Joni was so cute, like they wouldn't have absolutely rinsed her in primary school. Even Kayleigh told Joni she looked really pretty because Kayleigh it turns out was actually a snakey two-faced cunt.

Then Joni started sitting with us in lessons; it just happened one day, basically. And she was just with us every lunchtime, and it was normal. And then it was just like she was actually just there. She was just there all the fucking time. I used to partner with Annabelle for experiments in science and Annabelle literally picked Joni over me, and I had to work with fucking B-tier Stephanie. She was even with us in PE, even though she was shit and we were all really good and we always won at netball. Joni just started making a joke of it when she did badly. And

Annabelle and Lauren and Georgina would be creased up laughing. Even Kayleigh started to laugh with her.

I tried to tell Lauren again that Joni was really weird in primary school. I tried in Maths where we sat together. And Lauren was just sort of like . . . well, okay. I don't care because I like her. And she said my thing about Joni from primary school was really pathetic.

I didn't want to get on Lauren's bad side, so I started being nice to Joni. I didn't want to get kicked out of the group. But we weren't close and I seriously did not spend much one-on-one time with her. But yeah. So we were 'friends' or whatever.

*

Lauren Everett is now nineteen years old and studies Politics and International Relations at a Russell Group university. She was petite, pretty, and wore her dark, curly hair in a bob. She seemed surprised that I wanted to speak to her – she barely spoke to Angelica in the months leading up to the crime. She was the supposed leader of what Angelica termed the 'A-Tier Popular Girl Group', and the only member of that group willing to talk to me.

'Ugh, cringe,' Lauren said. 'I wouldn't call us that. That's so embarrassing.' Lauren told me Angelica often used strange Americanisms like that – they teased her (gently) for acting like she was attending a fictional high school in California. Angelica's accent even had a strange American twang. She once tried to tell people she'd picked it up after a month-long holiday in Florida.

The clever among you may remember that Angelica accused Joni of doing exactly this – of affecting American-isms. Lauren remembered that Joni would say 'Awkward!' but couldn't recall her doing an accent.

Lauren was also surprised that Angelica thought of her as a 'leader', and that Angelica expressed a need to remain on Lauren's 'good side'.

'Like . . . I always thought she hated me, to be honest with you. Especially after I made friends with Joni. But I suppose she did always . . . defer to me, in a weird way. Which – I dunno, I think it's really wanky to call yourself a leader, but . . . people have been deferring to me since I was really young. I'm the oldest daughter of an oldest daughter. I have three younger sisters, and lots of younger cousins so um . . . I naturally fall into leadership roles, is what my counsellor says. She says I'm decisive and I have natural leadership skills, I don't know. I don't think it's like I seek that role out. I don't want to be powerful, or anything, I'm just quite decisive, and I say what I think. I've always been quite confident, so I think that's why that's a very regular thing for me.' Lauren then apologised to me for rambling.

I asked her to take me back to the beginning – when did she meet Angelica?

She recalled her first day of Year 7 at CCHS. Arriving with Georgina May from a smaller primary school outside of Crow. Georgina (a self-confessed snob) wanted to be picky about her friends – Lauren wanted to make as many friends as quickly as possible. She was placed in a form group with Kayleigh Brian, and the two were sat together for a day of icebreaking games. They clicked – Kayleigh had her hair in

French plaits, which Lauren discovered Kayleigh had styled herself. She asked Kayleigh to plait her hair at lunchtime, and Kayleigh agreed. They were friends from that point onward.

'And yeah so . . . Angelica was just kind of there as well,' she said.

While Kayleigh braided Lauren's hair, Angelica quizzed Lauren about her favourite Disney princess.

'I said Jasmine but she said Jasmine was the worst one, because she doesn't have her own song and I was just like . . . okay . . .'

It was clear that Kayleigh and Angelica came as a package. Georgina and Angelica immediately clashed, and Georgina tried to convince the others to make Angelica 'go away'.

'But I just thought it was too mean. So we tolerated her. I'm not revising this because of what happened – and I'm not going to pretend we weren't friends with her but . . .' Lauren twirled her coffee cup, considering her answer. She was frowning. 'Have you ever had a friend . . . and this is really high school, but have you ever had a friend that you all just kind of hate? Like there's a group of you, and there's just one person that you . . . you all kind of take the piss out of. Everything they say is annoying, and you can kind of look at your other friends and roll your eyes and laugh about them when they're not there.'

Angelica was that to Lauren. That friend you hate. Angelica's status at the bottom of her particular social pile was solidified long before Joni joined her friendship group. Georgina resented Angelica's presence and Kayleigh's patience for her old friend was wearing thin. When the strikingly pretty Annabelle Moore joined CCHS partway through September, she was quickly absorbed into their small group. Angelica asked Annabelle (already 5'6" at the age of eleven) how big her feet were – when Annabelle gave her size (a six) Angelica cackled at her and announced to their friends that Annabelle had 'huge man feet'. Another day, she'd ask Annabelle how she'd gotten so 'huge', and told her to eat less – lest she grow any taller.

On a day that Angelica was off sick with a cold, Annabelle quietly asked the rest of the group: *does anyone else find Angelica . . . a bit annoying?*

They did. They did find her annoying. Even Kayleigh confessed that Angelica was 'a bit much'.

They made friends with Britney, Stephanie and two girls referred to exclusively as 'the Hannahs' – a small group of athletic girls. Britney was a swimmer, Stephanie was a gymnast and the Hannahs were both runners who went to the same athletics club. Because they were new to the group, Angelica dubbed them the 'B-tier' girls. And the 'B-tier' girls were confused as to why Angelica kept loudly calling them 'B-tier', when no one particularly seemed to like Angelica.

'No one considered Brit and Steph and the Hannahs B-tier but her,' said Lauren. 'I still see Brit all the time because she's at [another university in the same city]. We're all in a group chat together. They were never B-tier to me; we were all really good friends. I think Angelica called them that because . . . I don't know, I suppose they did just start sitting with us one day. It was a bit sudden, like they'd decided to be friends with us. It was probably a bit artificial, in the way making friends just is when you're twelve or thirteen. I suppose, I dunno, maybe she felt threatened by them or something? Because she could tell that me and Georgina and the others – we got on with them really well. We had a laugh.' I stopped Lauren to ask why she thought they all tolerated Angelica's behaviour. If she irritated them, and wasn't nice to them, why hang round with her at all?

'Well . . . Kayleigh told me about what had happened to Aleesha Dowd, and how it had fucked Angelica up a bit. Made her a bit weird and more like . . . I don't know, like more in her own head? Kayleigh said she got a bit babyish. Like she was all for acting grown-up in primary school, then she got to high school and she was back to talking about Disney princesses and making up dances and stuff.' Lauren paused. 'And she used to talk to Aleesha. Kayleigh told me once – she was at Angelica's house and they were playing Monopoly or something. And she made Kayleigh pick out a game piece for Aleesha and she like . . . kept looking to this empty space in the air when it was Aleesha's turn and asking her questions and pausing like she could hear an answer. That wasn't long after she died apparently but still . . . weird. And sad. But that was Angelica in a nutshell.'

I told Lauren this was interesting – Angelica's father was so resistant to the idea she'd had any interest in the occult. Lauren snorted.

'I don't know if I'd call it an interest, or anything. She totally, a hundred per cent believed in ghosts – but she never made a hobby of it, she just brought it up around Halloween or whatever. She was like someone who was religious but only went to church on special occasions, if that makes sense.'

Could Lauren think of any instances of Angelica 'going to

church' – did she ever publicly brag about seeing or speaking to ghosts?

Lauren said Angelica bragged about everything – and everything included *Most Haunted* et al. visiting her dad's hotel, and how her whole family was 'a bit psychic'.

Neither Simon Stirling-Stewart nor Angelica herself mentioned this behaviour. Lauren told me she thought Angelica was aware, to an extent, that what she was doing was strange. That she always was just a little bit self-aware, and that sliver of self-awareness seemed to cause a conflict in Angelica that made her even more difficult to be around.

'I think if she'd been completely delusional, she might've been a bit easier to deal with but . . . it was like she was kind of aware she was cringe and really didn't want to be. But she didn't know how not to be cringe. And she had this nasty streak but it was almost like – nasty in the way really little kids are nasty. I felt sorry for her. I did feel really bad for her. I completely pitied her. Like, aside from just Aleesha Dowd – there was the Vance Diamond stuff. That really wasn't easy for her – it was fucking horrible actually. Oh God, and her dad, he is just like so embarrassing. Like, relentless humiliation – no wonder she went mental, you know what I mean?'

Simon Stirling-Stewart's career as a right-wing rent-a-gob began following the explosion of sexual abuse allegations made against his friend Vance Diamond. Diamond died in September of 2012 (coincidentally, a matter of days before Angelica's thirteenth birthday) – by December, numerous accusations of sexual assault, child molestation and abuse had been made public.

Vance Diamond, for the uninitiated, was a nightclub owner,

radio and television presenter and a philanthropist. He was also a serial sex offender – possibly one of the worst in British history if one could quantify sex offences on a scorecard the way we might 'score' a serial killer.

In the seventies and eighties, he was inescapable – he had been Crow-on-Sea's most famous son. He was buried in Crow at the top of a large hill, facing the sea. His gravestone was an enormous stone prize wheel, a reference to *Steals on Wheels*, the game show that brought Diamond mainstream success. 'Spinning in my grave' read the epitaph.

Carved into each of the twelve sections of the stone prize wheel were the names of charitable organisations (mostly local to the area) Diamond had patronised. The Tomorrow Centre, Crow General Hospital, St Isidore's Hospital, Fox Family Children's Home, Crow Women's Shelter, Diamond Heart Hospice and more. It was massive, and obnoxious, and for the few months it stood, it was a popular tourist attraction.

'I actually remember when they removed the gravestone,' Lauren told me, when I asked her what she remembered about the Vance Diamond scandal, and how the incident fit in to her first years of high school. 'You could see the outline of it from the [school] yard, so we could all see the blokes and the van taking it away and loads of the boys were chanting like "nonce, nonce, nonce" when they did it.

'I also remember my mum's reaction. She was a bit shell-shocked. When she was eighteen, she used to work in one of his venues on the bar, and she was like, "I can't believe it. He was so nice when he came in. He bought us all drinks. I can't believe it. He did smack my bum once."'

Diamond's fame originated in Crow-on-Sea. He was born

in the 1940s to a wealthy family, owned several nightclubs in his twenties and became a DJ on local radio. He was discovered by the BBC in the mid-1970s, and began hosting the *Chart Show* on Radio 1.

Diamond really became a household name when he was hired as the host of BBC game show *Steals on Wheels* in 1979, the show airing in various early-evening time slots until 1989. Described warmly in Diamond's obituaries as 'needlessly convoluted' and 'unusually punitive', two families competed for the grand prize of a brand-new car or caravan, in addition to a (usually small) cash prize accumulated in the first two rounds of the show. Teams were asked increasingly difficult general-knowledge trivia questions. If Team 1 was correct, they earned a small cash bonus, and were asked another question. If they passed or were incorrect Team 2 was given the option to spin or steal. 'Stealing' by answering the question or 'spinning' the prize wheel. Spinning the wheel could net a team a maximum prize of £500, or a penalty loss of £500. Spinning the wheel could also trigger one of the show's various bonus rounds.

In 'Spot the Difference' Diamond would, at any point during the programme, change his tie, his shirt, or something in his pocket. The first player to notice would be allocated a 'Steal the Steal' card, which would allow this player to 'steal' another player's 'steal'. In 'Catch the Mouse' a small, radio-controlled mouse was released onto the stage, and players were given a bonus of £100 if they could catch it. The strangest round of all (only lasting for one year of the programme's total run time) was 'Get that Down You', during which players were offered the chance to reclaim lost money by drinking a tin of cold baked beans in fifteen seconds or less. When introducing this round, Diamond would say: 'You know that money you've lost? You want that back?' He would then produce a tin of beans: 'Well get that down you.'

Steals on Wheels was a notably chaotic programme, producing a number of legendary bloopers, in which Diamond swears, insults guests, completely zones out, or falls down drunk. He was a well-loved figure – the nation's slightly strange, alcoholic uncle – who was extremely popular among children. Diamond even hosted a watered-down version of *Steals on Wheels* for CBBC through the nineties.

Throughout all this, Diamond did a great deal of charity work, raising and donating hundreds of thousands of pounds for local causes in and around Crow-on-Sea. A true local hero, Diamond was given unrestricted access to many of the hospitals, care homes and children's homes he had patronised. He found his victims here, among the most vulnerable charges of these institutions. The vulnerability of his victims was what kept his crimes buried for so long. Those who came forward were ignored and dismissed – if they hadn't been scared into silence by Diamond or the institutional staff who collaborated with and protected him.

A staple of panel shows, Comic Relief, Children in Need and chat shows, Diamond was greatly popular and beloved. Crow-on-Sea even instated a Diamond Day before his death – the plan was to annually have schools and local businesses hold a large, town-wide festival to raise money for charity. Vance Diamond attended the first, and last, Diamond Day in June 2012. A huge mural was painted at the front of Diamond's, the gentlemen's club he had owned. It featured

Diamond and his distinctive dyed-black pompadour smoking two cigarettes at once and holding a hand of playing cards – the ace, king, queen and jack of diamonds, as well as a joker card. He was smiling, with two gold teeth, and winking. It would be painted over by Christmas.

The first accusations came via a *Panorama* documentary which aired in December of 2012. Not only had Diamond been abusing children for years, but a number of senior figures in management in the hospitals and care homes and in local government in Crow-on-Sea had been aware of the abuse and had taken steps to assist him and to cover it up, or had even taken part. Survivors were threatened, paid off, and often subjected to further abuse.

Initially, the people of Crow-on-Sea were defensive of him. After all, these alleged 'victims' coming forward were outsiders to the community – they'd gone from the care system to the prison system, or they'd spent their lives bouncing between psychiatric hospitals. It was not until more 'respectable' victims came forward that the tide turned.

Still: Simon Stirling-Stewart repeatedly took up invitations to defend Diamond in local media – despite mounting evidence against him.

Following the *Panorama* documentary (in which Simon had briefly featured), Simon was plucked from ranting on Crow's local radio station (Crow-on-Air FM) and given a slot on the BBC's *Newsnight*, where he enthusiastically argued in favour of Diamond's innocence.

I asked Lauren if she remembered the scandal's impact on Angelica. She did – clearly. Angelica came to school as normal following the documentary.

'There aren't many twelve-year-olds watching *Newsnight*, are there? So no one in our year really knew what was happening. But some of the sixth-formers did. There were some of them – I remember, because they mostly just ignored everyone in the lower school, but yeah – they were, like, looking at us. And I think Angelica knew what was going on because her dad had obviously watched it, and he was on the radio at school pick-up time, so a lot of us heard about it like basically from her dad in the car on the way home from school.'

The next day was worse for Angelica, with people shouting 'your dad's a paedo' at her in the hall and older boys asking her if she'd personally been abused by Diamond. The *Post-on-Sea* ran a story the following day titled: 'CIRCLE OF SILENCE: Who is Connected to Vance Diamond in Crow-on-Sea?'

Simon Stirling-Stewart earned a paragraph detailing his business and personal connections with Diamond, printing several photos of them together. As Angelica recalls:

There was a picture of me and my sister with him in the paper. He was dressed up as Santa and I was sitting on his lap and that was when things got really bad. Because mostly people weren't really paying attention to it, but when I was actually like literally in the paper sitting on his fucking lap, like yeah obviously people started saying 'Ho ho ho!' at me in the hallways and people were singing 'Diamonds are Forever' at me and shit which I thought was super weird and lame like, it wasn't even funny, it was just annoying.

There was an incident where a boy from Year 11 asked me if my dad was a paedo and how many times he 'let

Diamond rape me' which was SO dumb because my dad didn't even let me be alone in a room with him. It was a whole thing – if he was at a party they'd always make the kids go to bed pretty soon after he turned up, and my dad said if you're ever alone with him just say you're looking for your dad and leave the room.

Anyway a teacher overheard that horrible boy and he got excluded. Another boy got excluded for asking me the same thing and I snitched on him but you'd snitch too. But then people started calling me a snitch.

The school pulled my dad in about two weeks after me enduring all of this abuse, and they proposed a 'managed move' because my wellbeing was at risk. Which it was. Mrs White, the head teacher, made him come in an hour after the school had closed, so no one saw him.

He said he wouldn't move me because I wasn't the problem student, it was everyone else, and it wasn't fair to move me away from my friends. He said, 'She's not going to Amplefield, I'm not paying that shit hole another penny after my older girl got bullied there.' And Mrs White said there were high schools in Scarborough and Whitby.

And he said he didn't see how it could be any better in Scarborough or Whitby because they do have televisions there. Plus he didn't have time to drive me to another town every single day. He said because of the windy roads through Scalby[8] and Moorcock Hill it takes like forty-five minutes to get to Scarborough or Whitby and why should he have to go out of his way and make a ninety-minute

---

8 A village between Scarborough and Crow-on-Sea.

round trip every day because Mrs White couldn't discipline students effectively, and that he didn't 'plan on being silenced or censored.' And the head teacher was just confused and said this was about the Vance Diamond stuff and my safety, not his career. And also that it would take him as long to get to Scarborough or Whitby as it did to drive up to Amplefield. Which was a stupid point actually because Amplefield had a special bus which picked kids up, so he didn't even drive Lucie.

And this all really fucked my dad off. He asked her if he looked like a cab driver and said to discipline the people who were horrible to me or see how they liked it when he went to the school governors about this. And my dad was friends with like half of the school governors, AND he knows everyone on the city council, so Mrs White said she would try to find a way to work around it.

So then the school sent the letter home. Anyone 'invoking Vance Diamond' to harass or bully other students would be excluded – permanently if it happened twice. The school tried to make it seem like this was about their 'concern for those affected by the recent tragic revelations and their families' but everyone knew it was about me.

'I remember there was talk about her moving school yeah,' Lauren confirmed. 'She was actually a bit braggy about maybe having to go to the private school – like she was always telling us she could go whenever she wanted. But it didn't happen. I remember the letter home, and there was also an assembly, and some PCHE lessons. Just about how serious and not funny child abuse was, and like, basically threatening expulsion. A few more boys got temporarily excluded for a bit, and Angelica also didn't come in for like two weeks, and when she came back they let her spend lunchtimes in the classrooms – so we were all having our break with her in her form room for a while because at that point we felt bad for her. It sounds bad to say, but she was less annoying when she was sad. And then yeah I suppose people just forgot about it and decided it wasn't worth the bother. I'd say by the time we were back for Year 9, it just didn't get mentioned much.'

But Lauren noticed a change to Angelica's behaviour. She got worse. She seemed more detached from reality, more into her TV high school mean-girl character – and her behaviour got stranger again when Joni joined the group.

'I do think she got worse? She started calling Steph and Brit and the Hannahs "B-tiers" to their face all the time, when it was just something she'd mostly said behind their backs before. I remember Stephanie was once going to have a proper go at her – she was getting ready to corner her at lunch and tell her "you're the B-tier friend, not me, no one likes you", something like that – and I pulled her to one side and I told her about the Aleesha stuff and like reminded her about everything Angelica had to deal with, with the Vance Diamond stuff. I made excuses for her, basically. I said she was just insecure, just really sad and insecure and to ignore her. So Steph didn't say anything to Angelica. I did that a couple of times for her – talked people down from having a proper go at her.'

Lauren – now drinking a glass of wine – assured me she wasn't trying to paint herself as a saint in this.

'We did laugh at her behind her back. I definitely did. I said some really nasty stuff about her. We even took the piss out of her trying to talk to Aleesha, even though she was only about twelve when she was doing it and she did stop eventually. Still . . . we joked about it. And I think she did know we talked about her. But taking the piss out of her when she wasn't there helped us . . . get it out of our system. I think it stopped us properly having a go at her. But even if she wouldn't acknowledge it, I do think she knew that we didn't really like her, and we took the piss out of her. I think it did get to her a lot. And because of their history and stuff, Joni was a lot more . . . blatant about it.'

Joni's presence in the group only compounded Angelica's insecurities. Lauren met Joni in their English group – Lauren didn't know much about her, bar that she was one of the 'freaks' from primary school Angelica had made special effort to point out to her. The small handful of boys and girls that Angelica had picked on included Joni and Violet. I asked Lauren if that affected her view of Joni.

'Probably a bit, but honestly,' Lauren sighed, 'Angelica just talked so much shit. She talked bollocks all the time, so by the time I met Joni properly, I was mostly tuning Angelica out.'

Lauren was struck by Joni's hair: curly, like hers, but not well managed. It was frizzy and dry – Joni's mum had attempted to replicate her own hair routine on her daughter's far curlier hair, with limited results. Lauren had plucked at one of Joni's listless ringlets and asked her which conditioner she used.

'Not in a nasty way,' Lauren assured me. 'I genuinely just wanted to help. I think she could tell.'

That was the beginning of things for them. Joni cracked jokes over their shared copy of *The Curious Incident of the Dog in the Night-Time*, and did funny doodles in the margins of her exercise book. Lauren got in trouble for laughing and talking too much. When Lauren invited Joni to come to her house, and to sit with her at lunchtime, Joni was nervous. She told Lauren that Angelica used to pick on her, and Lauren confessed no one was really that keen on Angelica – if Joni sat with them, everyone would be nice to her.

'She was just so funny. I didn't understand how anyone could dislike her.' I asked Lauren if she ever found Joni overbearing. 'I mean, a bit? But honestly, who isn't dead annoying when they're like fourteen. Once she found a joke, she could be a bit relentless with it – so yeah, I could see her being a bit of a nightmare if you were on the wrong end of that, like Angelica was. Not that that's any excuse.' Lauren swallowed, her voice suddenly thick. 'But we probably should've been nicer to Angelica. I should've . . . I should've stopped the others from picking on her. I know, I know it's stupid to think that, I know there was a lot going on but. It's just hard not to have regrets. It's really really hard not to have regrets.'

I told Lauren that I didn't want to pick at her scabs. I told her that I didn't think she should feel guilty over things she did between the ages of eleven and fifteen. I told her that laughing behind the back of a difficult friend was not the worst thing a person could do. She did not know what Angelica was capable of at that time. But still, I asked her: was there anything in particular she regretted? Did she think her behaviour or the behaviour of her wider friendship group contributed at all to what had happened?

'I regret the . . . There was a couple of incidents um . . . around her talking to ghosts that we were quite nasty about.'

At a sleepover held at Angelica's house (possibly for a birthday – Lauren couldn't recall), Angelica convinced the other girls to play with a home-made Ouija board.

'She'd invited us all round – including Joni – and going to her house was always weird. You've seen how it's decorated, and her dad is so strange. He was a bit like – you know the "cool mum" bit in *Mean Girls*? Like he'd say we could watch whatever we wanted and drink and as long as we didn't wake him up he didn't care. Anyway we didn't drink, but we watched *Paranormal Activity* or something – some horror film with a Ouija board. And when it was done, Angelica brought out this one – this Ouija board – she'd made out of cardboard. I think Joni was taking the piss out of how ratty and half-arsed it was. And that she didn't have one of the pointer thingies.'

'Planchette?' I supplied.

'Yeah. She didn't have one of those so we had to use a plastic cup. And Angelica was ignoring the questions people were asking the board really obviously, like . . . dragging the cup to spell Aleesha's name. So Joni told her off – "I can tell you're trying to pull the cup and freak us out."'

Angelica and Joni argued – and to defend herself against accusations of cheating with the cup, she confessed that she'd spoken to Aleesha before. She wasn't pulling the cup, because Aleesha was there and she'd been there before. Angelica didn't have any proof, but she'd spoken to lots of ghost hunters, and she knew all about this stuff – and in the middle of this stammered explanation, Joni laughed at her. And the other girls laughed too.

'Angelica didn't cry, but she was just really quiet for the rest of the night. In school, Joni started trying to get us to call her like . . . I can't remember if it was Ghostbuster or Ghost Whisperer but Kayleigh said that was horrible and I agreed that was a bit much. It all made us really uncomfortable, and it was easier not to think about it and just pick on her for stuff that was like . . . less tragic.'

What did Lauren and the other girls consider to be within an appropriate realm to target Angelica? I asked, and I could tell Lauren was getting upset, so I shushed her. I reminded her I wasn't here to accuse her of anything – just to get the facts.

'We were pretty horrible to her in Drama,' she replied. 'I don't . . . I just want to say I don't think it's fair to suggest that it . . . that we contributed to her doing what she did because . . . But everyone knew how excited she was for Drama, and we were so bitchy to her.'

It was true that Drama seemed to mean a lot to Angelica, and she was particularly affected by how she was treated in those lessons.

The stage! I LOVE musicals, all types. I love Les Mis, *and* Glee, *and* Wicked, *and EVERYTHING Andrew Lloyd Webber. He is a GENIUS. I love the SONGS and the DANCES and I love how BIG they feel. I just always felt so so happy and like I was in a completely different nice place when I was watching them. But none of my friends were into them. I think Kayleigh once told me she thought musicals are cringey, so I didn't really talk about them much. But I was SO excited to start GCSE drama – I used to do drama at weekends when I was younger but I stopped going when my parents split up because Dad was too busy to take me I think probably. When I'm out of here*

I will audition for drama school because I am very very passionate. I really just want to act and sing and dance and I think I'm really good at it.

I did drama with Lauren and Joni and Annabelle from our group of friends. We always grouped up together and they never took it seriously. I actually stopped going into groups with them later on in the year because they just used to mess around, and I really wanted to get an A. We didn't fall out over it exactly, but it caused tension between us. They said I was bossy and weird, and they were always getting in huffs when I tried to get us to do scenes from musicals and sing songs instead of boring school stuff like Alan Bennett and Caryl Churchill.

There was a gay boy in drama who was the only gay boy at school (very brave in my opinion) – Calum,* and we started partnering together because he was also really passionate about acting and drama and we were definitely the best people in the class.

He told me that I should use Tumblr. We both watched Glee *and he said there were lots of people who liked* Glee *on Tumblr and I should try using it. So I set up an account, but I kept it secret from my friends because I didn't want them to laugh at me. I don't think I need to dwell on it too much because I was basically just doing normal fandom stuff on there, just like talking about* Glee *and Andrew Lloyd Webber and* Les Mis. *Reblogging fan art and analysis posts – just normal stuff really. But I obviously didn't really want my friends to find out because they thought I was a bit too into musicals and we were already bickering in drama and stuff.*

Honestly when I started working with Calum it was

really like the other girls weren't that bothered. Lauren and Annabelle were just happy pissing about with Joni. I did honestly start to feel a bit more left out at lunchtimes. After we started doing drama and bickering more, it felt like Joni was targeting me, and whenever I opened my mouth she'd make some comment and all the other girls would laugh. I could just say something super normal like that I was looking forward to drama and Joni would say 'I bet you are' or something boring like that, and they'd all laugh at me.

Whenever I would do stuff in drama they would giggle as well. If I had a scene to do with Calum they would sit and snigger at us and I think they would sometimes do impressions of me and the things I did in drama when I wasn't there.

So I started saying less at lunchtimes, and I would spend more time on my phone on Tumblr, or more time in the bathrooms doing my hair and stuff.

Lauren didn't remember exactly when Angelica disappeared into her phone, but she guessed it happened partway through Year 9. Angelica, more and more the subject of fun-poking in the group, began to keep her head down and spend more time on her phone. When Angelica did interject, Lauren felt it was often with a complete non sequitur, something about an episode of *Glee*, or a trip to London she was going to take, or something else. It was obnoxious. It made things worse. Angelica seemed to identify that she was part of the problem, but struggled to understand how to resolve it:

Sometimes I would think 'it'll be okay if I don't talk today.

Joni and the others will leave me alone if I just don't say anything.' But then sometimes I'd try to talk normally anyway and they would always say something, like I'd said something wrong or weird, so I'd just go back to my phone.

And it was okay for a while because I could just use my phone and stuff. That was fine. But then someone started sending me horrible anon messages.[9] Like stuff about me, very personal stuff, but also stuff about my dad. It was obviously someone from school because I'd never mentioned my dad on Tumblr because I'm not stupid like that. The horrible messages were on and off for years. Sometimes I'd reply to them but they seemed to come less often when I just ignored them. When I got a nasty message my followers were always really nice to me. I always got at least one or two replies or messages saying nice stuff when I posted one of the horrible messages. Maybe I got into a vicious cycle. I'd get the hate anons, and I'd post them so I could get replies to make me feel better. But I guess maybe that encouraged more mean messages to come in.

I asked Lauren if she knew who might have been sending Angelica abusive anonymous messages on her Tumblr – something which caused Angelica great distress.

'Who does she think it was?' asked Lauren.

9 Prior to 2015, Tumblr had no instant messaging function, and users communicated directly through long form 'fanmails' (rolled out in 2012) or their Ask boxes. The Ask box allowed users to send other users questions (or abuse). The sender could choose to remain anonymous provided the receiver had enabled the option to receive anonymous asks. This option could be enabled or disabled at any time. Anonymous questioners were referred to colloquially as 'anons'.

'Joni,' I replied.

'And who do you think it was?'

'I think it was probably a mix of Joni, and later Dolly Hart posing as Joni.' This is still my theory. Lauren nodded, and told me she thought that was probably the case. Angelica hadn't mentioned getting abusive anons – she didn't encourage her friends to follow her blog, and Lauren had no interest in it.

'Joni used to show it to people and read it out to us. She would read out posts where Angelica was getting like . . . heated about musicals in a really cringe way or posting about being like . . . how she was going to be famous and stuff. I didn't really like that. I think I told Joni it felt a bit . . .' Lauren shrugs. 'I don't know. Mean? Because it felt so private. I don't know. Because Angelica was so horrible to Joni in primary school, I didn't really push too hard because I understood why Joni found it so like . . . funny? You know, Angelica used to call her a freak, but here she was with a weird Tumblr and stuff. I didn't like it. But I didn't stop it.'

I reminded Lauren that it was not her job to 'stop' anything. I asked her about Dolly Hart.

She recalled when Dolly started the school. She joined half-way through the academic year, after the Christmas break. She was in Year 11, while Lauren and Co. were in Year 10. Dolly was pretty and confident and was soon the talk of the lower school – *have you seen the new Year 11 girl? Have you seen her hair? Have you seen her shoes?*

'God, I remember this girl in the year above who hated us, Carmen,* I remember her coming up to Annabelle. So, Annabelle and Carmen were both doing like, local modelling stuff. And Annabelle had beaten Carmen for a couple of Christmas jobs – so Carmen hated all of us but especially her. She came up to us, and poked Annabelle, and said, "Looks like you're not the prettiest anymore, so you can wipe that smug fucking look off your face." And that was how we were made aware of Dolly – this Carmen girl being like completely unhinged about it.'

Within a week of joining the school, Dolly had ingratiated herself into the Year 11 equivalent of Angelica and Lauren's friendship group. She then quickly 'stole' another girl's boyfriend and got into a physical fight over it. She was extremely aggressive, and a rumour began to circulate she'd gotten drunk and bitten her ill-gotten boyfriend on the arm because he'd tried to wrestle a bottle of vodka away from her. Apparently, she broke the skin, and the boy had stitches. Lauren insisted she saw the stitches.

'So obviously those Year 11 girls, and then the boys, they all stopped talking to her, so you just used to see her wandering around alone. Sometimes sixth-form boys would talk to her, but we weren't allowed in their common room, so she'd either be by herself or hanging round with some boys near the common room. Then Angelica started saying she was going to make friends with her. You know, all like, "She's so pretty, she should be in our group." We were all obviously a bit like . . . shut up, Angelica, because a lot of us were friends with the girl whose boyfriend she stole.'

Joni and Angelica argued about it. Joni said that trying to make friends with someone who was clearly insane just because she's pretty was weird and really desperate. She told Angelica that she needed to get over herself – apparently a common refrain.

'Oh my God, get over yourself,' Lauren hissed – her Joni impression. When she did it, she dropped her chin and looked up at me, glaring out from under her eyebrows. 'She'd do it just like that. You could tell you were really like . . . boiling her piss if she did that.'

Rumours soon began to circulate about Dolly's strange, religious parents, that she was thrown out of her previous school for either fighting or fucking a teacher. She got into more fights and kissed more people's boyfriends.

'It was weird, honestly. Because people hated her, but she kept getting invited to stuff. Like if you went to a Year 11 party, she was there. If you went to a sixth-form party – she was there. I got the sense she'd kind of alienate people and suck them back in – like there was a bit of a push-pull there. People did seem to be pretty sick of her by the next school year, though, when she went into sixth form. When that year started, she was mostly on her own at school, but she'd still be at stuff, you know?'

'Why do you think that was?'

'Well, boys would invite her to stuff, mostly. She was like . . . I'm not shaming her or anything, but she would apparently . . . she would give out blowjobs, and stuff. She'd trade blowjobs for drink and cigarettes and sometimes weed and stuff. The boys started . . . this was later on in Year 10 – my Year 10, her Year 11 – they started calling her Dolly Dick Pig.'

But this didn't put Angelica off.

Dolly seemed so glamorous to me because she was wearing

nice makeup and she had really shiny wavy black hair. But it was like naturally black not ugly and dyed. She also had a Michael Kors bag and the Vivienne Westwood ballet flats I had asked for for my birthday. It all looked really new. SO I assumed she was, like me, one of the non-poor people in the school. I introduced myself and I told her about how my dad owned the posh hotel and was friends with everyone. I told her I got to eat at the hotel restaurant for free, and could stay whenever I wanted, and I got to play for free at the amusements and when I was older I wouldn't have to pay for drinks anywhere in the town. And she seemed pretty impressed by that.

Obviously, at the time, I didn't realise how weird she was, and that all the clothes and hair and makeup was just a cover to disguise her weird life and her weird personality and family. But at the time I was taken in by her.

I didn't really talk to her for a while, like until she was in Year 12 and I was in Year 11 – after summer. She wasn't friends with many people anymore, and spent loads of time on her own – but she was still getting invited to everything. I really wanted to go to a sixth-form party or on a night out like, to go to a club and not just the Spoiled Princess. Joni, Kayleigh, Lauren and Annabelle had gotten invited to one and had CONVENIENTLY forgotten to invite me . . . so I figured if I made friends with Dolly she would take me to way more stuff than stupid Joni got to go to.

My old friends were a bit like 'gross why are you talking to her she bites people' but I was just like um . . . duh, because she gets invited to everything . . . obviously . . . So yeah I just *wanted to go to stuff with her, that was really the end of it.*

Angelica's account largely glosses over her friendship with Dolly, focussing more on her ongoing conflict with Joni. I ask Lauren if she was aware of the quality of Angelica's relationship with Dolly.

'No, I really wasn't that interested in her, to be honest. I remember Joni telling me she saw her hanging round the graveyard with Dolly, Violet and Jayde Spencer, and I actually remember thinking like . . . did you actually though? Because for however weird she was, I didn't really think Angelica would be caught dead with Violet Hubbard, never mind Jayde Spencer. She was so obsessed with her own made-up little hierarchy, I just thought Joni had made a mistake or was trying to start a rumour or something. But no I didn't know much about it, beyond Angelica occasionally bragging that they'd gone to X party or Y club together and drank Z amount of booze. I kind of doubt that was true though, because there were never any pictures of them out. If Angelica posted pictures of them, like on Instagram or Snapchat or whatever, they were usually just outside or at Dolly's house or something. She also told us that they smoked weed together – she was really trying to brag about it, like rub it in. But at the time I was very like . . . "Drugs aren't cool, Angelica." So she didn't mention it again to me once it was obvious that wasn't going to get her any clout.'

I asked Lauren if Angelica mentioned any of the occult aspects of her friendship with Dolly to her, or their wider group of friends.

'She never mentioned talking to Aleesha or ghosts or

anything like that again after the sleepover. I think she'd real-ised that we just thought it was quite embarrassing so she never mentioned it again. Oh, but in PCHE we did a few lessons about Myra Hindley and she was like "Oh I know aaaall about this." But um, no. Apart from that it was mostly just bragging about how much weed they smoked or what-ever.'

Finally, I asked Lauren how she has coped with Joni's death. Friends of the deceased are often left out of these narratives, as if we feel their grief must pale so much in comparison to that of the nuclear family unit, it is not worth mentioning. We like to ignore the shockwaves of a crime like this – we want the pain confined to a small space, lest it ripple out and touch us.

Prior to the murder, Lauren was thought of as outgoing, bubbly and kind. She had an active social life, and very aver-age grades. Lauren recalls her Year 9 History teacher telling her off for talking in a lesson, asking her to have respect for the students who wanted to learn, and were not destined for the beauty college.

She was bright, but a tad lazy – social and easily distracted.

'I think it hit me quite hard, to be honest, but it took me a long time to process it. We had gotten quite close. I didn't make a thing of it, because people will come out of the woodwork when something horrible like that happens. They'll come out and act like they were really badly affected. Loads of people who'd barely spoken to Joni were making out like they were best friends. They wanted to be seen to be upset, so they could act like they were part of the story – or so they could try and get time off school, or special exemp-tions in exams, which was so gross. There were even people bothering Amanda, trying to bring her flowers and pretend they knew Joni – I really hated that. I loved Amanda, I really, really liked her, and I knew she'd hate it. All this stuff just got to me, I couldn't stand to be around any of those people. The weak, toothless counselling shit we were offered in school – I couldn't stand that either. So I just withdrew.'

Following Joni's death, Lauren largely dropped out of social activities and spent the weekends of her GCSE year studying – doing practice essays and poring over her textbooks, even branching out into extra-curricular reading. She developed an interest in global politics through the grim, heavy history books she read. With a particular interest in the aftermath of World War Two, Lauren found herself sitting in on Saturday nights reading *Eichmann in Jerusalem* and *The Ethnic Cleansing of Palestine*; she read hefty books on the Cold War and John Hersey's *Hiroshima*.

She greatly outperformed her predicted grades and became one of the highest achieving students of that year.

'It was funny, my parents weren't really happy. I'd gone from a predicted C in history to an A* but yeah my mum came in to my room as I was sat listening to the Cure and reading *The Rape of Nanking*, and she was like "Right, I never thought I'd say this but you need to stop reading."' Lauren snorted. 'I think I found a lot of . . . like, I don't think it was healthy, but I think I found comfort in the idea of the banality of evil. I think I was so obsessed with the post-World War Two era, because I was living in the wreckage of Crow's own little nuclear bomb. Like, how can you go on after something like the Nanking Massacre? How do you go back to your life after that? I think just . . . I don't know, reading about this horrible stuff, knowing that life went on and the world just kept on turning. It was really fucking depressing but it also . . . it was quite comforting, as well. In like, a bleak way.'

Concerned for her wellbeing despite her newfound academic success, Lauren's parents made the decision to move to Scarborough. Lauren was able to have a fresh start in a new town at a new sixth-form college. Here, she managed to balance her social and academic life, make new friends, and secure a place at her current university. Though she assured me that she continues to read heavy books about gulags and concentration camps to this day.

Joni began to come to Lauren in nightmares when she moved away. Lauren, always prone to bouts of sleep paralysis, would often wake to find herself unable to move, with Joni burning and screaming at the foot of her bed. And Lauren, who had largely been protected from the details of the murder, began to read all she could about the case. She thought the details could not be worse than her imagination, and they might banish the spectre that came to her near nightly. But the details were so much worse. Joni was replaced in her nightmares: Angelica with a pair of pliers, sitting on her chest. Angelica dips the pliers into Lauren's mouth, then pulls the pliers out, repeating the movement until Lauren fades back into a normal sleep.

Lauren now takes a tricyclic antidepressant to treat her sleep paralysis, and the depression she has begun to struggle with. She is in talk therapy, which also helps.

'I just didn't realise how much it had affected me,' she said.

What follows is the first of four sections of my interpretation of a key event in the year leading up to the murder. These prose sections are adapted from interviews with Jayde Spencer, blog posts and my correspondence with Angelica and Violet, and serve to give the reader an emotional insight into each perpetrator's emotional life before the murder.

HALLOWEEN

In Drama, Joni and Lauren made her feel stupid and embarrassed. Angelica had worked with them, they were supposed to make a up a scene – a modern interpretation of a fairy tale the teacher had assigned them. They were given *The Wizard of Oz*, and the characters of Dorothy, the Good Witch and the Bad Witch.

'You're the Bad Witch,' Joni said to Angelica. She looked at Lauren, and they smirked.

'Good,' Angelica snapped back. She could feel her face beginning to flush. 'Like *Wicked*. She's the best character anyway.'

'No one has seen *Wicked*,' said Joni. 'No one understands what you're going on about. Nobody cares.'

Angelica tried to give the Bad Witch some nuance – she tried to talk about the things they did with the character in *Wicked*. But Joni kept rolling her eyes and Lauren kept smirking.

'The Bad Witch dies doesn't she?' said Joni. She held out an imaginary wand and said, 'Zzzap! Die! Zzzap! Zap!' Lauren giggled.

'She doesn't get zapped, she melts in water,' Angelica sneered back. So Joni grabbed her bottle of water and slopped some on Angelica. She hit her in the chest, so the small pink hearts on her bra were visible through the sodden blue fabric of her school shirt. The teacher didn't see. 'That's not fucking funny,' Angelica snarled.

'That's not fucking funny,' Joni said back, mimicking Angelica's accent. 'Get over yourself, no one wants to see your bra.'

At lunchtime they all sat together in the dinner hall, at a large, round table with space enough for twelve people. Angelica listened to the other girls talk. She was silent, a coiled spring, waiting for her chance to interject. She had sat out of earshot of Joni, hoping to have a normal conversation without anyone picking on her. She wouldn't say the wrong thing and no one would notice her damp shirt. She wanted to talk. She wanted the girls to talk to her. She convinced herself not talking was weirder than trying to talk. She could just ask a question. A normal question.

So she leant across the table and asked Annabelle what she was doing this weekend for Halloween now that her party had been cancelled. Annabelle was talking to the Hannahs. The three of them stopped abruptly and looked at Angelica like she hadn't spoken to them in English.

'What?'

'I said what are you all doing this weekend? You know, now you're not having the party, Annabelle.'

'Nothing,' said Annabelle. But one of the Hannahs, the stupider one, she blinked.

'The party's cancelled?' she asked. Annabelle's face was sour.

'Er . . . no, it's back on,' she said.

'I thought you said you couldn't have a party this year,' said Angelica.

'No. Well, yeah, I did. But my parents changed their minds, so it's back on. Didn't I tell you? I thought I had.'

'Yeah, I think so. I forgot,' said Angelica. But Annabelle

hadn't told her. No one had. And she could tell from the look on Annabelle and Hannah's faces that she wasn't supposed to have found out.

When she slunk away from the table to tip the contents of her lunchbox into the bin, she heard them giggling. Maybe at her. Maybe at another inside joke Angelica wouldn't get. Either way, she wanted to snap each of Annabelle's long, gangly limbs like a pencil. She imagined walking back over to the table and smashing their heads together.

She went to Biology five minutes early, and sat alone for a while. Kayleigh was a couple of minutes late and didn't even ask Angelica where she'd been at the end of lunchtime. Angelica waited for the teacher to stop talking, then asked Kayleigh if she knew about Annabelle's Halloween party.

'Because I thought she'd cancelled it,' said Angelica. Kayleigh shrugged.

'I think she wasn't sure if she was allowed to have it.'

'Because it sounds like it's happening now. Pretty weird that you wouldn't tell me TBH,' said Angelica. Tee-bee-aitch rolled easily off her tongue, even when she caught Kayleigh's lip curling slightly at it. 'Weird that she'd tell everyone it was happening but not me. Pretty bitchy.'

'Yeah, I suppose.'

'So you do think it was bitchy? You agree she was being bitchy?' asked Angelica. She was whispering, hissing, and the teacher glanced over at them. Kayleigh huddled closer to her exercise book. 'If you think Annabelle is a bitch, that's okay. I won't tell her.'

The teacher shushed them, and Kayleigh didn't answer. When Angelica texted her that evening to ask if they could get ready together to go to the party, Kayleigh said she probably wasn't going to go.

Angelica checked her Tumblr. She had five anonymous messages.

You're beautiful! Send this to three mutuals who you think are beautiful, spread the love x

You keep whining about getting NaStY MeSsAgEs but you NEVER turn anon off? how desperate are you for attention??? Lmao.

Have you seen the phantom movie?? From 2004??? you really should if you haven't. It's so bad lmaoo.

youre so sad, you actually make me sick to look at. you look like a rat and you cant sing and your dads a pedo.

Heard a rumour u think you can talk to ghosts?? Have you been tested for being retarded? :(

Angelica used to reply to the nasty messages like they didn't bother her, but she just started getting more. She ignored them. She kept anonymous questions on, though. She wouldn't get the nice messages if she turned it off. She wouldn't get any messages at all.

She replied to the 'You're beautiful' anon with 'aww' (but she did not send it on) and the *Phantom* anon with 'I've seen it LOADS and I honestly don't think it's that bad??? I think Gerard Butler is fine??? You're all just MEAN SORRY!! ALW can do no wrong!!! x'

141

She got another message:

have you thought about killing yourself? You really should if you haven't. How many times? What's your favourite method??

Another:

BATH TUB + YOU + HAIRDRIER = ZZZZAP! = the world + Lmao

She struggled to fall asleep that night. She listened out for Aleesha's voice, which often came to her as she drifted off, but heard nothing. She wasn't sure what Aleesha would have to say about this. She didn't really understand the internet much; before she died they only really used it to play dress-up games and *Neopets*. Aleesha had only just gotten her first phone. She'd probably tell Angelica to turn the computer off – like that was something you could just do now. Like the computer wasn't in your bag or your pocket all the time.

The following day, Angelica went to school wearing a clip-on bow on her ponytail. She'd put it on thinking it looked nice, and the other girls might compliment her for it. It was silky and baby-blue, and matched nicely with her blonde hair and her blue eyes. But Joni had immediately started taking the piss out of it.

'Yaaaas, queen!' Joni hissed, when she spotted it. 'Slay! Serving traction alopecia realness.'

Then Joni kept trying to unclip it, saying Angelica should wear it as a bow tie, that she'd be trend-setting, and calling her a fashion icon and saying 'yaaas' in a nasty way that made the other girls laugh.

Angelica was obviously going to cry, so Lauren told Joni to stop. But Lauren was still laughing when she said it – laughing up on her high horse.

'It's just a joke,' said Joni. 'She knows it's just a joke, don't you?' Angelica didn't say anything. She glared at Joni, her eyes prickling. 'Oh my God, you are so sensitive. You literally cannot take even the tiniest joke. Get over yourself.'

After third lesson, Angelica decided to go to the bathroom rather than the dinner hall. She couldn't face her friends at the lunch table; couldn't stand the thought of Joni's spiteful comments, or the other girls laughing at her. She'd waste some time doing her hair, fixing her ponytail and repositioning her bow. She walked through the hallway, self-consciously touching her hairline. She didn't have traction alopecia. She saw Dolly, who was sitting outside the secretary's office. Dolly was flexing her hand. Her knuckles were red, swollen and scabby.

Angelica hadn't seen her in a few days. Angelica had wanted to be Dolly's friend for ages, but Dolly got into loads of fights and drama.

Still, Angelica was intrigued. She and Dolly followed each other on Insta and Snapchat; they messaged and snapped back and forth, sometimes. Angelica spoke to her when she saw her, but not in front of her friends. Lauren said Dolly was scary.

'Hey,' said Angelica. 'Are you in trouble?'

'No,' said Dolly. 'Someone else is. I'm the victim.' She stuck out her plump bottom lip, stained with a dark red lipstick she'd been made to wipe off this morning. 'I'm trying to get sent home. They're ringing my sister.'

'Cool.'

A boy bumped past Angelica; people were streaming

through the corridor, entering and exiting the dinner hall. Some of them looked at Dolly.

'Are you doing anything for Halloween?' Dolly asked. Angelica felt her cheeks go pink.

'No. Well. I don't know. Annabelle said she wasn't having a party, but I just found out she is. I guess I'm not invited.' She tried to sound confident – like a girl on TV. Unbothered. She rolled her eyes. Dolly snorted. 'Like I totally caught her lying about it. Can you imagine being that pathetic?'

'What a cunt,' said Dolly. 'Do you want to crash it?'

'Crash the party?'

'Yeah. You can do pre-drinks at mine. And we can crash. And then leave and go somewhere better.' Dolly grinned, and beckoned Angelica closer. Then closer again. 'Do you smoke weed?' she asked. Her hair smelt of pineapple and coconuts; her breath was faintly alcoholic.

'Yeah, totally.' Angelica had never smoked weed before. 'I love smoking weed.'

At home, Angelica explained to her father that Annabelle's Halloween party was back on. Her mum had changed her mind yesterday – Annabelle came in this morning and told them all to come in costume. So she needed some money to get a cat costume.

She also explained she'd be going with a new friend and asked for a lift to Dolly's house. Dad said there was a private UKIP event at the hotel that evening, and he was busy. He gave her £60 for a costume and taxi and said she should take one of the cases of blue WKD in the garage left over from her birthday. She'd bought lots of blue WKD expecting a big turnout, but barely anyone had come.

On Saturday evening, she dressed as a cat. She hadn't spent much of the money her dad had given her – she just bought ears, a tail and some black liquid eyeliner.

She wore an old black unitard from her dance classes, which was now too small for her. She pulled her hair back into a tight bun, and doused herself in hairspray, till it felt rock solid. Then she fixed a headband with kitty ears to her head, and drew on whiskers with black liquid eyeliner. She tried to draw on a cat-eye too, but she couldn't get the liner sharp enough. She kept going, until she had huge wings ringing her eyes. But that was fine. It was Halloween. She applied mascara which claimed to be 'Better than Sex!' and red lipstick, and set it all in place with more hairspray, which made her cough and her eyes water.

She couldn't twist around enough to pin the tail on, so she called for Luciana, who didn't answer. Angelica stomped out of her room holding the tail aloft. It swung in front of her, looking like roadkill she'd scraped from the tarmac. She hammered on Lucie's door. No response – and when she turned the knob it was locked. The locks on their doors were shit; easy to undo. There were these little slots on the doorknobs which were connected to the lock mechanism – you could pick them with a penny or a long fingernail.

Angelica let herself in.

Lucie was wearing noise-cancelling headphones and playing her DS. She didn't notice Angelica, so Angelica threw the tail. Lucie jumped.

'Oh my God, you just absolutely shat yourself,' said Angelica. Lucie pulled off her headphones.

'What?' Lucie picked up the tail and then looked Angelica up and down. She rolled her eyes.

'Pin that on?'

'Your costume's too tight,' said Lucie. Angelica turned and felt Lucie fiddling with the back of her costume. 'You look like you're purposely trying to look slutty.'

'You're just jealous because you're sitting alone and I'm going out with my friends.'

'See what Dad says,' said Lucie. She stuck Angelica with the pin, but she fastened on the tail.

'He'll be too busy being pleased he's got one normal kid to worry about my outfit.'

'Fuck off.'

Their dad had gone out already.

Later, the taxi driver helped her with the case of blue WKD, which was quite heavy. Angelica wore a long coat.

'Are you meant to be a cat?' asked the driver.

'Yeah,' said Angelica. Her dad made her use local taxis, even though she wished she could just use Uber.

'I recognise that house you came out of – is that Simon Stewart your dad?'

'Yeah.'

'I voted for him,' he told her. 'We all like your dad down at the office,' he said.

He told her not to worry about the fee and to have a good night.

Dolly's house looked normal. It was detached (but only by a couple of feet) and had a small garden. There was a cross above the door. The car in the drive looked new, but not very expensive.

She rang the bell, and Dolly answered. She wasn't wearing a costume. When she saw the case of WKD, she looked panicked. She looked over her shoulder and rushed Angelica upstairs, helping with the box.

'What?'

'You should've told me you were bringing something so obvious,' she hissed.

Angelica was out of breath by the time they got up the stairs. Dolly set the box on the floor, and pushed it into her room, then under the bed.

'You said we were pre-drinking?' Angelica said. Dolly shushed her, then pulled Angelica into her room.

'Yeah, like, not in an obvious way though.'

'Well, sorry. My dad lets me drink in the house, I didn't think it would be a big problem,' Angelica said.

'We can do it at yours next time, then,' Dolly snapped. 'My mum used to be a massive alcoholic, so we're not allowed it in the house. Fucking hypocrite.'

'Are you supposed to be a cat?' asked another voice. Angelica turned. Violet Hubbard. She was sitting at Dolly's desk and squinting without her glasses.

It was weird to see her out of a school uniform. She was wearing skinny jeans, a turtleneck and a denim jacket. All black. No makeup. She looked strange in Dolly's very pink bedroom.

The room was a lot like Angelica's own, but it was smaller. Pink walls, white wardrobe and bedframe. Pink bedclothes. Pink desk. Dolly's room was tidier, though. It was almost spotless. And there were no posters. There was no personality. On the desk, Angelica spotted some Sylvanian Family frogs – but that was it for decoration.

'Why are you here? Why is she here?'

'Don't be a bitch, Angelica,' said Dolly, coolly. Violet snorted and sipped from a mug. Dolly explained they were drinking vodka, which was more subtle than a whole case of WKD. Angelica didn't come here to be laughed at, so she acted like this didn't bother her.

'I didn't realise your parents were going to be so weird,' said Angelica.

'You can talk,' Dolly said. 'But you're right, my mum and Paul are freaks. You'll see all their religious stuff when you go to the toilet. My mum never used to be like this, it's all him.'

Dolly opened two bottles of WKD with her teeth and tipped vodka into three mugs. She split the two WKDs between the mugs, and placed the empties in a plastic bag, which she stuffed under her bed.

'I like your room,' said Angelica.

'I don't.' She squinted at Angelica. 'Are you looking at my frogs?'

'No.'

'Don't look at my frogs.'

Dolly warned Violet and Angelica that they weren't allowed to act drunk while they were here. Angelica kept looking at Violet, and Violet kept looking at Angelica. No one looked at the frogs.

'I didn't know you two were friends,' said Angelica.

'Violet's cool,' said Dolly. 'She said you used to be a cunt to her all the time, though. But I said you were probably over that now all those other girls pick on you.'

'They don't pick on me,' Angelica scoffed.

'You're always saying they do. Even Violet said they're not

nice to you. That Joni girl bitches about you over text all the time.' Dolly turned to Violet. 'Doesn't she?'

Angelica felt her stomach lurch. Violet shuffled; she scratched the back of her head.

'Sometimes,' Violet said. 'She does, yeah.'

'I don't like her,' said Dolly. 'She's so annoying.'

'She is really annoying,' agreed Angelica.

'You know she keeps trying to talk to Jayde?' said Dolly. Angelica asked which Jayde – Jayde in Dolly's year, or Jade in Year 10. 'Jayde Spencer, obviously. Joni tries to talk to her so much – she even joined the same kick-boxing class. She's such a stalker.' Dolly stared at Angelica, waiting for a reaction. But Angelica didn't quite understand what she was getting at. 'Like she talks to her in a dykey way,' she said.

'Oh my GOD,' shrieked Angelica. 'That's disgusting.'

Violet and Dolly exchange a look.

'I'm seeing Jayde,' said Dolly. 'I'm bisexual.'

Angelica's foot was so far down her own throat she could vomit. She felt herself go bright red.

'Yeah I didn't mean disgusting like it's gross, I mean disgusting that Joni would like— I mean it's disgusting for Joni. I meant it's disgusting when she does it. I actually, um, I'm friends with gay Calum? So—'

'Don't have a stroke,' said Dolly. 'It's fine.' Dolly combed her fingers through her hair. It was long, and dark, and loose. She was wearing a black jumper, and a tartan miniskirt. Her makeup was sort of gothy – she looked much gothier than she did in school. Angelica could see her Michael Kors handbag and her Vivienne Westwood ballet flats shoved in the corner of her room.

149

'I really really do think your room is really nice, TBH,' Angelica said, trying to change the subject.

'Well *tee bee aitch*, I hate it? Mum decorated it before I moved here. When she got back with Paul – Paul is actually Heather's real dad—'

'Who's Heather?'

'My sister. When Mum got back with Paul, I wanted to stay with my real dad, so Mum and Heather left and moved here. And then my dad died so . . . all this shit, all that shit,' she pointed at the bag and the shoes in the corner, 'it's her trying to buy me back. Fucking embarrassing.'

'That sucks,' said Violet. 'I didn't know that.'

'It's whatever. She blamed my dad for making her an alcoholic and made out like he was horrible, but he wasn't. Pretty rich considering she's probably the reason he . . .' then Dolly held an imaginary noose above her head. She crossed her eyes, let her neck go limp, and let her tongue loll from her mouth.

Dolly sniggered. Violet smiled. Angelica thought about how weird this was. How weird Dolly was. Maybe the rumours about her were true after all.

'Anyway – you hang out with Joni all the time, right. Do you all know she's probably like . . . pretty gay?' asked Dolly. Angelica was relieved she'd changed the subject. She had no idea what to say to that other shit, but she could bitch about Joni till next Halloween.

Dolly bombarded her with questions: had Joni mentioned Jayde? (No.) Did she ever mention Dolly? (Not really. Only to agree with the other girls that she seemed mental.) She told Jayde she was really into sports – was that true? (No!) She'd joined Jayde's kickboxing class – did anyone know? (No.) Had she ever mentioned boys, or a boyfriend? (No, never.) Was she as stupid and pathetic as she seemed?

'Yes, totally. She used to be so fat and ugly, she used to just hang around with Violet – no offence – and she was so weird. She's totally fake,' Angelica said. She was grinning. She started to feel drunk.

'If we crash this party – should I invite Jayde? To see what Joni does?'

Dolly was already texting Jayde. She lay on her bed, on her stomach. She had a little smile on her face. Angelica felt sucker-punched by all of this. All of this gay stuff. She didn't have a problem with it, it was just a lot. Everyone knew Jayde was an absolutely massive lesbian, but Dolly and Joni . . . that was definitely weirder. If Violet was gay too – that would be less of a surprise. She seemed like the type. Angelica squinted at Violet, like there might be some kind of a giveaway – like if she looked hard enough, her gaydar might bleep. Violet played a game on her phone, pointedly ignoring Angelica's gaze. Angelica felt her lip twisting.

Angelica was friends with Calum. But that felt less weird – gay boys were less weird to her. Dolly was so pretty, and her room was pink. Her nails were painted pink, too. They were all raggedy and bitten, but they were polished and pink. Dolly bit the skin around her nails while she waited for a response, smearing nude lipstick on her fingertips.

'You're getting lipstick everywhere,' said Angelica. Dolly hopped over to her dressing table and topped the lipstick up – Angelica recognised the brand. 'Is that Kat Von D?'

'Yeah?'

'Isn't she like . . . a weird goth?' asked Angelica, sneering. Dolly blinked at her.

'You're so strange,' she said. She looked at her phone. 'Jayde said she'll meet us outside Annabelle's house. She doesn't want to go in. But we'll see about that.'

Angelica was suddenly very aware she was dressed like a cat. That her old dance costume was too tight. She probably had a camel toe. She glugged down everything in her mug and held it over her crotch.

Dolly's mother burst in, then. She had a bag of Doritos. She didn't look much like Dolly. She was fat and frumpy. Angelica thought of her own mother – slim, and polished – and felt superior.

'Hello, girls,' she said. 'What's your name?' she asked Angelica. Violet emptied her mug too and wiped her mouth.

'Angelica.'

'That's very pretty,' she replied. She was trying so hard to sound nice that she sounded sarcastic. She reminded Angelica of a dinner lady. She handed Angelica the Doritos. 'Those are for you, but I don't know if cats eat Doritos. Aren't you a bit dressed up for a film?' she asked. Dolly cut in for her.

'She came here straight from a party,' she said.

Dolly's mother told them she was going to her women's group.

'What time does the film finish?' she asked.

'About ten,' said Violet. 'I think my mum is picking us up.'

Dolly didn't look up at her mum – she didn't acknowledge her presence at all. Dolly's mum smiled at them and left. When they heard the floorboard creak down the hall, Dolly spoke.

'We should go before Paul gets back.'

Dolly packed her and Violet's backpacks with the vodka, and eight of the ten remaining bottles of WKD. Angelica couldn't fit any in her little handbag and had to shove a bottle in each of the pockets of her coat.

Dolly flattened and folded the box and stuffed it under her own coat. She didn't say goodbye to her mum and shoved the WKD box into her neighbour's recycling.

'I'm going to ring my dealer,' Dolly said. She had to shout over the wind. She'd come out in a leather jacket, rather than a proper coat. She had to shove her skirt between her thighs to stop it from blowing up.

'For drugs?'

'No, Angelica, for antiques.'

Violet sniggered.

'Shut up – like you've ever done weed before,' Angelica hissed.

'Violet's cool,' said Dolly. 'Be nice.' She walked ahead of them, shivering, her skirt now wadded up in her fist.

'How did you even start talking to her, anyway?' Angelica asked Violet.

'I could ask you the same thing.'

'Um . . . she's pretty and popular. Obviously I know her.'

'Sure,' said Violet. 'Well, me and Dolly have a lot in common.'

'Like what?'

'Stuff.'

'What stuff?'

Violet shrugged.

'You wouldn't get it,' she said.

'Get over yourself,' Angelica snapped.

They drank more vodka and more WKD on the walk. Dolly didn't say if she'd gotten hold of her dealer or not. It took almost an hour to get to Annabelle's from Dolly's house. Angelica should've offered her house for pre-drinks because it was much closer.

Annabelle said she lived on Moorcock Hill, but she didn't really. Her estate was still in Crow. It was at the bottom of Moorcock Hill, and there were some nice houses there but it wasn't Moorcock Hill. Angelica tried to tell the other girls: 'She tries to make like she lives somewhere posher than she actually does. Isn't that sad?' No one seemed to care that much. But when she told Dolly and Violet, Dolly laughed, so Violet laughed too.

'What a stuck-up bitch,' said Dolly.

The gate to Annabelle's back garden was propped open and covered in fake cobwebs and plastic spiders. Angelica marched forward, Dolly and Violet in tow. Annabelle *was* a stuck-up bitch, and Angelica was going to show her just how few fucks she gave.

Annabelle was dressed as a zombie schoolgirl. She looked cheap and freakishly tall in her short skirt and high heels. She rolled her eyes when she saw Angelica. She was standing with Kayleigh and the Hannahs. Kayleigh visibly cringed when she saw Angelica. She was dressed as a witch. When she screwed her mouth up, her green face-paint cracked.

'I came,' Angelica announced.

'Yeah.'

'Even though you thought you were acting like you're the queen bitch by not inviting me.'

'I did tell you about it though. I mean, you're here,' she said. Her voice was flat. She had her arms folded, and her mouth was smeared with lipstick and fake blood. She was trying so hard to look like she wasn't bothered. Angelica began to feel a bit frantic. She felt woozy and righteous.

'Well you obviously didn't want to, and I bet you felt so big and so clever,' Angelica blurted. Annabelle smirked.

'Okay, whatever, you're here now.' Annabelle peered over her shoulder. 'Did you bring Dolly Hart?'

'Yeah.'

'I didn't say there were plus-ones. She's not even in a costume. If she does anything weird, my dad is upstairs. He'll literally throw you out.'

'We probably won't be here for that long anyway. We're going to go somewhere cooler and *do* some weed, so,' Angelica shrugged. Annabelle smirked.

'*Do* weed. Well that sounds really cool. I'm so jealous of you.' She walked away, back to the Hannahs and Kayleigh. Everyone laughed but Kayleigh, who looked guilty.

'You're all so fucking two-faced. Kayleigh told me she thinks you're bitchy,' Angelica called. But they didn't hear her. Or they didn't care if they did.

Angelica went back to Dolly and Violet, who were themselves smirking and giggling.

'Because I'm such a fucking joke,' muttered Angelica. She tried not to sound hurt, but she failed.

'They're the joke, not you,' said Dolly. Her breath smelt of sugar and blue-coloured alcohol. 'Annabelle's skirt is tucked into her tights, look.' Angelica looked over, and it was. She looked fucking ridiculous.

They stood in the corner of the garden getting drunker and louder. Dolly and Violet laughed when they played Taylor Swift, and Angelica laughed too even though she liked Taylor Swift. Jamie Murgatroyd from sixth form came over and asked Dolly who she was dressed as, and she said Aileen Wuornos – another weird, private joke which she and Violet cackled at. Jamie told Dolly he had some beer and some cigarettes in the kitchen, but she said she was fine.

'You'll change your tune later,' he said, and he walked away.

'Let's go when Jayde gets here,' said Dolly. 'This is so lame.' Annabelle was laying out a Twister mat. The party *was* lame. There were hardly any boys. No one was dancing. 'Look, they're playing Twister. Oh my God,' she said it loud enough for Annabelle to hear. Her head whipped round.

'Just go then! You weren't invited,' Annabelle shouted.

'We are going.'

'Go sooner!'

Annabelle resumed setting up Twister. Angelica noticed Joni for the first time. She was dressed as a vampire, a masculine Dracula-type vampire. She was probably trying to be funny, or something. Angelica hadn't recognised her, with her hair slicked back like that. She started walking over to them, waving.

'Violet?' she said. 'Hey. I'm glad you came! You look nice!' Angelica gave Violet a look.

'She invited me,' Violet mumbled.

'Fuck off,' Angelica said. 'As if you were invited, fuck off.'

'I thought you said you'd bring Jayde?' Joni said. Dolly snorted.

'I said Jayde and Dolly, maybe. She's meeting us here,' Violet shrugged.

'Why do you want to speak to Jayde so much?' Angelica slurred.

'I wanted to ask her something about our kickboxing class,' Joni said, too quickly.

'Oh, gay,' said Angelica. Dolly sniggered.

'Excuse me?'

'I said okay.' Angelica smirked and Joni rolled her eyes. But it was hard to take her seriously. It was hard to care what she'd think, or what Joni might say about her when she was this drunk, and when Joni was dressed up like Dracula. She looked ridiculous. 'But you know, she's seeing Dolly. They're going out.'

'Okay, cool. I don't care,' she said. But she did care. Angelica could hear it on her voice.

'So sad,' said Angelica. Dolly sniggered, nodding along with Angelica. 'So sad for you. Tragic.'

'You're tragic,' said Joni.

'Jayde's outside,' said Dolly. 'Let's bounce.'

And they bounced. Joni watched them leave.

'Oh, don't you need to ask her about kickboxing anymore?' called Angelica. Dolly pulled her through the gate. 'SO FUCKING SAD!' she shouted.

Jayde was waiting across the road, in the light of a street lamp. She was bundled up in a man's coat and a scarf, the ratty toes of her trainers peeping out from under the coat. She waved.

She seemed familiar with Violet but didn't appear to know who Angelica was. She said hi to the other girls, then looked at Angelica like, *And you are . . .*

'Do you not know who I am?'

'No. You're in the year below at school, aren't you?'

'Seriously?' asked Angelica. 'My dad is like, famous. Everyone knows who I am.'

'Who's your dad?'

'The UKIP guy. With the hotel,' said Violet. 'He owns the chalets that keep burning down.'

'Oh,' said Jayde. 'My mum properly hates him. No offence.'

Her hair was short at the back and the sides, and bleached blonde. But she'd clearly done it at home. Her roots were white, but there were a few yellow patches in her fringe, which was clipped up. She looked like she'd just gotten out of bed, or something. Like she could be wearing pyjamas under her coat.

'Did you bring it?' asked Dolly. Jayde pulled a sandwich bag from her pocket. There were two long, weird cigarettes inside it.

'Is that the weed then?' asked Angelica.

'Yeah, obviously. What else would it be?' said Dolly. Angelica shrugged.

'I dunno. Cigarettes. I was just asking.'

She thought about her dad. Last week, he'd been on a local radio debate. Crow had a problem with heroin – he was arguing with Faiza Nawaz about what to do with the addicts. Faiza Nawaz was trying to be an MP for Labour, but she kept losing. Dad hated Faiza and hated Labour. Her sister taught English at the school, and Angelica's dad rang up to tell them to make sure his daughter wasn't in Ms Nawaz's class. He was told that wouldn't be a problem, because Ms Nawaz only taught the top and bottom sets, and Angelica didn't qualify for either.

On the radio, Dad said Faiza was too soft on druggies, and that they should be lined up and shot.

Jayde had also brought Dolly a pair of bike shorts, which she put on under her skirt. They started walking. When Angelica asked where, Dolly said, 'Somewhere spooky.' She held Jayde's hand and took her scarf. Her skirt blew wildly. The wind was so harsh, Angelica could barely hear anything.

'I don't want to go to the beach! It's too windy!' she shouted.

'We're not going to the beach!'

They went to the graveyard. They sat down on the damp ground, backs against the old church. They were protected a little from the wind here. It didn't feel as cold. From here, you could see the flat land where Poseidon's Kingdom had once been. The empty space made Angelica feel a bit sick.

Violet was staring into the same space as Angelica. She had begun to wonder if Dolly had taken them here on purpose when she asked: 'So, Angelica, you knew the girl that drowned?' Jayde was trying to light the weed cigarette. The lighter kept blowing out. Dolly cupped her hands around the flame like it was a butterfly, something delicate she wanted to protect. 'Violet told me about it.'

'Yeah,' Angelica replied. 'I did. She was my best friend.' *She is my best friend*, Angelica wanted to say. Hearing Aleesha's voice as she fell asleep at night, the little signs she saw around the house; Aleesha was still around.

'Violet said she was kind of a cunt, but everyone acts like she wasn't now she's dead,' said Dolly. Angelica shrugged. 'People do that all the time with dead people. It's okay if you think she's a cunt.'

'She was nice to me,' said Angelica.

'Violet said she was the spawn of Satan.' Jayde managed to light the cigarette and started smoking it. She passed it to Dolly. 'People act like it's a big deal when a kid dies, but sometimes I think, I don't know. If she was a horrible person, maybe it was for the best. Don't you think?'

She passed the weed cigarette to Violet, who smoked a little of it, but mostly just held it. Angelica shrugged again.

'And don't you think, maybe, she wouldn't have died at all if she'd been nicer? Like, sometimes shit happens. Sometimes bad things happen to good people. But when bad things happen to bad people, I don't know. It's like, I think it gets manifested. She was nasty to enough kids at school, and enough people wanted her dead that it happened. Just before you guys went to high school, too. She would've gotten worse there, I bet.' Dolly took the cigarette from Violet, and smoked it again, before offering it to Angelica.

Angelica took it. She put it in her mouth and breathed it. It didn't burn like she'd expected it to. So she sucked it again. It tasted stale and gross but not smoky.

'Wow, crazy. I can really feel it,' she said.

'It went out,' said Jayde. Jayde passed her the lighter, and Angelica struggled to relight it.

'I really believe this though,' Dolly continued. 'I think there's a lot of power in thinking. Like that Annabelle girl – don't you hate her? She was such a bitch, not inviting you to the party.'

'Yeah.'

'Don't you hope something bad happens to her? Doesn't she deserve it?' Angelica couldn't relight the cigarette, so Dolly took it away from her. She lit it, and let it dangle from the corner of her mouth. 'Let's try something,' she said.

She asked them to hold hands. She asked them to focus

hard on Annabelle. To picture her face. To really focus on how annoying she was. How she thought she was so much better than them, because she was sort of pretty and sort of rich. She thought she was the shit just because she'd done a couple of pissy little local modelling gigs. Everyone believed she was the shit just because she acted like she was. Wasn't that pathetic?

'Now, really focus on her getting taken down a peg. Think about something truly awful happening to her. What's the worst thing you can imagine?'

Angelica closed her eyes and cycled through a number of scenarios in her head. She imagined Annabelle snapping her ankle in Twister. She imagined her passing out on her bathroom floor and choking on her own vomit. She imagined her drunkenly insisting everyone go to the beach to skinny-dip – then her naked body washing up on the beach. She imagined someone throwing acid in her pretty face. Annabelle screaming, clutching at her cheeks: *I'll never be in another public safety campaign for Crow-on-Sea Council!* She started to laugh. And the other girls started to laugh too. They opened their eyes and let go of each other's hands.

'Now let's see what happens. Let's just wait,' said Dolly.

They kept drinking. Angelica managed to smoke some of the weed cigarette. It burned the back of her throat. It was dry and tasted smoky and muddy and bitter.

'How many dead bodies do you think are down here?' asked Dolly. 'We should . . . this is kind of dumb, but we should come back here and hold a séance or something.'

'I have a Ouija board,' offered Violet.

'Well I can talk to ghosts,' Angelica said. 'So you wouldn't

161

even need a Ouija board if I was here.' Jayde snorted. But Dolly said *Oh yeah?* Like she was interested, and didn't think it was stupid. 'Yeah. I can talk to my friend Aleesha. I can talk to her sometimes and she talks back to me.'

'How does she talk back?' asked Violet. Angelica suddenly remembered Violet had been there, in the slide.

'She never mentions you,' Angelica snapped.

'Um, okay,' said Violet, smirking. 'But how—'

'She moves stuff around in my room and I can hear her in my head sometimes. Like when I'm about to go to sleep, I can always hear her then.'

'That's cool,' said Dolly. 'So is it just her?'

'What?'

'You said you can talk to ghosts, plural, but then you've only talked about Aleesha.'

'Um,' Angelica said. She cleared her throat, thinking quickly. It didn't seem like Dolly was trying to take the piss, even if Violet and Jayde were sniggering. Dolly's eyes were big and interested. 'Yeah, well you know my dad's hotel is haunted. And it's been on *Most Haunted* and stuff. Well, I can hear whispering in there all the time. I hear all sorts of weird stuff when I visit.'

Dolly nodded and smiled.

'Cool. Maybe you can be like a conduit to the spirit world or whatever.'

'Yeah,' Angelica said, her chest swelling with pride. 'Maybe.'

Then her memory became a bit spotty. She remembered that they went to the beach. She remembered cold, wet sand between her fingers. Dolly hugged her and span her around – she remembered the smell of pineapple and coconuts.

She woke up in the downstairs bathroom of her own house – blue vomit in the toilet. But she didn't feel too bad. It was 6 a.m.. She was able to take a shower, and clean up, and drink a pint of water and go to bed. Neither her dad nor Lucie had noticed how late she'd been out or heard her throwing up. She got up at eleven with a headache, feeling no worse for wear otherwise.

On Monday, something good had happened, and something bad happened.

Kayleigh, obviously still feeling guilty, trotted up to Angelica before school started. Angelica wasn't even going to bother with those little bitches, but Kayleigh caught up to her before she could find Dolly.

'Did you hear about Annabelle?' she asked. She was smirking.

'Hear what?'

'Oh my God,' said Kayleigh. 'It was so funny. When you left – you know Jamie from sixth form? He was like, "Where did Dolly go?" And Annabelle was like so annoyed with him, it was so weird. She like snapped at him, "Are you mental? She's not even that pretty," and he was like, "She's prettier than you." And she cried and got her dad to come and chuck him out even though he was trying to leave. Then she started drinking loads and she was sick on herself. I think people took pictures. It was so cringey,' Kayleigh said. She was frantic, and grinning. 'She'd been being such a bitch all night. It was so funny.'

Angelica rushed to tell Dolly. They had manifested something. Angelica wasn't entirely sure they had done it – but she wasn't entirely sure they hadn't. Dolly had to know either way.

Dolly and Violet usually hung out in the corridor which connected the technology rooms to the rest of the school. Angelica found them huddled up together, sitting on the floor and charging their phones. Angelica excitedly told them what Kayleigh had said.

'I told you,' Dolly grinned. 'I knew it.'

That was the good thing. The bad thing came later in the day. It was in PE. Annabelle was off school. Kayleigh pointed this out while they were getting changed, and everyone giggled. Lauren asked Angelica if she'd heard what had happened and smiled at her.

'I think it serves her right. I thought it was a bit pathetic that she tried to keep it a secret from you and then she didn't even own up to it when she was blatantly caught,' she said. 'I said, either invite her or don't. She was so like,' Lauren rolled her eyes. 'You know what I mean? Like she was the first person to ever throw a party ever.'

Angelica felt like one of the girls again, even with Joni glaring at her. But the feeling didn't last.

In PE Angelica was on a team with her friends. They were playing basketball. She managed to avoid getting stuck with Violet, who was on the other team. Violet kept trying to catch Angelica's eye and smile at her, like they were friends now. Angelica was in a good mood, so she was trying really hard – trying to keep the ball and score. But she kept missing.

'PASS the BALL-UH,' Joni shouted at her. 'You are a BAD SHOT, you are making us LOSE.' She got in Angelica's face, so Angelica shoved her, and they were both sent out.

'Basketball is not a contact sport, ladies,' said the teacher.

In the hallway, they stood either side of the gym door.

'Since when do you care about sports?' asked Angelica, 'Since you started being a massive dyke?'

'Your dad's a fucking Nazi paedo. I hope someone burns one of his fucking chalets down with you inside it,' she said. And she was crying. Angelica didn't feel bad.

'I'm going to tell the teacher you said that. I'm going to tell everyone you're gay and you fancy Jayde.'

'Go for it. No one will believe you,' she said. 'It'll backfire. Just see if it doesn't massively backfire, like your little attempts to make people hate me always backfire.' She wiped her eyes on the back of her hand. 'Nobody even likes you.'

And Angelica started to cry as well. The teacher came out and said *oh dear*, and complained about teaching girls their age.

'Whatever it is,' she said, 'I promise you won't even think about this in ten years' time, you know.'

The teacher sent them to different rooms to calm down. She sent Joni to her office, and Angelica to Mrs Craig, the pastoral manager, who had dealt with Angelica a lot during the Vance Diamond fallout.

'I know you're friends,' she said. 'But you should tell me if she said anything about your dad.' But Angelica didn't say anything.

'We're both just stressed,' said Angelica. 'About GCSEs. And we argue sometimes. It's not a big deal.'

At lunchtime, Angelica sat with the girls and wished she had gone to the tech corridor instead. Joni came up behind her and hissed, 'You better not have said anything,' right in Angelica's ear.

All the hairs on the back of Angelica's neck stood up.

The girls talked about the party and laughed. They talked about how cringey Annabelle had been. They agreed to take the piss out of her *now*, and not to rub it in when she got back to school.

'She must be so embarrassed,' said Angelica. 'I would just die if I did anything that embarrassing.'

Some girls chuckled, agreeing with her. But others fell silent.

'You're that embarrassing all the time,' said Joni. Angelica glared at her. She thought they had a truce. 'You like, literally have a Tumblr account where you argue about musicals and dress up like a cat, so don't talk about her being embarrassing.'

'No I don't,' said Angelica.

'Yes you do.' Joni took out her phone. Angelica saw her open a browser, and type in the first letter of her Tumblr URL. It autofilled. Her stomach churned. Angelica told her to stop. Joni scrolled for a moment and found a picture of Angelica from earlier in the month. She was trying to do the stage makeup from *Cats*. But she looked ridiculous. She had thought it looked good at the time, but she realised now that she looked really stupid. It was a set of four selfies. She should've deleted them.

Joni put her phone on the table.

'I wouldn't call other people embarrassing if I did this on the internet, sorry.'

'That's not me,' said Angelica. Other girls leant to look at Joni's phone. No one laughed, but no one stuck up for her.

'You're in such a mood today,' said Lauren. She nudged Joni's phone back across the table. 'Let's stop being nasty about Annabelle. Let's all just chill out a bit.'

They sat quietly for a moment. Then one of the Hannahs asked Angelica:

'So how often do you dress up as a cat?'

'I don't. That wasn't even me.'

'Is it like a weekend thing? Or just special occasions. Like Halloween,' asked Joni.

'You *did* go to the party dressed as a cat,' said one Hannah.

'Oh my God, she's literally obsessed with being a cat,' said the other.

'Shut up,' she said. And the other girls started to laugh.

By the next day, they'd started meowing at her. Joni made the photo of her in *Cats* makeup her phone background, and she kept showing it to people. She kept showing it to boys.

At break time, Angelica snarled at her: 'That's not me in the cat photo.' And Joni just laughed. So Angelica announced that Joni was a massive lesbian. She was probably trawling Tumblr for more lesbians. She was probably obsessed with Angelica because she fancied her.

Joni laughed again.

'I mean, I'm not? But would it matter if I was?' she asked.

'Yeah that's really homophobic, actually,' said Britney. 'My brother is gay, I don't think that's cool.'

'It's really weird that you would say that,' said one of the Hannahs. Angelica didn't care which. 'Aren't you supposed to be friends with Calum?'

They all went to Joni's house the following weekend. Angelica wasn't invited.

GIRL B

Extract: *Creepy: A True Crime Podcast*, Episode 82

Hosts: Amy Floyd and Casey Hunter
01:01:00

HUNTER: Oh my God, I'm literally in tears.

FLOYD: I know. I'm so sorry, I said it would be rough. And do you know how long Violet got?

HUNTER: Life, right?

FLOYD: She's out.

HUNTER: What? You're fucking kidding.

FLOYD: Yeah, she literally went to a secure unit—

HUNTER: A what? Like jail?

FLOYD: No, I don't think they have juvie in England, just these secure units. She wasn't tried as an adult.

HUNTER: What?

FLOYD: Nope! She was in there for two years.

HUNTER: Two years!?

FLOYD: Because she didn't put her hands on Joni.

HUNTER: Fuck off. What the fuck. I don't give a shit if she didn't—

FLOYD: Oh, I know.

HUNTER: —put her hands on her, she didn't fucking tell anybody. She didn't fucking . . . She had so many opportunities to stop them . . . I literally do not care how old you are, that is disgusting. You'd have to be a pretty shitty, evil person to just . . .

FLOYD: Sit back and let some people burn your fucking friend? To death?

HUNTER: I feel sick. I feel like I'm actually going to vomit.

171

FLOYD: I know.

HUNTER: I hope she carries that with her every day.

FLOYD: She'd better.

HUNTER: I hope she wakes up every single fucking day of her life and thinks about how much of a coward she is and how her cowardice got someone killed.

FLOYD: Yeah, I can't imagine being that spineless. I'd rather die.

HUNTER: Same.

FLOYD: I would literally rather die.

HUNTER: I've had depression and I've had suicidal thoughts and I wouldn't wish that on anyone, but I don't know how she hasn't killed herself. Like I really don't understand how she hasn't killed herself.

FLOYD: Well, she probably got a bunch of free therapy in the secure unit.

HUNTER: I wonder if Joni's mom got free therapy.

It's hard to explain how I feel about everything. I watched
Paradise Lost not too long before all of this, and I identified
really strongly with Damien Echols. I identified with him
(and still do) in that he was persecuted for being different.
For his interests. People assumed that, just because he liked
dark things, had alternative interests, that he was guilty.

Though I suppose the core difference between me and
him is that he was innocent, and I'm not. But I suppose I'm
more innocent than some would suggest. Less innocent than
Damien Echols. But I think my point still stands.

*

Violet, from what we can stitch together, did not lay a hand
on Joni.

She was their ideas man, apparently. Dolly, and certainly
Angelica, would have it that Violet put the idea in their heads
to kidnap Joni – to teach her a lesson. It was Violet's idea to
burn down the chalet.

And it was Violet with internet browser bookmarks
clogged with YouTube videos and Wiki entries about horrific
murders. Three weeks before Joni Wilson's capture, torture
and death, Violet visited the Wikipedia page for the 'Murder
of Junko Furuta' on five separate occasions. She read about
the deaths of Sylvia Likens, Kelly Anne Bates, Jamie Bulger
and the Hello Kitty murder. She consumed hundreds of hours
of true-crime podcasts, creepypastas[10] (she would frequently

10 'Creepypasta' is a colloquial term referring to amateur horror stories
shared around the internet. The name comes from the term 'copypasta'
which refers to any memetic text which is copied and pasted.

comb the web for information on Slender Man, and would revisit the Russian Sleep Experiment over and over again) and horror books. She read *The Collector*, Jack Ketchum's *Girl Next Door*; anything she could find on Josef Fritzl, on Jaycee Dugard, the Ariel Castro kidnappings. Stories of prolonged capture and torture hummed in Violet's skull like a wasp nest.

But she also consumed a great deal of fantasy and science fiction. She watched just as many hours of *Game Grumps* videos, cat videos and anime as she did true-crime content.

And Violet did not touch Joni. And it was Violet who confessed. And it was Violet's mother who drove her to the police station. And it was Violet who expressed the most remorse at their trial.

*

Violet's mother, Dawn,* served me tea from her best china; delicate pink cups and matching saucers. The house was small, tasteful, and nowhere near the coast or Crow-on-Sea itself. Dawn herself was also small and tasteful. She looks like Violet, though appeared to have made a series of conscious aesthetic decisions to differentiate her appearance from her daughter's.

Where Dawn had once jokingly called Violet her 'Mini-Me' and leant into their matching dark hair and spectacles, at the time of our interview, she wore her hair short and blonde and seemed to favour contact lenses over glasses.

She served tea with cubed sugar. The house was neat, and orderly, and devoid of photographs of Violet. There were photographs of Dawn's stepson and her fairly recent wedding, instead. Dawn's new husband knows the details of Violet's case, but her stepson does not.

'He thinks she lives with her dad, and that we're estranged. That we had a big falling-out, and a generally bad relationship. I keep things . . . vague and so does my husband,' she said. 'Neither of them know her old name.'

Through the interview her teacup rattled against her saucer because her hands were badly shaking. Unlike Simon Stirling-Stewart, Dawn did not speak of her own accord. She answered questions when asked but offered nothing. It was an uncomfortable interview. She was not hostile, but I could tell she wanted me out as quickly as possible.

I told her she could be brief, and to start at the beginning.

Violet was born on 20 January in the year 2000. Not in Crow-on-Sea but in Berwick-upon-Tweed, to Dawn, aged thirty-two, and her husband Liam, thirty-five. Dawn and Liam had been married for three years, and together for five. Dawn was (and still is) a social worker, and Liam was (and still is) a civil servant. Dawn had two pregnancies before Violet. She miscarried the first, and the second was terminated due to a severe congenital abnormality.

'The foetus was anencephalic,' she said. I gave her a blank look. 'It was missing a large portion of its brain and its skull. The prognosis is very poor. If I didn't miscarry it, it was likely it would be stillborn. And if it wasn't stillborn, it was unlikely to live for more than a day or so. And even then, if it did happen to live beyond that, there'd be no quality of life. It wasn't a nice choice, but it was an easy one.' Dawn shrugged. 'Liam's family are very religious and weren't particularly happy with me, even when we explained.' This was one of the first cracks that would lead to her and Liam's eventual divorce.

'We didn't try again for another year. And then, Violet was very thoroughly screened and tested for everything. But she was fine. I wasn't fine, really, but she was.'

Dawn is prone to illness and loathed pregnancy. She told me that she'd come from a big family, a long line of robust working-class women who had no problem with their own pregnancies and thought Dawn was just being whingy. Dawn's mother had struggled around pregnancy but had passed away when Dawn was in her early teens. Her father was a quiet, reserved man who struggled with his mental health, but rarely discussed his feelings. Dawn was left only with her mother's brusque sisters to turn to for advice.

'They talked about my mum as someone who was . . . mostly they just talked about her being thin, and a bit stuck-up. My aunts are also thin – we're just small people, my family – but my mum was a size six to their size tens, and she was always ill. She was a bit like me. Always had a cold, couldn't put weight on, ate like a bird . . . quite whiny. People tell me I'm whiny. And I reminded them of her, they told me. They weren't very sympathetic to me.'

She recounted one aunt telling her that her prior difficulties and extreme morning sickness were the fault of Dawn's low weight and narrow hips, and she should've thought to 'get some meat on her' before she became pregnant again. When she struggled to put weight on, the other aunt 'jokingly' called her a lying bitch.

Dawn described carrying Violet as like carrying a brick of vomit in her stomach. By the third month, she knew Violet would be an only child, because she would not go through this again. She could barely move and had long absences from work. She remembers lying awake at night, hoping the remaining months would pass quickly – that the baby would come a few weeks early.

So Violet's premature birth was a panic and a relief. Dawn felt guilty – like she'd willed the baby out. Violet was born at thirty-two weeks, making her a particularly early baby.

Dawn showed me a photograph of newborn Violet on her laptop (her family albums are in storage). She was in a plastic cradle, wires erupting from her body, with tiny knitted socks and cap and near translucent skin. Dawn says, perhaps due to her professional training, that she'd coped better with the stress of the premature birth than Liam had.

'I do think he blamed me a bit,' says Dawn. 'Because, as I've said, I didn't enjoy being pregnant, and . . . logically I know you can't will an early birth, you can't make yourself give birth, but I think we both felt that my own . . . dislike of pregnancy, how poorly I'd been, that that might have caused it, somehow. When we were getting close to the divorce, I remember saying to him, "You think I'm the reason she was premature."'

While doctors told Dawn and Liam that Violet was unlikely to have any serious lasting problems, they were convinced there was something not quite right with their tiny, fragile baby. As she grew, they would even become secretly hopeful that there was something physically and definably wrong with her.

Violet wouldn't feed. She cried constantly. When she learned to walk (and she learned early), she climbed out of her cot. She wouldn't sleep. She would stand at her baby gate and wrap her little fists around the bars. She would scream, and rattle them, like a caged chimp.

Dawn took her to a GP and was told that some babies simply did not like to be babies. And that was that. No rash, no toothache, no terrible but identifiable internal problem; just some vague existential dread. She did not like being a baby. She was so distressed by being a baby that she screamed with the horror of it. She hated being a baby so much she couldn't sleep. Dawn told me that she felt cruel for bringing the child into the world; she resented the baby for resenting being alive so much.

Violet perked up when she learned to talk. She was bright, and jolly. She had a mop of black hair, and a polysyllabic vocabulary. She spoke in full, clear sentences by the time she was two, and she was tiny and adorable. Strangers were charmed by her in supermarkets, where she would pick up vegetables and shout their names.

'If she wasn't in the trolley, she would pick things up, and show them to strangers, then tell the stranger what she was holding. It was quite strange, but it was cute,' Dawn said. She demonstrated this to me. She leant over and tapped me on the knee. Holding eye contact, she mimed showing me something in her hand and said, very seriously, 'This is an orange.'

Nursery assistants were given lectures about frog spawn, and oblongs, and the life cycles of caterpillars. When Violet learned anything, she would make it her mission to inform everyone she came across of this new, important factoid. She became particularly interested in Henry VIII and then dinosaurs, and then *Pokémon*. *Pokémon* led to *Sailor Moon*, and

Sailor Moon later led to a pre-teen obsession with a variety of anime.

At four, she was happy, confident, talkative, curious and lively. At nursery, her advancement over her peers made things easy for her. They were still just babies, compared to her.

'Nursery reports were . . . I remember reading them and wondering how I could've possibly produced someone so remarkable. Liam and I are both just so . . . average. I know everyone thinks like this about their children but they said she was extremely bright, verbally more like a six- or seven-year-old – she could read first, she could write first. She had lots of friends. I was just . . . I thought a lot about the person she was going to become. Her potential. I really couldn't wait to see who she'd be.'

Violet's problems began the moment she entered school. She wasn't used to criticism, rejection or casual cruelty. She was incredibly sensitive. She became fragile. The children were unkind to her. Probably not especially unkind, but little Violet was so unused to unkindness that it ruined her a little. She came back from each day at school a bit more withdrawn, a bit sadder, and less talkative. Her curiosity turned inward; she no longer asked questions or lectured her peers and teachers about the things she had learned. She became painfully shy. Her reception teacher picked up on it – she was concerned there may be problems at home.

And there *were* some problems. Dawn's relationship with Liam's family was still strained, and Liam sided with them more and more. When Dawn floated leaving Berwick and exploring job opportunities elsewhere, Liam put his foot down and said absolutely not.

'Which I thought was ridiculous – he was working at the HMRC building in Longbenton in Newcastle, so he was driving an hour to work every day. I suggested we move to Newcastle, or somewhere nearby – Tynemouth, Ponteland, just . . . not Berwick. I thought Violet might do better in a new school because she'd gotten so . . . sad. She never kicked up a fuss or threw a tantrum, but she just became very sad whenever I took her to school or asked her how her day was. It was horrible.'

When she spoke to teachers, it became clear there was no individual child to blame. Violet's confidence had been eroded by many tiny slights. A girl calling her annoying, a boy laughing at her for her eagerness to answer the teacher's questions, a group of children who didn't want to play the same game she did, the teacher asking her to give someone else a chance to answer a question. For a five-year-old, this was a death by one thousand cuts.

Violet would spend more time with teachers and classroom assistants than her peers. She didn't quite lose her confidence with adults the way she had lost it with people her own age. She stayed that way. At her first school, she failed to make friends her own age, and looked for the company of adults wherever she could find it.

Dawn doesn't have any of Violet's old schoolwork in her house – everything of Violet's also in storage. But she has digital copies, photographs and scans of drawings and exercise books. She shows me an essay (more of a handwriting exercise) titled 'My Best Friend' that Violet wrote when she was six.

My Best Friend

My best friend is my mummy. I love mummy. We woch a film togehter it is called Shrek. We play games togehter like connect faw and imajinry games. I love mummy. Mummy is very kind to me and never shouts. Mummy makes nice teas for me. Daddy yousouly is nice to. But mummy is my best friend and we woch ready steady cook. I also am friends with Miss Murray and Miss Tracey.[11] Miss murray teaches us things and miss Tracey is funy and nice and plays with me at brake times. We play drafts and snap. Wen people are not nice to me miss murray and miss Tracey help make it better. Mummy makes it better to. I love mummy.

Dawn tells me she was incredibly touched by this when Violet gave it to her, but it made her extremely sad. She didn't think she should be her daughter's best friend. She didn't want Violet to have to play with her classroom assistant at lunchtime. The reference to other children being 'not nice' to Violet broke her heart.

Dawn felt robbed of her happy little girl. The baby was back. The baby that didn't like being a baby. She was a little girl that didn't like being a little girl.

'It got worse when she got older. I think people realised she was sensitive, so she became a bit of a target. She was also— Well. She was finding comfort in things like . . . in *Pokémon*

---

11 Violet's teacher and classroom assistant.

and in books and cartoons. And that's fine. I wasn't always into everything the other girls liked when I was little. But I think because she was so . . . into the stuff she was into, and not interested in much else . . .'

Liam's family were unamused by the new, shy Violet. Her paternal grandparents nagged her to cheer up, to make eye contact, to be more like her older cousins. They teased her about having boyfriends and compared her unfavourably to girl cousins who were more traditionally feminine. When Violet was quickly and inevitably pushed to tears, her grandparents never apologised, and instead told her to get a sense of humour. Dawn says it drove her 'mental'. When she asked Liam to speak to his parents about the way they treated Violet, he wondered aloud if they didn't have a point.

At school, Violet dragged unrelated conversations kicking and screaming back to *Pokémon* and *Sailor Moon*, back to Terry Pratchett books the other children hadn't read. She had difficulty understanding how she was supposed to talk to people. It didn't seem to click that conversations generally aren't two people talking at each other about the things they like; they are not two monologues with each person taking turns.

And then Liam and Dawn divorced.

Dawn applied for a job in North Yorkshire without telling Liam, having 'gotten it in her head' that she wanted to live and work in the kind of seaside town she used to holiday in as a child. The job came up, and she applied. She interviewed, and she got it. She told Liam who, rightly or wrongly, became extremely angry with her. Dawn told him she wanted a divorce. She wanted to get away from Liam's family and put Violet in a new school. They needed a fresh start.

'Things were quite acrimonious at first. Liam was very stressed and annoyed about having to sell the house – but we managed to sell quite quickly at a good profit, so that was a lot of stress off. We could both afford to buy something again, so Liam got a two-bed flat near his parents, and I got this little maisonette in Crow. The transition was smooth, and we had been quite unhappy pretty much the entire time we'd been married. His family were awful about it, of course, but once we'd spent a bit of time apart, I think we realised we'd both made the right decision.'

Violet and Dawn moved to Crow in January of 2008, just before Violet's eighth birthday. Dawn and Liam had a final Christmas together, at Dawn's father's house. Dawn remembers it as an awkward day she wished she had not bothered with – though her father and Violet enjoyed themselves. Her father taught Violet to play chess, while Dawn and Liam kept a constant flow of films on in the background, hoping to drown out the silence between them.

And things did and did not improve for Violet in Crow. She made friends for the first time – but she also acquired dedicated bullies. From Violet:

Joni was my first friend when my mum and I moved to Crow. On my first day at the primary school, I was buddied up with (would you believe it) Aleesha Dowd, and Joni protested because Aleesha was 'nasty'. The teacher told Joni to settle down and said something about Aleesha needing to have an opportunity to prove herself. And I remember thinking that I really didn't like where that was going. In my old school if someone was naughty, they'd have to come and sit next to me in the front row near the teacher. I didn't want to be the punishment seat in my new school.

Joni volunteered to look after me, and the teacher said no. I was too shy to speak up, but I really wanted to go with Joni instead. It was stupid that they didn't pair us up in the first place when Joni wanted to help me and Aleesha was such a little bitch. When Aleesha was supposed to be giving me a tour of the school at break time, she ended up locking me in a toilet cubicle. She turned the lock from the outside, stuffed a wad of playdough over the mechanism so I couldn't turn it back from the inside. Then she brought Angelica and Kayleigh through to laugh at me, then they left.

I was so embarrassed, I just sat on the toilet and cried until a teacher came for me. I'd gotten bullied at my last school, and I knew how upset it made my mum. She'd made quite a big deal about how this was going to be a fresh start, and how she was really looking forward to me having friends. I felt like I'd already really fucked things up for myself. From there, Aleesha consistently bullied me for being a grass. I hadn't actually grassed, it was just patently obvious that Aleesha (who had a penchant for locking girls in toilets and was banned from accessing playdough without strict supervision) had done it. The teacher let Joni look after me from there, and that's where our friendship began.

We mostly kept to ourselves and played imaginary games. We made friends with a couple of other quiet girls and Joni bossed us all around. Joni said 'let's play doctors' and one of us would lie on the ground, while Joni pretended to perform lifesaving surgery. 'We're playing cops and robbers' – and

Joni would chase us around with finger-guns, shouting
'BANG BANG BANG BANG!' I think the other girls (read:
Angelica and Aleesha) started getting a bit more vicious
with us around Year 5. We were playing 'baby games' and
wearing 'baby clothes' and had 'baby hair' because we
weren't giving ourselves ponytail-based traction alopecia
or forcing our parents to buy us crop tops with 'baby slut'
rhinestoned onto the front.

When I mentioned the bullying to Dawn, she got up to take painkillers. I didn't mean it as an accusation – 'why didn't you intervene' – I wanted to know if she knew; if she, or anyone else, had done anything about it.

'She didn't tell me she was being picked on. As far as I knew she'd made friends with Joni, and a couple of other slightly odd girls. I did like Joni,' said Dawn. Her mouth twisted, and her eyes filled. 'But . . . Violet was very passive. I was more concerned about Joni than I was the bullying – I mean, I couldn't be concerned about something I wasn't aware of. But knowing she was being bullied makes her . . . putting up with Joni make more sense.'

I asked Dawn to elaborate. I encouraged her to be candid. I was building a complete picture of all of the girls – not just the perpetrators. I mentioned that Joni's mother had told me she could be quite domineering. Dawn nodded.

'I did like her. I did. She was a nice girl. But my ex-partner, my boyfriend at the time, he used to call her the Bulldozer. Because of the way she'd just run over a conversation. She was domineering, like you said. They had a lot in common, but I do wish there'd been more . . . that things had been more even between them. Joni was in charge. And I didn't like that; I think Violet . . . I don't know. I'm sorry.'

Dawn took a break for a minute. She told me she was happy to talk about Violet, but she wasn't sure she could talk about Joni, or their friendship.

When I later interviewed Amanda, I asked her what she remembered about the early days of Violet and Joni's friendship, and what she remembered about Dawn.

'I do remember them together, yeah. Always liked Violet. She was very bright and very chatty with adults but really shy with other kids which I thought was quite funny. I felt sorry for her because I think it was obvious that the bullying got to her more than Joni and I'm comfortable enough with who my daughter was to admit that Joni wasn't always particularly nice to her. I once told her off for snapping her fingers at Violet and saying 'come here' to her. Violet didn't do herself any favours in that regard and did follow her around like a puppy. It was sad.

'I did like Dawn as well; I think we were similar in some respects. I told her not to let Joni run roughshod over Violet, to feel comfortable telling her off and stuff because it's the only way she'd learn but I don't think she did.'

Dawn returned to our interview shaking, and paler than she had been before. She frequently pinched the bridge of her nose, and told me more than once she had a migraine coming on.

Violet was, as you will recall, present at the accidental drowning of Aleesha Dowd, knocking Aleesha free from the waterslide she was caught in. From Violet:

I really don't like to talk about Aleesha drowning. I
still have nightmares about it. I'm really claustrophobic
because of it, and I haven't been down a slide since. After it
happened I was having really bad nightmares and I had to
go to the GP and have this weird short course of kid therapy
where they talked to me like I was a baby. I was also really
scared of water, which was quite inconvenient when you
live by the sea. There are a lot of water-based activities you
get roped into. And because my mum didn't want me to be
alienated from people's birthday parties and stuff she asked
the therapist what we could do about it. And the therapist
told her I should have swimming lessons to help me 'relearn'
to swim.

So Mum made me go to horrible swimming lessons and
they made everything worse. And because I associated
Aleesha's drowning with the swimming lessons I really
don't like to talk about it. I don't even want to talk about it
here because now the Joni stuff is piled into it and I can't I
can't I can't.

Violet didn't mention her swimming lessons in any great
detail again, at any point in her correspondence to me. She
would occasionally make a vague allusion to the 'swimming
thing' or 'the bad thing' but that's it.

I apologised to Dawn in advance and pressed her for a little info on the incident itself, and how Violet was after.

'I thought it was covered in sufficient detail at the trial,'
she said, becoming cold with me for the first time. I explained
that, yes, the basic details were covered at the trial, but I
wanted to hear from her.

'Okay. The pool staff were mostly A-level-age kids, kids going to uni soon, or taking a year off. They were working there as lifeguards and doing a bit of swimming teaching – something for their personal statement or their CV. I think a lot of them were competitive swimmers. Athletes – squeaky clean. I had absolutely no hesitation about booking her in for lessons with the pool. And Ryan Jameson had the best availability for me for work. I thought about going out of my way to book her in with one of the girls instead, but I thought I was being ridiculous and booked her in with Ryan.' Burying her face in her hands, and wiping away a few tears, she said: 'Obviously I've never regretted a single decision more in my entire life.'

Ryan Jameson was eighteen at the time of the incident. A former star swimmer, he'd been working on and off at the Crow Leisure Centre since he was fifteen; he was employed there as a lifeguard and swimming teacher. He had recently missed his chance to join Team GB for the London 2012 Olympics. Having attempted to swim a qualifying race hungover, he vomited in the pool.

After three weeks of lessons, during which Violet had seemed more or less happy, she came back one night complaining of pain in her stomach and saying she no longer wanted to take swimming lessons. When Dawn pressed her on this, Violet became aggressive. She turned to Dawn suddenly, shouting and in tears, and insistent that she no longer wished to attend lessons.

'I'm a social worker,' Dawn reminded me. Her tears dry, she clicked into a professional, businesslike tone. It was as if we were discussing a child who was not her own. 'So I knew something was wrong straight away. I asked her if something bad had happened at the pool, and she said yes. So I just took her straight to the hospital. I told them what I thought might have happened, and they examined her. They had to sedate her.' And then, Dawn's professional manner melted into sobs. She left the room again, for ten minutes or so this time.

The hospital confirmed injuries consistent with a sexual assault. The police were contacted, and, though all signs pointed to Ryan Jameson, they needed Violet to name him. It took her days to build up to it. Days to say his name. She sat up at night wailing, every night, for almost a whole year. She wouldn't speak to male police officers. She hit her father when she visited him. She never spoke about it, not even to friends. She didn't tell Joni, she didn't tell Dolly, and she never posted about it on her blog. As confessional as many teenaged girls are (and Violet occasionally was) on social media, Violet never posted about the incident, or made any allusion to it.

When Dawn came back into the room, I asked what happened to Ryan.

'He killed himself,' said Dawn. 'The police interviewed him, and for some nonsense reason, they let him go home totally unsupervised and he killed himself. He got very drunk and walked into the sea, I understand.' She snorted. 'A complete joke, honestly. I don't know what they were thinking. I have to deal with the police a lot at work, and I know they're generally pretty useless but this was just on another level. I put it down to plain ignorance. I thought – like from a mile off he looks like a suicide risk. You know, he's missed out on the Olympics, he's been caught hurting a child. Of course he'd kill himself. Why wouldn't you?

'His dad was one of those . . . local businessman types. He owned a few B&Bs, and I don't know. I got the impression – if you don't live on the council estate, and you were pally with the right people, the police would just let you . . . I don't know. You could get away with murder in Crow. Look at Vance Diamond. It's endemic. And . . . well, Diamond is different. The reason Ryan didn't get away with it – he picked normal, stable, middle-class girls to victimise. If he'd been more sly, like Diamond was, I bet he would've gotten away with it.'

I asked Dawn if Ryan's suicide helped or hindered Violet's healing process.

'Both. She was glad he wasn't out there anymore, because she was terrified. I think he might have threatened her, but she wouldn't tell me. She felt guilty – she felt responsible for it. It was a lot of very complicated feelings for such a young girl to carry around. She was only eleven. I'm glad his family were . . . they weren't in denial about it. The *Post* were going to run a big memorial thing like 'Olympic Hopeful Tragic Suicide' and the family stopped them. The pool had to quietly reach out to everyone who'd done lessons with him, and they turned up a couple more victims – a couple of other girls who were at school with her – which also helped Violet; it made her feel less alone.'

'Did she spend any time with those girls?'

'No. No, she didn't want to. She didn't want to talk about it or think about it, ever. It was her way of coping. I told her I was ready to talk about it when she was.'

Violet began regular counselling but wouldn't open up much to her therapist. She withdrew from adults – particularly men, struggling around young men more than any other demographic. Violet was private – she was already uncomfortable talking about her body, hearing about sex and puberty. Dawn assures me she tried to bring her daughter up in an open and safe environment, but too much of her conservative in-laws' attitudes to sex and her father's immense discomfort around anything to do with the body had rubbed off on Violet.

'So I think most of all . . . I think more than anything she was just humiliated by it. Absolutely humiliated. She just . . . she retracted. She . . .'

Dawn asked to stop. With a final blow of her nose, and a shake of her head she said:

'A fucking great start to high school.'

Joni was my best friend in primary school. We were friends with a couple of other girls too but it wasn't the same. She was my best friend. We went to birthday parties together, we played on the beach, we went to the amusements. And we got even closer when secondary school started. Our other couple of friends went to the private school outside of town, so it was just us at CCHS together. And I think you're not real friends with someone until you get a bit older. Children don't have real friendships, they're just together. But we had so much in common and I think we were friends on a deeper level for the first year of high school.

We talked a lot about where we sat in school. We talked about why people didn't like us so much. We got upset. I used to beat myself up and stuff and Joni would tell me we were just better than them. People like Angelica were just jealous of us because we were interesting and different. I think it's really cringey that we used to say stuff like that, but it made me feel better. I think because we'd been picked on so much it felt like it was us against the world.

And then I sort of don't really know what happened. I kind of remember that Joni got sat next to Lauren Everett in English, and Lauren was part of Angelica and Kayleigh's extended friendship group of blonde, skinny, bitchy girls. And Joni started telling me Lauren was really nice and I shouldn't be so judgemental – that I was being bitchier about Lauren than Lauren ever had been about me. And I pointed out that that's because Lauren doesn't know I exist, so she probably would be bitchy about me if she did. Joni said that I was making stuff up to be annoyed about. But I wasn't annoyed, I was just sort of hurt. We'd argued a little bit before but she never seemed as angry with me as she did here.

And then, it was like one day Joni and I were hanging round at my house and playing games, and the next, it was like we weren't friends anymore.

We'd been playing Heavy Rain together. I'd inherited a PS3 from my cousin, and my mum was kind of lax about video games. She would by any stuff for me – as long as it was fairly cheap and not obviously sexual. If it didn't have sexy women on the cover, she'd just get it for me. So I didn't play GTA or anything like that, but she got me Fallout 3 and New Vegas and Skyrim and stuff. Anyway, there's a part of Heavy Rain where you have to press X to shout 'Jason', because the main character's son disappears at a mall. The voice acting is a bit wonky, and you can sort of mash X and shout 'Jason? JASON?!' over and over again. Joni and I thought it was really funny. And we used to shout 'Jason?? JASON!!' at each other as we were passing each other in the hallway at school.

One Friday, I invited Joni round to finish our current run of Heavy Rain. We were trying to fail as many quick time events as possible (without killing the characters) to see what would happen, and we were a couple of hours off the end. But she said she couldn't because she was going to Lauren's house. I was a bit sad about it (and was sort of hoping she'd invite me along) but she just said, 'Well, bye!' and walked off.

Then, on Monday morning, she was just really off with me. She didn't answer my text when I asked if she wanted to walk in to school with me, and when I met her in the playground she was funny with me. Her hair was done. It didn't look puffy like it normally did, and she was wearing makeup. We never wore makeup – we called the girls that wore makeup normies and sluts and attention-seekers. But suddenly here she was. She looked almost like a completely different person. Older and prettier.

When she saw Lauren Everett she ran over to her, and just left me standing there. I was talking to her, trying to pretend things were normal but when I was like mid-sentence, she just walked off and went to stand with Lauren and her friends. Her friends including Angelica and Kayleigh, who we hated. They mostly ignored us, but we still hated them. We still used to talk about how stupid they were and laugh about them and how boring and pathetic and thick they were. But now Joni was standing with them, like that was normal. Like she fit in.

Then we passed each other in the hall between first and second lesson – I shouted 'Jason?' at her, and she was with Lauren. She just looked at me, like she was confused and a bit disgusted and didn't shout Jason back. That was when I knew we weren't friends anymore. I was kind of devastated? I didn't really have any other friends. I was too embarrassed to tell my mum. I remember crying in my room all night, because I just knew Joni didn't want to be my friend and I didn't know what I was going to do the next day. No one to sit or stand with at breaks, no one to pair up with in lessons. It was going to be horrible.

I pretended to be ill the next morning. I put talcum powder on my face, and dark eyeshadow under my eyes, and I pressed my head against the radiator before I told my mum I felt poorly. She touched my head and said I had a fever. I stayed off for the rest of the week with a 'flu'. I finished off our run of Heavy Rain by myself. It wasn't really as funny anymore and I just felt stupid. I kept wanting to tell Joni about stuff that happened in the game, I kept going to text her and stopping. And that made me feel sort of pathetic.

I had a really horrible few weeks at school after that, moping around on my own. I tried to sit with the other weird girls, but I didn't really fit in with them either. They liked books about horses and stickers and Taylor Swift, but only 'Love Story'-era Taylor Swift. Red was her newest album, and I remember them all complaining about how Taylor had changed and she was just a slut now. It was obvious we weren't going to be friends. They were obsessed with Frozen, and I had just started getting into Tim Burton films – which I know aren't exactly hardcore or anything, but to the sticker-and-horse crowd it was, and I was starting to get too scary for them.

Things improved for me when I got my first smartphone. I was still (in 2013, yes) carrying my mum's old Motorola flip phone, and I'd mentioned that the other kids were starting to get 'touch screens' – the holy grail of which was, of course, the iPhone. Angelica had gotten an iPhone 5 for her thirteenth birthday, and I remember it being this big thing that she had one, but she was very whiny about it because she'd wanted the brand new iPhone 5C.

An older boy from school saw me using the flip phone (to text my mum, because that was all I used it for after Joni started ignoring me) on the way home and knocked *it out of my hand. Because it was about a thousand years old, it broke, the screen detached from the keyboardy bit. I remember really clearly the way the screen popped off. Like it happened in slow motion because this was a disaster, and I was sure I was going to get in loads and loads of trouble. Then I came home in tears. But my mum just said she was due a new phone anyway, and I could take her iPhone.*

And because it was 2013, I immediately downloaded the Tumblr app. And it was life-changing. This was before I had my own computer, so I'd been able to use Tumblr a little bit on our family desktop in the living room. But now I had private, unlimited access. It was like I was instantly able to find my own little community of people into the same stuff as I was. That being, primarily: nerdy stuff like anime and video games, spooky stuff and true crime.

*

'I think it's fair to say I took an interest in Violet, yes,' said Farrah Nawaz-Donnelly, a former English teacher at Crow-on-Sea Community High School. We meet after school in her new place of work – a pupil referral unit in Birmingham. I asked her why she'd taken an interest in Violet, and she snorted, gesturing to her new place of work. 'No deep reason, I'm just a bit of a bleeding heart. I grew up in Crow as one of around seven brown people in town, and I was a goth. So I have a soft spot for outsiders.'

Farrah, now in her mid-forties, gave me a brief overview of her life. Her parents (both second-generation Punjabi Muslims born in Bradford) moved to Crow in the early 1970s, where they set up Taste of Punjab – Crow's first Indian take-away. Farrah was born a few years after Taste of Punjab opened. She is the middle child, one of three – an older brother Mahar and her younger sister Faiza. Her parents were, in Farrah's words, 'liberal and entrepreneurial': 'Very New Labour, before that was even a thing.' They wanted to make their money and send all of their children to university; they hated the Conservative government and campaigned hard enough for Tony Blair that, while on the campaign trail, he came to the restaurant and took a photo with them.

At the time of publication, Faiza is still a Labour councillor for Crow-on-Sea, and stood for Labour in the 2015 general election. It was thought that Simon Stirling-Stewart's UKIP campaign might split the right-wing vote enough to grant Faiza a victory – but she still narrowly lost to the Conservative's Barry Proud.

The photograph of Tony Blair and the Nawaz parents that had hung in pride of place in the restaurant – they had tacked a paper speech bubble to his mouth which read 'The best Indian in North Yorkshire' – now, apparently, sits on Faiza's desk in the council office.

'It seems like you're all very community-minded,' I said. Farrah shrugged.

'We're nice people,' she said. 'Can't say Crow always deserved it.'

While their parents built their business, Mahar, Farrah and Faiza each navigated the terrifying experience of being 'the only brown kids at school'. Mahar was athletic, funny and good-looking. Farrah tells me, with no offence to her brother intended, he 'acted and spoke as white as physically possible' at school – and acquired a large group of laddy friends, who dubbed him 'The Curry Man', a nickname which he pretended to take in good humour, but privately despised.

'That's awful,' I said.

'That's Crow-on-Sea,' Farrah said.

Faiza, charismatic, outgoing and light-skinned, also sunk more easily into the social fabric of their almost-all-white school – though she went through a phase of telling people she was Italian. Speaking as someone who is actually of Italian extraction, I found this surprising and sad.

'I sometimes used to get picked on for being Italian,' I confided. 'You know, for being *swarthy*.'

'It's not quite the same,' said Farrah.

When I explained that this was a private boys' school in the seventies, Farrah seemed to accept that the situations were more similar than she'd initially thought.

Farrah, for better or worse, was as shy as she was angry. Unable to tolerate the daily microaggressions she faced as successfully as her siblings.

'Though I don't like saying they put up with anything *successfully*, they just . . . I don't know, repressed their anger about the whole thing – because there's no doubt we would've been happier in Bradford, where we'd have had a community, and there's no way we'd have been the only Asian kids at school. My brother does therapy now, and Faiza moved to a city as soon as she turned eighteen. She came back, obviously. But I just . . . well, Mahar said I made life more difficult for myself than it had to be.'

Any jibes about curry or takeaways (or any of the other tired, disgusting racial tropes one might expect to hear in such an aggressively homogenous town as Crow) aimed Farrah's way were met with a sharp 'fuck off'. Farrah admits she developed the habit of responding to racism by rubbing her family's relative wealth in the faces of some of her severely deprived classmates.

'This obviously didn't win me any friends or allies – even the kids that ostensibly thought racism was bad also thought I was a smug, hostile cow and left well alone.'

Farrah spent her break times in the library, studying, reading and dreaming about going to university. She loved to read – she always had – and when she became a teenager, she moved on from children's books to the writers her newly beloved Morrissey sung about.

When she ran out of Keats, Yeats, Shakespeare and Oscar Wilde, she studied music magazines for examinations of Smiths lyrics, and read Virginia Woolf, Tennessee Williams and George Eliot – whose works were tenuously referenced in songs. She then discovered a *Sunday Times* list of '50 books to read before you die' so she read all of them while she listened to tapes of the Cure and Joy Division and channelled all of her energy into seeming romantically dishevelled and extremely well read.

'It went down like lead balloon at school, but I was pretty popular when I went to uni.' After 'smashing' her A levels, Farrah studied English Literature at Leeds University, where she initially entertained ideas of becoming an academic. Despite finding herself in another mostly white environment, Farrah was at first optimistic about her chances of fitting in. Her fellow students seemed almost unbelievably cosmopolitan and intellectual in comparison to her peers at high school, but her optimism quickly wore thin.

'They weren't as overtly racist but they were all still pretty fucking racist, you know what I mean? I didn't have the patience for the ex-private-school kids – I fell out with the first group of friends I made and ended up hanging round with the er . . .' she shrugged. 'I dunno, a couple of aggro Marxist white kids from state schools and the other people who weren't white? And I got quite radical. And I decided I wanted to teach English at state schools.

'I did quite a bit before I ended up moving back there. I taught at a couple of schools in Bradford – I got married to one of my uni friends, one of the aggy Marxists – and I moved to a pupil referral unit in Scarborough in the early 2000s when my mum and dad retired – to be a bit closer to them, and the business.'

Mahar (anointed with a business degree) took over the restaurant and rebranded it as the more upmarket Anarkali in 2003. Faiza and Farrah part-own the restaurant too. They were (and still are) far less involved in the day-to-day running than Mahar is but tried to pitch in where they could. Faiza (who was working in PR for the Labour Party at the time of the Anarkali rebrand) helped with events, hiring, marketing and advertising, whereas Farrah's role in helping her siblings was largely the organising of care for their increasingly infirm parents.

'My dad was diagnosed with vascular dementia within a month of my mum's cancer diagnosis – and that's how I ended up back at Crow, and back in my old high school. I was driving up from Scarborough every day – then I basically just waited for this absolutely geriatric teacher who'd taught me to retire and applied as soon as they went. Lucky timing – or unlucky, depending on how you look at it.'

Farrah began teaching at CCHS in 2007. I asked her how the school compared in the 2000s to when she'd attended. She told me it was both better and worse.

'I think the kids were less . . . I dunno. The student body is still 95% white, but I expected a lot more racist shit from them than I got. I think the kids are less . . . The socio-economic make-up of the school has shifted. I think because fees have shot up at Amplefield and the nearest grammar was closed, there are a lot more middle-class kids there than there used to be – so attainment rates are quite a bit higher. When I went I was one of the more well-off kids, and that wouldn't be the case now. There wouldn't have been anyone like Angelica Stirling-Stewart back in my day.

'And because of the Angelicas of the world there, I think there was more tension, and more class-based bullying. In the same way there'd have been no Angelicas when I went there, no one really would've batted an eyelid at Jayde Spencer. I mean, I went to school with Spencers and no one did bat an eyelid at them – they were just hard kids, there was no special stigma attached to living down the Warrens like there is now.

'But all that being said, girls like Violet Hubbard just get picked on wherever they are. Being a Violet kind of transcends race and class – there's not a Violet in every year, but there's at least one Violet at every school.'

I asked Farrah to define that for me – what makes a Violet.

'Well . . . I was kind of a Violet, I think. A bit mouthier than her but . . . I suppose I think a Violet is a student who is just kind of . . . weird and doesn't know how to do anything about it. They just don't fit in, and they don't understand why they don't fit in. The other kids probably don't either – there's something about them that's off. And so they do absolutely nothing to help themselves with that – apart from maybe melt into the background, which is sometimes the best you can hope for. In my experience it's just this intangible thing like . . . whenever I opened my mouth I said the wrong thing. I got the wrong haircut. I wore my tie wrong. I wore the wrong thing on non-uniform day. I walked wrong, I liked the wrong stuff. As far as my peers were concerned: I was just fundamentally incorrect. And kids, they're very instinctual, they're very primitive, in a lot of ways. And they can smell difference on you. It's difficult when you're constantly doing something your peers think is wrong and you don't understand what that is, or why.'

I asked her if she knew Joni – if she thought Joni was a Violet at any point.

'I only had her in Year 8. But I knew she was Violet's friend – so I noticed when they stopped hanging round together, and I noticed Joni's makeover, and I noticed the change to Violet for that period she was by herself.'

Farrah taught top- and bottom-set English for Years 8 through 11 – and took on second set for Year 8. Violet was in her top set, Joni her second. Joni had first flagged Violet to Farrah, because Joni had asked what she had to do to be moved up a set. Joni told Farrah her best friend was in top set, and she was sure she wasn't that far off being moved up. She told Farrah that there were too many normies in her current class, and she'd fit in better with the top-set kids.

'I wanted to tell her there were quite a lot of normies in top set as well – I think sometimes these self-identified geeky kids really underestimate the intelligence of those they deem "normal". I know I certainly did – so I try to help them with that a bit. But we didn't have a rapport – so I just told her she needed to do more practice essays and extra reading. I also asked her who her friend was – and she said Violet Hubbard.'

In Farrah's next lesson with Violet, Farrah made note of her. Farrah was yet to organise a seating plan. At first, she let the students sit where they wanted – to get an idea of who should be separated, and who needed to have an eye kept on them. Violet had sat in the corner in their first lesson together, and in their second, Violet chose the desk closest to Farrah's. She noticed that Kyle Richards* (a boy she describes as very bright, confident and outgoing, but with 'a horrible attitude') was periodically flicking very small pieces of paper into Violet's hair. Pieces so tiny that she couldn't feel them. When there were lots of pieces of paper in Violet's hair, the other children began to giggle. Violet turned around sharply, showering herself in tiny pieces of paper. Kyle pointed at her and said: 'Errr! You're getting your dandruff everywhere.'

Farrah sent him out of the room. Violet spent the rest of the lesson hunched over her exercise book – possibly crying, trying to make herself look as small as possible. It was like she was trying to fold herself up. Farrah held her back after the lesson and asked her if she was often picked on, or if that was just a one-off.

Violet said, 'One-off,' curtly. They both seemed to know it was a lie – but Farrah didn't press it. She asked Violet if she'd like Kyle to be kept away from her in the seating plan, and Violet nodded. Without being prompted, Violet also flagged a couple of other boys, and a girl she'd like to be kept away from.

'She said to me – like this really sudden outburst, she went really red – she said: "I'm not getting bullied, I just don't want to breathe in their stupidity miasma when I'm trying to concentrate." I think I was . . . I think I said you shouldn't call anyone stupid, but that miasma was an impressive word. And she smiled at me and told me she knew lots of impressive words because she loved English and reading. So I told her I was looking forward to having her in my class, and sent her on her way.'

Meanwhile, Farrah had created the seating plan for Joni's class. Considering Joni's comments, Farrah thought it might be productive to place her next to Lauren Everett.

'Lauren was sort of the Head B in Charge for their year but . . . I knew Lauren was nice – she was in my form group – and I thought they might expand each other's horizons a bit. They did end up getting on well – to the point I regretted sitting them next to each other. They weren't naughty enough to warrant moving, but there was a lot of whispering and giggling . . . Maybe if I hadn't sat them together, Joni would've concentrated a bit more, and she would've gotten moved up a set. But you can drive yourself insane saying *shoulda woulda coulda*.'

When Farrah drew up the seating plan for Violet's class, she kept Violet next to her, and shuffled the other students, keeping a ring of well-behaved girls around Violet as a protective barrier against flying pencils and pieces of paper.

Farrah had them do a creative writing exercise. It was something she liked to do to gauge her students' vocabularies, their general engagement with English and stories. Violet wrote furiously, all lesson. The next day, Violet turned in a fifteen-page story about a teenager who brought their dog back from the dead. An overt rip-off of Tim Burton's short film *Frankenweenie*, but Farrah found her cleverer writers did tend to steal ideas and do their own spins on them – rather than getting tripped up by the difficult task of making something original up.

The story was gripping, simple, and had a beginning, middle and an end – which made it head and shoulders above most of the work Farrah had been handed.

'So I gave her a couple of spare exercise books – I told her she could write stories in them whenever she wanted, and she could show them to me as often as she liked.' Farrah snorted to herself, then. 'She never showed me anything, but I know she appreciated it. I wanted to encourage her without badgering her. Mostly I just tried to talk to her about the books she was reading – particularly after I'd noticed she was by herself at lunchtimes.'

Joni had also stopped asking about being moved to top set – and happily sat in Farrah's lessons, cosy with Lauren Everett. They fiddled with lip gloss, and fiddled with each other's bouncy, curly hair. Farrah says that this was something she saw happen semi-frequently. An outsider who decided that they no longer wished to be an outsider; who wanted to be normal and look normal and blend into the crowd.

'It's sad to see the Violets of the world getting left behind like that, isn't it? But that's high school. I never judge the students who do that – rebrand themselves in the hope of fitting in – but I do try to look after the ones who get left behind. Within the line of what's appropriate, of course. I'm not their friend, or anything. But I try to make sure they know there's at least one friendly face in school. Though, in Violet's case I am a bit worried I might've made things worse.'

For the most part, Violet read a lot of true-crime and horror books that Farrah hadn't heard of, but she was able to connect with Violet over Stephen King. Farrah was a huge fan, and Violet had begun lugging around an old hardback copy of *It*. Violet's responses to Farrah's gentle attempts at conversation were fairly clipped – but once Violet realised she'd found a fellow horror fan, she opened up a little more.

I asked Farrah if Violet talked to her much about creepy-pastas, or true crime.

'She did, yes. I mean, I really didn't think there was anything that abnormal about it. Teenagers are morbid, and a lot of them – particularly in recent years, with podcasts and stuff – a lot of them make being into serial killers their entire personality. I just thought it was an affectation – there are a lot of very functional adult women with the same affectation. So again I just . . . I didn't think much of it. Hindsight is always 20:20 but . . .' Farrah gets a little bit upset for the first time. I tell her every single person I've spoken to has said almost the same thing – hindsight, regrets, 'I couldn't have known'. And Farrah tells me that doesn't make her feel much better.

And what did Violet have to say about this period of her life? In writing produced in the secure unit, she was open to admitting the extent to which she'd found refuge on Tumblr. A great deal has been made of her interests – both at trial and by podcasters and bloggers. It seems if anyone knew anything about Violet, they knew she was a little spooky.

During my interview with Lauren Everett, I asked her what she thought of Violet. She said: 'Oh, I didn't really know who she was. Just that she was sort of like . . . I dunno, like a goth but not aesthetically? Angelica said she was a freak and I knew she used to be friends with Joni in primary school and they were still kind of friendly? But that was about it. Joni would let her be on our team in PE sometimes.'

From Violet:
After Joni had ditched me and I decided I couldn't hack the sticker/horse girls anymore, I found somewhere to hide at lunchtimes. I found a spot that was out of the way of the dinner hall where people bought lunch, and further away from the benches where people ate packed lunches. It was this newly built corridor between the woodworking room and the lockers, and in the corridor there was a little alcove with a plug. I would tuck myself into the alcove, and have my phone on charge, and go through Tumblr.

Sometimes I would read a book, but mostly I just got into creepypastas – those are amateur short horror stories, intended to be copied and pasted and shared around the internet, in case you didn't know. Slender Man is the most famous one of these – you might have heard of him. I was never that deep into the creepypasta fandom, but I liked to read and discuss them and share fanart and stuff. I liked SCPs[12] a lot as well and sometimes I made up my own.

I'm not going to pretend I wasn't obsessed with them, because I was, but I just want to make it clear that I wasn't writing erotic 'Jeff the Killer' fanfiction, and I didn't think

12 SCP stands for 'Special Containment Procedures' and refers to the SCP Foundation, a fictional organisation which promises to 'secure, contain and protect' beings referred to as 'anomalies' or 'SCPs'. The SCP Foundation Wiki serves as a collection of user-submitted short horror stories, each describing a unique anomaly.

Slender Man was going to take me away to his Slender Mansion or whatever.

I also wasn't talking about them all the time. I didn't want to freak out my mum so I never talked to her about them. I did talk to Ms Nawaz about them, but only because she seemed to like horror and stuff. I think she felt sorry for me, because she knew I was on my own all the time. She used to talk to me a lot and I found it a bit embarrassing, but I suppose it was nice to talk to someone. I didn't really mean to talk to her about creepypastas, but I would just sort of blurt out stuff about things I was interested in.

But I did lose interest in them a bit after the Slender Man stabbing. Some of the artists and writers I liked a lot got abusive messages anonymously, and my American friends had their parents getting angry at them for being into creepypastas and started limiting their internet access or grounding them. A girl I knew's mum would check her internet history and take her phone away if she got caught reading creepypastas.

I was scared Ms Nawaz was going to tell on me to my mum because I'd talked to her about Slender Man before, but she didn't. I don't think she heard about the Slender Man stabbing, and then she got me into the local folklore stuff, so we talked about that more than the creepypasta stuff.

The Slender Man Stabbing and the local stuff got me a lot more interested in true crime than I had been before. I'd read a couple of books but I wasn't really in the fandom for it – but when things got less fun after the Slender Man stuff, I moved there.

I followed the Slender Man Stabbing really closely – which was, of course, used against me in court. But at the time I felt really angry at the girls for making the fandom look stupid and delusional. I was hoping some more information would come out, and we'd learn they were framed, or the Slender Man stuff was a fake defence they'd made up and they were really motivated by revenge, or something. I had news alerts set up for it, and I'd pore over every article I could find.

I was about to preface this paragraph with 'I'm aware of how guilty this makes me sound' but I am guilty. A lot of this stuff – my bookmarks, what I'd been looking at – they went over it in court. The whole thing feels like a dream. It's hard to remember that I don't need to defend myself anymore – I can just accept, and try to tell the truth as much as I can. I really don't think I got involved because of true crime – I don't want to blame the media I consumed for my actions. I won't deny that it fed into my mindset and influenced me, but I also want to take full responsibility for the extent to which I was involved in Joni's death.

From the Slender Man stabbing, I started reading about child murders – as in, murders committed by children. Obviously the Slender Man stabbing victim didn't actually die, but it was a really brutal attack, and I don't know, I guess I was just fascinated. It actually took a while for me to get into the really grisly stuff – the trashy websites and super-graphic crime podcasts – I was just reading Wikipedia. I started following some true-crime blogs on Tumblr, and someone put together this 'Killer Kids Masterpost' – which I had bookmarked. I went through every case in the post.

And when I ran out of content there, I went through the 'Torture Murder Masterpost', then 'Worst and Weirdest

Serial Killers'. I became encyclopaedic. If they were a child killer, cannibal or necrophile I've heard of them.

It all hit harder than creepypastas as well – it was real. The creepypasta I liked the most was the Russian Sleep Experiment, but that's because when I first read it, I thought it was true. I saw a Tumblr post where people were laughing about the amount of people who thought it was true, and that spoiled the story for me. When I found this trove of horrible stories that really were all true, I was just hooked. These were all real people that existed – the victims and the perpetrators. They'd endured and inflicted some of the most extreme acts a human could commit – how could you not be fascinated?

I obviously moved on from just reading on the internet, to reading books, watching documentaries and listening to podcasts. I started to engage a lot more with the 'true-crime fandom' – mostly in an ironic, edge-lordy way. I would never edit a flower crown onto Jeffrey Dahmer, but I would probably ironically reblog it – if that makes sense. I'd never actually sincerely read or write serial killer fanfiction, but I would go through fanfic websites as a joke, and screenshot wild stories to laugh at. But I was self-aware. I was determined that I wasn't like the other girls. I'd post a lot about how I was genuinely interested in 'the psychology' and how the girls squeeing about Harris and Klebold were embarrassing to us 'normal' fans.

I was pretty much just like a normal fan until I started posting about the local folklore and history? Ms Nawaz actually pointed me towards it because I'd been probably pretentiously spouting off about how I was really into *internet folklore and she asked me if I'd ever read much about Crow's history – any of the witch stuff or the Viking stuff. It took me a while to actually look it up (iirc it was the summer between Year 9 and 10 before I actually got into it) but when I did, I got VERY into it.*

And I guess being able to talk about more of the local stuff gave me a unique foothold. Like I could do posts about something that no one else had heard of, or had access to, so my posts used to do really well. There's obviously a massive crossover between people who like history and people who like true crime – because most true crime IS history. So I got quite a lot of new followers. I had eight or nine thousand, which doesn't sound like much NOW, but on Tumblr in a niche community that was quite a lot.

When I asked Farrah about getting Violet into local folk-lore, she looked at me guiltily. Farrah told me she had no idea Violet's interests were quite as dark as they were. Plus, she thought local folklore was kitsch – definitely more child-friendly than what Violet had been reading online.

'A lot of the local stories are quite artificial – you know Crow sort of piggybacked on the gothy Dracula tourism that Whitby gets – the ghost stuff, mostly? That haunting stuff is all so forced. But it was all Violet had heard of, so . . .' Farrah fiddled with the rings on her fingers. I reminded her I wasn't interrogating her. 'I thought it was interesting and fun. I don't know. I just didn't think anyone would or could take this stuff . . . literally.'

My blog got kind of popular on the spooky side of Tumblr. I started doing these #CrowLore posts – obviously there's not a huge amount of 'CrowLore' but enough for a few pretty popular posts. My English teacher told me about the Witch Hammer, and I did a post about it, and it went semi-Tumblr-viral (just a few thousand notes) and I gained loads of followers. I think the authenticity of it being this small fucked-up town in England no one had ever heard of, plus the seaside urban-decay aesthetic – people were really into it. I even took a historical walking tour – Terry's Tours – to get more content for posts. My English teacher recommended them to me, she said I'd like them.

THE WITCH HAMMER

When I stayed in Crow it was September – the last embers of summer were cooling in the air, and the off-season approached. Shops and amusements had begun to shutter for the coming autumn and winter, and fewer visitors seemed present with each passing weekend.

I had the opportunity to take the last ghost tour till next spring – and I was the only person there.

The tour's starting point is the statue of Hrókr the Crow down on Crow's North Beach. The statue depicts a generic Viking – he wears a horned helmet and is splattered with seagull shit. As I approached the small landmark for the tour, a gull was perched on the horn of Hrókr's helmet. A laminated piece of A4 paper was zip-tied to the railing behind the statue – the profile of a wide-eyed seagull captioned: 'I AM PUBLIC ENEMY NUMBER ONE. WATCH YOUR DINNER!' I am exaggerating, slightly, to call this a ghost tour.

It was advertised as 'A walk through Crow-on-Sea's Bloody history'. An older man named Terry Tatchell is the guide – the owner and operator of Terry's Tours. When he is not guiding tours, he works for the council's tourist board and has written several books on local history. He looks as one might expect a local historian to look: a small, older man with wild grey hair, an eclectic sense of style and little glasses.

When he greeted me, he appeared to be dressed as every pre-revival Doctor Who at once, and immediately launched into Hrókr the Crow's backstory.

Once he was finished, he told me about the Hrókr ghost sightings which were most frequently reported – that tourists and locals alike have sighted Viking warriors banging on the glass of the antique shop and leaving bloodstains behind, or spotted a black ship on the shore for a blink of an eye. Some have also reported the sight of medieval peasants cut into 'blood eagles'[13] suspended in mid-air by the statue.

Before the tour began, I took the time to ask the owner of nearby Viking Antiques if she had ever spotted the ghost of Hrókr. She said, 'It's rubbish,' and told me to leave if I wasn't going to buy anything.

Terry took me to the Empire Hotel next. He told me, speaking candidly, that he thought the hotel was 'a bit shit' and 'done to death' – so we quickly moved on. A distaste for the hotel is something he shares with Violet. The archive of Violet's blog shows she received repeated requests for posts about the hotel in her Tumblr Ask box – despite having written a post already. She replied on at least one occasion with a link to the previous post and 'i'm only doing ONE POST about the fucking hotel!! The story is so fake like lmao do I look like Derek acorah to you people??'

We walked past the site of Poseidon's Kingdom – Terry talked about the old graveyard and the waterpark. He recounted one of the haunting stories I'd read in the *Post*'s archives, but he

13 The 'blood eagle' was a method of execution allegedly practised by Vikings. The victim's back was cut open, the ribs severed from the spine and the lungs pulled through the incision, creating 'wings'. It is highly unlikely Hrókr made blood eagles of his victims, as it is highly unlikely the blood eagle was historically practised. Referenced only in sagas, it is entirely probable this method of execution was more literary device than historical fact.

didn't mention the drowning of Aleesha Dowd. He said the park was closed for safety issues, and implied interference from the afterlife.

'Didn't a child drown?' I asked.

'I try to keep things light,' Terry replied. He was sharp suddenly, an old schoolmaster ready to rap your knuckles with a cane if pressed.

We walked along the seafront for a while, past a few burned-out chalets and Joni's memorial. Wilted flowers and dirty soft toys are zip-tied to a lamp post; a faded laminated school photograph grins out from the centre of it all. Amanda doesn't maintain it – she can't bear to look at it. But she is touched that people continue to drop off bouquets and cards.

Terry asked me if I was familiar with Joni's case.

'I thought you wanted to keep things light?'

'I do, but it's become a bit of a draw, these days,' Terry sighed. 'I only asked because I assumed you knew – after you asked about the Dowd girl. I wouldn't usually bring it up.' I confessed that I was in Crow to write a book about Joni.

He was neither judgemental, nor was he particularly impressed or enthused to hear this – he told me he wasn't keen on the idea of a true-crime cottage industry springing up in Crow. Terry is from Crow but worked as a tour guide in both London and Berlin in his youth. He said he felt icky taking people on Jack the Ripper tours after a while. He did 'non-spooky' historical walking tours in Berlin and told me he'd periodically get 'some weirdo' who'd ask too many questions about the mechanics of the Holocaust and he hated that as well. He didn't want that to happen here.

But it kept cropping up. They'd inevitably walk past the

memorial on the way up to the castle – recently it felt like every other tour wanted to stop and discuss the case.

'I usually tell them I don't want to talk about it, because I know her mum and it's all still a bit raw. Well, I sort of know Amanda. My brother was friends with Freddy – so I say, "I have plenty of killings to tell you about that aren't as fresh for the community." Makes them feel guilty. Only had one group get really annoyed about it. They didn't tip me or nothing.'

We walked up a steep hill, toward the ruins of Gains-forth Castle. They sit precariously on a cliff between the two beaches, looking over the town and out to sea.

Before the castle was built, a military fortress stood here – it was constructed circa the 800s and destroyed during the Harrying of the North. A small castle was rebuilt in its place in the early 1200s, and was held by the noble Gainsforth family till the English civil war. The devoutly Catholic, Royalist Gainsforth family attempted to flee to France and were caught by Roundhead forces and executed. The Roundheads occupied the castle for a period, with the building suffering structural damage in clashes with both Scots and Royalists.

It was not reoccupied after the restoration of the monarchy and the small, ugly castle fell into disrepair. Still standing today, the building is mostly intact but not safe to enter. Attempts to secure funding for restoration have failed. The castle is not particularly popular with tourists, who tend to walk up to the site and say 'oh, is that it?', then head back down to one of the beaches.

The castle's outer wall is mostly destroyed, its towers are crumbled, but its keep is intact, bar a few holes here and there. What Terry wanted to show me, however, was not the castle itself, but a large, heavy device which stands in the grounds – the Witch Hammer.

There are several theories about the origin of the device. Another local historian, Victoria Jacobs, has posited that the Witch Hammer may have been crafted after townsfolk heard of the *Malleus Maleficarum* – The Hammer of Witches – a treatise on witchcraft written in 1486. The book was used throughout history to persecute and prosecute suspected witches. Jacobs, an archivist by trade, discovered the diary of local clergyman John the Pious – written circa the late 1400s – and was able to restore and translate some of the diary to modern English – an extract below:

We have heard of the scourge of sorcery here and great concern it has caused me and the other good folk of Crow. After the failing of our crops I think it best to seek out the witches hiding in our community. I have heard of a great hammer of witches, which can determine what makes a witch and what doesn't. I know not how such a hammer should look or how to construct one or what blessings should be put upon it to root out devils in our midst.

Jacobs, therefore, suggests the Witch Hammer was created from a complete misunderstanding – the assumption that the *Malleus Maleficarum* referred to a literal hammer.

Terry had a more fantastical story for me. The local legend goes that a woman named Benedicta – known for her physical strength, height and robust health – had survived an outbreak of a plague which had killed a significant portion of Crow's population, including Benedicta's relatively wealthy husband and her sons. Due to the extent of deaths the sickness had brought upon the town, Benedicta now stood to inherit a significant amount of land, property and money from her husband's family. And – spurred on by jealous, distant relatives of Benedicta's husband – Benedicta was blamed for the outbreak. How is it that one woman should not only be unscathed by such a terrible plague, but would even benefit from it?

So, Benedicta was put through a test. She was thrown in the sea from a height with stones sewn into her skirts to see if she would float. And according to local legend, she did not, but she was able to survive the fall, and swim to shore. Benedicta was hung from a tree by the neck – but (again according to legend) clutched at the rope, climbed it and then the tree branch she was tied to. She was able to untie her own noose.

Benedicta then taunted the townsfolk and declared that their petty tests were simply intended for women smaller and stupider than she. And so, the townsfolk put their heads together and came up with the Witch Hammer. Picture a guillotine – now imagine it bigger. Now remove the section in which the victim would place their neck and replace it in your mind with a small wooden platform. Switch the blade for a heavy metal 'hammer' – shaped a little like a church bell, but without any hollow space. A huge lump of solid metal shaped like a bell.

Benedicta was stood beneath the Witch Hammer, which three grown men were required to lift. The hammer was released, and Benedicta was crushed.

Whether this story is true or not, the Witch Hammer was used as a method of execution throughout the Middle Ages in Crow. For hundreds of years, women (and some men) were shipped from nearby villages to die by the hammer. Its last recorded use was as late as 1785.

The Witch Hammer is no longer usable – its wooden frame rotted away long ago and the hammer itself now lies flat on the ground, much too heavy for a single person to lift. A new iron frame was crafted for it; the frame is screwed into the ground, and the hammer is chained to it. A nearby plaque tells the story of Benedicta.

Once a quirky feature of local history, the hammer was recast in pop-feminist history book *Witches, Bitches and Hags: How Britain Punished Women Who Didn't Fit* by Hallie Smyth as a brutal instrument of misogynist oppression. Now it is common for young female visitors to lay flowers at the foot of the hammer.

I asked Terry if he was familiar with the extent to which the Witch Hammer had been folded into the events leading to the murder of Joni Wilson. He wasn't – he didn't want to know. This information seemed to upset him. I suppose he doesn't want such a key part of his tour associated with the death of a girl whose family he knew – I apologised for bringing it up. He finished his tour in good humour – I tipped him £30 and promised to mention his tour company by name in the book.

So that's a portrait of me in high school before I met the others. I was a girl on her own in a corner, injecting horror right into her veins. I was isolated, and I was becoming increasingly warped, and I was grotesquely lonely. I can admit that. I'm not going to pretend I wasn't chronically on the computer and in need of some IRL friends. The only person who paid any attention to me was an English teacher who obviously just felt bad for me, and my mum, who I'd lie to. I would put up a big front online, but I spent a lot of time alone in my room, feeling really shitty about myself. I would pretend to Mum I was going out with 'friends', then just sit on the beach on my phone by myself, or go to the library and read about local history, scouring for content for my blog and not finding much. I think my mum probably knew deep down I didn't really have any friends – but she always just accepted it when I said I was going out.

I felt like all I had going for me was my stupid little blog and my CrowLore posts. I also got really into modding The Sims. That was what I occupied myself with. I was so lonely. But at least, by that point, I wasn't getting actively bullied anymore.

There were easier and more obvious targets for bullying beyond Year 9. I was clean, and I kept to myself. I've never thought I'm pretty but I'm not so spectacularly ugly as to draw attention to myself. I'm plain. Inoffensive to look at. I stopped trying to personalise my stuff – I didn't carry a bag with buttons or patches, and I didn't cover my exercise books anymore. I became a totally blank person in school. The monochrome girl.

When people picked on me I just stopped reacting to it. I stopped attracting attention, and I faded into the background. I disassociated. I got through my lessons, and I looked forward to spending time on my phone at break. People just forgot about me, and that was exactly what I wanted.

And why the fuck would you bully me, when there was someone like Bella Chan* to pick on?

Bella was the only Chinese girl at school and spoke with an accent and I think that'd be enough to make her a target, but she was also an odd duck. Odder than me, even. She was part of the stickers-and-horses crowd – literally all of her school books were covered in horse stickers, and she wore babyish clips and bobbles in her hair.

And she always fought back. She was braver than me, I suppose. She stuck up for herself – she did it in a weird cringey way, but still. If someone made a comment about me I just ignored it, but Bella used to say 'Shut up, sluts!' to the girls, or 'Silence, morons!' to the boys. I'm just using her as an example. There were other kids, too – the boy with learning difficulties who used to wet himself sporadically, the girl whose family ran the fishmongers who smelt of raw fish and didn't know. They all got picked on, and they all fought back for some reason. 'I never pissed myself, I never ever did!' Or 'Fish doesn't even have a smell!' Fighting back just gave the bullies more ammo.

I learned quite quickly they just want a reaction, and I was able to just disassociate. Completely zone out. Bullying me became absolutely no fun, so I got left alone, for the most part.

Even Angelica got bored of picking on me. She used to try and trip me in the hallway, or she'd snigger whenever I spoke in a lesson. But the final nail in the coffin with her – even for petty shit like that – was in PE.

In PE I was last to be picked for netball (which I didn't even feel bad about – I'm really short and clumsy and my aim is really bad, so I was categorically the worst at netball) and I had to join a team with Angelica, Joni and Lauren Everett. And Angelica rolled her eyes and said 'So we're going to lose' and then Lauren rolled her eyes back and said 'Who cares if we win? Are you twelve?' And then JONI (who hadn't acknowledged my existence since Year 8) piped up like 'At least Violet doesn't hog the ball.' Then she did an impression of Angelica overenthusiastically making a shot, making the shot so hard that she tripped – this had actually happened the week before. She said: 'I'd rather have Violet on my team than you.'

This was late on in Year 10, I think. Me and Joni started talking a little bit again. And then I found Angelica's blog. She reblogged one of my CrowLore posts like 'omg I live here.' It was so obvious it was her blog. It was literally like ANGELICA – 15 – STRAIGHT – UK.

Like I said, I never posted selfies, and I never used my name online, I just went by Buttons or Butts (my URL was MurderxButtons) so I don't know, maybe she thought I was an adult. I used to deliberately imply I went to uni – like if I was posting about school I'd say 'seminar' instead of lessons or 'lecturer' instead of teacher. I didn't have my age listed, so most people assumed I was a uni student. A lot of my online friends were in their early twenties.

Anyway I figured it was probably that Angelica, so I dug until I found a photo. I was able to verify her identity via a Cats *makeup test* she posted. I thought it was really funny. Funny enough to save it. Collecting receipts from accounts you didn't like to collate and unleash as a 'callout post' was very normalised back then. Tumblr did 'cancel culture' before cancel culture was a thing. It just used to be 'getting called out'. I didn't think I was going to 'call her out' though. Like I said, I was just in the habit of saving things like that. Which I am now aware is extremely weird, but as one might have guessed, I was a weird kid, in a particularly weird period of my life.

I know I don't exactly have room to talk on the subject of 'Doing Weird Shit on Tumblr Dot Com' but I'd like to emphasise how truly demented her presence was aside from dressing up as a Cats *cat*. She was just constantly arguing about Phantom of the Opera, *losing her tiny mind over* Starlight Express, *talking about how horny she was for the cast of* Cats. *Someone sent her an anon saying 'Cats can suck my fucking balls' and she replied – I remember this quite clearly but I'm paraphrasing – with something along the lines of 'How fucking dare you, Andrew Lloyd Webber has more talent in his little finger than you have in your entire disgusting waste of a body you fucking oxygen thief!!!'*

When I was looking for a pic of her to confirm, I saw she was embroiled in this extremely vicious fight over someone else's Les Mis *fanfic. I'm not very into musicals – everything I know about them is just through cultural osmosis, so a lot of this was incomprehensible to me. But if I remember correctly, she was upset about someone shipping this Very Upstanding*

Very HetterowSeckshewal Male *with another male character.*
She reblogged someone's fic with a comment:

'it's disgusting to ship Jean Valjean and Javert. Javert is
an abuser and this is problematic. I'm done with sickos
forcing Jean Valjean to be with Javert' *(and I shit you not
here, I remember this word for word)* 'This is a rape of the
character.' *Huge argument. Loads of people telling her she
was problematic and homophobic – she shouldn't be casually
using the word 'rape'. All that stuff. Looked like she'd been
up all night fighting and she didn't even scrub the posts.*

*I just thought it was funny how rabid she was; all these
years picking on me for being weird or when she used to
pick on Joni for being too enthusiastic. And here she is, on
Tumblr dot com, doing this. She'd reblogged loads and loads
of thirst posts about the cast of* Cats *and I literally couldn't
believe it. I did judge her, despite what I was up to. I was
very very edgy back then, and I think at this point I'd even
decided I was too dark and edgy for the edgy stuff I'd liked
the years prior to that. I'd decided that Tim Burton was too
basic, and that I was a very high-taste teen, who consumed
only the bleakest true crime and the grimmest creepypastas
and the most demonic metal music (which I didn't really
like and was listening to for branding purposes more than
anything – I used to post a lot about Euronymous and Varg
and the Black Metal Church Burnings).*

*And I had kind of reconnected with Joni at this point.
I guess because she didn't really have THAT much in
common with her new friends, she started messaging me
periodically about anime and games and shit again. Texting
me or talking to me on Facebook messenger (because I*

refused to get an Instagram or a snapchat). We wouldn't really talk much in person but she did make eye contact with me in the hallway at school, and she'd sometimes say hi. But she'd never do it when she was with the others. I tried to be annoyed with her, but I was just so grateful she was talking to me again.

Joni also used to bitch about Angelica to me sometimes. She told me everyone else hated her in their group, but I guess she was freer to be meaner about her with me – Kayleigh and Lauren stuck up for her sometimes, apparently. So one day she texted me to say something like 'Angelica trying to make everyone in drama do Cats, *why is she such a closet furry' so I sent Joni the pic of Angelica dressed as a* Cat *and said I found her Tumblr. I gave her the URL and we were texting each other screenshots of mad shit she'd said.*

We could spend ages ripping into her. Angelica also started getting horrible messages. I felt a bit bad about that.

Tumblr was an awful website. I met Dolly via Tumblr. She was like an internet friend first. Sort of like Angelica, she reblogged one of my CrowLore posts, also saying that she lived here.

It was during the summer between Year 10 and 11. I was on Tumblr pretty much constantly. She sent me a fanmail (this was before Tumblr had an instant messaging system but it did have this weird 'fanmail' function where you could send a long message to someone they could answer privately) which was basically like:

Hey, love your posts about Crow. Do you live here?? hope you're not a middle-aged man.

I checked her blog. I didn't look at it very closely at first.
I just saw she was also into true crime and horror stuff –
but her posts were more basic than mine. She maybe hadn't
been mining this stuff for as long. She was still posting
about entry-level serial killers. There was a selfie which I
recognised. I was kind of shocked because I just figured
Dolly was this bog-standard pretty slutty popular girl.
Obviously not.

We started following each other, and I started noticing a
lot of . . . unironic-looking 'flower crowns on mass shooters'
appearing on my dash and I just gave her the benefit of the
doubt. Maybe it was ironic even if it didn't SEEM ironic.

We'd been talking for like a week before she asked me if
I was a 'creeker'. And I thought – oof. Yikes. Because every
creeker I'd come across was mental. Like mass-shooter
fangirls are considered pretty gross and weird even in true-
crime fandom circles so I was pretty surprised to hear that
she was one. Her URL was Cherrybobobomb – they all
had 'cherry' URLs – but I never put two and two together.
She changed the title of her blog to 'McKnight in Shining
Armour' pretty soon after we started talking – it'd been
CHERRYCHERRYCHERRY before and I'd figured she was
just a Lana Del Rey fan or something.

The Cherry Creek massacre was a pretty obscure case –
it still kind of is outside of true-crime circles, honestly.
Another American school shooting – it feels like there's
one every five minutes so it's like who cares, big deal, even
the most obsessed people can barely keep up with them.
Two white boys killed seven people at their high school in
Montana – Matthew McKnight (in shining armour) and

Brian Cooper. Without knowing the details of the case it sounds like a snoozefest but it is actually interesting – I can understand why it caught on.

No one really cared about Cherry Creek till the footage of Matthew McKnight's sentencing went viral and made a bunch of people kind of rabid. The footage was from 2008; no idea why it got reposted when it did, but it did. It was McKnight making his closing statement and he said something like: 'I jack off with the hand that killed your kids' or something like that. And suddenly people were like 'oooh who is this beautiful murder boy?'

To me, McKnight just looked like a generic white American boy. Not handsome at all, just . . . a guy. But all the creekers talked about him like that – he was a beautiful dark twisted avenging angel, that kind of shit.

And what really made people go nuts wasn't that McKnight was 'cute' (he wasn't) but that after he and Cooper did the shootings, Cooper shot himself in the head and McKnight fucked his body. ALLEGEDLY. A bunch of Columbiners lost their minds about it, and within like seventy-two hours of the McKnight footage going viral they'd created this whole new fandom and this fantasy about the case in their heads.

The creekers made McKnight and Cooper these tragic boyfriends who were innocent victims of smalltown homophobia. I don't really think that was the case myself personally. McKnight seems to have been motivated just by being a psycho and wanting to be famous – he was actually pretty homophobic (and really racist) based on his diaries and stuff. I know that doesn't mean much but

I don't really think it adds up to someone who's a tragic, oppressed closet case.

It felt kind of awkward, Dolly asking me that, because I actually spent a lot of time dragging those kinds of . . . you know, DO NOT CONDONE, JUST WANT THE BOYS TO KISS mass-shooter fans on my blog. So I just told her it was an interesting case, but I wasn't a creeker. She said that was a shame.

I even muted her blog because I thought all the creeker stuff was fucking weird. She reposted loads of cutesy fanart of McKnight and Cooper; she read and wrote fanfiction about them. She didn't make personal posts very often, but when she did, she deleted them. I remember that she had a recent post with a few hundred notes that said some shit like: whenever i feel alone i just think about how matthew is really out there and hes real and i feel so connected to him like he might be lying in his prison bunk and knowing that im psychically reaching out to him.

She used to get a lot of messages – anonymous and from accounts like 'BloodyCherryGirl' and 'the-mcknights-sword' – telling her how much they loved her writing. She used to post her fanfic all the time. It wasn't on any mainstream fanfic websites (I assume school shooter fanfic is banned on AO3??), just this crunchy LiveJournal clone called 'DethJournal'. Once I'd recovered from the unrelenting cleverness of a serial killer fanfic site called 'DethJournal', I scrolled through. She was in the middle of writing a long story set during the build-up to the Cherry Creek massacre, in which Matthew McKnight is horrifically sexually abused by his father.

228

It *was* super graphic. I didn't tell her I'd read it because it kind of grossed me out. I only skimmed it, but in between all the child abuse stuff, her version of McKnight was having this torrid romance with Brian Cooper. It was really flowery. Like her prose was so purple I felt embarrassed I'd stumbled across it. It was all stuff like 'the rippling crystalline pools of Brian's eyes were so impossibly, royally blue.' 'A thought lit up Matthew's midnight-dark brain like a burning fire', 'It should be illegal for a boy to be this beautiful' – very cringey to be honest.

But I was pretty cringe too, so I kind of thought she was like . . . a kindred spirit. So, different taste in murder-stuff aside, we kept talking. I found out we lived on the same estate. We went for a walk together a couple of times over summer, but we didn't really get close till we started hanging around in the tech corridor together at school.

I'd just tell her about stuff I'd seen on the internet. It was . . . I don't know. I guess it was weird. Even though she was really into Cherry Creek, her true-crime knowledge level was pretty shallow. She knew the basics on Dahmer and Bundy, but she hadn't even heard of Richard Chase or Dean Corll. So I'd tell her about stuff like that. I think we were closer after Halloween. I think we were even closer after the Christmas break.

CHRISTMAS

'This is fucking gnarly,' said Dolly. She kicked the Witch Hammer. 'That's totally solid.'

'Yeah,' Violet replied. 'They used it on witches and I think other criminals, sometimes.' She made sure to do air quotes around the word *witches*. 'They – like the town and the church people – they would put them beneath it, and they'd drop it on them. Try to lift it,' said Violet. On school trips, tour guides would always pick a volunteer to try and lift it. She did it once. She wrapped her tiny arms around the hammer and tried to make it budge. It was freezing cold and smooth, and so immovable it may as well have been screwed to the ground.

Dolly did the same. She hugged the hammer and tried to move it.

'This must weigh a tonne,' she said.

'It does weigh a tonne.'

'Whoa. Did anyone ever survive it?'

'There's a story about one girl who survived,' Violet said. 'They said she was a witch and they had her under the hammer, chained up. But she broke out as it dropped, and it didn't crush her completely. The story is really vague because it's really old and word of mouth. Apparently it – the hammer – crushed one side of her body but not the other, and she lived like that for a few days.'

'No way,' said Dolly. 'That's so cool.'

Violet had asked about that story on a different trip a few years later. She raised her hand and asked about the girl who'd gotten half-crushed. Was that true?

And the tour guide said it was just a made-up story – just an urban legend. Still, Violet made a post to her blog about it: she titled it 'Semi-Squashed Sally', and made a bunch of stuff up.

'This place has such a vibe,' Dolly said. She crouched and touched the freezing ground with her fingertips. 'It feels really evil.'

'You think?' asked Violet.

Dolly said she felt it in the ground. Bad blood. Witch blood. She said it was soaking the earth. That between Hrókr the Crow (who she called 'the Viking guy') and this and even Vance Diamond, Crow had evil in its foundations – probably running through its water supply. The wind whipped her hair dramatically around her face.

'I think this is a thin place. Like . . . the barrier between the living and the dead, and between here and hell . . . I think it's thin here. In all of Crow, but here especially,' she said. Dolly looked at Violet; her eyes were wide with excitement. Dolly made a show of being cynical and grown-up in front of others but she loved stories – she loved playing pretend, playing in the space a story would create for her. She could pretend to touch the ground and feel something; she could pretend to summon and dispel spirits, to psychically project herself. Violet could pretend to believe. It was fun.

Wrapped up in her coat and peering up, with her face nestled between her scarf and her hat, Dolly looked like a little girl. 'Do you feel it?' she asked.

'Yeah,' said Violet. 'It's like . . .' Violet tried to think of something to say. Something Dolly would want to hear.

Something that would impress her. 'It's like so thin . . . that it could tear any moment. Maybe it's tearing all the time. Maybe that's why so much fucked-up stuff seems to happen here.'

'Exactly.'

'Do you think if we brought Angelica here, she'd be able to talk to anyone from the other side?' asked Dolly. 'Do some conduit shit?'

'Maybe,' said Violet. 'You don't . . . Do you actually believe she can talk to dead people?' Dolly thought for a moment.

'Why would anyone lie about that?' asked Dolly. 'She's annoying but I dunno. She told me some of the stuff Aleesha said to her. It was pretty creepy stuff.'

'Yeah,' said Violet. 'I bet.'

They walked around the perimeter of the ruined castle together and they talked. They said the word 'thin' a lot. They talked about the barrier between worlds, between life and death. Good and evil. Hell and earth. Hell on earth.

'I really think hell is real,' said Dolly. 'But I think we make it. I think people create tiny hells. Little pocket dimensions, little hell dimensions. You can physically and literally enter hell. Matty and Brian – they totally made a hell in their high school. You can't tell me when they barricaded themselves in the library something totally supernatural didn't happen in there.'

'Yeah, obviously.'

'Like you told me about Dennis Nilsen's flat? Where he had the bodies stored, and he was trying to boil them and dispose of them and process them. But he really wanted to keep them too. And I think that's a perfect example of a tiny hell, isn't it. Like, that flat was literally a piece of hell, wasn't it?' She looked over to Violet, and her eyes were big and expectant.

'Yeah, I suppose. Yeah. When you put it like that,' said Violet. 'Crow is kind of hell, too, isn't it.'

'Totally.'

'Wet, seaside hell.'

'Tacky hell.'

They talked about other thin places in Crow: the graveyard, the site of Poseidon's Kingdom, the beaches, the Empire Hotel. Maybe the Astro Ape's amusement park. They had a little back-and-forth on that – whether it might actually be a thin place, or if they were just thinking in horror-movie clichés.

Dolly said she wanted to try manifesting something again. That Annabelle girl, embarrassing herself at the Halloween party – Dolly was convinced they'd done that. By holding hands and focussing in a thin place, they'd made it happen.

They'd tried other things, since. A girl in sixth form that was nasty to Jayde – they tried focussing on making something bad happen to her, but it didn't work. It didn't *really* work.

Dolly said it did because the girl broke up with her boyfriend. But there was no way of knowing if the girl they were targeting was that bothered about the break-up or if he'd even been the one to break up with her. Violet didn't think it counted. Violet wasn't convinced it worked at all. She was supposed to pick someone, but she couldn't think of anyone to target, really.

'Do you think Angelica's dad would let us stay at the haunted hotel? Like for free?'

'Probably not. But it's not the original hotel anyway. I think most of the stories about it are made up,' Violet said.

'Maybe we should just try Astro Ape's. I don't know, maybe it'd be fun, at least,' Dolly said. 'I've heard it's really easy to get in there.'

'I don't know, it's really dangerous. Like, it's probably a thin place now because so many homeless people die in there. People freeze and overdose all the time,' Violet said. 'What's wrong with here?'

'I think we should save it. I think the Witch Hammer is too powerful,' Dolly said. She sounded so serious.

Dolly had to leave for a driving lesson, so Violet stayed at the hammer. She plucked a half-dead flower from a bunch laid by it and put it in her pocket. It was ugly and purple. She took it to press at home.

While she walked, she tried to pick a 'target'. She tried to think about someone who had annoyed her recently, but she lacked the kind of focussed rage Dolly or Angelica had. The anger she felt was shapeless and general; a low-level buzz aimed at nothing at all and everything at once. A lot of people were a little bit unkind to her – she couldn't hold a bully's attention for long enough for them to form any special hatred. She didn't have any love rivals to aim her ire at; as much as she didn't hate anyone, she didn't particularly like anyone either. Nothing inspired particularly strong feelings in her.

Sometimes she wondered if she was a psychopath. She googled it all the time and tried to make the diagnosis fit. But she was too sad, and too fearful and too well behaved to qualify. She was another lightly depressed, middle-class-ish teen. A poster girl for the 'Teen Mental Health Crisis Plaguing Our Youth' – a girl among a million other somewhat sad girls, with no real problems beyond a vague existential angst.

And yes, arguably, the bad thing had happened to her. But much worse things happen to people every day. Statistically, she was really nothing special.

Did hanging around with Dolly make her feel something? Sort of, she supposed. Panic was a feeling. Adrenalin was something. It reminded her of the feeling she had when she read about a particularly nasty murder case or watched a really horrible film. That feeling of things being wrong, and bad, and yucky in a very internal way. Dolly only wanted to hear about terrible things, and think about them, and chat about them like the weather. It was why they got on. But it was Dolly's interest in channelling and manifesting that made it feel strange.

The creeker shit didn't help either. The fanfiction, the way she called Matthew McKnight 'Matty', like they were friends. Violet thought of herself as a pretty non-judgemental person. She wasn't really in a position to question the weird shit other people did on the internet. But she did judge the creekers. The same way she judged the Columbiners or the girls who thought they could have 'saved' Elliot Rodger if only they'd met him instead of the shallow sluts who ignored him at college. It all set her teeth on edge.

When Violet got home, her mum asked her where she'd been. Violet told her she'd been out with Dolly, and they'd walked around at the castle. Mum smiled; it was nice not to lie to her about having friends. It was nice when Mum didn't worry.

Violet took the purple flower from her pocket and asked her mum if she could use some of her books to press it. Violet had got rotten flower gunk on one of the chunky, expensive books her mum had used at uni, so she had to ask now.

Mum carefully wrapped the flower in kitchen roll and cling film (to 'contain the goo') and fetched Violet a couple of thick textbooks about the history of social care in the UK.

'You could've picked one that wasn't quite as battered,' her mum said.

But Violet liked battered things. Nothing was so delicate and precious as that which had already begun to fall to pieces. She wanted to preserve its last gasp of colour and beauty.

Violet shrugged.

'I suppose it has a bit of character like this,' said Mum.

Violet went to her room. It was painted in a neutral colour – a duck-egg blue. She liked that you probably wouldn't be able to tell if it was a girl's room or a boy's room at a glance. She sat at her desk and turned on her desktop computer. She listened to a podcast, and played *Sims 4*, which her computer was just about new enough to run comfortably.

The podcast was about Slender Man as a 'tulpa'. An expert in Tibetan religious practices and mythology explained to an internet historian what a 'tulpa' actually was. He said that the West's idea of a tulpa was just that – the West's idea. That the internet's concept of a tulpa was much more like our idea of a Golem – or the version of the Golem that had entered Western, cultural osmosis. A monster from Jewish mythology, the golem is often characterised as a creation which turns against its master; though its role is more complicated than that. In the way we had mischaracterised the golem, we had gone on to mischaracterise the tulpa. We have collectively misunderstood the complexities of the tulpa (we were not even pronouncing the word correctly) and projected our own mythology onto it.

'We've made it into a sort of Frankenstein's monster. In Western, Christianised cultures, we have this knee jerk hostile reaction to the idea of people playing god. You can see it pre-Christianity, even, as far back as the Prometheus myth,' he said. 'And that just doesn't have anything to do with the Tibetan tulpa.'

They mentioned a subreddit where people discussed their tulpas, creatures the users believed they had manifested – either physically or inside their own heads. So Violet went to the subreddit. Bearing in mind what had been said on the podcast, she thought these people sounded pathetic and insane. Adults ten years older than her were claiming to be able to manifest cartoon characters, and romantic partners and terrifying monsters. They were publicly reporting on the intense and special relationships they had with imaginary friends.

There was no way of knowing how many posters were genuine, and how many were trolls. But this did seem like the kind of thing Dolly might like, even if she just took the piss out of it. Violet didn't send her the very sceptical podcast (Dolly wouldn't like that), but she did send a link to the subreddit, and a couple of articles from some more credulous paranormal websites.

In *The Sims*, Violet built a house for a family. She followed a guide she found online. The house was pretty. It had white decking, and flowers, and three bedrooms. It had an office and three bathrooms and a big kitchen. It had a living room, a dining room, and a recreational room. It also had a basement. Where the main house had fussy, pastel decor; the basement had naked concrete walls, with cracked stone and spiderweb decals. It was fitted with a toilet, a basic bed, a sink, a fridge and a microwave. She used a mod to give the basement a door you could lock and unlock with a key.

The family she created to live inside the house consisted of a mother, a father, a little girl and a teen boy. She wanted the boy to have the key, but Violet knew it didn't make much sense for him to be the only person with a basement key – so she killed off the father. She drowned him in the pool so the boy would be the 'man of the house' and he could inherit the key.

Violet made another teen girl, unrelated to the family, and moved her into the house. Violet unlocked the basement and had the girl walk inside. Then she locked the door behind her.

Violet had the boy visit the girl. She made them fall in love, with the girl locked in the basement all the while. Violet thought about installing a sex mod, but she was too embarrassed to download it. Violet placed the father's gravestone in the basement, and sometimes the ghost of the father scared the girl in the basement until she wet herself. The mother and the sister didn't know about the girl in the basement. When the girl and the boy aged into adults and started having babies, the babies also stayed in the basement.

Mum knocked on the door at 11 p.m. and told Violet to go to bed. Violet handed over the power cord from her computer.

She read for an hour, then took out the second power cord she'd bought months ago from its hiding place at the back of her wardrobe. She plugged her computer back in, and booted *The Sims* back up.

The boy's mother died and his sister moved out, so Violet decided to give him an upstairs wife. The upstairs wife had an upstairs family, while the girl in the basement took care of the basement children. Violet used a mod to turn off social workers, to make it so the downstairs children didn't have to go to school.

As the oldest basement child had aged into a teen, Violet considered downloading a mod to enable incestuous relationships, then felt grossed out with herself and decided to go to bed. It was 3 a.m.

When her mum knocked at 7 a.m., she felt exhausted. Mum made her a weak coffee and complained about how silly it was to make teenagers start a school day before 9 a.m..

'If we had it my way, you wouldn't start till eleven,' she said. She used to go to work before Violet, but now she waited for Violet to go to school.

Last year, Violet began feeling particularly anxious about a chemistry mock exam she hadn't revised for. She'd had the idea to call in sick, to put on a voice and pretend to be her mum. It took four days for her to be caught. On the fourth day she'd called in sick, the school rang her mum at work that afternoon to reorganise the chemistry mock she'd missed. Violet had assumed they'd just let her miss the exam. She didn't really get in trouble; her mum was mostly annoyed it had taken the school almost four full days to notice. But this was it now. Mum started and left work an hour later, and she made sure Violet definitely went to school.

Mum had told her about school refusers before; a lot of the kids she worked with did it. Violet thought about doing it as well – refusing to go – but she couldn't quite bring herself to. It was too embarrassing to make that much of a fuss.

She walked to school rather than getting the bus like she

was supposed to. It took longer, but not that much longer. The bus was always sat in traffic for ages, and Mum had her out of the house so early she could easily walk in good time.

She ducked through the Warrens, which she wasn't supposed to. Her mum said it wasn't because they were especially dangerous, just that she did a lot of work down there, and she didn't want any of the families she worked with to recognise Violet. She had an 'adversarial' relationship with some of them.

The Warrens didn't look terribly different from her own estate, really. Like Violet's estate, they were densely packed terraced houses. But the ones on Violet's estate had three or four floors, and were generally bigger. The houses on Violet's estate had front gardens, but most of the Warrens houses opened straight onto the pavement. There were a couple of bigger, semi-detached houses. She walked past one with a sign reading 'TRESPASSERS: BEWARE OF THE DOGS' over a picture of a cartoon dog foaming at the mouth.

The door to the house opened, and Violet heard barking. Not aggressive big-dog barking, nothing that would belong to the dog in the cartoon, but yappy barking. A boy was leaving the house when a greyhound streaked out, making a beeline for the fence. Violet was terrified of dogs and stopped in her tracks. But so did the dog. It reached the fence and skidded to a halt, suddenly unsure of itself. The boy caught the dog by the collar and began to guide it back inside.

'Oh. Hi, Violet.' It was Jayde. Easily mistaken for a boy at a distance (especially with Violet due an eye test and squinting behind her glasses), but still, Violet felt embarrassed.

'Hi,' she said.

'Do you walk this way?'

'Sometimes.'

'Well hang on and I'll walk with you.'

With the greyhound deposited back in the house, Jayde and Violet walked to school together. They hadn't spent any one-on-one time together – Dolly was always there, and Jayde didn't talk much.

'How many dogs do you have?' asked Violet.

'We've got Baby, Coco, Skinny, Spaghetti and Dave at the moment,' she said. 'But we're just fostering Skinny; someone else is going to take him eventually.' She explained that her mum, who owned the bookies round the corner, rescued them. 'She used to be really into racing when she was a kid; her dad had a couple of racing dogs. But she found out when she was a teenager that they get treated really badly and they get put down all the time, so she takes them off people when they get injured. We've had absolutely loads. We're always fostering dogs but Mum kept bonding with them, so we kept keeping them and now we've got four. We've had Baby the longest.'

'Do you like having that many dogs?' Violet asked. 'No offence intended, it's just a lot of dogs.'

'Sometimes. I like all the dogs on their own but I don't know. I'm a bit allergic to them, so I sleep in our caravan sometimes, when my allergies get bad. Not in like a shit way or anything, like mum likes the dogs more than me. I'm just normally like . . . fine, but sometimes when we get a new one it sets me off. Especially if it's spring, and my hay fever's going. I'm like . . . aww I'll just sleep in the caravan for a bit, you know what I mean?'

This was a rumour Violet had heard before, that Jayde slept in a caravan outside. It sounded much worse when she heard it at school. That was probably why Jayde was explaining it to her like this – she knew people knew about the rumour. Violet wanted to say everyone probably had something a bit weird like that – something a little bit odd their family does, which would sound really bad if people from outside found out and didn't understand why.

She wanted to talk about something weird her family did to make Jayde feel less self-conscious, but she couldn't think of anything on the spot. So she just said yeah, and they kept walking. They talked about Jayde's dogs a bit more. Baby was her favourite, and Coco was the least favourite. The dog that had run out of the house was Skinny, the foster dog, who was unpredictable, fluctuating between being meek and anxious, and exuberant and aggressive.

They arrived at school; Jayde went to the sixth form common room, and Violet went to the tech corridor. She plugged in her phone. She had fifteen minutes before she'd need to go to her form room.

She had a text from Dolly, who seemed excited about the tulpa stuff Violet had sent. She said they were 'SO COOL' and that she wanted to 'discuss' them at lunchtime. There was also a text from Joni, one that had just come in, asking Violet if she'd walked into school with Jayde. Violet smirked at the message. She hadn't entirely believed Dolly when she'd said that Joni liked Jayde. Joni just didn't seem . . . gay to Violet. She wore all that makeup and she fussed with her hair and nails and stuff. It wasn't just that she was feminine – it was more that she was feminine in a basic, boring way. Dolly was feminine but she wasn't basic the way Joni was, and basic people were straight.

She replied to Joni: *ye why?*

Three dots appeared on her screen.

Idk

was just wondering

shes friends with you and dolly

ye

are they still going out?

Yeah. why do you care? Lol

Just wondering omg

K . . .

K?

Didn't mean anything by it just k . . .

W/e

Violet decided to twist the knife a little. She sent a raised eyebrow emoji, which Joni didn't respond to.

She had English second lesson. Ms Nawaz waved at her, and gestured to the front seat, like there was no seating plan and she was inviting Violet to sit with her.

Ms Nawaz was nice – a bit 'How do you do, fellow kids?' But mostly nice. She was interested in local history, and she liked hearing about Violet's blog. She would ask about the stories that had done well, wanting to know 'how many upvotes' her posts got. She had no idea that it was notes on

Tumblr and upvotes were just a Reddit thing. But she was clearly so impressed with herself for knowing what upvotes were, Violet didn't have the heart to correct her.

Today they talked about A-level options – Ms Nawaz wanted assurance that Violet would do English.

'I don't know. Do you think they'll let me if I get a B?'

'You're not going to get a B. And even if you did that'd be fine,' Ms Nawaz said.

'Okay.'

'Your marks are flagging a bit, yeah? But you just need to focus. Get a good night's sleep, you're always yawning. Spend less time on your computer, okay?' said Ms Nawaz. 'It'll still be there for you over summer.'

Violet yawned because Ms Nawaz had mentioned yawning. Then *she* yawned and they both laughed. When the lesson finished, one of the boys that sat in the back giggled, mockingly, in Violet's face.

'You loooove Miss Nawaz,' he said. Violet just looked at him. 'You loooooove her.' She tried to walk away. 'She admitted it!' he jeered. She flipped the boys off over her shoulder, rising to it for once. They laughed at her.

Break, French, then lunch. *La récréation, Français, puis déjeuner. Une heure de 'ou est la piscine' et 'mon chat est très noir' et puis déjeuner.*

She'd forgotten to pick up her packed lunch. Her mum sent her a text shortly before lunch: *Did you remember your sandwiches?* And when Violet replied with a sad face, she asked Violet if she'd remembered her debit card. She had, luckily. Mum sent her £5 to get the bad, sweaty pasta they served in the dining hall.

Mum said they were having spaghetti tonight, so Violet sent back a screenshot from *The Simpsons* – Kirk Van Houten saying 'I don't like the idea of Milhouse having two spaghetti meals in one day.'

Mum said: *sorry Milhouse :(*

She queued for the pasta. It was overcooked and bad, served in a styrofoam pot. Someone shoved her in the queue. Maybe by accident, maybe on purpose.

They were supposed to eat hot food in the dining hall, but Violet hated eating alone there. She felt exposed, and lonely. So she took a fork, and smuggled it out with the pasta. She ate alone in the tech corridor. Dolly appeared as she was finishing up. Dressed for the sixth form, she wore a black pencil skirt with a white shirt and a grey blazer. She carried what she described as her 'stupid straight-girl handbag' and black high heels which were an inch too high for the school's uniform rules. She usually got in trouble for wearing them – once she got sent home and told to change shoes.

Dolly said she wanted to go to the college in Scarborough and do an Art BTEC, but her mum wanted her to be 'academic'. So here she was at CCHS sixth form. She dragged around a big portfolio like the other A-level Art students. She also took Biology, English and History.

She clomped in, dragging the portfolio.

'Tulpas,' she said. 'I want to make one. I bet we could. I know it's supposed to be your turn to manifest a thing, but I thought because you sent me the stuff about tulpas that you'd probably want to make one as well.'

'Yeah, totally,' Violet lied. 'So cool, aren't they? I mean. Metaphorically speaking.'

'What do you want to make? Let's not do weird shit like the retards on that subreddit,' she said. 'Like I wouldn't want to try and make Matty or something. Not yet, anyway. Did you see the guy who said that he'd made a Pinkie Pie tulpa and he fucked it and now it's all fucked up and sad and it keeps screaming.'

'No. That's minging,' Violet said.

'Yeah I know. Let's try and make something cool,' she said. 'Something scary.'

'Yeah,' said Violet. And she really wanted to add 'but just for fun, right?' But she imagined saying it, and Dolly snapping back 'obviously just for fun, duh', and making her feel stupid for having asked.

Dolly was mean about Angelica when she wasn't with them. Even if Angelica could talk to ghosts – at least one ghost – she still didn't *get it*. Even though she acted like she did, she didn't *get it* the way Violet did. Angelica wasn't on their level or their wavelength. She didn't understand what Dolly and Violet were talking about half the time. She didn't have any interest in the occult, not really, not beyond the little ghost story she'd made up about herself and Aleesha. Frankly, Violet thought Angelica was an idiot. But Dolly was convinced they needed her. She was a conduit.

'Maybe we should ask Angelica what tulpa she wants to make,' said Violet. Dolly grinned.

'Yeah and we'll be stuck with Rumblefuckins the Horny Cat, or whatever,' she replied.

Angelica did arrive soon after that. Dolly had sent her the tulpa stuff, the articles and the subreddit. She seemed pretty bought in.

Violet thought that Angelica had very little control over the things in her life. Her dad was always being embarrassing in public, none of her friends seemed to like her, and now people knew about her stupid Tumblr blog. Violet regretted showing it to Joni. She'd sent it to her last year after coming across Angelica by chance. For a while, it seemed Joni would only respond to Violet if she was feeding Joni a steady stream of cringe from Angelica's blog.

Joni didn't use Tumblr, and Violet would send her a link to all of Angelica's most embarrassing posts. As soon as Violet sent something to Joni, Angelica would then post screenshots of, or responses to, a series of abusive anonymous messages she'd received. Violet once messaged her anonymously suggesting she turn anon off (*I don't think it's worth keeping anon on when you get all these mean messages, please think about turning it off?*) but Angelica didn't acknowledge or respond to it.

'So this is real, this really works?' Angelica asked. Like a little kid who really wanted to believe asking if Santa was really really real. Then Angelica said she didn't want to 'make' anything scary. She'd read about the Slender Man stabbing and didn't want them to go crazy and try to sacrifice her.

'I wouldn't want to stick Slender Man with you,' said Dolly. She looked at Violet and waited for her to say something.

'Yeah . . . I don't know if you can give back a human sacrifice, but he'd probably try,' Violet said.

What kind of scary thing should they try to make? Should they create something powerful, or something weak? If Crow was a 'thin' place, a tiny hell, did they want to embrace the darkness, or attempt to combat it? Should they sink further down into the depths, or attempt to lift themselves out from underneath it?

'Embrace chaos,' said Dolly. She was quoting from Matthew McKnight's diary. 'Fuck this place. What's the point in trying to fight it. Let's make things as shit as possible for everyone here. We know it's hell, everyone else should feel how we have to.'

'So you want to make some kind of like . . . I don't know. Some kind of bad thing to like . . . release on everyone,' Violet said. Dolly nodded. And they returned to lessons with this idea in their head – an amorphous bad thing, to throw at the town.

What shape could it take? Violet spent History doodling in the margins of her exercise book. The teacher showed them a documentary about the Beer Hall Putsch, and Violet drew a stone golem, a vampire, Adolf Hitler and Slender Man. Real people were scarier than monsters, she decided. She wrote the phrase down in her exercise book, then scribbled it out. Fake-deep, stupid thing to say. Obvious.

Back at home, safely in front of her desktop computer, she googled 'scariest tulpa stories'. She found a Reddit thread titled 'Your tulpa horror stories please?'

It read:

I'm debating over whether or not I should manifest a tulpa.
I read a lot of success stories but not so many stories of
failures. Can you share any stories you personally have
or have heard about tulpas failing? It will help me make a
decision.

A lot of the replies from the community's 'Tulpamancers' were smug, and annoying.

– A tulpa is just like driving a car – it'll never be 100% safe tbh.

– why would you even ask? too much bs is posted here. this sub has a rule about low effort creepypasta for a reason lmao. bs stories about tulpas are easy to find yourself.

– I might be an old fogey, but a lot of newer 'mancers handwringing about 'Hostile tulpas' or 'MALICIOUS tulpas' is silly. As other commenters have pointed out it is like 'driving a car' and few (if any) manifested Tulpas are going to be evil or hostile for no reason. However, if you're manifesting with ill-intent or you have a lot of personal demons I'd suggest you reconsider. Take some time to deal with your issues and lay them to rest before playing around in this space.

Violet noticed a lot of the 'tulpas' these people had mentioned didn't really seem to exist outside anyone's head. A lot of them seemed more like split personalities – a lot of talk about being possessed or allowing 'mind-forms' to 'walk in and take over'. She laughed out loud when she realised the subreddit had a rule asking individual posters not to create threads just so their tulpas could respond to each other.

She texted Dolly.

> Spent more time on the tulpa subreddit

> starting to think this is all a bit . . . Idk daft?

Yeah those people are retarded

But we won't be doing retarded stuff

Yeah okay if youre sure

I don't think youre supposed to say retarded btw

Lol ok snowflake XD

Sozzzzzzz

Any way we wont do it in a STUPID way

Can I still say STUPID

ha ha lol

Yeah

No trying to create imaginary friends in our heads

Yeah exactly

More like an energy or a vibe

Ye like a vibe

Yeah

We can go to astro apes this weekend??

Okay

They made plans. They were all telling their parents they were going camping. Dolly told her mum that Jayde had loads of camping equipment and they didn't need to worry about buying anything – Violet told her mum the same thing.

When Violet asked if they were actually going to camp out somewhere, Dolly said she was going to borrow her sister's car. They could hang out at the twenty-four-hour McDonald's in the service station outside of town until morning.

> But you're just taking lessons

Yeah but I can pretty much drive

It's not far

We're not going to get pulled over

> Okay

Violet had a look at the *Sims* subreddit, where users were discussing a mod which enabled 'Extreme Violence' in the game. The mod added a number of ways for the player to kill Sims and allowed Sims to steal from, kidnap and murder one another. The guy who made the mod had also created a 'Torture & Chaos' mod – so Violet downloaded both.

The mods opened up huge possibilities for her basement-girl game. Would she have the basement girl's captor begin to torture her? Would she have the basement girl break free, killing him and his upstairs family? She could do this to take the place of the upstairs wife. She could murder her children to spare them a life in the basement. It was a lot to consider.

For the time being, Violet decided to create a town serial killer. She was going to base the Sim on her favourite serial killer (who was Jeffrey Dahmer, even though it was cringey

Columbiner shit to have a favourite, and especially for that favourite to be a sad, blond, white boy) but she decided that was too predictable. A creepy loner guy as a serial killer? That was so overplayed. So she made a woman – a girl. A girl who maybe looked like Violet if you squinted. She had black hair, and glasses, and wore unassuming clothes. She named the Sim Dahlia.

Violet had Dahlia get beaten up by other teenagers. She could do that now – with the mod. Then she had Dahlia hunt those teens down, one by one – murdering them in secret with different methods.

When the police were called on Dahlia, Violet had the Sim commit suicide. The mod had a few choices – a gunshot to the head, hanging or wrist-cutting. She had Dahlia slit her wrists.

'It's time for bed,' said Mum, at 11 p.m., as Dahlia's story came to its crescendo. Violet handed over her power cord. 'Do you have anything to add to your Christmas list?' Mum asked.

'No, I don't think so,' said Violet.

'You haven't asked for much.'

'No.'

'So could you think of some more things, please?'

'Why?'

'Your dad is annoyed that I've gone ahead and bought most of the things from it,' she said. She tried to hide her disdain, but she didn't do a very good job. Violet knew her mum hated her dad. Violet didn't like her dad very much either, but they both pretended this wasn't the case to one another. She didn't get the sense her father particularly liked her either – attempting to get her an equal or correct-seeming number of presents was all about how it looked. How it looked to Violet's mum and his family and to Violet herself.

Now he lived in London, he wanted to trot around the Westfield centre with some big shopping bags and look like a good dad to total strangers.

Violet promised to think about it.

Instead of using her secret power cord, she lay in bed googling 'present ideas'. She made a list on her phone of things she didn't particularly want but supposed she could probably use. Soap from Lush, chocolate, good-quality colouring pencils and a sketchbook. Last year, her dad had gotten her some quite babyish gifts – this 'make your own bracelet' set with strings and little colourful plastic beads, and this unicorn stationery set. She'd heard her mum tell him 'She's fourteen, not four. You need to go off her list.'

In his defence, Violet supposed she probably would've liked the bracelet thing a few years ago.

On Saturday, Violet walked over to Dolly's; it was around the corner, only five minutes away. Dolly's mum answered the door, and Violet was polite and tried not to think about the weird stuff Dolly had told Violet about her mother. Just the odd comment, the occasional reference to strange behaviour. She usually wouldn't elaborate, but sometimes she did.

What really bothered Violet was some of the stuff in Dolly's upsetting creeker fanfic. There was this part where Matthew McKnight confronted his mother about his father's sexual abuse and screamed at her: 'You didn't do anything to protect me from him you dumb drunk cunt' and the mum responded 'Why does he want to fuck you when he should want to fuck me? What's so special about you, you fucking slut?'

This sexual abuse stuff was central to the plot of Dolly's story, even though by all accounts McKnight's parents were nice and normal. No history of abuse at all. McKnight's lawyers would've used something like that if they could have. There was no reference to sexual abuse in McKnight's diaries, and he recorded every minor slight. Someone even left Dolly a review that said: *cool story I guess but I don't think this is fair to matty's parents tbh.*

The implication bothered Violet enough that she deliberately ignored it. Still Dolly's mum had a *bad vibe*, even though she was always nice to Violet.

She and Dolly walked out of the estate and met Jayde, and then the three of them walked to Heather's flat. Dolly's older sister lived on her own and had a car. She was three or four years older than they were – she was an apprentice hairdresser or went to college for it or something. Maybe both. Dolly rang the buzzer of her flat and Heather came to meet them downstairs.

'Can I borrow your car?' Dolly asked.

'What for?' Heather replied.

'We're camping tonight.'

'All night? Nah, Dolly, that's a piss-take.'

They argued back and forth. Heather started to get angry, and Dolly started to get whiny. Eventually Heather agreed on the condition that Dolly got the car back to her before 7 a.m. and sent regular text updates.

They drove to Angelica's. Jayde complained that Angelica was coming.

'She's bringing snacks and booze and stuff,' Dolly said. 'She always talks about how rich she is. At least she's putting her money where her mouth is.'

Sometimes Violet thought Dolly liked having Angelica around so she had someone to pick on. While Violet knew it wasn't exactly nice, she decided Angelica probably deserved it. She was a horrible person, after all.

Angelica didn't want them to drive up to the house, so they had to wait at the gate at the bottom of her huge driveway.

'This house is insane,' said Jayde.

'It's mental inside,' replied Dolly. 'Her dad's fucking tapped. He has loads of pictures of himself with that paedo. When I went round he was like . . . trying to tell me about the paedo and how he was a great man, like it wasn't national news that the fucker was a paedo.'

Angelica came down the drive, dragging heavy bags. She was dressed like they were actually camping, in heavy, out-doorsy sporty clothes, rather than just a normal coat.

'We're not really camping, you know,' Dolly said.

'I know. But it'll be cold,' she said. Her clothes looked new, like she'd told someone she was going camping, and they'd been bought for her.

They drove around for a while. They talked about getting food somewhere, but Angelica complained that she'd brought stuff for a picnic, even though it was freezing outside. Violet suggested they sit in Greaves Park, by the pond. Jayde said that'd be a great idea, if they wanted to get mugged (or worse).

'Let's just go and sit by Astro Ape's,' said Angelica. 'People only use that field in summer.'

They pulled up the car on the edge of the large, unkempt field – the rickety outline of Astro Ape's could be seen a few hundred yards away. They could see the top of the rusting Ferris wheel, the tip of a helter-skelter and the top third of a drop tower. They ate bread and hummus and crisps and watched the sun go down. They drank alcopops and Dolly and Jayde smoked cigarettes. It was windy, and Violet's face and fingers were numb. She suggested they get back in the car to warm up but Dolly said Heather would go mad if they got crumbs on the seats, or spilt anything.

'Know any scary stories about the old, abandoned amusement park?' Dolly asked. She said 'old, abandoned amusement park' in a spooky voice.

'There was a stabbing here a couple of years ago,' said Violet. She told the story (which she did not particularly believe) and only exaggerated parts of it. She'd told the story on her blog and tried to remember the way she'd phrased everything because the post had done quite well.

A group of homeless people had moved into the park, defending their territory aggressively. According to urban legend, everything went a bit *Mad Max*. The biggest man declared himself king of the park and made the others serve him. He ruled the amusement park with an iron fist and locked his subjects in the old rides if they disobeyed. Someone disobeyed too hard, and there was a big fight. Someone was stabbed, but they lived.

Violet made it sound like the king was violently deposed – executed by his former subjects. Her story was surreal and medieval. She thought about her mother hearing the story and being disappointed with her. 'You shouldn't talk about homeless people like that,' she would say. And she would probably add, 'Addiction is a disease, not a moral failing.' And Violet felt bad. She wrapped up the story quickly and sheepishly.

'Sick,' said Dolly. But she didn't sound that impressed. They got drunk and talked about tulpas. Dolly kept saying they weren't going to 'do anything retarded'. And she looked at Violet pointedly when she said the R-word. She warned Angelica, especially, not to try and manifest anything too obvious, too stupid.

They agreed the idea was to try to draw on the energy of the park and create some kind of force. A wind, a plague of disease or pests or bad luck.

'Just like, a bad vibe,' slurred Dolly. 'Like Matty was always saying he was like . . . this force of evil. And I'm thinking like . . . yeah. Like. Evil. I don't know.'

'Who's Matty?' asked Angelica. Dolly snorted at her.

They went to the park at midnight. The half-arsed security fences had huge holes, sections of the chain-link pulled down to allow access. They climbed through easily and entered the park. They did a quick sweep with the torches on their phones. Violet checked the inside of a food stall shaped like a banana and peered through the filthy windows of the abandoned restaurant.

'Someone we used to go to school with – a few years above us – got stuck on the roller coaster,' said Angelica. 'He climbed up it at night and they had to call the fire brigade to get him down.'

This wasn't entirely true. Violet had been hearing this story since she was kid – if it even was true, they didn't know the boy who did it.

'That's so fucking dumb,' said Dolly. 'Where did the stabbing happen? We should gather there.'

'I don't know, maybe let's just go to the middle of the park,' Violet said.

They walked roughly to the centre of the park, following the old maps and signposts. It wasn't particularly big – and a large fibreglass chimp statue made the centre easy to find. The statue was placed on a large map of the moon on the ground, which was now so scuffed and dirty it just looked like a plain grey circle.

'Can you hear anything, Angelica?' asked Dolly.

'Just whispers,' said Angelica, in the mysterious tone she adopted when she was pretending to commune with the spirits.

'Is that it?' asked Dolly, unimpressed. She'd never asked Angelica to perform for them before – she'd just taken Angelica's little stories about hearing Aleesha Dowd's voice and seeing stuff at face value. They all looked at Angelica expectantly, and Angelica looked around, then closed her eyes, making a sort of calm, mystical face that almost made Violet laugh out loud.

'The whispering is actually . . . much louder here. I think this is the best place to do it, yeah.' She reached out her hand, as if touching something. 'Yeah, really loud. The veil is so thin and skinny here.'

Violet almost said: *yes the veil between worlds is a known skinny legend*, but bit her tongue, knowing Dolly would be annoyed with her making a flippant remark right now.

Dolly seemed satisfied with this. Angelica looked relieved and pleased with herself. They turned off their phone torches. Jayde pulled some plain tea lights from her pockets and lit them. They sat on the floor around the candles and held hands.

'Concentrate on making something bad. Don't get too specific. Just think about like . . . manifesting something with a really bad energy. Something that would really fuck up the town.'

Violet cycled through various figures: a stone golem, Jeffrey Dahmer, a witch, a zombie, someone with the plague. They stayed like that until Jayde started to snigger.

'Sorry,' she said. 'This is really daft.'

'No it isn't,' snapped Dolly.

They heard a sound. A grotesque, hacking cough. A figure shuffling out from between a pair of rides coughing and spitting. It yelled something. It screamed.

The four of them legged it. Absolutely legged it, shooting through the fairground in the pitch black, screaming.

Violet got to the chain-link fence and caught her coat, ripping the soft fabric as she tore herself free. She ran and ran straight forward, toward the distant sound of cars, and the sparse lights of the town below them. She managed to find Heather's car.

She climbed onto the hood of the car and tried to look out over the field. She heard distant shrieking but saw nothing. She turned on her phone's torch and waved it, yelling, 'I'm at the car, I'm over here. I'm at the car, I'm over here.'

She was in tears by the time Dolly and Jayde found her. It was only around ten minutes, but it felt a lot longer. She wiped her eyes and hoped they didn't notice how upset she'd been.

'What do you think it was?' Dolly asked, frantic and clearly still drunk. Violet felt horribly sober.

'I think it was just a homeless guy,' said Violet.

'That's what I said,' Jayde replied. She was trying to reassure Dolly, rubbing her shoulder tenderly. 'See? It's okay.'

Dolly aggressively shrugged Jayde's hand from her shoulder.

'No. Are you both thick? That obviously wasn't just a guy,' she said. 'With the timing of us summoning it? No way.'

'Dolly . . . no offence but that is mental,' Jayde said.

'Fuck off. No offence? Fuck you. You don't know what you're talking about. You're mental. Violet, you seriously think that thing was just a homeless guy? Seriously?'

They both looked at her pleadingly, Dolly and Jayde. It made Violet think about the way she was often presented with binary choices like this in video games. She thought about Telltale Games, Y *Character is grateful* or something, paired with the stern X *Character will remember that* pop-ups after you make a choice.

'I . . . I don't know. Maybe you're right. It was really weird. I need time to think about it.'

Jayde's brow crinkled. She looked disappointed, not angry. Dolly nodded frantically.

'See?'

Dolly is grateful you sided with her.

Jayde will remember that.

They found Angelica with her foot stuck in a rabbit hole, crying and claiming she was trapped, and had probably broken her ankle.

'I can't get it out,' she said, yanking her foot.

'Have you tried taking your foot out of your shoe?' Jayde asked. She hadn't. She was free in seconds, putting her filthy shoe back on after easily pulling it free from the hole, now her foot wasn't in it.

Angelica agreed that the probably-homeless-man they'd seen in the park was definitely, definitely something supernatural. Not a man, but a manifestation. Whether she was saying it because she actually believed it, or just to please Dolly, Violet couldn't tell.

Dolly decided they'd go to the service station to get McDonald's. She drove too recklessly and much too fast, swaying in the road.

The staff glared at them when they arrived. Jayde quietly drank a coffee while Dolly and Angelica frantically exaggerated the shape (which they started calling 'The Shape' with great reverence) over sugary lattes and McFlurries. Violet joined in. She didn't want to be left out.

It was no longer the size of an average man, but seven or eight feet tall. It'd been too dark to make it out, really – but now they agreed that it very clearly had no eyes. A face without eyes, that's what they saw. A mop of dirty hair. What was it wearing? Probably a parka – but this became a fur cloak. It was an ancient, eyeless being. It was what had possessed the king of the homeless men – it was probably the spirit of Hrókr the Crow. It was the evil and chaos which was about to rain down on Crow.

Jayde sipped her coffee, unimpressed, occasionally raising her eyebrows at Violet. *Well done*, her face said. *You could've nipped this in the bud.*

FORMERLY KNOWN AS GIRL D

Extract: *I Peed On Your Grave*, Episode 341, 01/07/2018

DOYLE: So we're at the part I know Andy's been waiting for.

KOONTZ: [*in a cockney accent*] Hello, guvnah?

DOYLE: Yes, hello, Andy.

KOONTZ: [*in a cockney accent*] Is it time for lesbians now, guvnah?

DOYLE: Yes, it is time for lesbians. But it's also time for ads.

ALAN: Smooth. So smooth.

KOONTZ: Paragon of professionalism.

DOYLE: Men's health is important to us here at *I Peed on Your Grave*—

KOONTZ: Oh my God, not a boner-pills ad!

DOYLE: Yes, it's an ad for boner pills.

[*all laugh*]

ALAN: This isn't the worst ad-to-episode combo we've had.

DOYLE: No, I think Fred and Rose West and the ads for LoveToys dot com is always gunna be the head of the pack here.

KOONTZ: Hey maybe if you're into murderous teen lesbians you won't need the boner pills after this episode.

DOYLE: Don't say that. If you're struggling with boners you should absolutely buy our sponsor's boner pills. Can I please read the copy before they refuse to sponsor us again.

ALAN: Zero per cent chance we're getting paid for this episode.

KOONTZ: They knew what they were signing up for.

[*Doyle reads the ad copy*]

DOYLE: Okay, now we're back at it again with the lesbians.

KOONTZ: WOO!

ALAN: So there's a fourth chick that's kind of involved here?

DOYLE: Yes, and we really shouldn't dunk on her because she was falsely accused of being involved and it totally ruined her life for a minute there. I mean I think she's fine now – it's really easy to find her Instagram. She's into MMA and shit, she seems fine.

KOONTZ: Oh my God, that's fucking hot, dude. Assuming she's legal now. I'm googling her, what's her name.

DOYLE: Jayde Spencer. And Jayde is spelt with a Y.

KOONTZ: Classy.

ALAN: This chick *is* legal, right?

DOYLE: Yeah she's like twenty.

KOONTZ: [*laughing*] I mean, for my tastes, she's maybe a little uh . . .

ALAN: Show me? . . . Oh yeah.

KOONTZ: This absolutely does not look like a heterosexual woman.

DOYLE: No. Not to be stereotypical. We love our lesbian listeners, of course. But no, this lady does not look straight at all.

KOONTZ: Still kind of hot though.

ALAN: Dude.

KOONTZ: What? I'd let her fucking . . . kick me in the face and shit. So what, they murdered the victim like . . . over this chick?

DOYLE: Sort of. Uh. Not really. Well . . . you'll see if you let me finish.

KOONTZ: Well if you let me finish jerking off at literally any point in this episode I'd have been able to concentrate way better.

DOYLE: Dude . . .

ALAN: We apologise again to the fine purveyors of boner pills who sponsored this episode.

I went to the bookies that the Spencer family owned a few times before I managed to speak to someone. The first time it was closed; the second time I was scared off by a couple of regular customers; the third time I'd intended to go was the day of Terry's tour. It overran and the bookies closed before I had a chance to go.

My fourth attempt was successful.

I asked the young girl at the counter for Diana Spencer and was immediately asked if I was police. No one calls her Diana Spencer, locally. It's Lady Di. Over the girl's shoulder, I could see a Princess Diana commemorative plate hung up, but with a picture of Crow's own Lady Di pasted over the princess's face. Crow's Lady Di is a hard-faced, handsome woman in her early fifties, and sticks out very pointedly in the soft pastel of the memorial plate. She has a heavy jaw, and the leathery, lined face of a working woman who has lived her life in the sunshine and rough salt air of a seaside town.

The girl behind the counter scowled at me.

'I'm not a grass,' she said.

'I'm honestly not a policeman.'

There'd been quite a bad fight here last week – both the men involved were friends and regular customers, and no one wanted any trouble. When I told her I was a journalist and I was working on a book on the Joan Wilson murder she said:

'Oh, are you the phone-hacking guy?'

I admitted to it. Yes, I was indeed the phone-hacking guy. And I was writing a book. And I wanted to speak to Lady Di.

'Nah, no way,' said the girl. Di had been dodging my calls – the girl was not about to get it in the neck for passing her boss's details over to me. She wouldn't even tell me if Di would be in today. So I waited.

I waited, and I stuck out like a sore thumb. I looked like a clean plate in a sink full of dirty dishes. Men glowered at me as they put in their bets, and wandered between here and the nearby pub.

Di came in after several hours. She recognised me immediately and asked me to leave. Her daughter had not been involved in the murder. There was no reason to continue to persecute her. She was more victim than perpetrator – victimised by the police, prejudice against the family, and false accusations.

And I told her I had no intention to further those misconceptions. I wanted to give her and Jayde a chance to speak. To tell their side of the story. To talk about how they fit into Crow-on-Sea, and how they'd been treated by the town. How Jayde had been treated.

I'm very convincing. She relented and agreed to speak to me – but only if Jayde was comfortable with it. And I wouldn't speak to Jayde without her there. Even though Jayde was an adult now – no longer living in Crow – Di was extremely protective of her.

After a week of waiting, we set up a meeting. I'd speak to Di first, in the house, for a chat about the Spencer family, and Jayde would come up in the afternoon.

Their house was a modest semi-detached with three floors – it was ex-local authority and one of the larger houses on the estate. When I entered, I was immediately greeted by a collection of greyhounds, who varied in confidence and aggression. Two ran and whimpered and hid from me – Di called:

'Baby and Bingo are scared of men.'

Two different dogs stayed to bark at me. Di appeared and pulled them (gently but firmly) by the collar into the kitchen where she closed the door.

'But Biscuit and Coco hate men,' she said. Spaghetti, a dog which was particularly long and skinny, even for a greyhound, stood and watched me. He sniffed me and seemed to accept that I was not a threat. Spaghetti stayed with us through the interview, and Lady Di called him a series of sweet nicknames: Spagoo, Spaggy, Spagspog, rarely calling him by the same name twice.

Despite her reputation (and her initial hostility) it was immediately clear that Lady Di was an extremely kind woman. Not particularly nice in the false, performative way the British often expect, but genuine and kind. Her walls were lined with photos of her legion of rescued hounds, past and present, and photographs of her children: Jayde, and her son Connor.*

We drank tea, and she told me about her dogs. She'd been rescuing them since she was a teenager. She knew it was 'a bit mad'.

The bookies had been her dad's. As a girl, she loved dog racing, advising her dad's customers on the best dogs to bet on. Then she discovered how badly the animals were mistreated and she started to hate dog racing. She refused to help the customers with their bets anymore (although she still took their money), and rescued her first dog when she was seventeen. She got into an argument with one of her dad's friends when he said he was going to have an injured dog put down, because he was no good for racing anymore.

'I still took over the bookies, obviously. I just started glaring at people when they put bets on the dogs,' she chuckled. 'The blokes used to whinge to my dad. They said: "Everything's starting to feel a bit vegetarian in here."'

Lady Di was upfront with me about her father. He was involved in organised crime in the area. She wasn't – she's always been a law-abiding citizen. But her dad and two of her three uncles were involved in illegal activity and her grand-dad was 'a hard, nasty bastard'. She doesn't know exactly what they were up to, just that a lot of their business was wrapped up in gambling and illegal tobacco. She showed me a photo of her father and uncles – they were all big men, arms around each other in front of the bookies. She pointed one of her uncles out:

'That's Uncle Bob. Mad Bob.' She said this as if I would know who Mad Bob was. 'Local character,' she said. 'He's been in the paper a couple of times.' Lady Di said I probably didn't want to hear it. But, of course, I did.

MAD BOB

In 2011, the Pearl, a block of 'five-star luxury vacation homes', was erected. Only ever intended as holiday apartments, the block was built to serve the high number of tourists trafficking through the town from June to August. From September to March, they would sit empty. They do sit empty. No one in Crow could afford to live there. They were not locally owned, nor would they create jobs, or attract too many additional tourists. Coverage of the Pearl in the local paper was limited, unenthused and brief.

The complex is four storeys high, and contains around sixteen apartments, each with a balcony, all facing the sea, and placed evenly across the northern and western walls. The stairway for the apartments is built into its southern face, visible through large, floor-to-ceiling windows.

The eastern wall, however, is a different matter. There are no windows there because the Warrens are immediately to the east of the Pearl. The Pearl is far enough away from the Warrens, yes. But it is at an elevated height, and were someone to look out from a hypothetical window on the eastern wall, they would be overlooking the Warrens in their entirety. Thus, no windows.

Canada geese make their home in the cliffs around Crow, while a variety of ducks and grey geese roost in and around the enormous man-made pond in Greaves Park. All these birds travel back and forth from their nesting spots to the sea, where they fish. The eastern wall of the Pearl was not visible to these birds at night.

At first, it didn't seem to be a huge problem. Crow residents found a few dead ducks, dead gulls and dead pigeons crumpled on the ground at the east wall of the Pearl – but this was in spring, before the return of the Canada geese.

When the geese returned to Crow, it was carnage. Following a particularly busy night during the geese's migratory season, Crow residents woke up, left their homes and walked past the Pearl on their way to work to be greeted by the scattered bodies of around twenty-five dead geese. 'INVISIBLE WALL OF DEATH', screamed the *Post-on-Sea*'s front page in June of 2011. Then, a week or so later: 'INVISIBLE DEATH WALL TO BE ILLUMINATED AT NIGHT – PEARL LANDLORDS OUTRAGED'.

An article followed about how the leaseholders of apartments at the Pearl (the majority of whom were landlords, leasing the flats out as holiday rentals) were protesting the installation of lights. They were concerned that renters would be affected by light pollution.

A few pages into this issue: an article titled 'That's Dinner Sorted!' accompanied by a photo of Di's uncle, Robert 'Mad Bob' Spencer.

Pictured holding a goose by the neck in each hand, Mad Bob was a big man with a large, square head and a cheerful, yellow smile. 'Local resident "Mad Bob" Spencer celebrates prospect of luxurious goose meal' read the caption.

What followed was a short interview – Mad Bob was excited to eat goose because he'd never had it before. The article casually referred to Bob's known hatred of birds, and had a smirky, unpleasant tone.

273

This, as it turned out, was not Mad Bob's first run-in with Crow-on-Sea's avian population. A few years prior to the Wall of Death incident, Mad Bob declared war on Crow's seagulls.

'In fairness, they are like fucking pterodactyls,' said Di, as she told me the story. And she was right. Signs littered the seafront: 'DO NOT FEED THE GULLS'; 'PROTECT YOUR FOOD! GULLS STEAL!'; 'CAUTION: AGGRESSIVE GULLS'. One takeaway van had a sign taped to the side: 'NO REFUNDS. IF A SEAGULL EATS YOUR DINNER THAT IS NOT OUR PROBLEM!!'

A particularly popular design featured the slogan 'PUBLIC ENEMY NUMBER ONE' paired with a cartoon or a photograph of a seagull. One could even find it on postcards and T-shirts.

Even I have fallen prey to Crow's wild, enormous seagulls. I lost a box of chips one day (knocked from my lap and promptly stolen) and had an entire Greggs Tuna Crunch Baguette plucked from my hand on another.

Bob did not have permanent housing – he tended to rotate between the homes of his siblings, as well as his nieces and nephews. Bob was significantly younger than his brothers, and closer in age to his eldest niece, Diana. He'd spend a few weeks in a family home, until he inevitably wound them up, and was told to bugger off.

'He obviously had a lot of mental health issues. But he was a massive pain in the arse. He just refused to be looked after,' said Di. 'He should probably have been in care or had a carer or something, but he didn't want it. We all offered to club together and pay for something for him, an assisted living

274

facility or something like that. He said – he'd been sectioned before, you see – he's not going back to hospital and he'd rather sleep rough.'

Bob made a meagre living doing odd jobs for family friends. He was also an artist, and sold watercolour landscape paintings on the seafront during tourist season. Di points to an extremely competent painting of Gainsforth Castle on her wall and calls it a 'Mad Bob original'.

'When he was well enough, he was quite popular you know. He was very bubbly and outgoing – people liked chatting to him,' Di said.

Bob's feud with the seagulls grew gradually, over the course of decades. If they weren't shitting on his paintings, they were stealing his lunch or scaring away his customers. His frustration with them built as he grew older, and his health deteriorated.

'Even though the gulls were a nightmare for everyone, he got it in his head the gulls specifically had it out for him,' Diana said.

In the summer of 2008, Bob borrowed money from each of his siblings, marched into an army supply shop, and bought a crossbow. And early in the morning, he began patrolling the seafront, and shooting the gulls.

'PUBLIC ENEMY NUMBER TWO?' asked the front page of the *Post-on-Sea*, above a photo of Mad Bob pointing his crossbow at the camera.

Meet the local character determined to rid Crow-on-Sea of its 'biblical plague'.

After about a week of Bob's attempted culling, someone contacted the RSPCA. Mad Bob wasn't charged, but he was arrested and cautioned for animal cruelty. If the seagulls weren't such a pest, he might have faced greater legal consequences.

Still, Bob seemed to enjoy his moment in the sun, and would sit with his crossbow by his side when he sold paintings. He would tell customers about his war on the gulls.

'It was all well and good when people were just . . . taking the piss out of him like behind his back and stuff. But not in the fucking paper. I mean obviously it was horrible and embarrassing and . . . People, locals, they knew he wasn't well. This was a disabled man they were bullying. I rang them up both times he was in the paper and said *he's disabled and he's been sectioned before and I think this is just bullying* but they didn't give a shit, did they?' Di said. 'You know they'd always say he was connected to the local crime family, even though by the time he was shooting the seagulls, my dad was dead, and his other brothers were in their seventies. There was no crime family anymore, just some old men and their poorly younger brother. But the tone of all this – all this "local character" stuff – took a turn when the donkey stranglings started.'

I had to double check I'd heard her correctly. From my recording of the interview:

ME: Sorry – donkey stranglings.
DI: Yeah, donkey strangling.
ME: As in . . . strangled donkeys?
DI: Yeah, you know the beach donkeys that kids ride?
    Someone was strangling them at night.

ME: How do you strangle a donkey?

DI: With a rope, I suppose. Sorry, I'm just used to people knowing what I mean when I mention this. I should say – the donkeys didn't die. I think it's quite hard to strangle a donkey. They have them penned up near the beach, and over a couple of weeks – I think this was around 2012 – a couple were found erm . . . attacked. With ropes tied really tight round their necks, like someone had tried to choke them.

ME: What the fuck?

DI: Yeah, it's weird isn't it.

The spate of attempted beach donkey stranglings occurred in 2012. No one was ever caught – but Mad Bob was a prime suspect. The *Post-on-Sea* never publicly accused him, but they implied he might have been responsible in an article titled 'SICK: WHO WOULD HURT THE DONKEYS?'

They included an interview with a local RSPCA volunteer, who said: 'It's not surprising this is happening when we have a clear culture for the disregard of the safety of animals in Crow-on-Sea. We treat animals as rides and playthings and let people who shoot birds with crossbows roam the streets.' The *Post-on-Sea* added, 'We queried the local police constabulary to ask if those with a known history of animal cruelty had been arrested, but they refused to give details.'

Bob was arrested the next day – but he had a hard alibi. He'd spent the night at Di's. The front of Di's house was in view of a council-owned CCTV camera, and her back garden was in view of a neighbour's personal security camera. Bob could be seen arriving home with Di on the relevant day and could not be seen leaving from either the front or the back of the house.

'I can't say I like that my house is pretty much under surveillance, but . . .' Di shrugged. 'It's certainly been handy a couple of times in the last few years.'

Bob was released without charge, but he never quite shook off his reputation as a suspected donkey strangler. People used to be kind to him (at least to his face) and that all stopped in 2012. People wouldn't chat with him anymore; children ran away from him and he was beaten up by a group of drunk young men shortly after his arrest.

Bob became even more aggressive in his paranoia. He was hostile and erratic. After a fight with the brother he was staying with in early 2014, Mad Bob stormed out, and insisted he'd rather sleep on the street. It was a freezing night in January, and a sudden snowstorm hit Crow. He died of hypothermia.

'It was horrible. It was absolutely horrible. I'm sorry I went on about him like that but . . . I mean, that's . . . my family's reputation in a nutshell, I suppose. Criminals – possible donkey stranglers,' Di said. 'People have never been nice to me. I'd never get any shit, but in school, teachers were all prejudiced against me, and I didn't have many friends. A lot of other kids' parents had had run-ins with my dad or my uncles so . . . I had this reputation that I didn't even ask for.'

I asked if she thought it was that way for Jayde. Did Jayde feel the ripple effect of the Spencers' reputation in Crow?

'It's no fun being a name in a small town like this,' Di said, nodding. 'We should've moved but . . . the bookies. It's always done well. It was steady, secure. Family business – it's hard to leave something like that behind. And I suppose . . . I know who I am here. I thought Jayde would be fine, even if things were a bit tough for her in school sometimes.'

Jayde was born in 1998 in Crow's hospital. She was the younger of Di's two children – Connor was born in 1994. Connor had quite the reputation with teachers.

'He's got ADHD. So does she. I probably do as well, I don't know, I've never bothered to find out. But he has very . . . stereotypical ADHD. He was exactly the little boy most people think about when you say ADHD. He's more settled down now obviously, but he was climbing up the walls all the time when he was little. The teachers acted like he was a nightmare, but I don't think they did very much to help him – to make it better,' Di said.

Connor was a bright, high-energy boy, who complained constantly of boredom and could not sit still for longer than a few minutes at a time. Di admitted he could be difficult. He never seemed to run out of energy and he was exhausting to keep up with – but the teachers made no attempt to accommodate him. He was told off and dismissed as a 'naughty boy'. He was probably the kind of boy my own daughter would have complained about on her way home from primary school.

Being called 'a naughty boy' hurt his feelings. Di told me he was extremely sensitive to rejection (a typical symptom of ADHD), and that it badly affected his self-esteem.

Di thought about sending him to special school – but decided that, ultimately, the stigma of having gone to a special school would affect him more than going through mainstream school with a disability.

'He had a diagnosis – he got extra time on stuff, and he had a classroom assistant, sometimes. But I probably should've bit the bullet and tried to take him out of mainstream school,' Di sighed. Connor left school for college at sixteen. He trained as an electrician. Though he is currently happy and settled with a partner (having recently had his first child) he has struggled with his mental health as an adult.

Jayde entered school, much as her mother and brother had, with the Spencer label hanging over her. On her first day of reception, her teacher asked her: 'Connor Spencer's sister?' And when Jayde nodded, the teacher said: 'Oh dear, not another one.'

Jayde was more settled than her brother – but that wasn't saying much. Jayde was also high energy and fidgety, and also complained loudly of boredom. On a surface level she was a lot like her brother – and she was unfairly targeted by teachers because of it. Di also thinks Jayde being a girl led to special hostility from the school.

'Little girls aren't meant to be gobby, are they?' said Di. 'Not meant to whinge that they're bored or play football with the boys. She was always really athletic – despite her allergies – really talented. But no one ever treated it like it was a good thing. They acted like it was another thing wrong with her,' Di huffed. 'If they'd actually bothered to encourage her, I bet she could've gone to the Olympics for something.'

'That's a massive exaggeration,' Jayde snorted, from the doorway.

Jayde had entered the house without either of us noticing. She got herself settled down, and Di continued to recount Jayde's experience in school with the odd interjection or correction from Jayde.

When she started high school, things got worse. Teachers would generally ignore her ADHD diagnosis and harshly punish her and single her out for displaying benign, typical symptoms.

'I remember she kept getting told off for doodling in lessons by this one English teacher – and I explicitly told this teacher that she actually listens and concentrates better when she can occupy her hands.'

'He made me hand my pens and pencils in at the start of the lesson and would only give them back to me when we started to work,' Jayde added. 'So I used to fidget loads, or fall asleep, and then I'd get told off for that.'

As her GCSEs rolled round, Jayde was predicted unreasonably low grades. A D in English (certainly not her best subject but a D was harsh) and Cs in Maths and Sciences – even though she had always been among the best in her year at STEM subjects.

'Every fucking year they'd put her in middle set, or set four of five, and I'd ring up and say, "Are you fucking joking?" And they'd make her do some mock test, and she'd get really good marks, and they'd put her up into second or top set like *well, let's see if she can behave herself and maintain a standard of work.* And their definition of behaving yourself was always just fucking . . . sitting still and not talking back. They didn't give a fuck about her work.' Di went red in the face. 'Sorry, it just absolutely boils my fucking piss how they treated her. I know Connor was at least a bit of a pain in the arse, but it was a piss-take with her.'

'I ended up getting all As in Maths and Sciences, by the way,' said Jayde. She still kept her hair short and blonde. Removing a beanie hat, she scrubbed her hands through it. 'They said I'd never go to uni, you know. Said maths would be too hard for me at A level.'

'Piss-take,' snarled Di.

Teachers and students alike were unfair with Jayde. A couple of her classmates had older siblings who'd been picked on by Connor. She was a tomboy. People assumed Jayde was hard.

'They thought I'd be a bully because Connor was a bully.'

'Connor never bullied anyone,' snapped Di.

'Oh come on, Mum,' said Jayde.

'He didn't.'

Jayde explained that he used to make a habit of kicking balls at the less athletic children in his class, and Di said, 'Oh he was just trying to get them involved.' When Jayde said Connor would name-call and push around any kid who looked like an easy target, Di cut in to tell me that 'they called him stupid, they were probably asking for it, but nobody ever mentions that.'

However deserved Connor's reputation was – Jayde's wasn't. However she appeared to her peers, she was shy, sensitive, and just wanted to fit in.

'I was always quite butch, to be honest. I've never liked having long hair, and I hated skirts. The girls wouldn't have anything to do with me. The boys would usually let me play football with them but only because I was good. If I had one crap game they'd exclude me for weeks. And they didn't want to sit with me in lessons or invite me to their birthday parties.

'I've never suffered fools gladly. I dunno, I probably was a bit like . . . annoying and awkward. I wouldn't make an effort with the girls because I wasn't interested in playing imagination games, or whatever. I used to play with them when they were doing skipping ropes and hula hoops, but I'm quite competitive and I got asked to go away sometimes when I got too into a game. I think that no one really knew me or wanted to know me much beyond . . .' Jayde shrugged and apologised for repeating herself.

Diana tried to intervene, at first.

'I used to try and chase up the other mums, when she was at primary school. I'd go up to them on the playground and ask – why did every other kid in class get invited to your daughter's birthday party, but not my Jayde – and they'd always give some excuse. I just wanted someone to have the balls to admit the real reason.'

I asked: 'And what was the reason, as far as you're concerned?'

'The Spencers are scumbags. I just wanted one of these . . . jumped-up, aspirational cows – half of them used to live down the Warrens themselves, by the way – to admit they were just . . . doing it to make themselves feel like they've moved up in the world,' said Di. She did an accent – not unlike my own. 'Oh no, darling, we don't want Jayde Spencer at your birthday, don't invite her,' she said. 'It was the same shit with Connor but I suppose I can admit that was a little bit more justified, because he was a handful.'

Jayde's short hair, preference for sport and more masculine dress sense had gone from tomboyish quirks to something that placed a target on her back by high school. She looked gay. She was gay. And it made her stick out.

She explained that she'd never had a fraught relationship with her sexuality. Her family were always supportive.

'I think because I'd basically grown up with my mum saying "you know if you wanted to have girlfriends instead of boyfriends I wouldn't care", I really didn't think it would be a problem for me in school. So when I was about thirteen and people noticed I was different and started giving me all that "Are you a lesbian? Why do you look like such a fucking lesbian" stuff I was just like . . . well that's because I *am* a lesbian,' she said. 'And maybe things would've been a bit easier for me if – I'm not whinging that you weren't homophobic enough, by the way, Mum – but if I did have a bit more like . . .' Jayde paused to scratch the dog, Baby, who had padded through to investigate. The dog curled up between Di and Jayde, keeping a wary distance from me. ' . . . fear about being out, maybe it would've saved me a lot of shit.'

She says after effectively 'coming out' in high school she

went through a phase of trying to conform to a more feminine gender expression. Hoping to avoid some of the harassment she'd had for being masculine, she grew her hair into a bob, and tried wearing skirts.

Di found the school photo from Jayde's 'femme year', as Jayde calls it. It was, like most school photos, unflattering and awkward. Jayde's dark blonde hair was tucked behind her ears and clipped at the front, as if she hated the length. She was wearing too much eyeliner, and a perfunctory smear of lip gloss.

'Yeah so that summer – that was GCSE year and I wanted it off for going into sixth form – I got it chopped at Connor's barbers and then went to my mum's salon to have it bleached and I've never really looked back.'

I asked her if the bullying was sustained through sixth form.

'Not really, no. This was like . . . a lot of people went to college somewhere or started an apprenticeship instead of the sixth form. The people who stayed were like, the more academic people who wanted to go to uni and stuff – people who knew me a bit better from lessons. And this is so stupid, but that was also the year that Ruby Rose got cast in *Orange is the New Black*.' Jayde snorted. 'So suddenly a couple of the girls – I won't name names obviously – but a couple of them were like . . . you look just like the model Ruby Rose – I obviously don't, but I don't know – it suddenly seemed like being gay – and specifically butch – was a bit cooler and a bit less like . . . No one was openly calling me a dyke anymore. It was now uncool to be homophobic in sixth form.'

I asked her if she was able to make friends now hostility toward her had reduced.

'Er . . . no. Because I started going out with Dolly. No one really knew we were going out but yeah, if my reputation was shit thanks to years of er . . . my family doing crime stuff and my uncle shooting seagulls then like . . . hanging round with someone who'd gotten pretty much everyone to hate her in less than a year wasn't going to do me any favours.'

At this point, Lady Di excused herself from the conversation. I told her she was welcome to stay – but she said that she now trusted me not to be a complete bastard after speaking to me. She found hearing about Dolly too depressing, and still struggled with anxiety around Jayde's proximity to the murder. I asked her to elaborate on this, quickly, before she left.

'I'm not religious obviously. But Jayde was arrested, and I really thought she might've been involved for a minute there. So it's just . . . having to hear about something so awful and thinking there but for the grace of God goes my daughter . . . I mean with her possibly being a victim, not getting involved. There's no telling what might have happened to her if she hadn't split up with that girl, or if she'd pissed her off.' Di shook her head. 'It makes me feel fucking ill,' she added, before leaving me with Jayde.

Jayde relaxed a bit now her mum was gone. She explained that, even though her mum didn't seem it, she was very sensitive, and Jayde was always worried about upsetting her when she talked about high school.

Her mum's indignance at the way she was left out and picked on really hadn't helped things for Jayde. If you're already something of an outcast, having a mum who was happy to be very confrontational with teachers and parents really didn't help Jayde's case much. She loved that her mother was so fervently defensive and protective of her – she always felt supported and safe. But she was also frequently embarrassed by her mother who, fuelled by a deep sense of injustice, would publicly and dramatically lose her temper.

'It reminded her of the way she was treated in school,' Jayde said. 'There's a bit of you that's always a teenager, isn't there? It's the most traumatic time of loads of people's lives, and . . . even the most mentally healthy and put-together adults are still . . . there.'

I told her that was a very astute observation. That even in my fifties, I still felt that for myself and many of my peers. A good friend of mine failed to invite me to his birthday party when I was thirteen and I still get upset on a base, animal level if I'm passed over for an invitation. I started crafting outrageous lies to impress my peers, hoping to be whatever I was needed to be to acquire attention and friendship from the other boys at my school. It didn't work – people saw through me.

'That's very Dolly of you,' said Jayde. 'She had a very flexible relationship with the truth.'

I asked Jayde what she remembered of Dolly joining CCHS and she recounted it to the best of her memory.

Dolly came to the school about halfway through Year 11 – either just before or just after Christmas. She stuck out immediately, because she was so pretty. She seemed outgoing, too. Rather than putting her head down and waiting for people to come to her, she was bubbly and seemed to make friends easily. She took advantage of people's natural interest in her.

She made friends with the kind of girls who would pick on Jayde in lower school but who would be telling others that homophobia was *literally so not cool* by sixth form. She made friends with, in Angelica's parlance, the 'A-tier' popular girls.

But it didn't last long. Dolly was a whirlwind – a chaotic force, ripping through friendships and teenaged romances.

'She was . . . She was the person people thought I was. Really aggressive if you wound her up. There was stuff she did that was a big enough deal that it even got back to me, when I had no pals to tell me this kind of school gossip shit. I know she got with some girl's boyfriend, and then she fought the girl and bit the boy when he tried to break up the fight. Something like that,' Jayde said. She did not seem comfortable talking about Dolly. She dropped eye contact with me, and focussed on stroking the family dogs, who whined in solidarity with her distress.

In the time between Dolly joining the school up to their actual GCSE exams, Dolly completely tanked her own reputation. She'd gone from being invited to every party to someone who was whispered about in the hallways. Jayde remembered classmates speculating – hoping – Dolly would go elsewhere for sixth form. She remembered entering the sixth-form common room on their first day back, and Dolly walking in, and hearing another girl loudly go 'URGH'.

I asked Jayde if she knew much about the rumours of promiscuity – the Dolly Dick Pig nickname.

'She would go with boys if they offered her something. Cigarettes or alcohol or sometimes drugs, but there wasn't much of that floating round the school. And they started calling her that nickname. She was really weird with boys and she knew she was. Even when we were going out she would still text boys – and she'd tell me it was just because she thought it was funny and they'd buy her stuff . . . I knew

288

it wasn't just that. In one breath she'd tell me it wasn't that big of a deal and then she'd have a couple of drinks and she'd be almost in tears telling me she didn't know what the fuck was the matter with her.'

Dolly was fragile. Jayde could sense that much about her before they got to know each other. She reminded Jayde of Connor, sometimes, in the way her sensitivity manifested as cruelty and aggression.

I asked her how they got to know each other.

'Dolly started talking to me before summer break in 2015. She was weird at first, but . . . I suppose I was patient with her. Like I said, I could tell there was . . . that something wasn't quite right there. She seemed really fucking sad. No one behaves the way she did if there's not something fucked going on . . .' Jayde trailed off. 'Anyway, because she'd alienated everyone else in our year, she started spending more time with weird kids with no friends. If someone was on their own, she'd talk to them. And I was on my own a lot. The first conversation we had was in a lesson – I can't remember which – and she said she'd seen me playing football with the boys, and asked if . . . if I was fucking any of them, basically.'

Jayde told Dolly that she wasn't interested in boys – she was incredulous about it. Everyone knew Jayde was gay. And Dolly told her that was cool, and she was actually bisexual. She then began to quiz Jayde about the gay scene in Crow, a question that Jayde laughed at.

'There is no gay scene in Crow-on-Sea. There's one gay bar. It's called The Pink Dolphin and it's fucking shit. They have one single tragic lesbian night a month called Muff-diver Mondays, and the six gay women who live here will go because they feel obliged to go. I never actually went that much because . . . everyone here knows who I am. So it wasn't much fun for me. Who knows, maybe Muffdiver Mondays is a right laugh for anyone whose high school girlfriend didn't set someone on fire.'

Jayde admits she initially dismissed Dolly. The only thing Jayde knew about Dolly was that she stole people's boyfriends and slept around. Jayde thought Dolly was taking the piss out of her.

'But then she started following me on Instagram and Snapchat and messaging me over summer.'

Jayde did not use Tumblr, like Angelica, Violet and Dolly did. After having been somewhat patronisingly encouraged to seek out other gay people on Tumblr by well-meaning straight people, she'd been rather put off the idea. She used Reddit, and knew people thought Tumblr was cringey and annoying. She didn't like any of the geeky stuff Tumblr seemed to be centred around, anyway.

She had resigned herself to the idea of finding a community when she moved out of Crow – though was somewhat resistant to the idea she needed a queer community at all. Even though she'd outgrown trying to fit in at school in the way she dressed, she did still want to be normal. She was conscious of becoming one of the annoying SJW[14] gays that people took the piss out of on the subreddits she browsed.

14 'Social Justice Warrior' is a pejorative term for someone obnoxiously concerned with issues of social justice. In the early 2010s, people proudly proclaimed they were 'anti-SJW'. The term was synonymous with hysteria and hypocrisy – it has now been replaced in popular parlance with 'woke' or 'wokeist'.

An interest in normality was part of what interested her in Dolly. Dolly was, as Jayde said, completely tapped, but she was very pretty and very feminine. Jayde liked the idea of having a pretty, feminine girlfriend.

'I'd er . . . internalised a lot of er . . . respectability politics shit,' she said, still a bit uncomfortable with using the language of social justice. 'But my Instagram presence was obviously gay. That was basically where I met and talked to people. I'd talk to girls but not always romantically – it was how I made friends. Like Violet and Tumblr, I suppose. Not exactly like that, though. Obviously Instagram is still pretty weird but it was less . . . mental than Tumblr was at the time.'

Jayde said she had a pretty normal internet presence. She had online friends and niche interests, but she wasn't 'internet poisoned' the way the others were. She was deep into sports: men's and women's association football, as well as both the NBA and the WNBA. She was also into mixed martial arts and the UFC, with a particular interest in women's events.

Watching the UFC made her want to take up fighting herself, but the only gym in Crow that offered mixed martial arts classes didn't have one for women. The only 'female' classes were for karate and kickboxing. Jayde explained to me that this was a disappointment, as MMA took the most effective parts of all styles of fighting – she said that even the best kickboxer would lose to a mediocre mixed martial artist. Still, she made do, and joined both the karate and kickboxing classes.

This was what made up most of her Instagram feed. Videos of her training, pictures of athletes she liked, and selfies. She followed barely anyone from school, mostly interacting with 'sports gays' (her words, not mine) and other teen girls involved in sports and martial arts in the north of England.

Jayde was surprised when Dolly followed her, and even more surprised when Dolly messaged her. She DM'd Jayde in response to a selfie Jayde had posted with a few heart-eye emojis.

And though Jayde was surprised – maybe even a little bit uncomfortable – she still messaged back. Dolly was pretty – and Jayde liked the idea of a pretty girl messaging her more than she liked Dolly.

'I don't know if I'd say I fell for her . . . Maybe I've ret-conned all this in my head. But I really liked the idea of having a girlfriend, and I really liked the idea of having a pretty girly girlfriend – at the time – and so . . . even though she was weird, and I found a lot of stuff about her unsettling and off-putting, I still messaged her back. And I still flirted with her – and I asked her out.'

Jayde invited Dolly to the beach with her over summer. To 'hang out' and 'get ice cream' – I use quotes because Jayde did. Like most of their dates, they just ended up huddling up somewhere private to smoke weed and kiss. Dolly asked her if she could get weed, and Jayde said yes even though she couldn't. She told Dolly her brother dealt her drugs.

'But he wasn't dealing to me, I was nicking it. He didn't deal at all and he was fuming when he caught me. I said if he didn't start giving me some, I'd tell Mum he had powder drugs in the house – which he did. Mum didn't like that he smoked weed, but she tolerated it. But she told both of us when we started drinking: no pills or powders. Zero tolerance. Anyway – Connor said I at least had to start giving him some money. Which seemed very fair at the time. And Dolly really liked that I could get access to drugs. She sometimes used to ring me when she was with Violet or Angelica and pretend she was ringing an actual drug dealer.'

Jayde didn't even like smoking weed that much, at first. She was concerned about the effect smoking would have on her ability to play sports, particularly with her pre-existing allergies. She even bought special herbal 'nobacco' to roll joints with.

'It felt like the only thing we had in common. Drinking and smoking weed and stuff. Like I honestly really didn't give a shit about the scary shit they were into, and Dolly had no interest in sports. Like properly couldn't care less to the point she was rude about it. I remember before we were properly girlfriends, I tried explaining the NBA draft to her while we were on this date over summer. And she had this fucking . . . glassy look on her face the whole time, and when I was finished she literally said like "Babe I'm sorry but I actually couldn't give less of a fuck about American basketball." And I really remember thinking . . . I should break up with this bitch.'

'Did she ever talk about Cherry Creek?' I asked.

'Oh you mean Matty and Brian?' Jayde asked, rolling her eyes. 'A bit. The first time she mentioned Matty to me I thought she was talking about an ex. And when she explained who he actually was, I thought it sounded really weird, and it must have shown on my face. She didn't mention them around me much, but she slipped up when Violet was there.'

They really didn't have much in common. Dolly was a little mean to her. Sometimes Dolly was a bit scary, and unsettling. But still . . . Dolly was the only other gay girl her own age she knew in real life. She did like Dolly. She really did. Even if their relationship was a little artificial – a little high school – Jayde did like her.

'I was very lonely,' said Jayde. 'It took me going out with her to realise how lonely I'd been.'

They began 'officially' dating in September of 2015 – just after they started at sixth form. But Dolly told Jayde not to post about her on Instagram or tell people, as her mother would disapprove.

'I never properly spoke to her mum – I wasn't really allowed in their house if her mum and stepdad were there. Violet and Angelica would go over but I usually had to wait outside. Dolly said her mum and stepdad wouldn't like it. So I don't know if she actually was homophobic, but I took Dolly's word for it. I know not all Christians are homophobic but her mum was so strict about drinking – weirdly strict, especially for round here – and she was born again and shit. Why would I question it?'

For Jayde the secrecy was annoying but not totally unexpected. Ultimately, she understood if Dolly didn't feel safe or comfortable being out to her family. She was happy to guard that secret, even if it was inconvenient, and sometimes a little hurtful.

'It was a secret but totally to her convenience. So I wouldn't tell anybody, and I'd make an effort to talk around it in conversation, and someone would casually drop in like "oh so Dolly said you and her are going out" which was a bit . . . Like I know if I told someone she'd be fuming, but I suppose it was her that was closeted or whatever, so it made sense she'd want to have control over who knew . . . But I don't know. It was one of a few things where the rules were different for her than they were for me.'

Most of these differing standards revolved around who Jayde was and was not allowed to speak to and hang around with. Dolly was controlling and possessive toward Jayde in a way that was unpredictable and unpleasant.

'She'd go through my Instagram messages and my Snapchat and block people I was friends with because she didn't want me to talk to them. Even though I'd explained to her like fifty times I had no interest in boys – like I wasn't even remotely curious about them – she'd come up to me after I'd played football and be like "oh who the fuck was that, who the fuck were you talking to" – and she'd be talking about some lad who had literally been screaming at me about how I'd totally fumbled a shot and how I wasn't good enough to play football with the boys. I literally was not on anything beyond the most basic good terms with any of those boys. She was so fucking . . . weird about it.'

I asked if they fought about it.

'No, because I'd roll over. I'd always apologise. I thought it was normal – and sometimes I even thought it was quite cute – for your partner to be jealous if they cared about you. In my head, I thought she was protective of me and she couldn't help being jealous because she liked me so much. But I started to get fucked off with her about it when I found out she was still messaging and texting boys. Like the same boys she'd be shouting at me for playing football with she would text. And then she acted like I was being unreasonable, and I was being unfair and I was being scary and jealous. She kept telling me she was just texting them because they'd buy her stuff. And I didn't find that very reassuring because obviously . . . I would bring her weed. So, what really made me that different from those boys, you know what I mean?'

Jayde said this was not something she would tolerate in a relationship as an adult. But at the time, she didn't understand Dolly's behaviour as particularly troubling. It was upsetting and annoying, but Jayde did not view it as anything beyond that. She explained that she is not a very anxious person – she's just not prone to worrying or going straight to a worst-case scenario. She was relaxed, not easily bothered or easily distressed. It took a lot to annoy her so it also took a lot for her to stand up for herself.

This idea of Jayde as someone who was so relaxed they'd become something of a doormat doesn't quite fit with other things Jayde and Di had told me. She was overly competitive and she 'told it like it was' when she thought something was pointless or stupid. Why wasn't this the case for her relationship with Dolly?

'Er . . . I don't know. I'm not annoyed when I think something is daft and say it. Like I'm not angry or kicking off, I'm just stating a fact so . . . I dunno. If Dolly did something and I knew it was definitely wrong, I would tell her. There was this time we broke into the . . . well, I say broke into – it's really easy to get in there. But we broke into the Astro Ape fairground thing and . . .' Jayde recounts the story of their break-in at Astro Ape's – how Dolly was convinced they'd summoned a creature, a terrifying monstrous shade, rather than coincidentally encountering a homeless man.

'Like I was very firm with her then – that I didn't think he was a monster or anything. With that stuff, when she asked me directly, I was always really clear. I didn't believe in any of the weird mystical stuff, and I thought it was okay if she wanted to believe in it but I just didn't. She would get really annoyed with me, and rather than argue I'd say it was fine and ask to drop it.'

As Dolly became more 'mystical', Jayde had more and more concerns about continuing their relationship. Particularly as the 'mystical' began to intersect with her issues around jealousy and control.

I flagged to her that this would probably be a good time to talk about Joni. And Jayde agreed, though told me she wished she didn't have to.

As far as Jayde was concerned, Joni was just some girl in the year below who popped up in her kickboxing class. She was a little overweight, and she wasn't very strong or coordinated, but she was friendly and funny. Jayde had no idea Joni's joining kickboxing had anything to do with her until Dolly insisted that that was the case.

'I didn't believe her. Even with the stuff Violet and Angelica said . . . They were making a big deal out of nothing.' Jayde shrugged. 'So what if Joni was trying to make friends with me? I don't know. At the time I thought she probably didn't even fancy me, she probably . . . she was probably just gay or bi and wanted to talk to literally the only other gay person she knew. I had no problem with her and zero issue with her messaging me. But Dolly had to make it something sinister, like Joni was plotting to steal me away or something. But Joni didn't even know I was going out with Dolly when she joined the kickboxing class.'

And then Jayde shook her head. She didn't want to talk about this with me right now. I pressed her, but she refused.

When I asked her if she wanted to talk about the build-up to the murder, she said no, and that she didn't want to talk about the murder itself, either. She knew this interview was coming, but she didn't really have time to get her thoughts into place, to get her ducks in a row. She asked if she could have some time to think. I asked if I could email her a list of questions. She wasn't sure about that. I could tell she wasn't comfortable talking about this, and I said I'd be happy to speak in a way that was comfortable. She said she wasn't sure she'd be comfortable talking via email either.

Still, I emailed her a list of questions. It took her three weeks (and several nudges) to get back to me.

SPRING EQUINOX

Violet's room was small and a cursory attempt had been made to tidy it. She'd pushed clothes and books and stationery against the walls or under her bed to clear space for the four of them to sit. Jayde thought about how annoyed her mum would be if she had people back at the house and didn't clean properly. The room wasn't dirty, there were no mouldy mugs or plates – nothing wet. But it was messy, dusty and dark. Dusty enough to set off Jayde's allergies, a bit. The longer they sat, the itchier Jayde's eyes and nose became.

Violet's curtains were drawn – they had been since they'd arrived and the sun was still up. Even with a few candles lit, it was stuffy and unpleasant. Jayde wasn't even sure why she'd been invited. Violet and Angelica were Dolly's friends – Dolly didn't always drag her around to stuff like this, but she seemed to want Jayde there whenever they were doing anything especially mystical or weird. When Jayde questioned the need for her presence when Dolly was hanging around with her Year 11 friends, Dolly said four was a good number. North, East, South, West. Earth, Fire, Water, Air.

Today they were talking more about manifesting things. Summoning stuff. Something about tulpas again. Jayde wasn't really listening. She watched UFC videos on her phone and nodded and hummed occasionally. Violet's mum went out after an hour, so Violet let Jayde smoke a joint in the back garden. Dolly came outside for a couple of drags, but it was mostly just Jayde smoking. She smoked half the joint herself (which was a lot for her). She took a photo of herself with the joint hanging out of the corner of her mouth and posted it to her Snapchat story.

Jayde carefully crushed the joint out on the wall of Violet's house and cleaned the little burn mark off with her fingers. She placed the joint back in the small sandwich bag she'd brought it in, sealing the bag and carefully rolling it up.

She went back into the house, and looked dizzily around for her backpack, which was tucked beneath the kitchen table, then deposited the sandwich bag inside of it.

She was delaying going back upstairs – she knew she was.

She drank a glass of water in the kitchen and thought about how to excuse herself – how to leave early.

Jayde stumbled back into Violet's bedroom, wanting to ask why they couldn't sit in the garden or the living room – why did they have to be sealed into this gross little room?

The three of them were mid-conversation; they spoke in hushed and serious voices. Jayde sat on Violet's bed, then lay on it – head at the foot. She stared at the ceiling, which still had little-girl glow-in-the-dark star stickers on it, now alight with a soft, sickly green as the sun had set.

Dolly was speaking. Jayde's hand was dangling off the bed, and Dolly held it. She had soft hands. She was always complaining that Jayde's hands were rough and dry.

'I think it hasn't worked because—'

'It has worked,' Angelica snapped.

'Yeah. It has worked, obviously,' Violet agreed. Even though Jayde knew that was a lie. Violet was not bought in on this shit the way the others were. She always sounded unsure; always like she was saying what other people wanted to hear.

'But maybe the reason it worked best in the graveyard and the theme park was because they were thin places – we tried it a couple of times at home and in school and it didn't work. We were being lazy,' Dolly said.

Jayde had been forced to take part in a couple of deranged in-school summoning circles. She didn't hugely care what people at school thought of her – she was past that point. But she still really didn't want to be seen doing this shit. It was all embarrassing. Baby, pretend games.

'But at Christmas it sort of worked too well, don't you think? I mean, if it really was a tulpa and not just . . . a guy,' said Violet. Doubting Thomas, unable to resist poking her fingers into the holes of their silly ideas. Ideas Violet gave them in the first place.

'It wasn't,' said Dolly.

'I know, but . . . don't you think that was kind of scary?'

Dolly let go of Jayde's hand. Jayde knew she'd be glowering – that horrible, starey face she made when you said something that didn't fit with what she wanted to hear.

'Every time I talk about us trying to manifest or make another tulpa you are so fucking negative about it,' she said. And she said it like it was a sane, normal sentence.

'Yeah, Violet. You're so fucking negative,' Angelica said. Funny, of course, because Angelica was the most hostile, negative person Jayde had ever met. Angelica hated everyone and shat on everything and brought out the absolute worst in Dolly. The way the two of them could go on and on about that Joni girl drove Jayde insane. 'It's no wonder we're having trouble, the spirits literally seem quieter when you're around.'

301

Oh my God, thought Jayde. She could no longer tell if Angelica was just saying she could talk to ghosts to impress Dolly, or if she actually believed it herself.

'Well . . . I don't know. I just don't want to make . . . a Frankenstein's monster, type thing,' Violet said. And Jayde had looked at the Wikipedia page and the *SparkNotes* for Mary Shelley's *Frankenstein* the other night, because Violet was always talking about 'making a Frankenstein's monster' and if any one ever said 'Frankenstein' she would always correct them and say 'Frankenstein is the doctor, not the monster'.

After reading the *SparkNotes*, Jayde now understood that it was far too late for Violet to get anxious about having created a monster. This stupid game they were playing – that Violet was having to carry on with – that already was a monster. And it was getting bigger and more unruly with each day. Still, Violet kept feeding it. Digging up more graves, adding more limbs and grafting on more bits of skin. More violent stories, more fucked-up Wiki pages, more insane subreddits.

Jayde wanted to articulate all of this, but had no idea how she possibly could while she was this high.

'Jesus Christ,' she mumbled. Down on the floor, Dolly sighed.

'Oh my God, the Frankenstein thing again,' Dolly said. 'Look, it's going to be cool. It's not going to be like a Frankenstein – I know Frankenstein's the doctor, shut up – because we're not trying to manifest a physical-body thing this time, okay? We're not going to be setting it on people, it's going to be like . . . a plague, like a miasma, it's going to be like . . . chaos, just like pure chaos,' Dolly said.

And she really was just saying words. When they did this, it always got to a point where Dolly seemed to just be saying this nonsensical shit. And the others nodded and agreed like she wasn't just saying stuff that made no sense to anyone but her.

'Full offence but what the fuck are you talking about. What the fuck,' Jayde said. Out of her mouth before she had a chance to stop it – almost thinking aloud. The other girls stopped talking, and there was an outraged silence that Jayde was too high to really care about.

'We're just talking about the same things we always talk about,' offered Violet, her voice weak and soft.

'I know but like . . . it's just a joke, isn't it? Like it's just for fun,' Jayde said. She was also too high to make this point properly. 'Like you seriously can't believe this shit.'

'What the fuck is your problem?' Dolly snarled. And Jayde was done with that – done with that tone and done with her talking shit unchecked. Jayde sat up. Her phone slid out of her pocket and bounced off Violet's thick, dusty rug, practically into Dolly's lap.

'What the fuck is your problem, all of you. Jesus Christ,' Jayde said. She didn't bother looking at Angelica – who was just tapped and a massive cunt and beyond Jayde's help – but she shook her head at Violet, who responded by looking at the floor.

'Why is Joni messaging you?' Dolly asked.

'She's probably just replying to my story, it's nothing,' she said. Jayde tried to snatch her phone back, but Dolly moved away.

'Why is she replying to your story?' Dolly asked. She unlocked Jayde's phone (she'd need to change her passcode again) and looked at the message. It just looked like a smiley face, something totally inane. 'I fucking hate this desperate little bitch,' said Dolly. And Angelica agreed, squawking like a parrot behind her. *Yeah, yeah, she's so desperate.*

'It's nothing – it's fine, I'm not even – I don't even reply to her,' Jayde stammered.

'You don't reply? That's so pathetic that she keeps messaging you then,' said Angelica.

'It's really sad,' agreed Violet. *Don't you start*, thought Jayde. Dolly muttered something dark under her breath, grinding her teeth.

This was always so jarring for Jayde. Because Jayde generally got the sense that Dolly was a bit . . . indifferent to her. She never seemed to care about Jayde more than when another girl had DM'd her, or replied to her Snapchat, or something.

'That must really piss you off,' said Angelica – just to Dolly, not even looking at Jayde. Angelica only acknowledged Jayde when she could shit stir. She hated Joni Wilson – absolutely loathed her. It was like she really wanted to start something between Dolly and Joni; she was really hoping Dolly would start on her – fight her at school. 'It would piss me off soooooo much,' she said. 'She needs such a massive smack.' And Angelica clapped her hands together, her palms connecting with a loud crack.

Jayde grabbed her phone back from Dolly. And Dolly looked hurt – really hurt. And Jayde was a sucker for it, for Dolly looking at her with these big, sad, kicked-dog eyes. Because Dolly was a kicked dog, in a lot of ways. She never talked about her parents, but Jayde knew there was some shit going on there. Outside of her mum and stepdad and the weird religious stuff, Dolly was always making weird jokes and comments about her real father's suicide. It was so uncomfortable.

She made Jayde think about her mum's dogs. Her mum never thought there was a dog beyond help – that even the most aggressive, unpredictable greyhound was just a product of a horrible owner. You couldn't just abandon something like that; you couldn't just give up on an animal because it wasn't acting how it was supposed to – especially when it wasn't the animal's fault.

'Look,' said Jayde. 'I'm sorry. I don't really want her to message me, but I'm not going to be like . . . I don't want to embarrass her, okay? I'm sorry.'

'It's okay,' said Dolly. 'It's fine.'

Jayde said she was going to go and was met with minimal protests. As she walked home she got a series of texts from Dolly – oscillating between apologetic and angry. *Sorry I looked at your phone, sorry I got angry, but seriously why the fuck is she messaging you, I hate her, I'm sorry, I love you, I hate her.*

Jayde texted 'love you too' back, even though she didn't. Not really. She liked Dolly – but she was also probably going to break up with her soon. If she could be arsed to deal with the fallout. Maybe they could just stay together till one of them moved or went to uni or something – or until Dolly decided she wanted to break up. Jayde felt an overwhelming sense of dread and turned off her phone. She thought about throwing it in the sea, and wished she could.

When she got home, her mum immediately asked her if she'd been smoking weed. She said *no?* But it was obvious. Mum said her name. *Jayde.*

'It's just my allergies.'

'Don't blame the dogs,' snapped her mum. So Jayde admitted it, and got the standard lecture about how her mum didn't *really* mind, but she needed to think about her developing brain and be responsible given the mental illness running in the family and *I'd prefer if you didn't until you were older.* Jayde tuned her out, and her mum clicked her fingers in front of Jayde's face. 'We'll talk about this tomorrow, when you're sober.'

She made Jayde a cup of tea, and they watched *Take Me Out*.

'If you were going to dump me, how would you do it?' asked the hopeful bachelor.

'It'd be "Mambo No. 5" – because I want you to have a little bit of Monica in your life,' replied Monica, 23, Coventry.

'What? What kind of an answer is that?' Jayde said. Her mum gave her a look. 'Sorry – what was the question?'

'I think it was: if you were going to play one song to get my attention in a club, or something like that. What did you think he said?'

'Nothing, I just didn't hear it properly.'

Jayde didn't turn her phone back on until Monday morning – she had a handful of texts and a missed call from Dolly.

Heyyy xx

whatchya doin? x

jaaaaaayde xx

im watching minions x

> have I said my mum won't let me watch anything above a 12A lmao x

> its minions or bust x

> okay fine then i suppose you're still annoyed

> whatever see you in school

> Sorry I missed you x

> Got food poisoning x

> Still really ill probably not in today x

Jayde waited for her mum to leave for work, then didn't leave for school. The sixth form had an absence email which was listed in the 'parents' section of the CCHS website. Jayde emailed from a Gmail account she'd made in her mum's name. She'd done it a couple of times before and it always worked.

To whom it may concern, she typed, knowing that was the adult and professional way to begin an email.

Jayde is sick with food poisoning and will not be in today. She will probably be back tomorrow but I will email or call again if not. Please call if you'd like to confirm or have any questions.
Best regards,
Diana Spencer.

'Please call' was a good way to call their bluff if they did doubt it – but the school wasn't very strict with this stuff.

There were enough serial truants in the lower school that Jayde bunking off the odd day here or there went pretty much under the radar.

She only had three lessons on a Monday anyway. Two in the morning and one fourth period – she'd put on her school clothes and drop by her mum's shop at about half twelve and say her last lesson was cancelled because the teacher was off. It was a bit extravagant just to avoid Dolly, but it was worth it. Jayde ate toast in her pyjamas and watched repeats of *Friends*. Connor came downstairs at about eleven, looking extremely hungover.

'Aren't you meant to be at school?' he asked.

'Aren't you meant to be at work?'

'I'm ill,' he said. Jayde shrugged.

'So am I.'

Mutually assured destruction guaranteed their respective silence. Connor went back to bed and Jayde watched more crap television; not quite relaxed, but certainly feeling better than if she'd gone to school. She felt better after she'd gone to speak to her mum at the bookies at lunchtime.

Dolly texted to ask if she was still sick.

> Not throwing up anymore lol
>
> Ate some dry toast
>
> Will probably see you tomorrow x

She did go in on Tuesday, and Dolly didn't even seem suspicious. It was a normal day. She deliberately avoided Dolly at lunchtime, but not in an obvious way – she got away with it.

After school she had kickboxing. She walked straight from school to the gym; it was around half an hour away on foot. She usually had to wait around a bit for class to start, but it made more sense than going home first.

'Hey, Jayde?' someone called behind her. Joni Wilson. Jayde winced. She needed to find a polite way to brush her off. She needed to discourage Joni from trying to get too pally-pally with her. She didn't want to upset Dolly. But then, the more Jayde thought about Dolly, the more she resented her. If she did work up the courage to break up with Dolly, she wouldn't have to find a way to brush Joni off – she could just talk to her, like a normal person.

While Jayde turned this over in her mind, Joni made small talk. She asked Jayde if her toe was okay. Jayde had mistimed a kick last week and hit a wall – her little toe went black.

'It wasn't broken, was it?' asked Joni. She had a round face, big eyes and a snub nose; she reminded Jayde of one of those soft dolls you give to babies.

'No. It looked a lot worse than it actually was.'

Joni smiled and said 'cool'. She was twiddling with her phone, holding it out and checking it nervously as they walked.

'Hey, sorry if this is weird. I got a message from er . . . Dolly Hart last night?' she said. She unlocked her phone, opening Instagram.

'What kind of message?'

'Like an angry one.'

Joni showed Jayde her phone. A message request on Instagram from Dolly which read:

Hey! Seems like you have been talking to my girlfriend a LOT. I know you do kickboxing together and I know you like her. I want you to stop talking to her and messaging her. She doesn't like you and it's weird. Thanks!!

Jayde sighed, and felt her face go red.

'I'm really sorry. That's so fucking embarrassing,' she said. 'Has she done this before?' Joni shrugged, like she might have, but she didn't want to admit it. 'Sorry about this.'

'It's okay. Did she look at your messages or something?' Joni asked. Jayde said she didn't know. 'I'm sorry if I made you feel weird, or anything. I was just – I reply to everyone like that. I honestly do.'

'No, it's fine. I know it's nothing, it's just like . . . normal stuff. It's not you, it's her, she's just a bit weird with this stuff. She said she's been cheated on before, so I understand, but she goes way overboard.' Dolly hadn't actually said she'd been cheated on before, but Jayde felt the need to make the excuse for her.

'Okay,' Joni smiled at her. 'She's really jealous, then?'

'Sometimes.'

'She must really like you.'

'I suppose.'

'That's kind of toxic, though,' said Joni, cautiously. She blinked up at Jayde innocently with that faux-sweet stuffed-doll stare, quite obviously trying to goad her into saying something bad about Dolly. *Wow, it sounds like your girlfriend is really crazy . . . maybe you should talk to someone . . . less crazy.* Jayde wasn't stupid; she knew what Joni was trying to do.

She wanted to warn Joni off, but she didn't want to embarrass her. Jayde felt bad for her. Even if Jayde was just the target of some experimental infatuation, she didn't want to hurt Joni's feelings.

She was torn, and she could not wait to live in a place where she was no longer the only out gay girl in a ten-mile radius.

Dolly being jealous was probably making it worse – she'd turned Jayde from an idle object of fascination to forbidden fruit. Joni had probably gone from *I am choosing to fancy Jayde because she's the only 'available' girl to fancy* to *I must have Jayde because I can't have her.* Something like that. Then Jayde started to feel embarrassed for thinking like this. It was so big-headed of her.

This was all a bit complicated to articulate to someone you didn't know very well about fifteen minutes before your kickboxing class. So Jayde didn't say anything. Probably sensing that trying to needle someone into slagging off their girlfriend (even if she was mental) was a bad look, Joni changed the subject and asked Jayde if she watched *RuPaul's Drag Race*.

She didn't. Joni told her that Season 8 had just started airing. She should catch up – it was good. She awkwardly asked Jayde about other conspicuously gay media – *Glee* ('It was bad but I'm kind of sad it's finished!'), *The Legend of Korra* ('So cool that they went there!') and *Steven Universe* ('It's for kids but it's soooo good.'). Jayde hadn't seen any of it and didn't know anything about it apart from the fact it was, somehow, gay and that well-meaning people had asked her if she liked it before. It was all nerd shit, as far as Jayde was concerned. Weird, nerdy, Tumblr stuff she had no interest in.

'I'm just really into sports,' said Jayde. 'I really like basket-ball and football.'

'Maybe you would like *Drag Race*. It's really competitive – it's basically a sport. Even though drag is not a contact sport,' she said that last part in an American accent.

'Is that from the show, or something?'

'Erm. Yeah, sorry.'

Joni couldn't let a silence linger.

'Do you hang round with Angelica?' she asked.

'Dolly does. I don't like her,' Jayde said.

Enthused, Joni replied that she hated Angelica as well. That people only hung out with her because they felt sorry for her – but Joni didn't feel sorry for her.

'She used to be such a bully in primary school, and she tries to be a bully now but everyone is like *ew*. Have you ever seen her Tumblr?'

'No,' said Jayde.

'It's so funny. She argues with people about musicals and dresses up like a cat. Um . . . sometimes I send her these messages – anonymously – to wind her up, and she gets so annoyed,' Joni chuckled. Jayde didn't quite know what to say to that. 'Like, do you know she thinks she can talk to dead people? She never tells anyone, but Kayleigh – do you know Kayleigh Brian? – she told me she does. She made a tit of herself at a sleepover pretending once so she's usually really quiet about it. But she's been posting about it on her Tumblr recently, so I sent her this message like "do you have any info from the spirit world for us" – and she actually seriously replied. Hang on, I'll see if I can find it.'

'No,' said Jayde. 'That's okay.' And then, because she

couldn't help herself: 'You know, some of the messages she gets – I've heard her talking about them; they really upset her.'

'I don't send all of them. Hardly any of them. She never turns anon off, you know. I think she likes the attention.'

'Yeah that sounds like her,' Jayde conceded.

Kickboxing was a bit awkward. Jayde was very aware of Joni looking at her, and also very aware of the fact that Dolly was probably texting her loads because she'd remembered Jayde was at kickboxing.

'Come on, Spencer,' said the teacher, in response to what was honestly a very half-arsed kick. 'It's like you can't be arsed today!'

'Sorry,' she said. 'I had food poisoning over the weekend.'

At the end of class, Joni said bye to Jayde and gave her this awkward punch on the shoulder, like she wanted to hug but couldn't quite bring herself to do it.

Jayde put off checking her phone till the walk home – and she was right. She had a bunch of messages from Dolly.

How's your girlfriend today lmao x

Jk jk x

You have to tell me if she's being tragic tho x

Missed you at lunch but we're going to do some spooky summoning at the witch hammer on saturday if you're up for it? X

Meeting at mine for about eight x

Its the equinox on Sunday which would've been much cooler but SKOOL NIGHT isn't it x

Jayde replied: *sounds good!* Even though it didn't sound good. Tempted as she was to have a bit of a whinge about Joni, Jayde didn't want Dolly to message her again.

Connor was out, so Jayde thought about asking her mum for some relationship advice over dinner. Then she remembered her mum only went out with twats and approached men the way she approached her sad, abused greyhounds. Every man was deserving of her patience, every man was deserving of her empathy – never put a good dog down (even if he's a bellend and you met him at the bookies because he's got a really bad gambling habit). Knowing her mum, she'd probably side with Dolly.

But then, it wasn't like Jayde had anyone else she could ask for advice.

'How do you know if you want to break up with someone?' Jayde asked.

'I was just thinking you hadn't mentioned your girlfriend in a while,' said her mum. 'Haven't seen her round in months.'

'Yeah,' said Jayde. 'We're still going out. But . . .'

'Cooling off a bit?' she asked. She said it in that smug, know-it-all way adults did when they asked you about your relationships. Like just because you're seventeen they can predict everything you'll do. Everything's always *I was obsessed with my first high school boyfriend, it's just like that when you're your age* until it's *I totally lost interest in my high school boyfriend after two months – it's just like that when you're your age.* Like everything Jayde did was going to be stupid and trivial and obvious until she was twenty-five.

Even then she'd probably still be hearing *well, when I was twenty five . . .*

'You don't know everything, you know,' snapped Jayde. Her mum rolled her eyes. 'Never mind.'

'You asked,' she said. She looked over at the dogs, who were sat in a line, staring at them hungrily as they ate dinner. 'At least none of you will ever give me backchat like that.'

'Skinny bit you two days ago,' said Jayde.

'It's just his separation anxiety. You didn't mean it, did you?' she said in a baby voice. 'No you didn't, did you, ducky? You're a good baby, yes you are.'

All of the dogs woofed or snuffled or whined, unable to distinguish which of them was the good baby in question. Her mum chattered to the dogs for the rest of the meal, and Jayde ate in silence, stewing.

She spent the rest of the week feeling apprehensive about what the fuck they were going to do on Saturday. It wasn't as nerve-wracking as breaking into the park (which Jayde had really not enjoyed) but she still didn't want to hang around the Witch Hammer or the castle at night.

Crow got nastier at night. Her Mad Uncle Bob had put the shits up her about it, those times her mum had him on the sofa for a couple of nights to get him off the street. And he used to mutter to himself, or to no one in particular: 'Nasty place at night. This is a nasty, nasty place at night.' He'd have this faraway look in his eye, like he'd seen some shit.

And her mum would usually say, 'Yeah, well, when you're hanging round with the junkies and begging for drink it will be.' And maybe she was right – but it didn't make Uncle Bob wrong. It was particularly bad at the weekends. It was one thing walking back and forth from hers to Dolly's, or whatever. But she hated walking through the town centre, and past the North Beach – and you had to go through both to get to the Witch Hammer.

A lot of people came from out of town for a night out – and the kind of sad fuckers who'd come to Crow to drink weren't the kind of people who took very kindly to Jayde. Jayde didn't think of herself as cosmopolitan or anything, but a girl with short hair to some of the blokes who came in from the countryside – she was like a red flag to a load of provincial bulls. She'd had grown men screaming in her face, calling her a dyke; she'd once had a bottle thrown at her.

It would probably be fine – but she couldn't get the idea of some group of blokes finding them while they were doing weird shit outside (in a pretty public place) out of her head. Angelica was always worrying about junkies and tramps, but Jayde was more worried about stags.

Jayde spent most of Saturday in a shit mood. She kept snapping at her mum for no reason. She snapped at Connor as well, when she was trying to get him to give her some weed.

'Nah. Mum was whinging about you smoking it and being like "you set a bad example for her" the other day. Not worth the shit if she finds out I'm giving it to you.' And that was fair of him. He wasn't being a dick about it, and she still had half a joint left over from last weekend. Still, she snarled at him.

'Why are you being such a twat? Like you're a responsible adult now. Get fucked.'

'Tell me to get fucked again, and see what happens,' he said.

'Threaten me again and see how quick Mum chucks you out.'

'See how well that works when I tell her you were asking me for drugs and swearing at me.'

That was stalemate. Jayde stomped off. She sat in her bedroom and started to cry. Bickering with Connor hadn't really set her off – the stress and discomfort of the last week had. Still, she'd cried loud enough for Connor to hear her. As she was beginning to calm down, she heard shuffling and rustling in the hallway, as Connor tried to push a joint under the gap in her bedroom door. The gap was just wide enough for it to fit through.

'Thank you!' she said. 'Sorry for swearing at you.'

'Sorry for trying to be a responsible adult,' he replied.

'I'll give you some money.'

'It's fine. Just don't smoke it all at once.'

She stuffed the fresh joint (thoughtfully rolled with fake tobacco) into the sandwich bag with the other. She still felt anxious, but at least she could get a bit high before she went to Dolly's.

She probably ended up getting too high before she went to Dolly's. She finished the old joint without really thinking about it and did so on an empty stomach. She didn't feel relaxed so much as she felt edgy and fuzzy and a bit detached from her own body.

She felt like she'd teleported to Dolly's house. She was in her own back garden – then she was at Dolly's front door. And her mum was answering – which was weird, because Jayde had been kept at an intentional distance from Dolly's mum. And having met Dolly's glamorous sister, Jayde was shocked by how plain this woman was. She was dowdy, and conservative: her hair was very short and unfashionable, her skin was dry and dull and her clothes were baggy and boring. She had Dolly's big, pretty eyes but they were tired and unfocussed.

'Hi,' Jayde said.

'Hello,' she replied. 'Are you Jayde?'

'Yeah.'

'That's . . . very cool hair,' she said. 'Very funky.'

'Thank you,' Jayde said back. She was trying not to stand or speak in a butch way, but also realised she didn't really know how to stand or speak in a girly way. Dolly's mum let her in, and about three different illustrations of Jesus and Friends stared beatifically down at her. 'You have a very nice house,' said Jayde, in a weird, high-pitched voice. She'd been here before, but not with the mum or the stepdad around. 'Sooo nice,' she said, trying to copy Angelica's weird, girly intonation. She even flicked her fringe – the only part of her hair long enough to flick.

Dolly barrelled down the stairs and seemed horrified Jayde and her mum had interacted at all. Without acknowledging her mother, she dragged Jayde back up the stairs, and into her room.

'Are you fucking high? Are you talking to my mum high?' Dolly hissed. Jayde blinked. She felt as though she'd blinked really slowly, like a chameleon. She tried to think of something to say back, and just went 'uh' for ages, while Dolly glared at her.

'I don't think she'd know,' Jayde said.

'Of course she'd know. She's a fucking ex-pisshead; she used to go to raves and shit in the nineties – are you fucking thick?'

'Don't get in my face like that,' said Jayde. Because Dolly was in her face. She gave her a little shove (not an aggressive one) and stepped back. 'Don't get in my face and swear at me.'

'You were talking to my mum high,' Dolly said, still close enough that her spit landed on Jayde's face.

'I said like two words to her,' Jayde said, now hiss-shouting back. 'You don't have a right to be angry with me anyway – not after what you did. Fucking embarrassing me.'

'What do you mean?' Dolly asked. Hiss-shout gone – now she was shifty-eyed, ready to move into kicked-puppy if need be.

'Joni told me you messaged her.'

'Did not. She's a fucking liar.'

'Yes you did.'

'How do you know she wasn't lying?'

'She showed me the message.' Jayde watched Dolly's face shift from hurt, to sad, to angry, back to hurt again. 'It's not on. It's scary, you can't do that,' Jayde said, before Dolly could get anything out. Dolly went back to anger.

'Or what?'

'What do you mean *or what*?' Jayde asked. Dolly didn't have an answer. 'We'll have to break up if you keep doing that. Because it's not cool,' she said. Her face was red, and her heart was beating much too quickly. It ached in her chest – pure panic as she anticipated Dolly blowing up at her. But Dolly didn't. Her face melted, her eyes welled.

'I'm sorry for caring,' she said, theatrically. 'What, so, some girl who we all know likes you – she's just allowed to keep messaging you even though everyone involved has made it clear you're not comfortable with that? I'm just supposed to be okay with her making you uncomfortable?' Fat tears ran down her face, streaking her cheeks with dark eyeliner and mascara. Jayde felt awful. 'Yeah, exactly,' Dolly hiccupped – like she knew Jayde felt bad.

She realised then that Dolly was wearing a bracelet Jayde had won her from a 2p pusher machine in one of the arcades. She went through almost a tenner, feeding so many 2ps into the machine that her fingers went black from handling the change. It was a horrible bracelet – this ultra-cheap Pandora knock-off thing – but they'd had so much fun together that day. They played air hockey and shot basketball hoops and Dolly said 'win me something'. And Jayde knew the claw machines were rigged – so she went for the pusher.

'I'll keep it forever,' she'd said. And she'd kissed Jayde on the cheek.

Jayde gave Dolly a hug. She hadn't meant to make her cry.

'You can't message her like that though,' Jayde said, into Dolly's hair. She smelt of artificial coconut. 'I appreciate it, that you're trying to make sure I'm comfortable and stuff. But you can't message her like that, it's really embarrassing, and you know . . . you might get in trouble. What if she tells some-one?' Dolly pulled back from the hug, looking incredulous.

'She's not going to fucking tell anyone,' she said. 'Whatever. If she stops messaging you, I'll stop messaging her. She'd have to be pretty fucking thick to keep doing it.' Dolly wiped her eyes and immediately started fixing her makeup.

'Yeah, I suppose,' said Jayde. And that was true – it would be a bit weird if Joni kept messaging her. But then: why should she stop? Why should she have to?

Angelica arrived, ostentatiously, in a big black cab. As always, she was carrying a large, rattling bag of alcohol and crisps. Jayde immediately commandeered a large bag of Doritos. She ate as Dolly and Angelica bickered over whether or not to start drinking.

'We're leaving as soon as Violet gets here,' said Dolly. 'Literally just give it five minutes.'

'Are you okay?' asked Angelica. 'You look like you've been crying.'

'Joni told Jayde I messaged her and made it seem like I sent something really mental and aggressive,' Dolly sniffed. Jayde attempted to focus on the Doritos while Angelica made things worse. Joni was such a shit-stirrer, such a bitch, such a pathetic loser – message someone else's girlfriend then play the victim? What a joke. What an absolute joke.

'It's done,' said Jayde, around a mouthful of Doritos. 'Don't get wound up over it again, it's done.'

Violet arrived, and the subject of Joni was dropped. They left Dolly's house (without acknowledging her mum) and began walking through town, up to the Witch Hammer.

As expected for a Saturday night, town was full of drunk men. Shouting and swearing and moving from bars to pubs to amusement arcades. Jayde knew she was being paranoid, but she felt like they were being looked at, being watched.

'Let's have a go on the gamblers,' shouted one man back to his friends. Jayde jumped, as if she'd been addressed. She huddled in close to Dolly, even though Dolly didn't feel very safe. They passed another group of blokes who were arguing strategy for a 'skill cut' machine; inside, a large Clifford the Big Red Dog plush appeared to be hung by the neck from a string. One of them made a sudden, angry yelp and Violet jumped and gasped.

Violet was very jumpy around men, Jayde had noticed. They went over to Jayde's once, before Christmas, and Violet wouldn't even look at Jayde's brother. She tensed up whenever she heard his voice.

As they walked past, Jayde was sure the men had pointed and laughed at them.

'Can we get off the promenade, please,' she said.

'Yeah, fuck this,' said Violet.

'We're nearly there,' Dolly replied. 'Chill out.'

But Jayde could not chill out – because it was loud and there were strange men everywhere. There were bright lights and colours and several different songs blaring out from several different sources. The air smelt of cigarettes, candy floss and curry sauce. She was tempted to stick her fingers in her ears – then remembered her hands were still kind of covered in spicy Dorito dust, and she probably shouldn't.

But they were off the North Beach promenade soon enough and trekking up the hill to the castle and the Witch Hammer.

Angelica had opened the bottle of vodka she'd brought with her; they passed it round between them and drank. They made faces. Jayde said no. Her mouth was so dry and her stomach hurt; she couldn't imagine drinking alcohol right now without throwing it straight back up.

They stopped at the top of the hill, and Jayde grabbed one of a couple of cans of soft drink Angelica had packed. A Fanta. She sat on the damp grass and drank the can and tried to calm down a bit.

'Are you okay?' Violet asked her. She gave a thumbs up.

The other girls sat with her. They took their own cans of soft drink, sipped from them, then topped them up with vodka.

'Did you only bring Diet Coke?' asked Violet. 'Is there any normal?'

'Normal Coke makes you fat,' replied Dolly. Angelica nodded.

'I only drink Diet,' said Angelica.

'Same,' said Violet. 'I was just asking.'

All three of them were so thin. Jayde, tall and broad-shouldered and muscular as she was, always felt huge around the three of them. She felt bulky and out of place and distinctly irritated to hear them talking about Diet Coke and getting fat.

Violet was too skinny and Jayde thought she looked ill. She was pale, with a blue, anaemic undertone to her lips and eyes. Angelica was thin enough to feel confident in saying she could 'probably be a model if she didn't want to be an actress'. Even though she was far too short and plain to model. Not ugly – just nothing to write home about.

Dolly was the only one of them with a figure of which to speak – and she watched it obsessively until she didn't. It was all Diet Coke and skipped meals until it was McDonald's and Doritos and alcopops. And her junk food habit was fine with Jayde. No judgements here. Dolly was meaner when she didn't eat.

Jayde didn't want them to get stuck on this: what does and doesn't 'make you fat'.

'Do yous feel like you have to be drunk for this ritual thing to work?' asked Jayde. 'Because yous always get shitfaced beforehand.'

'Some people do hallucinogenic drugs before they do stuff like this. Like ayahuasca or LSD or mushrooms or whatever,' said Violet.

'But then you'd probably just hallucinate that something had happened, wouldn't you? That seems stupid,' Jayde said.

Violet shrugged. 'I don't know much about it.'

Dolly told her off for being negative.

When the other girls were drunk enough, and Jayde's high had calmed down a bit, they approached the Witch Hammer. There were a few flowers laid there – Violet said it'd probably be busy here tomorrow anyway, with the equinox. She said she knew some Wiccans who liked to come and pay tribute to their fallen sisters, and she said it with a bit of a sneer, which surprised Jayde.

'I think for a certain type of woman,' said Violet, 'witches and stuff, this is like . . . their holocaust, or something.' Dolly and Violet laughed; Jayde and Angelica didn't really get the joke.

'You're so fucking mean,' said Dolly, grinning. Dolly pushed the Witch Hammer with her toe. 'And you said this thing weighs a tonne?'

'Yeah.'

'I know a few people I'd like to stick under it.' Dolly clapped her hands, suddenly. 'SPLAT.'

They held hands and closed their eyes. Jayde was holding Dolly's and Violet's hands. Dolly told them all to focus. To focus hard. To think about everything and everyone they hate in Crow-on-Sea. To think about a huge, dark fog enveloping the town. But Jayde wasn't really thinking about that. She was thinking about how it'd be the WNBA's draft in a few weeks. She'd read the names of the top picks and tried to remember them. She remembered that one of the women was really tall, and one of them was surprisingly short – a bit shorter than Jayde. Like 5'6" or something. And WNBA players do tend, on average, to be a bit shorter than people assume they are. But still. 5'6" was pretty small.

'This isn't working,' Dolly said, after a few minutes. Jayde felt her heart speed up – like Dolly would know she wasn't thinking about the great and terrible fog or whatever. She tried not to look suspicious; she frowned, like she was really concerned. Like she actually thought it might be 'working' or might have 'worked' any time they did this stupid shit.

'I think it worked. I totally think it worked,' said Angelica. 'I can hear a voice. A witch's voice, I think. She's talking about getting killed here and I'm a conduit so—'

'No, Angelica, it's not working. Violet, did that work?' They all looked at Violet, who flinched under their gazes.

'I . . . No, I don't think it did.'

Dolly huffed and kicked the Witch Hammer.

'It's just baby shit. Stupid shit, holding hands and . . . Fuck,' she said. 'If we want to make it a hell here, if we really want to make it . . . if we want to rip down the veil . . . we've got to manifest the chaos ourselves, you know? Like Matty and Brian.' Jayde forgot who Matty and Brian were for a moment and couldn't stop herself from rolling her eyes when she remembered. 'You can't just keep like trying to make something like . . .' She was rambling. Worse than usual. Maybe it was just because she was drunk. Jayde looked at Dolly and Angelica, who were nodding along intently, like anything she was saying made sense. 'Matty and Brian hated their shitty town so much that they literally made a pocket hell.'

'Yeah but, they killed people, didn't they?' said Jayde.

'Yeah. But okay, like Fritzl – that basement, that was a tiny hell. He didn't kill anyone,' she said. Jayde shook her head. 'Look, I'm not saying we should do something bad, I'm just . . .'

'What are you trying to do here, Dolly?' Jayde asked.

'Pocket hell. Tiny hell.' Like that was a suitable answer. Like that made any sense. And Dolly had explained this shit to Jayde before but that didn't mean she understood any of it.

'Yeah, but why?'

'Because,' Dolly said. And then she fell silent. 'Because . . . it's a fucking shithole. It's like Matty says in his diaries, it already *is* hell—'

'Oh my God, who cares what Matty says? If it's already hell, why do you need to make it worse? Like, I just don't get this stuff, and I don't think you two get what she means either,' said Jayde. Angelica and Violet shook their heads.

'It makes sense to me,' said Angelica. 'It makes perfect sense.'

'Yeah,' added Violet, weakly.

'We're just trying to . . . to fuck things up! God, why are you being such a bitch about this?' Dolly was practically shouting at her now. Frustrated and indignant and too wrapped up in all of this to understand how mad she sounded.

'And I can like, I can hear the witch spirit, Jayde, and she's saying—' Angelica began – but Jayde cut her off. She was done.

'This is stupid, I'm going home,' she said. She pointed at Angelica. 'You can't fucking talk to ghosts.'

Angelica gasped, offended.

'Good,' Dolly replied. 'We don't need you. You're probably fucking things up anyway, with your . . . vibes.'

'Whatever,' Jayde called back. She was already walking down the hill. She went home, cutting through the dark back streets, which felt safer to her than the promenade.

Dear Alec,

Thanks for sending over the questions. I have answered them as best as I can and have tried to be detailed. This was really difficult to write and I'm a bit dyslexic so sorry if most of this isn't very good.

What was your relationship with Dolly like after you had the falling-out at Easter? Am I to understand you didn't really break up? Did you continue to communicate with Joni?

Well to start off with yeah I did still keep talking to Joni. She was at my kickboxing class and she was friendly so I couldn't really get away from her. I had no problem with her though. I talked to her a bit and she messaged me a couple of times but not in like a DM slidey kind of way, just normal stuff. Dolly and the others really had it in their heads that she fancied me and maybe she did. I don't know it almost doesn't really matter.

After the whole thing round Easter (when I found out Dolly had sent Joni this angry message and I asked her to stop because it was embarrassing) I didn't hear from Joni for a while on snapchat or insta but she kept talking to me a bit in Kickboxing and just didn't mention the Dolly stuff. Around when the Year 11s went on study leave she started replying to my snapchat stories and stuff again.

I thought about telling her to stop because Dolly would get wound up, but I didn't want to make it like this big secret thing. I felt like if I gave it that kind of attention I was proving Dolly right? I don't know if this makes sense but I felt like if I said 'you can't message me because my gf will get annoyed with you' it would prove that Joni was doing something wrong or I was doing something wrong by messaging her back.

The fact is there's just nothing wrong with talking to someone you go to school with a little bit. Even if she did fancy me, she didn't say she did or ask me out or try to get me to break up with my girlfriend so why would it matter? I bet loads of people innocently reply to DMs from people who fancy them a bit and it doesn't become this huge ridiculous thing.

After we had the fight around the witch hammer thing, I don't know. We just sort of didn't break up. I was kind of hoping she would dump me but she just acted like nothing had really happened and stopped inviting me as much. We still texted and spoke in school, and we still saw each other outside of school but we cooled off. Then when the Year 11s went on study leave we got a bit closer, a bit more like proper girlfriends again. We were a bit on-and-off again really it was just that we never officially broke up or got back together.

How did Dolly, Violet and Angelica's behaviour change after the Easter break? Describe their mental states as you entered summer.

I don't know. I was on the outside of it. After Easter they excluded me from it because I was 'negative' and I didn't believe in it anyway – even though Dolly liked having four people there, it was just like . . . I was probably bringing the whole thing down, anyway. I know they were still trying to 'manifest' stuff and I know Dolly said she thought Crow was like evil or something.

328

I don't know how to explain it because I didn't understand it at the time. But she thought it was really haunted and full of evil energy she could harness to make things worse and like open a hell portal or something. I didn't really understand what she was trying to do. Like I never really got if the goal was for them to punish bad people or just make things worse for everyone. I think it changed a lot, to be honest, depending on what she was interested in at the time.

If they were planning anything they didn't tell me about it. Dolly tried to get me in on what they were doing but she gave up when she realised I just wasn't interested. A few weeks before we broke up when we weren't talking much she sent me a picture of the school shooters she liked, Matthew and Brian, and she captioned it THIS COULD BE US BUT U PLAYING :(. It was at like 3 a.m. and I ignored it.

I didn't see Violet and Angelica as much, I just saw Dolly on her own and not very regularly. I suppose I would say that Dolly seemed to be getting worse. When I did see her with Violet and Angelica, Violet had stopped pushing back at all when she used to question Dolly sometimes, and Angelica was just constantly acting like she could hear ghosts and was talking to ghosts and stuff.

I think Dolly was more paranoid and more aggressive and she was generally talking more shit. She wasn't trying to convert me but when I did see her she would often not make a lot of sense and ramble about stuff. She would say that she had been 'channelling matty' and she wanted Angelica to help her channel Brian. She started saying that in early May, I think, and I had no idea what to say to that or what she meant. I asked her like . . . what the fuck, and Dolly was just like 'oh I just want to see if she can speak to him, I want to see if I can reunite Matty and Brian' and I decided I didn't want to hear any more of it and it was too creepy to think about.

I should probably have properly broken up with her in spring. Even though we were more 'back together' in summer we weren't seeing each other that much and I was starting to get annoyed with her and sick of her just talking about weird mystical stuff and her pretend mass shooter boyfriend and then she would get annoyed with me if I didn't agree with her or pay attention. Like I said we'd argue and not talk for a bit and then she would text again or turn up at my house and act like nothing had happened.

Can you describe the night of the murder and the morning after from your point of view?

It's basically a normal day for me except I'm finally really thinking it's time to break up with Dolly. I think she's gotten so jealous at this point that I really can't be arsed with her. I was past thinking it was cute or it showed that she cared about me, because we were barely talking even though she was still being really possessive of me. She was also just talking mad shit all the time and she was freaking me out. On all levels she was weirding me out and making me feel uncomfortable.

There's some Joni stuff which was the last straw because it's so weird and she was so hung up on it. I know Angelica hated Joni and I know Violet and her had some weird shit as well, so I know it was probably just the three of them winding each other up and making really petty high school bullying a much bigger deal than it actually was.

The day before the murder I'd met up with Dolly at my house and when I'd gone to the loo she went through my fucking phone again. I had changed my passcode for like the tenth time, but she would always watch me really carefully to work out the new one. She would look over my shoulder and I wouldn't think to hide my phone because that's just no way to live.

We had this big argument where I say about fifty times 'I don't fancy Joni and I'm not interested in her' and that this time Dolly doesn't need to message her to tell her to stay away from me or whatever. Because it's mad and embarrassing behaviour and I'll be friends with her if I like. And then I told her I was sick of her and she was dumped.

Dolly said I just wasn't a loyal person and that I didn't understand her, and she stormed out.

I remember thinking 'I hope she doesn't try to do some kind of weird ritual shit on Joni' but then I thought . . . they don't fucking work do they so who cares? At worst it'll just be cringey. Mostly I felt relieved. My mum asked what the argument was about and then why I looked so pleased.

Joni messaged me later on the same day to say that she appreciated that I was defending her to Dolly and she's sorry if she ever made me feel uncomfortable. Which meant Dolly had messaged her AGAIN. I was fuming. And I told her I was really sorry and embarrassed about it and not to worry. And then Joni sent Dolly a screenshot of what I'd said like . . . oh look at that even your gf thinks you're being a mad bitch right now. And I know that because Dolly sent me a screenshot of the screenshot Joni sent so I just said WE ARE BROKEN UP. THIS IS NOT MY PROBLEM.

And she blocked me. And I was pretty annoyed and I just

thought . . . well fine, we're DEFINITELY broken up now. GOOD. But we were supposed to all be going to this house party – this boy in the upper sixth Dolly had fucked a couple of times invited her and she invited us. And she rang me the next day (the day of the actual murder) like are you coming to this party and I was like:

No? I dumped you? And we had a back and forth, me saying we are broken up, her saying we're not, and eventually I just hung up.

Joni also texted me inviting me to this party and I said 'no, I don't want to go because I just broke up with Dolly, she's going and I don't want to see her'. And Joni said 'fair enough, see you at kickboxing' and that was the last time I spoke to her.

I had a really quiet day. I watched some telly with my mum. Later on (not sure if she was at the party or not at this point) Dolly started texting me:

If Joni is at the party then I'm going to kill her/I want to kill her/she's going to die tonight.

I didn't say anything to anyone because I didn't think she actually meant it.

When someone says 'I'm going to kill her', am I always supposed to take that literally? Do you take that literally? Because people have actually said to me 'if you were getting these threat messages texted to you why didn't you tell the police' and I'm sorry but can you fucking imagine telling the police every time you got a message like 'Oh I'm going to kill this person who's annoyed me' because I think that'd be pretty fucking ridiculous.

Especially if you're a teenager being texted by another teenager. People act like I wouldn't have been laughed out of the police station like I was this insane attention seeking lesbian walking in like 'My ex-girlfriend has threatened that she is going to kill a girl who fancies me.'

Grow up. That's fucking stupid and anyone who thinks about it for five minutes knows it's fucking stupid.

She kept ringing me so I turned off my phone and went to bed. I know this off by heart because I had to tell the police so many times. I turned my phone off between 9 and 10 p.m. I watched a film at around 10 (*Furious 7* which is 137 minutes long), took a shower once that was finished and went to bed a bit after midnight. Really boring.

As far as I was concerned that was my night.

Then I get woken up at like 6 o'clock in the morning, police banging on the door, sent the dogs absolutely wild. One of the dogs bit a policeman even though my mum told them to let her get them shut in the kitchen but they just ignored her and barged in. It was Skinny, the foster dog – they took him and had him put down which is extremely fucked up.

So while they were ignoring my mum warning them about her fragile and unpredictable rescue dogs that hate men, a couple of them came up the stairs and basically dragged me out of bed. Handcuffed me when I had no idea what was happening. My mum was really upset and my brother was really panicking and told me he flushed all his weed and hid in the toilet until they were gone.

They took me down to the police car and they put me in the back and told me I was under arrest on suspicion of conspiracy to commit murder. This is all going to be a bit all over the place because it was a really confusing few days and I can't remember much of it.

333

I got interrogated for hours and I kept telling them I hadn't done anything, but they kept asking me where I was last night, and didn't believe me when I said I didn't even know who was dead, or what they were on about. They told me what had happened and showed me these really graphic photos of Joni's body. I don't remember much about the interrogation but I remember the photos. I couldn't even tell who it was, it was like something from a horror film.

They checked all the CCTV cameras near mine and confirmed I hadn't left the house but they still said I was involved. They went through my phone and they were really aggressive and horrible to me – they said loads of stuff about my family and they talked like Dolly had started this mad lesbian murder cult. It felt really homophobic and targeted. They asked me loads of pointless details about our relationship and if we'd had sex and stuff. It was humiliating. I was at the police station for 24 hours before they let me go. But they gave me a cannabis warning because they found weed in my bedroom.

My mum was hysterical because they'd trashed the house and the *Post-on-Sea* took photos of me leaving the police station and posted them to their website, even though I think some kind of anonymity order had come through from the court. They had to pay damages to me but it was a bit late because it was out there. My face and the murder.

People still repost the picture with blog posts and podcasts and stuff and say that I'm one of the murderers because they get my photo mixed up with Violet and Angelica's all the time. My face is a google result when you search both of their names.

The more people cover it and the more people are talking about the case, the more it happens and the more I get recognised. Part of the reason I said I'd talk to you is just because people will at least have this book as a reference. I can live with being recognised if they're not recognising me as someone who did or organised a murder. I was just going out with the wrong girl at the wrong time and that's all that's relevant. If anyone wants to write about it or make another podcast they'll at least read the book first or something and they'll know that I didn't do anything.

GIRL C

'Cherry Lips, Black Eyes' Chapter 3

By Cherryb0b0b0mb
Rated: Explicit

Author's Note: I do not condone, don't like don't read etc. etc. Some people complained that I used the F slur in my last chapter sorry but Matty used it in his diaries all the time. I have censored it for this chapter but if an actual word that Matty used in his diaries triggers you maybe this isn't the fandom for you lol.

Brian didn't know much but he knew one thing. He was obsessed with Matty and every moment that they weren't together was agony. He thought about Matty every minute that Matty wasn't there and he burned with desire for the taller boy. Matty was charismatic and handsome and brian was small and pathetic compared to matty. He wanted to do something to impress matty but he didn't know what. He knew Matty was hardcore and dark and he wanted to be like Matty as well as be with him. He was gay and that was really hard. He thought maybe that Matty was too but he didn't know. At home one day Brian put on eyeliner that he stole from the store and he did that before school. He looked at himself in the mirror and admired the way the eyeliner made his eyes look bright green. Then he cut his arm and the blood was bright red.

XxX

Matty was angry just like he was every day. It was so hard every day to be him. He wanted to die but he wanted everyone else to die more. Especially his dad. His dad was the worst piece of filth in the entire rotten town. That disgusting pedophile piece of shit was a drunk, and his mother was also a drunk. At night his dad came into his room even though Matty didn't want him to and said no. That was when Matty wanted to die the most even though his dad said it was okay. His mom didn't do anything to help him she just drank and that was the worst part of it sometimes that his mom didn't seem to care. Or she drank so much that she couldn't care about him anymore because it was like her brain was damaged. Her brain was damaged just like Matty.

Matty wished there was some body out there who loved and understood him and didn't want to hurt him. It was the only thing he wanted in the whole world.

XxX

At school Brian tried to get Matty's attention. Their lockers were near each other so he tried waiting at the lockers. He hoped Matty would notice his eyeliner when he saw him in the morning.

'Hey,' he said when he saw Matty. Matty looked so sad and so sexy his blond hair hung over his impossibly blue eyes which were so blue it was like staring into limpid icy pools.

'What do you want?' said Matty. 'You're that Brian kid, I heard you were a real f*g.'

'So what about it,' said Brian and he blushed.

'I hate gays,' said Matty.

340

'Whatever,' said Brian but his eyes burned with painful tears of embarrassment and shame. He ran into the bathroom and locked himself in the stall. He took out a knife that he had brought to school with him and he cut himself. He wanted to die. Then he heard knocking at the door. 'Fuck off.' He said.

'It's me . . . Matty . . . I can see blood . . .' he said. Brian looked down and saw that he was bleeding all over the floor.

'I want to die, go away.'

'I love blood,' said Matty. 'Are you cutting yourself? That's really dark. And really hardcore.' Woah, that was all Brian had wanted to hear. He unlocked the stall door and Matty came inside. There was so much blood on the floor he almost slipped in the blood.

'Sorry I bled so much,' Brian said.

'It's okay,' replied Matty. 'I think that the blood It's really beautiful.'

XxX

Author's note: sorry this chapter is kind of short, but I needed to post as soon as I got them together aaaaa . . . I will try to post again soon.

*

On 30 June 2016 a post titled 'DRAMA: Creeker sets random girl on fire irl, fandom melts down' was uploaded to the DethJournal community 'TCC Wank Report' by user Emperor-Dahmertine. This post is likely what was sent to the hosts of *I Peed on Your Grave*, ultimately triggering public interest in the case.

341

Errrm yeah . . . I'm not getting into graphic detail but Trigger warnings apply. If you read this and get upset take it to therapy not my comments section pls.

So what's important to know here is I'm a) from a small town in north yorkshire in the UK and b) I hang out undercover in creeker spheres on tumblr. you may recognise my handle from my previous reports on creeker wank: 'New McKnight Diary Entries Leaked, Fangirls Scramble to Explain he's NOT a Nazi' and 'Creeker discourse meltdown over BNF[15] "Necrophiles are LGBT" post'.

Basically about a week ago in a town near me three girls set another girl on fire. Local news isnt reporting on it in detail (ie: no perp names just victim). There was one article with names/pics on the post-on-sea but some kind of gag order came through and now the article is inaccessible and there are no screenshots. (EDIT: Screenshot here. We decided to censor names and the face of someone who was falsely arrested to cover us legally. Also a link to the side-by-side of this pic and a selfie from Dee's blog to prove its deff her.)

Through the local social media grapevine it turns out one of the killers' older sisters is a friend of a friend. I look up the girl on facebook and i am not kidding – i recognise this girl from the creeker fandom. I dont want to get in any legal shit and use her name so lets call her Dee for the purpose of this post. I'm able to

15 The phrase 'Big Name Fan' refers to fans with large followings within their fandom communities. Prior to the advent of social media websites like Tumblr and Twitter, Big Name Fans were always fan artists and writers of fanfiction. Now some fans can amass a large following simply through posting about their TV show/book/game/ serial killer of choice.

confirm bc her FB profile pic is a selfie she posted to her blog a couple of months ago.

Dee writes fanfic and posts constantly about 'MATTY' and is a hardcore McCooper[16] shipper.[17] I realise the police haven't found her blog yet so I do what any self-respecting true-crime fan would and go through her blog. I have downloaded all her fanfic (all McCooper lol) and I tried to download her blog but couldn't w/o the login so screen capped as much as i cared to.

again I don't want to get in any legal trouble here so any identifying info has been censored but please enjoy this window into the very stupid mind of a killer:

Screencaps (About page, blog layout, sidebar etc)
Screencaps (choice text posts and reblogs)
Shitty fanfic

The blog has now been deleted but some of it is still viewable on the way back machine. Can't give much more info on the case as everyone involved is a kid, plus there's so much focus on Brexit r/n you'd think there was no other news in the UK atm. But I am 100% sure it's her and the fandom knew something was up too. Screencap of the last 2 posts she made below with timestamp. CW AGAIN please this is obviously very disturbing stuff. I've censored the victim's face but obviously still upsetting.

16 McCooper is the portmanteau ship name for Matthew McKnight and Brian Cooper.
17 A 'ship' refers to a romantic relationship between two (usually fictional) characters. A 'shipper' supports, consumes and sometimes creates content for a 'ship'. For example: I might want Mulder and Scully from the *X Files* to get together. Therefore Mulder/Scully is my 'ship' and I am a Mulder/Scully 'shipper'.

I'm also in a creeker discord server she used to use (I just lurk I don't post) and I've got screencaps/chat logs from there. Plus caps of people figuring out in real time she set someone on fire. Wild stuff.

The content of user Emperor-Dahmertine's post was voyeuristic but insightful. Dolly was deeply embedded into a fandom dedicated to two teen murderers – she'd become a teen murderer herself. For all the other creekers insisted their interest was healthy and harmless – that they did not condone, as their blogs commonly state – this was clear evidence to the contrary. With Joni's murder coming relatively hot on the heels of Tumblr user and true-crime fan Lindsay Souvannarath's failed mass shooting plot against the Halifax Shopping Centre in February of 2015, the creekers melted down.

The last two posts on Dolly's blog were a photograph at 1:46 a.m. and a text post at 5:37. The 1:46 a.m. photograph was captioned 'creating a miniature hell dimension ama', which appeared to show Joni curled up in the corner of a small, dark room, possibly unconscious.

The 5:37 a.m. text post read: 'have you ever done something really bad then you realise you cant take it back but you already did it. going to sleep and hoping this all goes away when I wake up like a nightmare'.

Engagement on these posts was minimal. I find people often refrain from interacting with strange, distressing posts. I remember sorting through my daughter's laptop shortly after she took her own life. I couldn't stop myself from looking at her social media posts.

Frances also had a Tumblr, and despite having a few

thousand followers, the posts she made in the middle of the night expressing extreme distress netted half the engagement her funny jokes and 'outfit of the day' posts did. But those netted even less engagement than a 'callout post' I found linking her to me.

Tumblr user Frances-farmer-420's dad is a fucking gross journalist who hacked dead kids phones. She asks for people to donate to her Kofi and buy shit off her wishlist but her family is rich AF . . . please stop supporting this manipulator, she's gaslighting you all into thinking shes poor and vulnerable when she's not . . .

It had hundreds of 'notes'. Frances reblogged it, adding:

I don't ask my family for money and my MH is really poor r/n so I lost my job. I genuinely need help making rent and I don't condone my dad and barely speak to him. Please delete this????

The shock of finding this digital footprint was gut-wrenching. The fact I'd been tied to something so stressful for her was worse. I realised this 'callout' had been made about a week before Frances's suicide.

Frances's flatmate, Lizzie, found her login details and announced her death on Frances's own blog. Lizzie and Frances had met on Tumblr, then went to the same university. They were friends, but they weren't especially close. They'd drifted apart after graduation but continued to live together – Lizzie was no longer as 'online' as Frances. She had a steady job and a long-term boyfriend. She had been at her boyfriend's flat the night of Frances' suicide.

> Hi this is Fran's flatmate. She killed herself three days ago and I hope you're all happy. <u>Link to a news article if you don't believe me.</u> Congratulations and i hope you got what you wanted.

The original poster of the 'callout' could be found in the replies, begging for forgiveness. I went to their blog, and discovered this 'callout poster' was now being harassed – called out themselves for 'bullying people to suicide'.

For all the people who seemed to be sorry Frances was dead, talking about her on the 'dashboard', sending private 'rest in peace' messages to her blog, few reached out to her when she had posted cries for help in the dead of night.

Those who reached out to Dolly did not seem particularly concerned for her, or the girl in the photograph. Replies ranged from the cynical ('stop larping girl this is cringe') to the actively distressed ('wtf is happening????? This is so scary pls put a trigger warning on this wtf.').

Over the next twenty-four hours, Dolly's mutuals became more and more frantic, with posts like '*Has any one heard from dolly/Cherrybobobomb I'm really freaked out? I know its early in the UK but wtf???*' gained replies like '*I think she knows murderxbuttons irl but she hasn't posted in days this is really weird*'. Something similar happened with Frances too.

Scrolling back in her inbox, I found messages from the day after her suicide: *Hey girl!! Haven't heard from you in a couple of days hope you're doing good.* Then *Fran plz respond to my texts are you online???* then *Fran I don't wanna message Lizzie and worry her but I will* then *Fran please don't make me call the police idek how to call the cops in England.* Then *I'm so sorry I didn't do more to help you.*

These online friends of Frances, of Dolly, they had such intimate access to young women in such extreme states of mind – yet they lacked any real access to them. They could reach out via text. That may have helped Frances – it might have helped Dolly, at one point.

Dolly often posted about how angry and lonely she felt. She posted about boys treating her 'like a cum disposal unit' and often seemed to openly post about suicide. She'd delete these posts quickly – but the ones she managed to relate to Matty and Brian would get good engagement. She'd leave those up.

Posts like: 'im so pissed off rn i just randomly started biting stuff. It is now my headcanon[18] that matty bites stuff when hes angry lol' acquired hundreds of notes. Posts like this were how she amassed most of her small following.

And that following scrambled to find out what had happened to Dolly in the days following the murder. Why had she stopped posting? Were her posts part of some sick new story or prank? Or had she actually done something terrible?

In a private Discord server Dolly had been relatively active

18 From Merriam-Webster: '*Headcanon generally refers to ideas held by fans of series that are not explicitly supported by sanctioned text or other media. Fans maintain the ideas in their heads, outside of the accepted canon.*'

on, her online friends investigated – and Emporer-Dahmertine watched and recorded their chat logs.

Brianlovedpocky: can any1 remember where she was from??

PoppedCherry: She's probably just trying to get attention! Like one of her dumb edgy art projects. Remember when she posted that picture she drew and smeared with her own blood?? Made it seem like she'd slashed her wrists then posted later she just had a fucking nosebleed. She's just a fucking edgelord, I think everyone should calm down!!!!

Snarf: she was from a beach town iirc
Snarf: shut up erica this is serious

PoppedCherry: w/e

Harambevengence: I'm from the UK she was from scarborough or something.

Snarf: not there it was somewhere with a bizarre name

Kai: Same here also in the UK remember! It wasn't scarborough but it was somewhere like that
Kai: blackpool? maybe
Kai: She knew Murderxbuttons didn't she??
Kai: like irl??

Harambevengence: oh i like that blog

Brianlovedpocky: Yeah I think so gimme a minute

Harambevengence: idk tho I think murderxbuttons is at uni

Brianlovedpocky: I found the pic of two of them together

Brianlovedpocky: [a link to one of Dolly's posts, a picture of her with her arm around Violet at the Witch Hammer]

Snarf: ye

Kai: okay its Crow-on-Sea then

Haramevengence: YES THAT WAS IT!!! also lol as if murderxbuttons is like 12 wtf.

Kai: Ikr. Theres only one high school in town we could try ringing it?

Harambevengence: yeah maybe. What would we say though?

Snarf: checked the local paper
Snarf: [pasted a link to a *Post-on-Sea* article titled: '16-Year-Old Girl Brutally Slain By School Friends']

Kai: fuck

PoppedCherry: what the fuuuuuuuuuuck
PoppedCherry: lol I take it back I guess

Harambevengence: this is so fucked up

Snarf: maybe it's not her. No names in the article.

Brianlovedpocky: im gunnathrow up wtft

Harambevengence: Unfortunately the victim had the same hair cut/colour as the girl dolly posted the fucked up torture hell dimension picture of

PoppedCherry: looks like the girl in the pic

Harambevengence: I'd say maybe coincidence but her hair is pretty striking. Red and curly I don't think many people have hair like that.

Brianlovedpocky: imn frekjing the gfick out rn

Snarf: not looking good

Brianlovedpocky: you gusy aim having an opanci attak;

Snarf: not everything is about you skyler please log off if youre just gunna cry type into the chat

Brianlovedpocky: fukc you guys fcujk oFF

Harambevengence: no body post about this on tumblr please in case it's not true

PoppedCherry: AGREED.

Snarf: no way

Kai: obviously not

Harambevengence: Skyler?

Kai: he went offline after he told us to 'fjuk off'

Snarf: 0% chance he won't post about this sorry

PoppedCherry: I just banned him RIP Skyler you were so annoying </3

Kai: ffs you guys
Kai: there's been a lurker in here this whole time

Kai: who tf is @trashtrashtrash make yourself known asap or you're banned

PoppedCherry: Ban hammer coming OUT today

At this point 'Emperor-Dahmertine' lost access to the Discord server. They went to user brianlovedpocky's blog, where he posted:

Cherryb0b0b0mb actualluy fcking killed snomebine im freaking out I jused to talk 2 her all the time fdgyhujik

When other creekers expressed disbelief (and users of the Discord server replied 'delete this skyler you fucking idiot') he posted the link to the *Post-on-Sea* article. While some were reluctant to accept that Dolly had been involved in this murder, most creekers who had seen the picture Dolly posted put two and two together. Someone from their fandom had killed someone. A friend of theirs had killed someone. Someone who'd been nice about their stories or their fanart – someone who'd messaged them happy birthday and who'd consoled them at 3 a.m.

To return to Emperor-Dahmertine's 'TCC Wank Report' post:

They could ban me from lurking on their discord but they could NOT ban me from lurking on tumblr. the next 24 hours were a fucking bloodbath. Nuclear level discourse. Moms threatening to psych-ward, people trying to dial-up a Matthew McKnight fact-kin[19] for his take, people mad that the murderer 'made the fandom look bad.' Weirdest shit I've ever seen in my years down the creekercoal mines.

Weeaboobribri

People posting about dropping out of fandom after this . . . I can feel matty cringing from jail you guys are pathetic. He'd probably be happy for her so grow a fuckin spine. It's like none of you even care about the real matty just the uwu yaoi softboy version of him in your head. Losers.

Vriskadidnothingwrong

Yeah okay watching everyone do mental gymnastics around this . . . you guys really are nuts. I feel dumb for burning bridges w people for being in this fandom. Sorry if you're an old mutual from homestuck or w/e and you've been watching from the sidelines like 'wtf' I now see why its wrong to be in a fandom like this. I'm blocking all the creeker accounts and scrubbing my blog.

Tunneloflove-enjoyer

The way some of you are acting like this is okay or not a big deal it's not fucking okay and it is a big DEAL. People are ALWAYS saying that we're fucking psychos and we have to

19 A factkin is someone who identifies either very strongly *with* or literally *as* another real person. Many factkin appear to be trolls, however 'real' factkin can be found scattered through online fandom spaces. They are closely related to the more common 'fictionkin', who do the same with fictional characters. Both are related to 'otherkin', who identify as something other than human – be that as a wolf, a vampire, or a dragon, etc.

FIGHT to justify our LIVES and now they have PROOF that we're psychos because one selfish BITCH was probably trying to get matty's attention. Fangirls like this make me SICK all we do is study the case and discuss matty and brian in PEACE and now people are going to act like we're the same as HER. Its not fucking FAIR. SHE IS GOING TO FUCKING RUINED EVERYTHING.

Softxxmatty

yikes I think I'm going to delete in 24 hours. My mom was really mad at me when she found out I was a columbiner and if she finds out about this blog/the murder it'll be back to the psych ward :/

togetherfoureverandever

I think before we rush to judge Cherryb0b0b0mb we need to ask: was she being bullied? How was her mental health? Did WE as a community let her down? Y'all claim to be radically empathetic to killers and the mentally ill but none of y'all stopped to think for a minute what else was going on in her life. All you care about is your little fanfics and Tumblr followers and getting in trouble from your parents. Y'all make me sick.

Scout-and-the-system

Hey, a couple of people have contacted me (this is Scout) to comment on this situation because of the Matthew McKnight factive in my system. He's refusing to front right now I guess because he's taking the news pretty hard. I think he's upset that someone would make our fandom look bad like this.

353

Starsinthemcknight

I knew cherryb0b0b0mb and she was really nice. we were mutuals for years and she went through a lot of shit you guys will never understand. Fact of the matter is is that I believe she would not hurt someone unless pushed to do so. I think it's very likely this so called 'victim' bullied her and deserved it. Its cr*zy to me that you could be in this fandom and not instinctively understand that hurt people hurt people and that often their 'victims' are not victims at all but deserving ab*sers. I wouldn't judge someone for killing their ab*ser so it really upsets me that some of you would say that you think it was bad that she did this without knowing the facts. really disgusting that so many of you are out here potentially supporting an ab*ser.

*

At 10 a.m. on 9 May 2006, Matthew McKnight and Brian Cooper walked into their Montana high school with a pair of loaded semi-automatic rifles. They were seventeen years old.

McKnight had slept over at Cooper's house the night before the massacre. They murdered Brian's parents that morning, making Michael (40) and Katherine Cooper (38) the first of their seven victims. The boys shot Michael and Katherine in their bed sometime between 5 and 6.30 a.m. They used a handgun Michael kept in a shoebox under the bed. Katherine didn't know it was there – but Brian did. It was his dad's 'emergency gun'.

Brian and Matthew had been planning on killing Sally Cooper (12) too. But Brian's little sister was spared by a

354

last-minute sleepover at her cousin's house. The final entry in McKnight's extensive diaries read:

At Brian's now preparing for D-day tomorrow. He is trying to get out of doing mommy and daddy but he knows he has to for all this to go down. Brian's bitch sister is sleeping at her cousin's place tonight. Surviving by a cunt hair. If she has to come home and shes here tomorrow morning I'll do her first.

Michael Cooper was a keen hunter and collector of guns; he was also a paediatrician and member of the Democratic Party. He was chapter president of the local branch of the NRA and campaigned to repeal capital punishment as hard as he did for the relaxation of gun laws.

He was a contrarian and a libertarian – in his early twenties he played in a grunge band and called himself an anarchist. Katherine was a good girl who'd had a crush on Michael since high school. She was shy. Michael's personality was overpowering, and she sank into his shadow. She worked menial jobs and carried and raised their children (with help from their parents) while he went through medical school.

She loved Michael, but she didn't like the guns. They were locked away in the basement with a key Michael kept in his bedside table.

Dolly wrote on her blog about the boy's parents. She often speculated (she was sure, in fact) that McKnight's parents were abusive – but she also identified similarities between her own parents and Brian Cooper's.

I know a lot of you are mike and kathy stans but their dynamic
is off to me tbh sorry. Y'all know I'm more of a matty than a
brian but tbh sometimes brian's mom and dad remind me
of my parents. I think the way brains mom just threw her life
away for their dad is really sad. I get he was the big man about
town (lol) and everyone loved him but it reminds me of how
my mum basically flushed her life to be with my dad and how
obsessed with him she was. They broke up when I was a kid
but still idk, reading about mike and Kathy makes me think of
them. My parents relationship was kind of fucked so I wouldn't
be surprised if theirs was too.

After murdering Michael and Kathy, Brian took the key
to his father's arsenal downstairs. They took a pair of semi-
automatic rifles and stored them in a sports bag, lined with
towels. Matthew took possession of the 'emergency gun',
storing it in the front of his jeans – the way he'd seen people
do it in movies and on television. He pulled his shirt over
the gun.

At 7:30 Brian called in sick to his father's office. He did
not pose as his father and told Michael's secretary that the
entire family was sick with severe food poisoning and his
father was too sick to make the call himself. Katherine was a
homemaker. While she was a busy volunteer at church and a
local horse sanctuary, Katherine was not expected anywhere
that day and did not need to be covered for.

Brian used his father's phone to text the secretary, asking
her to call in sick to school on behalf of the boys. Brian then
used his father's phone to text Matthew's mother:

7:44

Hey Amy hope you're well. We got Chinese food for the boys last night and were all laid up with food poisoning including matty. I called the school. Come pick him up when you get the chance but please don't rush or leave work early. I don't know if anybody is leaving the bathrooms any time soon.

Amy McKnight (the owner of a small arts and crafts supply store) replied at 8:00.

Oh no! Hope you guys aren't too sick. I'll be over as soon as my part-timer gets here. Thanks for calling the school, I will call too.

Amy was friendly with Michael Cooper. Their brothers had been close in high school. She called the school to confirm Michael's story. Amy would discover Michael and Kathy's bodies at around 10 a.m., missing the boys by forty-five minutes. The Coopers left a key under a flowerpot in their front porch, which she used to let herself into their home. She called 911: when Amy told the dispatcher there'd been a shooting in Cherry Creek, he replied, 'Another one?'

There'd been no discussion as to whether Amy McKnight should die. When Brian suggested they kill Matthew's parents too, Matthew acted as if this was a stupid suggestion. From his diary:

He said should we kill Amy and Nick too? So stupid. My parents are total losers and nobodies. What do my mom and dad have to do with shit? Nobody cares about my mom's craft store and my dad just drives a truck. My dad is gunna be in fucking Canada on D-day any way. But everybody loooooooves Kathy and Mike. Everyone will go <u>NUTS</u> if we ice mike especially.

This framing of his parents as 'losers and nobodies' was exaggerated. Amy and Nick McKnight were popular and well-loved in their small community. Matthew's relationship with his father was as strained as you might expect, being that Matthew was a moody teen and Nick was an oft-absent long-distance trucker. But Matty was unusually devoted to his mother.

This was something Dolly got into frequent arguments about with other creekers. She didn't tend to engage with 'drama' much on her blog (she was self-righteous about it) but she would argue in the comments section of her fanfics.

An example exchange below:

Fenrisbinch43

Hey I like this fic but idk if I agree with you characterising amy and nick as abusers. everyone knows matty is a total mommas boy and it really jars with me honestly. Not trying to be rude but wondering if you've read Massacre At Cherry Creek by A. J. Rossi bc that makes it pretty clear.

Cherryb0b0b0mb

Lol please leave your flame reviews elsewhere. Obviously I've read MaCC but Rossi is a total hack. I have a real empathetic connection with Matty which is basically psychic and goes beyond what Rossi and her agender have to say. Amy

McKnight gave her matty's diaries (if you didn't know that fyi)
so Rossi has to be nice about the McKnights. Btw I think giving
up his diaries was a disgusting invasion of matty's privacy and
abuser behaviour. You can tell if you read between the lines in
his diary entries what amy and nick were really like to him and
how they mistreated matty and drove him to the edge.

Fenrisbinch43
What is your evidence for that sorry? Really not trying to flame
review you but your interpretation is bizarre to me

Cherryb0b0b0mb
In his APRIL 12 entry Matty says: 'dad is gone again, wish
he'd never come back.' Why wouldn't he want his dad to come
back unless his dad was an abuser. Also on March 9 enry he
says 'Mom being drunk and annoying tonight' sorry but march
9 2006 was a Thursday what kind of good mom is drunk on a
THURSDAY

Fenrisbinch43
Okay whatever but just so you know in RPF[20] it's really
disrespectful to say stuff like that. These people aren't fictional
characters you can't just make up headcanons about them. In
most RPF communities we don't tolerate that kind of thing jsyk
maybe creekers are different. I've heard this fandom is toxic
so thanks for confirming that.

20 Real Person Fiction.

Cherryb0b0b0mb

Get off your high horse bitch youre literally reading school shooter fanfic.

After organising their excuses, and before Amy McKnight arrived, the boys ate breakfast together. They ate sugary cereal which turned the milk blue; Brian wasn't usually allowed to have it. It was a cereal saved for special occasions: his birthday, or the morning of big tests. They watched episodes of *South Park* on DVD and remarked on the irony: Trey Parker and Matt Stone had attended Columbine High School. Matthew and Brian were both obsessed with the Columbine massacre.

They exited the Cooper home at 9:15 a.m.

It would've taken McKnight and Cooper two hours to walk to Cherry Creek High School, so they took Michael Cooper's jeep. Neither of the boys had a driver's licence, but Brian had been taking lessons.

The roads were wide, and clear. This thirty-minute drive from the Cooper household to the high school is referred to, in fandom, as 'the tunnel of love drive', because the road connecting the Coopers' house to the high school was known locally as 'the tunnel of love': densely planted cherry trees either side of the road made an archway, a tunnel. In spring it was dramatic and beautiful. Dolly made much of the drive in *Cherry Lips, Black Eyes*. From Chapter 11:

They drove through the tunnel of love. Brian always imagined driving through this one day with someone he loved and the day was finally here. He still had his mom's blood under his finger nails. This moment was so sad and so beautiful. He knew nothing would ever be the same again but that him and Matty would be bonded together forever in history and in life and in death.

'Do you think they let people in love share prison cells?' he asked.

'What?' said matty back.

'Nothing.'

'Did you mean us? When you said that?'

'Maybe . . . I don't know. Is it okay?'

And it took a really long time for Matty to say anything back. Brian was scared he'd ruined the whole moment and the whole day. He was scared it wasn't going to be D-day any more because he couldn't keep his mouth shut. But then matty stopped the car.

'I love you too Brain.' He said. And then they kissed under the cherry trees. Pink blossom got on the car and it was beautiful.

A thousand versions of this scene have been written and rewritten by creekers over the years. A confession of love in the ride to the school seems to be an accepted piece of the story for fans. Dolly even once posted to her blog:

Sorry asdfghjkl did they actually kiss in the car?? Bc it seems like we all think they did and I'm just wondering if that comes from something somewhere? Whatever as far as im concerned they did asdfghjkl lmao

They arrived at the school at 9:47. They can be seen pulling into the car park on the school's CCTV system, and sitting

361

there for approximately ten minutes before exiting the vehicle and collecting their duffel bags from the trunk.

The ten-minute conversation between arriving at the school and entering it is also a popular topic of discussion and exploration for fans. Some save the confession of love for here; some have one of the boys (usually Brian) lose his mettle and beg to hand themselves into the police, while the other (usually Matthew) convinces him to go ahead with it. In *Cherry Lips, Black Eyes*, Dolly skips over this standard point of conflict. In her story, both boys are excited, vengeful, and raring to go.

First period at Cherry Creek High would let out with a bell-ring at 10:15. At 10:01 Matthew and Brian entered the school and walked together to Matthew's English class. They spent the walk shedding their duffel bags and the towels swaddling their weapons. They slung the guns over their shoulders with long, matching straps.

At 10:07 they entered the classroom.

Macey Rivers (33), Matthew's English teacher, was killed first. She was standing at the front of the classroom, cleaning the whiteboard with her back to the door. Matthew opened fire, spraying bullets wildly, hitting Macey in the back of the head.

While Brian kicked the door closed and fumbled with his gun (Matthew later said that Brian was supposed to barricade the door), Matthew shot at two students he had intentionally targeted.

Jenna Morgan (17) had laughed in Matthew's face when he'd asked her on a date two years prior to the massacre. She had a boyfriend already – everyone knew it. She'd thought

Matthew had been joking. She took a bullet to the shoulder and was smart enough to play dead. She went limp and rolled her eyes to the back of her head, lolling her tongue from her mouth. This performance would save her life.

The fandom was not kind to Jenna Morgan. As a survivor, she was fair game. She was the villain in their stories – a normie bitch who would've seen what a kind, sensitive soul their beloved Matty was, if she'd given him a chance. The existence of her boyfriend is often written out of these stories – she's not confused about being asked out, she's a malicious, nasty bitch who thinks she's too good for Matty.

Dolly particularly disliked Jenna Morgan. She would often make references to the idea of 'a Jenna', using the term the way incels might use the term 'Stacy' – a 'Jenna' was a pretty, popular girl who thought she was better than everyone else. She was hyper-feminine, and probably a bully.

Pfffff theres a girl in my year whose a total Jenna I wont say her name but she's gross just imagine jenna. any way I've been texting her bf and I tHINK I'm gunna kiss him in front of her at this party tonight?? Gunna imagine matthew fucking w real jenna while I fuck w this fake jenna hehehehe.

Next, Matthew shot Kareem Foreman (16). Matthew shot Kareem (the only Black student in his grade) because Matthew is a racist. The creekers like to gloss over this victim choice and ignore the diary entries where McKnight scrawled swastikas and racial slurs over his own racist cartoons.

Sometimes they frame Kareem as a bully and a jock when Kareem was (by all accounts) a good-natured geek. He had good grades: he was particularly strong in English and History. He was a big boy but not very athletic. Now and again, peers and gym teachers would try to bully him into playing football, only to find him timid and slow on the field. The creekers make him a football player in their stories anyway. Dolly usually ignored him in her stories and her posts – she ignored all aspects of this story which clashed with her mental image of Matty. But the other creekers – the ones who acknowledge his presence – draw Kareem in a letterman jacket and write him as a douchey athlete. Sometimes he is Jenna's boyfriend.

He didn't know Jenna. He was too gentle for football. He was dead at sixteen because Matthew McKnight shot him in the neck at point-blank range. He didn't have a hope of survival.

Matthew intended to shoot a student named Sam Mackintosh (known to his peers as Smack or Smacky). From Matthew's diaries:

I think I'd also like to shoot a fatty. I'm fucking sick of staring at smacky's neck fat in English. He thinks we are friends? I think he's better off with a bullet in his skull before the diabeetus gets him.

What saved Sam's life was the poorly timed re-entry of Becky Little (17) to the classroom at 10:11. She'd been to the bathroom, almost passing Brian and Matthew on her way there. It is not clear why she entered the classroom. It is presumed she did not hear the gunshots and mistook the sounds of chaos after the shootings for the sound of people packing up for the next period.

She opened the door of her English class and stepped into hell.

Brian shot her in the face. Tate Carey, a ninth-grader, was also on his way back from the bathroom. He heard the shot and saw Becky's body flop back into the hallway. He pulled the fire alarm and ran. Students began filing into the hall-ways, running back into their classrooms and toward the nearest fire exits at the sight of Becky's body in the hall.

McKnight and Cooper ran for the library. This was their plan B – if they got caught, if someone pulled the alarm, they'd run to the library and barricade themselves in.

It was nearby, just a short run. They pulled down a large bookshelf, and threw desks and chairs and tables on top of it.

James Garrett (13) was collecting a book for a Geography project – he was going to give a presentation on the Gobi Desert. He didn't leave the library as soon as the alarm was pulled – assuming this was a fire drill, he'd gone to grab his bag. He saw the barricade, but he didn't see Matthew and Brian's guns. He asked: 'Is this just a drill?'

It was not. Matthew shot the boy in the chest. James would die three days later in hospital. Matthew found Ethel Malloy (64), the school's librarian, hiding behind her desk a few minutes after James was shot. He shot her with the handgun, pressing the barrel to her forehead.

Brian, meanwhile, discovered Taylor Schwartz (15) and Jessica Spicer (18) hiding in a stationery cupboard. Taylor been grabbing a new stapler for her Maths teacher, Jessica had dropped her car keys in the library that morning and was looking for them. They hid together when the boys entered the library.

They begged Brian for their lives when he found them. Taylor would tell the media later that Brian whispered to them: 'I have to make it look like I killed you both. I have to shoot you guys. I'm really sorry. I'll try not to kill you but you have to make it look like I did.'

Jessica rushed Brian. She tried to grab the gun. Brian shot her in the chest and neck during the struggle, then shot Taylor in the abdomen. Taylor survived with permanent damage to her spine – Jessica did not. She was their final victim.

Here we have Brian's identity in the fandom solidified. Merciful, reluctant, enthralled by Matthew. Misunderstood, repentant, lovestruck and terrified. Matthew was the tempest, the tortured mastermind, the Byronic anti-hero, the 'dark-fuck-prince of Montana'.

Jessica and Taylor were shot at approximately 10:30 a.m., and Brian Cooper was dead by his own hand by 11 a.m. According to Matthew, Brian wanted out early. The plan was to get arrested; to go to prison, and influence and inspire together. To write to their followers, to publish manifestos. To embrace chaos and to promote the darkness. Much like Dolly's, Matthew's ideology is incoherent.

They weren't supposed to take the easy way out like Harris and Klebold – whom they alternated between worshipping and mocking – they were going to live to see what they could inspire.

They were supposed to take out as many people as they could, maybe take a hostage (a role filled by Taylor when McKnight realised she was still alive), wait it out for a few hours, then calmly surrender to the police.

But Brian couldn't cope with the weight of what he had

done. He couldn't cope with the guilt or the oncoming consequences. He wanted to die. His automatic rifle was out of bullets, so he fought with Matthew over his father's emergency handgun. Matthew, allegedly, tried to talk him down 'calmly'. Taylor Schwartz recalled them arguing, screaming at each other. But she admits she was only half-conscious and may not be a reliable source.

Matthew – who was ultimately smaller and not as strong as Brian – lost the gun. Brian shot himself in the head and died instantly.

Here the story is muddied: rumours of Matthew undertaking necrophilic activity with Brian's corpse abound; in part, thanks to Matthew McKnight. During his trial, while recounting Brian's suicide, he announced: 'Then I fucked his corpse and I'd fuck it again.' During Taylor Schwartz's witness statement she said it was possible Matthew engaged in sexual activity with the corpse. From the court transcripts:

MS SCHWARTZ: I was pretending to be dead, but I could see through a gap, like an opening, in the closet door. I heard the gunshot and I heard Matthew scream. And I heard weird noises after that, like dragging. I looked out of the closet and I saw Matthew um . . . rolling around on the corpse. I think he was trying to get blood all over him. I don't know.

MR MOODY: Was it possible McKnight was engaging in sexual intercourse with Cooper's body?

MS HOFFMAN: Objection, relevance.

THE COURT: Overruled.

MS SCHWARTZ: I guess it's possible, yeah. Whatever he was doing it was weird.

Matthew also alluded to 'corpse fucking' several times in his diaries and during the trial. The diaries seemed to contain genuine necrophilic sexual fantasies; the statements during the trial seemed intended to shock.

The fact that McKnight may have engaged in sexual intercourse with Brian Cooper's body is an important part of the fan lore around the case. There may have been no 'creeker' fandom without this. The creeker fandom first emerged when an old clip from Matthew McKnight's sentencing went viral.

While being led from the courtroom, he shouted: 'The hand that killed your children jacks me off to the memory of their pain and suffering; just like the way God jacked off to my pain and suffering.' In the clip, his hair has grown long and lank. He is unshaven, but too young and fair-haired to have any significant stubble. His cheeks are flecked with freckles, and small purple acne scars.

This caught the attention of the true-crime fandom at first – particularly the 'Columbiner' subsection of it. What really elevated the creekers to a fully fledged fandom of their own was when Tumblr users collectively discovered that McKnight had a male partner in crime and that he may have engaged in sexual activity with that partner's corpse.

A. J. Rossi's previously overlooked book *Massacre at Cherry Creek* gained a significant sales bump – heading up to number three in Amazon's true-crime chart.

It seems Dolly discovered the fandom around when she moved to Crow-on-Sea. Prior to her discovery of the creeker fandom, she had a bog-standard edgy Tumblr. It was full of creepy aesthetic posts – ghostly faces in static televisions, pictures of other people's self-harm, pro-ana[21] images and edgy jokes. She dipped her toe into the true-crime fandom – then apparently got into the Cherry Creek fandom when an online friend of hers began posting about the massacre.

Her rebrand was swift and all-consuming. While Dolly was not as heavy a Tumblr user as either Angelica or Violet, she posted at least a few times per day and almost always about Cherry Creek.

Increasingly, she seemed to identify with Matthew McKnight. At first, she posted only about the broad strokes of their personalities. They seemed to share explosive tempers as well as teenaged nihilism and ennui. She wrote:

In matty's diary he says he feels like nothing good is ever going to happen to him. He said that he felt like everyone hated him and was laughing at him and that he got mad and they laughed at him more and he couldn't control himself. I just started crying because it was like he was writing about my life. I felt like his hand was coming out of the page to touch mine. I really felt it.

She wanted to write to him in prison, but couldn't work out how. This is when she started to write fanfiction about him and Brian Cooper. She thought that writing 'self-insert' fanfiction was embarrassing and didn't want to think about McKnight with other girls – so Brian was the perfect vessel for that.

---

21 Images which promote and encourage disordered eating, particularly anorexia.

Even though Dolly tried to identify more with Matthew, Brian seemed to become her self-insert in her fanfiction. Her version of Matty was ultimately a romanticised version of herself: the person she thought she was, and whom she wished to be. Her version of Brian perhaps made up a more realistic portrait of Dolly – in her stories he was magnetic, wrathful and charismatic but he was also scared, lonely and easily led.

She used to pick apart the small ways that she and Matty were similar and post about them. She found an old photograph of Matthew McKnight in an orange cap and a grey T-shirt – then found a picture of herself in an orange cap and a grey T-shirt at about the same age. She posted the pictures side by side, simply captioned: *wow*.

Then she began to post about how she felt Matthew's presence, that sometimes she felt she was able to psychically reach out to him, and that he was reaching back. '*Some days I feel like Matty and I are two halves of a whole,*' she wrote. '*I really feel like our souls are the same. We are both children of chaos and ruin. We are rage.*'

In reality, Matthew McKnight and Dolly Hart were nothing alike.

Matthew McKnight's stable, middle-class family were supportive and caring – Dolly's home life was chaotic and fractured. McKnight's behaviour changed dramatically at the age of twelve when he sustained a serious head injury – Dolly had no such incident in her past.

While Dolly had anger management issues, they were not as prolonged or severe as McKnight's. Matthew McKnight was extremely racist and had seemingly been radicalised online by his heavy use of shock sites and imageboards like

4Chan. He also consumed huge amounts of extreme pornography. The only websites Dolly seemed to frequently use were DethJournal, Tumblr and *Neopets*. Even though she was prone to bouts of rage and cruelty in her day-to-day life, Dolly's writing reveals a personality which is romantic and empathetic to the point of delusion. McKnight was harsh, narcissistic and sadistic.

The idea that McKnight and Dolly were in some way kindred spirits was sheer fantasy. The version of Matty in Dolly's head was a lost soul and an abuse victim who had reclaimed his power through an act of extreme violence. The real Matthew McKnight was a violent, sexually sadistic neo-Nazi.

It is one thing to identify with a killer – strange, but I feel not out of the sphere of ordinary behaviour for teenagers, even when taken to the extreme of imagining yourself and this killer as two halves of a whole. Teenagers can be extremely strange, especially as they experiment with the boundaries around societal norms.

But it is entirely another to become so wrapped up in your fantastical relationship with a killer that you follow in his footsteps and commit an unspeakable act.

In the 1961 book *Man, Play and Games*, French sociologist Roger Caillois defines 'play' as an act which is '(1) free, (2) separate, (3) uncertain, (4) unproductive, (5) regulated, and (6) fictive'. Play is something which can be corrupted: 'any contamination by ordinary life runs the risk of corrupting and destroying its very nature'. The boundaries between real life and play are blurred, and the purity of the act of play is corrupted by the mundanity of everyday life. It ceases to be play.

Japanese sociologist Ikuya Sato built on this in his 1991 book *Kamikaze Biker*, in which he examines the behaviour of Japan's delinquent youth – specifically within the '*bōsōzoku*' biker subculture.

Essentially he posits that these youthful delinquents begin their careers merely playing at delinquency. They play the role of the violent biker – but, as Sato says: 'The playlike definitions of the situation, however, cannot entirely keep playlike action from becoming serious'. That is – that the biker who 'plays' as the kind of a boy who might rob a stranger at knifepoint may find himself one day actually robbing a stranger at knifepoint.

'Action often produces deep enjoyment, especially when it approaches the pole of serious action and creates a truly engrossing alternative reality.' Consider Dolly's summoning circles – the thrill of conducting invented rituals with friends, of staying out late and breaking into an amusement park; the appeal of choosing to believe that one has the power to manifest consequences for one's enemies, or an evil force.

'In such a case the corruption of play and irrevocable consequences often ensue.'

Dolly's family were the most difficult to locate, and for good reason.

I asked around Crow, but few people knew the family. The people at their church who'd known them wouldn't speak to me.

I left Crow-on-Sea shortly before lockdown began, and after months and months of internet sleuthing, I could not find a trace of Dolly's mother. She and her husband had left Crow-on-Sea, and are completely off the grid.

I could not find them myself and used some of my old contacts (not all of them entirely savoury) to attempt to reach them. The only contact who found anything said his leads dried up instantly and that she must have left the country. All he could offer me was the old work address of Dolly's half-sister Heather.[22]

She had no social media presence and used a new last name, something she'd made up completely, alongside her (common) middle name.

Via her old place of work, I was able to discover her new place of work. Heather was a hairdresser – in the summer of 2020, when some services had begun to reopen, I went to the salon that had previously employed her. I pretended to be the husband of an old customer who loved her and asked if I could book my fictional wife in with her as a birthday gift. Her former colleagues cheerfully directed me to her new employer – they were extremely helpful (and a GDPR nightmare).

22 Editor's note: All allusions to 'Heather's' employer, real name or location have been removed or anonymised for legal reasons.

She called me a creep when I found her, and I felt like one. I was, ultimately, a strange middle-aged man attempting to track down a girl in her mid-twenties – weird behaviour, regardless of my motivations.

And perhaps I should've left her alone. But I needed to speak to someone from 'Dolly's camp' and Heather was one of the stand-out figures from the trial.

The trial was short. We knew who was responsible for Joan Wilson's murder – it was only the degree of criminal responsibility for each perpetrator that was up for debate. Heather spoke on her sister's behalf, insisting that Dolly's father had sexually abused her. Heather claimed she had witnessed the abuse – then scaled her claim back. She had witnessed Dolly's father entering and exiting Dolly's bedroom at night on numerous occasions throughout the years, beginning when Dolly was eight years old.

Dolly denied everything. Even though this was exactly the kind of extenuating circumstance she'd benefit from being heard – she denied it. In front of a judge, going against the advice of her lawyer, she called her sister a liar.

Dolly's personal history seemed like an important piece of the puzzle – and it was a piece I was currently missing.

It took several weeks for Heather to agree to speak to me. Unfortunately, I had to be quite persistent. Eventually she agreed to be interviewed on the condition that I never contacted her again.

I met her at a hotel on a sticky summer day.

Heather is three years older than Dolly and cut a glamorous figure. She worked at a glitzy salon and looked a lot like her sister, but her hair was straight, and bleached blonde.

Her upper lip was swollen with filler. She met me in a full face of makeup, including fake eyelashes, despite her intense dislike of me.

As we spoke, she continually looked over her shoulder, as if she was afraid we were being watched or listened to.

I explained where I was at with my project. By this point I had spoken directly to the victim's mother, to the perpetrators and to their parents. I had spoken to teachers and friends, and even to Dolly's ex-girlfriend. I had pored through Dolly's blog, I had read her fanfiction – but she remained a very mysterious figure.

'She always was a bit of a mystery,' said Heather. 'I'm not going to pretend I'm an expert when I'm not.'

She and Dolly were never close. Never really friends, and barely sisters at times. They were divided by their wildly different temperaments and interests – and by their different fathers. To avoid confusion I will be referring to Heather's biological father as Mr Smith and Dolly's biological father as Mr Hart.

Mr Smith and their mother were high-school sweethearts. Their mother was a party girl; Mr Smith was straight-laced and religious from a young age. Their mother became pregnant with Heather while they were both in their early twenties but she did not want to marry Mr Smith, which caused a huge crack in their relationship. They broke up soon after Heather's birth.

When Heather was born, their mother did not cease being a party girl. Heather spent a lot of time with her father and her maternal grandmother during the early years of her life. Her mother worked and maintained an active social life

– when Heather was two, her mother met Mr Hart.

Mr Hart was a DJ; he was fun and charismatic and their mother quickly moved in with him and fell pregnant with Dolly. They married within weeks of discovering the pregnancy.

'But your mum got back together with your dad?'

'You're jumping ahead quite a bit – but yeah. I know it's a bit complicated, but that's who we were living with when it all happened, the murder. So Dolly's dad was my stepdad, then my dad was Dolly's stepdad,' Heather said.

'And . . . what was your relationship like with him? Er . . . with Dolly's dad, I mean.'

'Well . . . he didn't abuse me, if that's what you're asking. I think he was only interested in Dolly. Maybe because he had more control over her, I don't know,' Heather said. I opened my mouth and she immediately snapped, 'I know you're going to ask how I know. Well I just know. I always thought it was weird – him going in and out of her room at night. I saw him, and he knew I saw him. And I never said anything, because I didn't know what he was doing in there. Well, I'm just saying, I seriously doubt she would've done that if something awful wasn't happening to her behind closed doors, do you know what I mean?' She threw back a cocktail and clenched her fists. 'It just makes me so angry that people who weren't even there try and tell me what I saw. I know what I fucking saw.'

I asked Heather to calm down – I told her I was not here to judge. I was not here to call her a liar, only to hear her account. I asked again if she could tell me about Dolly's father.

At first, Mr Hart was all fun and games. The cool, fun stepdad. He and her mum were always at parties and always on nights out – which was fine for Heather and Dolly. They were babysat by a cool, teenaged cousin who let them stay up late and eat sweets.

Their mother adored him. She was obsessed with him, in fact. Heather simply understood, as a child, that Mr Hart was her priority, not the children. She thought that was normal, in fact.

But, as Dolly and Heather grew older, so did their parents – and the party began to go sour. Mr Hart got a day job: he left DJing behind, and became a police officer. He found the job extremely stressful and drank to cope with it. Their mother, who had always been something of a problem drinker, drank to cope with Mr Hart.

'He was never physically violent, but he was a fucking nightmare. Tightly wound, always moments off shouting at you. He was only cheerful when he was drinking, and that never lasted. He used to get in these screaming arguments with Mum when she went out with her friends, because he basically couldn't go out at all anymore with his work. It was fucking horrible. I started spending more time at my dad's, and he was trying to get full custody of me. And Mum also started spending more time with my dad. She was coming back and forth to pick me up all the time, and they started spending loads of time together again. To be honest, I think they started having an affair.'

After a couple more years of misery in the Hart household, disaster struck. Mr Hart was sacked for gross misconduct.

'I don't know what he did exactly,' said Heather. 'I just remember my mum screaming, "What do you mean, gross misconduct?" at him, and then telling me to go to my room.'

Heather thinks this is when the abuse started – this is when she remembers Mr Hart going in and out of Dolly's room at night. His drinking also got much worse; Heather once walked into the living room before school to find him covered in vomit on the sofa.

Seeing her husband at rock-bottom seemed to inspire their mother to clean up her act. She stopped drinking and started going to AA. Things improved for a bit – their mum was more stable, and more present – but Mr Hart became furious with her.

'I think he was jealous. He couldn't kick the habit, and he felt like Mum was lording her sobriety over him. She chucked all the booze in the house, and they had this horrible argument where . . . he actually did hit her. And then she took me and Dolly to Grandma's for a bit. And – again, I don't know all the details, because I was just a kid – he actually got himself sorted, and tried to get her to come back to him. But then she told me and Dolly that she was going to go and live with my dad for a bit.'

Dolly was a daddy's girl. She'd always had a combative relationship with their mother – even as a toddler. She would kick and scream at Mummy, then burble and coo for Daddy. Dolly was enraged at the prospect of the move. 'But we live with *my* daddy,' she said, sounding younger than her ten years.

'Originally, we all moved in with my dad. He didn't live that far away – about a half an hour drive. We didn't even move schools and my dad's house was bigger and much nicer. But Dolly would not stop fighting with Mum about it. She wanted to go back to her dad's – when she was visiting him at the weekend, she used to kick off about having to come back.

378

She was really, really difficult. These long, horrible tantrums where she'd be up half the night screaming. It was absolutely deranged. She was like the girl from the fucking *Exorcist* – you'd think she'd been taken away from fucking . . . Tom Hanks, rather than some nasty, alcoholic nonce.'

So they swapped arrangements: Dolly would stay at her dad's during the week, then at Mr Smith's during the weekend.

'She did hate coming to church with us so that was a bit of a bone of contention – she'd still kick off about that. I mean, I didn't really like going to church either, but Mum had got so into it when she got back with my dad – I didn't want to hurt her feelings. Dolly didn't give a shit though. The church really wasn't that bad. Dolly used to make it sound like they were fire-and-brimstone Catholics or Baptists or something. But it was all very limp, very C of E.'

Dolly was often very huffy and pouty with their mum, outside of her forced church attendance. Heather once got Dolly to admit she was in a huff because 'my daddy said that Mum called me stupid behind my back. My daddy said that Mum says all sorts of nasty things about me.'

'He was always a liar, you know,' Heather said. 'When I was little I believed him. He used to say things like that to me, sometimes, to get me on his side. But he wasn't my dad – he was just . . . By the time I was ten, he was just this horrible man who shouted at me. So I told my mum and she explained he was like . . . well that she'd never say anything like that about me, and tried to make out like it was just a nasty joke, not this mad manipulation tactic.'

Heather tried to explain to Dolly that this wasn't true

– that Mr Hart was being horrible. But Dolly didn't believe her. 'My daddy doesn't tell lies.'

'He would lie to us about stupid stuff as well, you know,' she said. 'Not just serious stuff. He'd make up stupid shit, just for fun.'

When Dolly was living with Mr Hart, Dolly once asked Heather if she'd ever seen a horse fly. Not a horsefly but a horse fly, because Mr Hart had told Dolly, in great detail, that horses and zebras and donkeys could all fly. They had small wings, which folded back into their spines when not in use. It was a rare behaviour – they didn't fly very often now, because they'd mostly evolved to walk on the ground.

When Heather said this wasn't true, and that Mr Hart was just winding her up, Dolly didn't believe her. Even after them sitting together and reading the Wikipedia pages for horses, donkeys and zebras, Dolly still didn't believe Heather.

I asked if Dolly displayed any other concerning behaviour during this period of time. And Heather said yes, she did think Dolly got gradually weirder as the months passed. Heather had no way of knowing what was going on at Mr Hart's house – and her mum seemed to bury her head in the sand.

'But she was odd, yeah. I think . . . I know most kids are a bit odd. And maybe I'm reading too much into it now, after everything. But she was really weird, sometimes.'

Dolly seemed to live in her own little world, at times. She had lots of small dolls, and dollhouses, which would come with her everywhere.

'She liked Sylvanian Family-type things. And she always used to bring them to ours from her dad's. She would bring loads of little animals and sometimes a little plastic dollhouse – if she was allowed, which she usually was because her dad never told her off for anything.'

'No Barbies, then?'

'No. But she did love Polly Pocket.'

When Dolly was purchased Barbie dolls, she would generally damage them. She would cut their hair or throw them down the stairs – Heather recalls Dolly microwaving a doll a well-meaning aunt bought her for her birthday. They were too big and too real. Large, human dolls had no place in Dolly's tiny little universe.

The smaller her toys were, the better. She amassed a large collection of Polly Pockets and used to talk about going to Pocket Land. She would take her little Polly Pocket sets and lie with them under her bed. She would pretend she was in Pocket Land and that she was also very small, and in her own little set. Heather said if you hadn't seen Dolly in a few hours, you could generally find her under her bed, whispering to her Polly Pockets, or her little animal dolls.

When distressed, Dolly would often climb into small, dark spaces and close her eyes. You could find her under tables or in cupboards and wardrobes. She would sit in there with her eyes shut, whispering to herself – presumably pretending to be very, very small. Heather also recalls that Dolly was obsessed with the Borrowers, and Terry Pratchett's *Nome* trilogy. When Dolly was little, it was a quirk. But in high school she was still having trouble letting go of 'Pocket Land'. When her father died, Dolly moved with all her Polly Pocket toys, and continued to play with them even when they moved to Crow.

Heather also remembered that Dolly's games with her animal families had long, strange storylines – which became creepier after her father's death. If Pocket Land was a place of comfort for Dolly, the animal families were where she acted out her distress. An animal family who seemed particularly to suffer in Dolly's pretend worlds was a group of six frogs. One large frog, Daddy Frog, and his daughters – who all wore tiny little dresses. Except for when they didn't. Heather was unaware of the details of the frog family's tribulations, but the baby frogs could often be found naked, floating in small cups of water, trapped under glasses or being poked with little pins.

Not because the little frogs had been bad by Dolly's judgement – Dolly was merely acting on the will of Daddy Frog. When Heather asked why Dolly didn't stop Daddy Frog, she cried and said she didn't know. Heather found it disturbing and stopped asking Dolly about the frogs.

But Dolly made comments about the frogs, nonetheless. She would smirk at dinner time – when asked 'What are you smiling at?' She'd say: it was something the frogs said. Something Daddy Frog did. An idea she had for the frogs.

'Was there anything leading up to his suicide? Anything Dolly did or said that stuck out, anything that you can remember?' I asked.

'No. I think he told her not to tell us anything. I think he made it seem like we were scheming to separate them, so whenever Mum asked how her dad was getting on she always said fine. It actually came as a real shock when he did it. We all tried to get it out of Dolly, what had been going on. But she wouldn't talk. Not to Mum, not to me, not to her counsellor.'

Dolly's father committed suicide when she was eleven. Heather can only tell me that Mr Hart had apparently been prescribed antidepressants very recently, and hadn't been monitored very closely by his GP after he began his course. He'd been working two jobs: he was security officer for a private company, and drove a taxi in his off-hours. He began to struggle with depression, stress and chronic pain.

'But that's all I know. One day he was there and he seemed fine, the next day he wasn't. She really didn't want to move in with us, and for the sake of ease, Mum let her move in with Grandma – Mum's mum. But Dolly was a total nightmare. She just ran roughshod over Grandma and she was in loads of trouble at her school. She got even worse during the summer holidays, between her finishing primary and starting high school. They got into a fight about Grandma not letting her watch something on telly, so Dolly bit Grandma really hard.' This incident was the straw that broke the camel's back. Their mother put her foot down and insisted that Dolly move in with the family.

'I wasn't looking forward to it. I'd started finding her so creepy, with all her weird dolls, and . . . I was so embarrassed that she was going to be going to high school with me, and she was like . . . urgh, she just wasn't right.'

Dolly would believe anything. She still believed in Santa and the Tooth Fairy, and it caused major problems for her at school. Heather was aware of at least one incident where Dolly was told it was non-uniform day by other students (it wasn't) and arrived at school in her own clothes.

There'd also been some uncomfortable incidents with a few older boys who lived on their grandma's estate. Heather was not fully aware of the details of these incidents, only that Dolly had been 'tricked' into trading a sexual service in exchange for something on more than one occasion. Heather told me her mother would know the details but would be very unlikely to share them.

'This was around when we moved to Crow-on-Sea. My parents made it seem like we were moving . . . just because. But I'm sure it was to put Dolly in a new school. That was fine with me; I wanted to go to beauty college and the one in Crow was quite good.'

Before they moved to Crow, their mother attempted to intervene. Tiny animals and Polly Pockets were seized, to Dolly's extreme distress. She was told 'you're too old for these' and 'if you want to act like an adult you can't play with toys' and Dolly screamed and howled and begged for mercy. Heather didn't understand what her mother was trying to achieve; why Dolly couldn't just keep her weird little toys. She remembers that Dolly screamed, 'You're killing them! If you take them away from me, you're killing them!' Dolly clearly took the life she'd imbued into her toys extremely seriously.

She called her mother a murderer, and Heather wasn't sure she was being histrionic. She felt like Dolly really, really believed it.

Heather stole the baby frogs back (not Daddy Frog, who she thought was best consigned to oblivion) and a handful of Polly Pockets. Their mum (who felt too guilty to throw them out) was keeping them in a box in her wardrobe. Heather hid them under Dolly's duvet – she probably should have left a note, or something, but she assumed Dolly would work it out.

Dolly did not work it out. Engaging in an unexpected level of magical thinking, Dolly seemed to think the toys had made their way back to her. They were resurrected, by the force of Dolly's will. Heather knows this, because Dolly called Heather

384

into her bedroom and, whispering frantically, told her that she must have brought them back. Magicked them back, maybe.

Heather didn't have the heart to tell her that she'd rescued the toys.

'How old was she when this happened?'

'Fourteen? Probably fifteen, actually.'

'Hmm,' I said. Even though I was well aware of the time-line, I was expecting to hear Heather say 'twelve' at most.

'Yeah,' said Heather. 'Strange, isn't it? My mum tried to get her all this nice new stuff as well. A grown-up handbag and shoes I'd recommended. My dad had a lot more money than Dolly's dad, so we could afford that low-end designer stuff teenagers go mad for easily. But she just wanted these dirty old frogs.'

Heather shrugged. She thought that was probably all she could help me with. After all, when the family moved to Crow, Heather got her own place.

'I know that she said she wanted to make an effort to have friends and be popular and stuff but . . . I don't know. She had anger problems so I understand that all went out of the window pretty quickly. But there's really not much more I can help you with, now. Can I go?' she asked.

I said I had a couple more questions to ask her, and one more point to make.

The first question: Did Heather or her mother have any idea about Cherry Creek?

'Erm, no. I think my dad probably would've had a complete nervous breakdown over it. As I said, they weren't fire and brimstone or anything near it, but they were really suspicious of anything a bit . . . morbid or scary. They were funny about

Halloween – they wouldn't even let Dolly watch 15-rated films, they would've gone mad. I had no idea either – like I said, we weren't that close and Dolly was really secretive. I remember my mum complaining she was spending too much time on the computer, and I thought, well, that's what happens when you buy a fifteen-year-old a laptop. Mum said she needed it for school,' Heather rolled her eyes.

I asked Heather why she had let Dolly borrow her car. Heather tensed – I imagine it was a question she'd been asked a lot.

'I'm not judging you – I know she stole it from you the night of the incident, very little you could do about that – just trying to understand why you'd do it. It seems odd that you would lend it to her.'

Heather sighed. I expected her to lose her temper with me for asking, but she didn't.

'When you live in Crow-on-Sea, you get a lot of birdshit on your car. Constantly. I hate cleaning my car. When Dolly borrowed it, she had to clean it.'

'Even after she'd repeatedly failed her tests?'

'Well she'd just kick off with me if I didn't give it to her. I'd seen her drive and she always looked fine to me. I failed my test a few times – it's normal to fail a couple of times. And she never went very far with it. Mostly just drove her friends to the McDonald's and back. I just didn't see it as that much of a problem. It was stupid but I was only nineteen, twenty myself. How good is your judgement meant to be at that age?' she asked.

I shrugged. I didn't want to grill her about the car, and this all made sense to me. It was irresponsible, yes. But not insane.

'The last thing I want to mention is just . . . the sexual abuse claim. I just want to point something out.'

'Here we go,' said Heather. She started gathering her things, finishing her drink and picking up her handbag. I followed her as she left the table.

My point was that Mr Hart entering Dolly's room may not have been as sinister as it appeared. I am a father myself. I sometimes used to look in on my daughter at night. I would tuck her in. During a period of poor mental health, I would become extremely paranoid she would stop breathing, and I would stand over her for hours, watching her.

'It's not necessarily malicious, checking on your child. That's all,' I said.

'I don't really care what you think. He wasn't checking on her, he was doing something.'

'How do you know, Heather?' I asked. Heather was flagging down a cab.

'Because she fucking killed someone, okay? Because she fucking set someone on fire. It's not normal behaviour. You don't do that for no reason. I'm not a fucking liar,' she snarled. I had frustrated her to the point of tears. When I tried to hand her money for the taxi, she smacked my hand away. 'Creep,' she said. 'You're a creep. And I want you to write that into your nasty little book.'

LEAVING

Dolly was pacing her room like a caged animal. She squeezed her phone in her fist and thought about smashing it, slamming it against the wall in a blind rage.

She called out to Matty for guidance. What would he do? She knew exactly what he'd do – but what should *she* do? She felt nothing and she heard nothing. She closed her eyes and concentrated, and tried to imagine his face. He was smiling – smirking. That meant nothing. He was just fucking with her.

Her phone kept buzzing in her hand. Not Jayde but Jamie. Stupid boy messaging her winky faces – *Are you still coming to my party tonight? Hope I'm going to see you.*

The Year 11s and Year 13s had broken up already. Most of them had had their last exams. Dolly and the rest of Year 12 were still in school, but she would just bunk off on Friday.

Yeah I'm coming, she replied. *Going to get FUCKED UP tonight.*

And she was. She was going to get fucked up. She'd already started drinking, breaking into the small bottle of vodka she kept hidden beneath the drawer inside her bedside table.

She summoned Violet and Angelica. *Get ready at mine. Come over now.* And Angelica replied with some wishy-washy excuse, some *maybe I'm not coming tonight, my dad's really busy with Brexit* shit. And that was pretty annoying, because Angelica had promised to get them the keys to her dad's private beach chalet. They were supposed to go there, down to the beach, after the party – make a real evening of it. Use all the bad Brexit vibes in town to make something, manifest something, embrace the chaos. She thought about Jayde calling it stupid. She tried to think about Matty instead. She tried to think about all the power inside of her. She thought of all of the things she could do, and how no one could stop her.

She was powerful, and evil and angry. And they would all be sorry. All of them.

She texted Angelica, sweaty thumbs slipping against the phone.

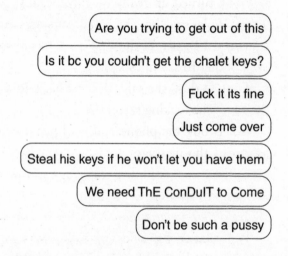

Are you trying to get out of this

Is it bc you couldn't get the chalet keys?

Fuck it its fine

Just come over

Steal his keys if he won't let you have them

We need ThE ConDuIT to Come

Don't be such a pussy

Dolly went to Tumblr, then to Angelica's blog. She opened her 'Ask' page, checked 'Anonymous' in the question box and typed:

Excited for daddy's Brexit you nazi nonce rat baby

Then, struck by inspiration, she sent another anon:

Hey anonymous info do not publish!! I am a long time
follower of murderxbuttons, we message sometimes and
she says someone called Joan Wilson brags about sending
you nasty anonymous messages? Wtf.

She texted her sister asking to borrow the car. Heather said
no, because she needed it early in the morning, and it was too
late at night now. It was only half eight. It was practically still
light outside. Dolly wasn't taking 'no' today.

Violet turned up really quickly, because when Dolly said
'jump' Violet said 'how high'. She was dressed for the night in
jeans and a T-shirt. Boring and black like always. Dolly didn't
even bother to say hi to Violet.

'Look at this,' she said, shoving her phone in Violet's face.
'Read it. The fucking screenshots.'

Violet took the phone and read her messages with Jayde
and read the messages Joni had sent her. Violet hummed,
placid and expressionless. Where was the indignant anger
Dolly had expected to see from Violet? *No, I can't believe
she'd do that, what a two-faced shit-stirring cunt.*

'Well that sucks,' said Violet. 'But you were fighting anyway. Didn't you even say that you wanted to break up with
her? Because she was negative?'

'No. Well. Yes. Yeah I did, but it's the fucking principle of
it,' said Dolly. She and Jayde had nothing in common, and
Jayde had started looking at her like she was insane and stupid. She was annoyed because Joni had gone out of her way
to break them up. Even if Dolly didn't care that much. It was
the principle of it. It wasn't fucking on. It was snaky behaviour. Dolly explained all of this, and Violet nodded.

'Do you still want to go to that party tonight?' Violet asked. And she sounded a bit hopeful because she hated being dragged along to parties. She liked staying in with her phone and her murder stories and the torture basement she'd made in *The Sims*. She'd shown Dolly once. It was sick – sick like cool, and sick like fucked up. Sometimes Dolly doubted Violet's belief in her. But when she saw the basement, she knew Violet understood. That basement was a pocket hell, a digital pocket hell.

'Yeah. Obviously. Angelica's coming as well.'

'I thought she was busy with her dad's Brexit stuff tonight,' Violet said.

'Nah. We'll go and pick up her up. We might need her for the beach. And we're going to go to the party and I'm going to . . . Joni's getting what she deserves. Angelica wouldn't want to miss it, would she?'

'Probably not,' said Violet. 'I don't have money for a cab all the way to Moorcock Hill, though.' She started looking at her phone, not making eye contact. 'Maybe we just shouldn't go.'

'It's fine, we'll just take Heather's car.'

They finished off the little bottle of vodka. Well, Dolly finished it off. Violet had a few sips.

Dolly's mum had a spare set of keys to Heather's flat. She kept all the keys on prissy little hooks shaped like seashells.

'Why do you need her flat keys?' Violet asked.

'In case she's not home.'

'She knows we're borrowing the car though, doesn't she?'

'Yeah, obviously,' said Dolly.

They walked to Heather's flat, avoiding the Warrens and avoiding the risk of bumping into Jayde.

They arrived at the small block of flats Heather lived in and Dolly told Violet to wait outside.

'And Heather *definitely* knows you're borrowing it?'

'Yeah, obviously,' whispered Dolly.

Dolly let herself into the block, then into Heather's flat, hoping her sister was in bed already or wearing headphones or something. Dolly heard the shower. It was perfect. She barely needed to go in the flat – Heather kept her car keys hanging on a hook by the door, the same seashell hooks their mother used. Dolly took them, locked the door behind her, and slipped back outside.

She and Violet drove off quickly. Heather couldn't see her car from her flat; her windows were on the opposite side of the building to the car park. Dolly was home free as long as Heather didn't go to the shop, or something.

When they pulled up to Angelica's house, it was past nine, and the sun had just gone down. She honked the horn and hung out of the car window to call their ridiculous intercom.

'Hello, Angelica Stirling-Stewart speaking?' she said. 'My dad's not home – if you're a journalist or something you have to go away.'

'Hi, this is the Remain campaign? Just wondering why you're such a fucking Nazi?' said Dolly. 'I'm just joking! It's me and Violet. Come down!'

Angelica huffed then hung up the intercom. She came down to the gate scowling, and wearing her pyjamas.

'Get in, loser, we're going to the party,' said Dolly.

'Um . . . my dad said I can't have the chalet keys or go out tonight,' said Angelica. 'I'm supposed to record the Brexit coverage for him and he's worried I'll get attacked by Remainers when they lose.'

'That seems kind of . . . paranoid,' said Violet.

'Your dad literally thinks he's the centre of the universe. It's going to be a big nothing,' said Dolly. 'Just steal the keys. You're not going to get attacked by Remainers, we'll just have some spooky Brexit beach fun.'

'But the recording,' she said.

'Can't he just rewatch it on iPlayer?' said Violet. 'He's probably going to lose anyway.'

'Or you could just start the recording now? Or your sister could do it? Come on, you're going to look like such a sad little Brexit twat if you spend the night hiding here. I think like, everyone is going to this party. It'll be kind of embarrassing for you if you don't go.'

'He doesn't trust Lucie to do the recording,' she said.

'So? She can just do it, who cares. We *actually* need you. Like how are we supposed to get anything cool done at the beach without the conduit.'

'But . . . Okay. Fine.' Angelica sighed and went back up to the house. She came back down to the car with the bag of alcopops and spirits she knew was the cost of admission. She'd hastily applied some sparkly red, white and blue eyeshadow and red lipstick, and had changed into a Union Jack dress. She sat in the back, cradling her bag of booze.

'I don't think the party's Brexit-themed,' said Violet.

'I don't care. This is my outfit,' Angelica replied. Dolly sped off. Jamie had texted her his address and a picture of his abs. 'Did you know Joni was sending me anons on Tumblr?' Angelica asked.

'What?' Violet said. Her voice cracked, because she was a terrible liar. Dolly grinned in the front seat. Angelica was jiggling her leg with this barely concealed rage, and Violet had gone red.

'Well, Violet, someone told me that you said Joni sends me nasty anons.'

'Who told you?' Dolly and Violet made eye contact in the rear-view mirror.

'It doesn't matter,' snapped Angelica.

Violet stared pleadingly into the rear-view mirror.

'What are you looking at? It wasn't me,' said Dolly. 'I don't know what that bitch's problem is.'

'Joni texted me once to say she'd sent you some stuff, but it was like a year ago. Before we were hanging out,' said Violet.

'We don't hang out,' Angelica scoffed.

'I mean, we *do*, but okay,' said Violet. 'To be fair though, like, who the fuck did you think it was? After she started showing your *Cats* pictures everywhere, wasn't it obvious?'

'Shut up,' said Angelica. Her voice sounded thick. She changed the subject. 'Where's Jayde?' she asked.

'She dumped me because I messaged Joni again telling her to fuck off and she snaked and sent Jayde a screenshot.'

'Oh my God, I hate her so much,' said Angelica. She was boiling with fury. Dolly could feel it. 'She's literally evil.'

'She's the fucking worst. She's literally . . .' Dolly trailed off, thinking. Cogs turning in her head. What would Matty do. 'She's fucking dead meat, is what she is. She's hell meat.'

'Hell meat?'

'Yeah. I'm feeding her into fucking pocket hell.'

They got to Jamie's party and made their way through

Angelica's bag of booze. They stood in the corner of his garden. He'd hung fairy lights on his fence and around his washing line. It was surprisingly busy – a lot of Year 11 girls and a lot of Year 13s – not so many people from Dolly's year. A handful of people had had their last exams today – they were the drunkest. They 'cheersed' to freedom, and chanted 'gutted, gutted' when they came across people whose last exam was not till next week. Jamie was distracted by one of the girls from this group and wasn't bothering Dolly. That was good.

Dolly didn't want to drink too much or get pulled away from the main party. She didn't want to be totally unable to drive. She would need to drive for this.

Angelica and Violet both talked to her, but not to each other. They chattered. Angelica was complaining about Joni, and Violet was muttering about the extent to which a Leave or Remain Brexit result could contribute to a Crow-centric pocket hell dimension. Dolly sipped her alcopop and scanned the crowd for Joni. She was supposed to be here tonight. One of Jamie's friends was going out with that stuck-up Annabelle girl, and she'd invited all their little friends. She was supposed to be here.

'There she is,' hissed Angelica. 'What are you going to do? Are you going to say something? Are you going to hit her?'

'Maybe,' said Dolly. Joni was standing with Lauren Everett and Kayleigh Brian. They were also drinking alcopops, but they were smiling and laughing. They were probably celebrating Joni breaking up Jayde and Dolly.

'I bet they're laughing at you,' said Angelica.

'Angelica . . .' Violet murmured.

'What? That's what they do. They do it to me all the

time – they're probably just practically pissing themselves at the thought of Joni breaking you and Jayde up. So homophobic, TBH.' Violet rolled her eyes at that. But Angelica was probably right. Those girls practically made sport out of picking on Angelica – why not Dolly?

One of them snorted. Maybe with laughter, maybe a pig sound. Dolly Dick Pig. That was all she was to girls like Lauren.

Dolly decided to go over, telling Angelica and Violet to stay back. To back her up if needed. She tapped Joni on the shoulder. Joni visibly jumped at the sight of her, squirming.

'Can I talk to you for a minute?' Dolly asked. She sounded very calm. Very even. But her jaw was clenching, her fists were balled up.

'Um . . .' Joni looked at Lauren and Kayleigh, who looked confused and concerned. 'Okay,' she said. She told Lauren and Kayleigh: 'It's okay, it's fine.'

'Well, shout if you need us,' said Lauren.

'She's not going to need you,' said Dolly, smiling. Trying to smile in a breezy *honestly it's nothing!* kind of way.

She led Joni over to the garden shed, so they could speak without the prying eyes of Lauren or Kayleigh.

'Hey, so Jayde broke up with me. I hope you're happy,' said Dolly. And Joni looked shocked and panicked. She choked on the alcopop she'd been chugging.

'No. No, I didn't—'

'It's fine. Honestly it's fine, no hard feelings. We were going to break up anyway, it's really not a big deal. Sorry about the messages, it's honestly . . .' Dolly smiled her nicest, friendliest smile. Joni looked tense, still, but less like she was actively

397

about to shit herself. 'Look. It's water under the bridge. I know I am a crazy fucking bitch . . . so . . .' She laughed. Joni laughed as well, nervously. 'You know . . . we're going to go to the beach soon. I think Jayde's still going to be there.'

Joni cleared her throat.

'Um . . . well, maybe. If Lauren or Kayleigh—'

'I only have space for one more person in my car, so maybe they could come later.'

'Um . . .'

'Violet's coming. And Angelica – you're friends with them, aren't you?' Dolly said. She was keeping all of this very casual. She was being gentle. She'd managed to unball her fists and everything. 'It's okay if you don't want to, though. Just thought it might be nice. Fun.'

'Well . . . okay.' Joni smiled. 'Sure.'

'Do you want to go now?' Dolly asked. She made a show of checking her phone. Half ten. 'Oh shit, we need to go, actually, Jayde is on her way.'

'Okay, sure,' Joni said. She peered around the shed, and couldn't seem to see Kayleigh or Lauren anymore. 'Sure, fuck it.'

'Fuck it?'

'Fuck it!'

They smiled at each other and giggled. Dolly linked arms with her and led her over to Angelica and Violet. Dolly gave them a big, fake smile like *follow my lead*.

'We're going down to the beach, galz,' said Dolly. 'Let's hop to it.' She clapped – it was awkward; her arm was still linked with Joni's.

They got in the car. When Dolly started the engine, Joni took her phone out, and started texting.

'Get her phone off her,' Dolly said. Angelica snatched it and started laughing.

'She was messaging Jayde,' Angelica snorted. 'That's so fucking sad.' Dolly opened the back window on Angelica's side – Joni was now scrambling to grab her phone back.

'Get rid of it,' said Dolly. Angelica threw it out of the window.

*

In Violet, Angelica and Dolly's police statements, things begin to vary wildly here.

All (more or less) agree on what happened until the phone went out of the window. Until the violence began to escalate.

Dolly began to drive up to the castle. Either Angelica or Violet tied Joni's hands up with a scarf Heather had left in the glovebox, depending on who you ask. Dolly says Angelica did it of her own accord; Violet says Angelica did it at Dolly's behest. Angelica says Violet did it.

Then Angelica gagged her with a pair of spare socks – Angelica admitted she did this after initially blaming Violet. The socks were hers; they had been in her handbag. Angelica had to wrestle her for a bit, but Joni began to comply when Angelica threatened to push her out of the moving car. Violet and Angelica said that Dolly made a show of unlocking the car doors, saying *she'll do it*. Dolly did not mention this.

They drove slowly through the town centre, then up the North Beach promenade. It was a weeknight, so the arcades were closed and quiet. Either Angelica or Violet kept Joni's head down, so no one could see her. Angelica said Violet held her down, Violet said Angelica did it – Dolly said both of them did.

When they arrived at the castle, they marched Joni in front of the hammer, where all agree Joni sustained her first serious injury of the evening.

Dolly was joking about testing the hammer on her – honestly joking, according to her. She knew she couldn't lift it. But she wanted to scare Joni. They made her lie down on the floor with her head next to the hammer. Violet said that Dolly seemed to be genuinely trying to lift it, encouraging Angelica to help her. How sincere she was is impossible to tell.

Then Dolly sat on Joni's stomach and (according to Violet) recounted the story Violet had told her about the woman who was half-crushed. Dolly and Angelica, however, said that Violet interrupted Dolly to correct details, and took over the retelling.

Then, Angelica found a brick. Broken in half, but still a brick. She and Dolly discussed dropping it on Joni's head. According to Violet this discussion was mutual; according to Dolly, she tried to convince Angelica that it was a step too far – Angelica said that Dolly tried to convince her to drop it.

Joni, who was crying and quite drunk, twisted violently, and threw Dolly off of her. She scrambled to her feet and tried to run.

Angelica threw the brick and hit Joni in the back of her head.

'Now who's a bad shot? Now who's a fucking loser?' Dolly and Violet claim she shrieked. Angelica said she just threw the brick because she panicked. She didn't want Joni to get away and tell on them. She didn't mean to hit her in the head, just to slow her down or scare her. She thought she'd probably miss.

The impact knocked Joni to the floor and left her gurgling, face-down in the dirt and the grass. She was semi-conscious, but it was obvious even to the other children she was badly hurt.

At this point, all three girls knew they had crossed a line. They were going to get into real trouble.

'We should take her to the hospital.' Violet alleged she was the one who suggested this but Dolly said *she* did. Angelica said that she was the one who wanted to take Joni to the hospital. Each is the could-be hero of her own story.

Everybody said they wanted to take Joni to the hospital, but they didn't. No one wanted to get into trouble. If they took her to the hospital now, it'd be a 'whole thing'. Maybe if they took her to the beach chalet, she'd be fine in like an hour. They'd just scare her a little. They'd teach her a lesson about shit-stirring and bitching and camping out in inboxes you didn't belong in. They'd convince her not to talk. Everything would be fine. Each girl repeated these talking points at interview – none attributed to anyone in particular. This must've been a group discussion, a circle of justification and reassurance.

Violet asked, 'Is this real? Are we doing this?' And Angelica replied, 'Doing what? We're not doing anything.'

And then they drove down to the chalet. They arrived at around quarter past eleven. Angelica and Dolly carried Joni down to the beach. Angelica held her feet, and Dolly held her wrists. Violet was too physically weak to assist, so Joni swung between Angelica and Dolly, while Violet looked on. Dolly said that Angelica mocked Joni's weight: *She's so fat that Violet can't even hold her legs.*

Violet followed them. She said she repeatedly told the other girls, 'Guys, that's enough,' and asked them to pack it in, to put Joni in the car. She said: 'We can just push her out at A&E and drive away,' because she'd seen people do that in films.

Angelica denied that Violet had said this. Dolly corroborated that Violet did make the comment about pushing Joni out of the car at A&E.

Dolly admitted that she told Violet to 'shut the fuck up'.

If anyone noticed the four girls, they assumed Joni was drunk, or they were just messing about, and didn't think about it much. No witnesses came forward.

Down in the chalet, Joni was yet to regain full consciousness, so the girls began to argue about what they should do. Violet said that she vomited outside. She said she tried to convince the others to stop, but they weren't listening. Angelica locked Violet out of the chalet while she and Dolly discussed what to do.

Though Angelica and Dolly deny that Violet was ever locked out of the chalet, here a witness can corroborate Violet. She was spotted by a late-night dog walker knocking on the door of the chalet.

The dog walker didn't intervene – just some teenager messing about. Why would you? When the dog walker made eye contact with Violet, she slunk away from the chalet, and went back to the car.

Back in the chalet (depending on who you believe), Angelica was egging Dolly on, saying they should mess with Joni while she was unconscious. She told Dolly that no one would believe Joni anyway – they might as well have some fun. Dolly said that she was angry – but she was also scared. She told the police that she thought about Matthew McKnight and wondered what he would do, but she struggled to make her mind up.

Angelica said that she was the indecisive one. She was trying to work out how they could cover this up – she suggested covering Joni in alcohol, so the police would think she'd just wandered off. They could go to the police and say 'Our friend is really drunk and she hit her head, and we lost her, and she stole our chalet keys' – or they could dump her at A&E. Angelica was trying to work out how they could get out of this. Dolly was rambling about Matty and pocket hell and *this is our chance* and *I can do this.*

Dolly began slapping Joni extremely hard across the face until her lip split. Dolly claimed this was a genuine, desperate effort to wake Joni up. Angelica disagreed.

Violet's phone records show that she rang 999, then hung up after two seconds. She was panicking. She didn't know what to do. She said she thought Dolly and Angelica would hurt her as well. She was scared of the police, too. She didn't want to get in trouble. After the bad thing happened, the police weren't nice to her. They'd spoken to her like she was a liar – they'd asked her (without her mum or anyone else there) what she'd get out of lying about a young man with his whole life ahead of him.

Violet turned her phone off at around 1 a.m. She said she doesn't really know what she did in the car, or what she was thinking. It started to feel completely unreal to her. Before the murder, she had a recurring nightmare where she'd killed someone, and needed to bury the body. The whole while, she'd just wish she didn't have a body to bury. She'd wake up anxious, and sweaty, and then utterly relieved it had all been a dream.

She said she sat in the car and willed herself to wake up.

Back in the chalet, over the course of the next four hours, the violence escalated. Angelica and Dolly hurt Joni with the scissors, a corkscrew, small rocks found on the beach, and a small set of tools Simon Stirling-Stewart was keeping in the chalet. The toolset included a hammer, and screwdrivers of various sizes.

Dolly neglected to mention when she stopped trying to 'wake Joni up' and when she started to torture her.

I won't go into great detail here. If you want specifics you can look them up online. There'll be a 'Murder Wiki' entry or a podcast which will happily provide you a complete list of Joni's injuries – a list of what Angelica said Dolly did or what Dolly said Angelica did.

Angelica said Dolly did most of it, of course. Dolly kept getting worse and worse, and kept challenging Angelica to top her. To think of something more fucked up to do. Angelica said that Dolly kept asking if she could feel it, did Angelica realise they were in hell, now. They were literally in hell.

Dolly didn't dispute that she said that – that she felt she had finally, literally created her tiny hell. She admitted she was exhilarated by it. She felt powerful, in control, and in touch with Matty. She understood him now more than any other creeker would. She disputed that she led on the torture. She said it escalated gradually from the slaps which had split Joni's lip.

Dolly said that Angelica found the scissors her father kept in the chalet (for opening bags and boxes and cutting up plastic rings on cans of beer) and used them to chop off Joni's hair.

Dolly spat in Joni's face, and says that Angelica egged her on. 'Do something that'll really make her wake up.' So Dolly bit her.

And it went from there.

Where was Violet? She was locked out for the entire four hours in her version of the story. In the car for most of it, sometimes on the beach banging on the locked door of the chalet and begging Dolly and Angelica to stop.

Angelica said Violet was in the chalet watching, cheering them on. Though she was never able to keep this part of the story straight. Violet tended to appear and disappear, depending on who asked and when. Dolly couldn't remember if Violet was there or not.

Joni did regain consciousness, eventually. Her hands had been unbound. She grabbed the hammer and hit Angelica in the shin with it. Angelica screamed, and Violet began banging on the chalet door.

Violet's phone was switched back on – she made and aborted another 999 call.

Dolly tried to wrestle the hammer from Joni's hand, while Angelica squealed and hugged her injured leg. She opened the chalet door, and demanded that Violet help. Violet watched, frozen, phone in hand.

They didn't struggle over the hammer for long. Angelica said that Joni was weak, and Dolly snatched the hammer right off her. Dolly said that Joni had attained a feral, adrenalin-fuelled strength, and seemed primed to hit Dolly with the hammer.

Dolly won the struggle, and hit Joni right on the head, with a sickening crack. Violet said this was all she remembered – this final blow. She thought Dolly had killed her.

Joni wasn't moving. Violet rushed over and pulled out the gag. She held her hand over Joni's mouth and said she couldn't feel her breath. She tried to check her pulse and said she couldn't feel anything.

Immediately, Violet said they must burn down the chalet. Joni would take the fall for the chalet burnings, and it'd be ruled a death by misadventure. Violet denied that she had been cooking this worst-case scenario plan up in the car. She said it was spur of the moment – Dolly and Angelica said it didn't feel spur of the moment.

Dolly remembered her sister had a canister of petrol in the boot and ran to grab it. In their panicked state, the girls did not notice Joni's shallow breaths.

If one of them did, they did not say anything to the others, or admit this in interview or at trial.

There was not much petrol in the can. Enough to soak Joni's clothes, but not enough to spread around the chalet.

Angelica and Violet waited outside.

Dolly doused Joni in what little petrol she could, stuffed the canister with the scarf they'd used to bind her hands, and lit it with a lighter Dolly had stolen from Jayde. She threw the canister into the chalet and they all ran.

And now we're back where we began, aren't we? Back at the end of the story.

They set the fire. They drive to McDonald's. The fire burns out. Joni crawls from the ashes and onto the beach. She staggers into the hotel. Arrests. Limited coverage. Cult status. Podcasts. Reddit threads. Chumbox articles. And now, me, here, writing this. You reading it.

AFTERMATH

I do still have some gaps to fill, of course.

We know that the girls were arrested – the unfortunate and completely innocent Jayde Spencer along with them. Violet's mother took her to the police station, where she handed herself in. Angelica was arrested in the early hours of the morning, and Dolly was arrested a bit later, when they found her sleeping by the side of the motorway in Heather's stolen Fiat 500.

Dolly slept at the police station too. When she woke, she rambled. She practically spoke in word salad, explaining gleefully that she had finally created her pocket hell. She had finally gone to the depths of horror and terror she had been seeking to create. Duh. Obviously. And the police could not make head nor tail of her. Nor could anyone, really. She mentioned 'Matty', of course – but this wasn't a copycat. She seemed to have no real motivation. She had buried the regret she displayed in her 5:37 a.m. Tumblr post deep in the mud of fantasy and delusion.

Angelica immediately blamed Dolly. No, Angelica insisted, she was not driven by revenge. She was not angry at Joni for bullying her, because she was simply not the type of person who got bullied, got it? Angelica was an A-tier popular girl – she wasn't like Violet. No, this was all Dolly. And no, there was no crazy devil-worship stuff or whatever, because Angelica wasn't dumb enough to believe something like that. No, Dolly was driven mad by jealousy – she was just going crazy over the break-up. She wanted to kill Joni, because Joni had, like, stolen her girlfriend. Angelica was just along for the ride. They were just winding Joni up. The death was a complete accident. They started the fire because they panicked. The whole thing was an accident.

And they hadn't tortured her – if Dolly said that she was just lying. Because she was fucking crazy. And if anyone had tortured Joni, it would've been Dolly, while Angelica looked on helplessly. And while Violet egged her on. Because these were all Violet's ideas – Violet was obsessed with this stuff. She even had a house on *The Sims* where she captured people and tortured them. Sounds like a total psycho, no?

Violet was hysterical but seemed to lay out everything as honestly as she could. She still tried to paint herself in the best light possible, however. Her own fascination with torture-murder would not be cited here, no no. It was a purely academic interest. She stayed in the car the whole time, and she rang 999 twice. Why didn't she let the calls go through?

She didn't know. She couldn't answer the question. She didn't want any of this to be real. She tried to make them stop. She was sorry. She was just so sorry – but it was Dolly and Angelica. Even if she'd told Dolly stuff, even if she'd encouraged the whole 'pocket hell' thing – she just thought they were messing around. Speaking metaphorically. Plus, Angelica was the one who really hated Joni. She was the one who wanted to set Dolly on her like a pitbull.

Pointing their fingers at each other to varying degrees didn't get anyone off the hook. The offence was considered serious enough that all three girls were tried in Crown Court, rather than in the juvenile court system.

The trial was relatively short – no one plead not guilty. Angelica and Dolly were murderers, kidnappers and torturers; Violet was a kidnapper and an accessory.

Despite the guilty plea her legal team had insisted on, Angelica spent much of the trial in denial, avoiding questions, and frequently being chastised by the judge.

Dolly spent most of her trial talking nonsense. Manifesting, magic powers, pocket hell. She did a good job of making herself look unfit to stand trial. She also loudly objected to her sister's sexual abuse allegation.

Violet broke down on several occasions. At sentencing, the judge described her as a coward. Though she was receiving the lightest recommended sentence, the judge told her that she wanted her to think about the fact that she could have intervened at any time. Between Joni being bundled into the car, to the moment her frenzied schoolmates bashed Joni's skull with a hammer. She could've stopped it all with one phone call.

Because of Simon Stirling-Stewart's status as a public figure – and his increased prominence around the Brexit vote in particular – the judge made the decision to waive Angelica's anonymity. Then he decided to waive the anonymity of the other girls, too. Logic being that it would be easy for the public to seek out and discover the names of the anonymous assailants with Angelica's name out there.

At the close of the trial the judge said, 'I did this because I felt the public interest overrode the interest of the defendants.' This decision was later criticised by senior government figures, including the director of the Government Communications Headquarters. Because of this decision, each girl would now have to be granted a new identity upon release at great cost to the British taxpayer.

Though the girls were to be detained at Her Majesty's Pleasure, they would likely be released. Violet had been granted a far lower recommended sentence than the other girls. While Dolly had fifteen years, and Angelica had ten, Violet's recommended sentence was only four years. It was unlikely she would graduate to the adult prison system.

Violet was released in 2019, after two years in a secure unit. She was granted a new identity. She will be on licence till 2029, at which point she will be almost thirty years old.

Angelica was allowed to remain at a secure unit past her eighteenth birthday. It was felt that she had made significant improvements. She was contrite, remorseful and engaged in therapy. It would be inappropriate to put her into the adult prison system, or in a psychiatric hospital. Despite her ten-year recommended sentence, she was released in late 2020 after three years. Angelica will remain on licence for the rest of her life.

When Dolly Hart is released (if she is released) she will also remain on licence. Dolly did not make the improvements in the secure unit Angelica did. She was first moved to a medium-security psychiatric hospital, then to one of the UK's three high-security psychiatric hospitals.

I think on Dolly's handful of hell. The tiny pocket of horror she was determined to create, to mire herself in. The extreme she wanted to experience, the fire she wanted to swallow her. And I can only think about how well she succeeded.

Amanda Black, Joni's mother (now using her maiden name), was not particularly satisfied, or dissatisfied with the outcome. She did not wish for the prison system to lock the girls up and throw away the key – but she did doubt Angelica had truly had time to 'rehabilitate' in less than four years. How could someone even begin to atone for such a terrible crime? Amanda felt sure that Violet would carry this around with her, that she would never forget and move on. But Angelica probably would. And maybe she deserved to have her life upended as much as Dolly's had been.

But then, they'd never live normal lives. None of them. Never again. Maybe that was enough. Maybe it never would be enough. Nothing would ever bring her daughter back. Or her husband. Or anything from her life before the murder.

The crime itself, however, will live on. It will live on for as long as podcasts which covered it are available. It will live on for as long as this book is in print. A Murderpedia page with a complete list of Joni's injuries is available to view, bordered with ads for 'BEST EVER 18+ ONLY online games' and the latest superhero franchise movie. It will live on in the chumbox ads that first led me to this crime. It will live on in the memories of everyone who comes to Crow – and everyone who sees Joni's sun-bleached memorial.

It will live on online. The same type of young people Dolly and Violet discussed scary stories and brutal slayings with now talk about Violet and Dolly. Under the hashtag 'Chaos-Girlfriends' is a picture of Dolly with her arm around Violet in front of the Witch Hammer. Someone has edited the image to clean up Violet's skin and make Dolly's eyes pop. They have added flower crowns to both of their heads.

I love them so much wtf, reads the caption.

A collection of Dolly's posts circulates captioned: *she just like me fr!!* With a line of crying emojis.

There are numerous text posts too:

Username redacted:
You: virgin, columbiner, no bitches
Me: Chad, Chaospilled, dolly/vi shipper

Username redacted:
I wish dolly and violet had just dated theyre so cute I actually want to cry

Username redacted:
Angelica is so overlooked in this fandom its like you all pretend she just didn't exist lol

Username redacted:
Heard some chaos gf shippers messaged Jayde Spencer on instagram actually going to kms yall are so embarrassing!!!!!

Username redacted:
HELLO SICKOS IN THIS HASH TAG, I just got done listening to the Creepy episode on this case and just wanted to come here to say you are all DISGUSTING. How dare you use a CHILD'S death for your own shipping amusement. Hope you honestly all get set on fire wtf.

And that new-found fandom wasn't just contained to the internet. As Terry of Terry's Tours had feared, as of publication, true crime is Crow's new cottage industry. After checking out

412

the various Dracula-centred attractions, travellers to Whitby now take a visit to Crow-on-Sea for the (usually sold-out) Crow-on-Sea Creepy and Criminal Tour – you can even book this tour as a package alongside certain Dracula tours.

Between an uptick in domestic tourism and its new-found infamy, Crow-on-Sea seems set for a small economic resurgence, but who knows how long that might last.

Local business owners hated the murder at first, openly complaining about the morbid tourists hanging around the site of Joni's murder when I visited in 2019. If they're still complaining, no one does it openly. Even Terry of Terry's Tours will talk enthusiastically about the murder on his walks – perhaps forced to in order to compete with the Crow-on-Sea Creepy and Criminal Tour.

That tour will take you to the Witch Hammer – where you'll hear the same stories Violet told Dolly – then to Poseidon's Kingdom, where you'll hear about the drowning of Aleesha Dowd.

You'll then move on to the unmarked site of Vance Diamond's grave and Diamond's gentlemen's club (now named Porky's) and – the last stop, the star of the show: the site of Joan Wilson's murder.

A tonal whiplash: immediately after hearing about the seedy life and times of Vance Diamond, you are taken to the spot where a burned-out chalet once sat. It is now an empty space, marked with flowers. You can walk where she walked – up to the hotel – while the tour guide asks you to imagine doing this walk barefoot – then without skin.

The snake has eaten its own tail.

Interview: Alec Z. Carelli – 'I admit I have no scruples', as told by Shruti Tewari

Originally published in the *Guardian*, October 2022.

A few months ago, a shocking scandal rocked publishing, resulting in lawsuits, police investigations and re-traumatised victims. Lives and careers were shattered, reputations were ruined and a lot of money was lost.

Before me sits the man responsible: journalist and author Alec Z. Carelli. A middle-aged man to whom controversy is not unfamiliar, Carelli cuts an unassuming figure. His dark hair is grey at the temples, he is of average height and slender build, and his tan indicates a recent foreign holiday.

Who is Alec Carelli?

Carelli was born in Hampstead, London, in 1968 to an Italian father and a British mother. His father, Vittorio, was a high-ranking executive at Ferrari, and his mother was the modernist sculptor Euterpe Campbell-Lyon, a second cousin of the Queen Mother. Campbell-Lyon committed suicide in 1985.

Carelli was educated at the Westminster School alongside cultural contemporaries Louis Theroux, Adam Buxton and Giles Coren. Initially known for his left-wing 'Gonzo' style political journalism, Carelli moved to tabloids in the mid-1990s.

After an interest in crime and the criminal justice system was instilled in him by prison reformer Frank Pakenham, 7th Earl of Longford (famous for his anti-pornography crusade and friendship with Myra Hindley), a family friend who mentored Carelli, he began to cover major crimes for national tabloid *Polaris*, where he worked as a staff writer until 2011, when he was (in his own words) 'made collateral damage' in the News International phone-hacking scandal. Despite his minor role in the scandal, Carelli was dismissed from *Polaris* over his involvement. Carelli left newspaper journalism behind and went on to write several books recounting and examining cases he'd covered on the major crimes beat at *Polaris*. His books *How Could She?* and *Into the Ether* (on the murders committed by Raymond and Kathleen Skelton and the Molly Lambert disappeared respectively) were met with critical and commercial success – but were not without controversy. Molly Lambert's parents were victims of phone hacking – illegally acquired information used by Carelli in his *Polaris* coverage of the Lambert disappearance was then used again in *Into the Ether*.

After his exit from journalism, Carelli was inspired by writers like Brian Masters and Gordon Burn to become a true-crime writer. He wrote two successful (and by all accounts accurate) books based on crimes he had covered at the time of their discovery and investigation. His books *How Could She?* and *Into the Ether* were met with critical and commercial success – despite protests about the latter.

Carelli's daughter Frances committed suicide in late 2014, shortly before the publication of his memoir *My Life in Crime* in spring of 2015. Carelli was unable to promote the book, which performed poorly, both critically and in the charts. A third true-crime book, *The Spider's Web*, completely flopped despite positive reviews from critics.

Carelli became a fixture at true-crime conventions, on

podcasts and as a talking head in documentaries. He seemed to develop an antipathy toward the scene, however, periodically invoking the wrath of the community many pointed out was 'paying his bills' by firing off critical (and often insulting) tweets aimed at other writers and podcasters.

His most notable bust-up was with Andy Koontz, host of true-crime podcast *I Peed on Your Grave* (transcripts of which featured prominently in *Penance*), in mid-2018 after Carelli tweeted:

Who signed off on the title 'I peed on your grave'?
Disgusting podcast and deeply disrespectful to victims of violence. You could not pay me to listen to this drivel. Two hours of 'Hur hur hur multiple women dead' dressed as 'dark humour.' Vile men.

Reception to this tweet was not positive and Carelli was dog-piled by *IPOYG* fans. Andy Koontz quote-tweeted Carelli with four screenshots of news articles regarding his involvement in the phone-hacking scandal. The headlines: 'SICK: JOURNO HACKS PHONE AND BAGS BOOK DEAL'; "LET HER REST" MOLLY PARENTS BEG FOR BOOK CANCELLATION'; 'LOONY LEFT'S CARELLI NAMED IN HACKING SCANDAL'; 'MOLLY LAMBERT'S PARENTS TARGETED BY SICK JOURNALIST' were paired with the simple yet damning caption: *this u?*

Carelli then became Twitter's 'main character' for the day, and his appearances at upcoming conventions were all cancelled. He was dropped by his literary agency and a book deal he'd recently signed (according to *The Bookseller* this would have been 'an exploration of his own daughter's suicide') was cancelled.

Things were quiet for Carelli after this public humiliation: until his book *Penance* was announced.

Released to much fanfare – the book was incredibly well timed; a Netflix documentary on the case had just been announced – success and popularity would be short-lived for Carelli.

A number of interview subjects represented by Farrah Nawaz-Donnelly – one of the few people featured in the book who opted not to be anonymised – came forward to claim that they'd been misrepresented or inaccurately quoted. They called on Carelli to release his original recordings of the interviews. When Carelli refused to provide the recordings, Simon Stirling-Stewart released his own recording of his interview with Carelli to the *Daily Mail*. He tweeted:

Hate my politics all you like, I would NEVER ridicule a man's dead daughter as @alecZZZcarelli alleged in his latest pulp novel. Read the truth HERE: [link]

While the majority of the interview content in Carelli's book could be found in this recording, the alleged digs about and references to Frances Carelli's suicide were entirely absent. The tone of the interview was also far less hostile than implied in the book.

There was more: Farrah Nawaz-Donnelly was told the information she gave about her siblings would be 'off the record'. Her sister Faiza, the newly anointed MP for

Crow-on-Sea, also took to Twitter to mock Carelli. She tweeted:

My sister: being the only brown people in a small northern town isn't the same as people making jokes about spaghetti at your private school

@alecZZZcarelli:
[A screencap from the season 4 episode of The Sopranos 'Christopher' – the image depicts the character Silvio Dante saying, 'This is Anti-Italian Discrimination']

The tweet received thousands of likes.

Jayde Spencer was unhappy with the way her mother had been described and presented and was deeply uncomfortable with the way Carelli adapted the information she'd given him into prose.

She claimed that many of the anecdotes she'd told Carelli about key events leading up to the murder of Joan Wilson were dramatically elaborated on, with a great deal of artistic licence taken in his writing and presentation of these events.

Amanda Black, the victim's mother, also came out loudly and publicly against the book, calling Carelli a 'manipulator' as well as 'deceitful and immoral'.

'Alec told me lots of very personal information about his daughter to get me on side. I'd never think someone would levy their own pain like that to disarm another grieving parent. While I do not feel I was inaccurately represented and most of the information is correct, I found the way he wrote about me, my daughter and my relationship with my ex-husband

419

invasive. I feel Carelli used the shared experience of losing our children to throw me off guard, and harvest me for content. He told me I would be able to sign off on the book before publication but I never heard from him again after the interview. The man is a vampire.'

Then, the final nail in the coffin: the 'correspondence' Carelli claimed to have had with Angelica Stirling-Stewart and Violet Hubbard was therapeutic writing created while they were incarcerated. Whistleblowers from Hubbard and Stirling-Stewart's respective secure units anonymously contacted the *Guardian* in September of 2022 with evidence to suggest this material had been purchased by Carelli from members of staff at the secure unit.

For legal reasons, I was unable to question Carelli on these allegations.

The book was pulled from shelves by its publisher days after the *Guardian* exposé was published.

The Interview:
I meet him in a café, and he orders a latte with oat milk, explaining to me that he has recently become vegan as part of a 'health kick'. He had 'fallen off the wagon again' around the time of the book's release and informed me he was twelve days sober.

He opens: 'Now I wouldn't compare myself to Truman Capote, but a lot of people have.' He looks at me, waiting for me to make the comparison myself. 'Capote was a liar and a gossip. But he was also very talented,' he says, and the unspoken 'I'm just saying' hovers in the air.

How much of the book, in your estimation, is fabricated?
Well, in terms of emotional truth, I would say it is 100% true. Fact and fiction have been blended as they often are in real life. I pulled lots and lots of things from the girls' blogs, you know. I had tons of material to pull from, I just gave some of it a clean-up and a more literary spin. Most of the prose sections – which everyone loved on publication by the way – were based directly on things they'd posted and stories Jayde Spencer told me. And a lot of the writing from them – it really was from them, I barely touched it. When I did I just supplemented it with material from their own blogs. Their own words edited with their own words.

But you did fabricate a lot of it?
It was all based on very real and very true material.

I've got a quote from Jayde Spencer here I'd like you to address – I'll just read it for you: 'Alec bothered me and spammed me with emails for months and months and he kept asking for more stories. The bits in the book: Hallow-een, Christmas and Easter – those are mostly based on stuff I told him. I never gave him that much detail and he took the equivalent to three or four sentences in an email and turned it into an entire short story. He never said he'd do that.'
Well I disagree that I bothered her. I sent a couple of follow-up emails. Of course I elaborated on her stories a bit – I feel I made that clear to her.

I think the issue is the extent to which you editorialised a couple of anecdotes she told you. Why not present the

material as it was? Why not keep it in her words? Why elaborate so much?

Would you rather read the words of a professional writer, or a few misspelt anecdotes from a twenty-year-old who wouldn't know good prose if it smacked her in the face?

Alec.
What?

I really want to know – I think a lot of people who trusted you want to know as well – why did you lie? Why not tell people you were going to write a non-fiction novel or just . . . take your material and create a piece of fiction. Why write half a novel and present it as a thoroughly researched definitive account of a major crime?

I don't like the word 'lie'. And it *was* thoroughly researched; I really resent this idea that I made lots and lots of shit up off the top of my head. I stayed in Crow for months and spoke to locals off the record and read hundreds of archived newspapers. I read every single archived post on Dolly and Violet and Angelica's blogs – and a fascinating tale began to emerge.

One of corrupted play – girls who were playing at being villains, playing at magic, playing at killing – and then they acted out in real life what they had merely played at. I did not make any of this up – on the various podcasts about the case, the ones built from material on the girls' blogs and so on, they all touch on this aspect. I just wanted to explore it, because I really felt this was an explanation for this crime, which was so horrific and seemed so unknowably violent. True-crime writing can also be quite boring, I suppose. I wanted to create something with real, tangible literary merit. So I took a bit of artistic licence, yes. I don't see the harm in that.

I think most people would agree that what you did was beyond a bit of artistic licence and was quite harmful to your interviewees and the families of those involved.
Yes, well.

Well?
Well!

Again, Alec, why not write a novel based on the case? Why go to the research lengths you allegedly did and then make up huge swathes of the material?
Huge swathes – no, it was not huge swathes, thank you. And I resent 'allegedly' there. There's great emotional truth in the book. I consider this to be a non-fiction novel in the vein of the work of Truman Capote. Simply put, I enjoy a story more when it is grounded in fact. As a novel, I think this would lose a great deal of its truth. Because it would be a piece of fiction. I think what I've done is really elevate a true story with beautiful prose and emotional explorations of the killers' mindsets. You come away from my book with a much greater understanding of this case, and of the conditions that created it.

I'm confused, Alec. I understand what you're saying, but I don't understand why you, as a trained journalist, are comfortable with this level of plasticity around the truth.
I've always thought of the truth as quite a plastic thing. I admit

I have no scruples when it comes to splitting hairs over tiny details, because what I'm interested in is emotional truth. I'm interested in getting across a higher understanding of a story.

And this has nothing to do with the amount you were paid by your publisher to write about this case?
Yes, it is always going to be about money. I am not a particularly rich man, but I have a lifestyle to which I am accustomed and yes, money is important. But the proper and emotionally truthful telling of a story is important too, no?

I feel more importance should be placed on purely factual and accurate reporting, I'm afraid.
And that's why you're not a very elevated writer, Shruti.

Ignoring that – how do you then justify your contact with the family of the victim and the families of the perpetrators? All of these people have suffered terribly around this horrific child murder. You approached these families and told them you planned to write a sensitive and accurate portrayal of this case, which seems beyond unscrupulous to me.
Well to be fair, I paid them all enough to be interviewed. I told them all I would write the definitive book on the case and they all got a nice payout. After my book came out, no one would bother them again. They would just read my book. I think that was appealing to them. So they did get something out of it; I don't think you can present them as . . . having been bamboozled by me. Because they weren't. They knew what they were getting into.

I disagree with that. I think you lied, and . . . you can't promise your book will be the only one. You don't control the media – there's nothing stopping more writers or journalists reaching out; in fact, now that your 'definitive' book on the case has whipped up all this additional interest, aren't these people more likely to get harassed?

It's worth pointing out that being on this true-crime circuit can actually be quite lucrative. Simon Stirling-Stewart got a book deal out of it – did you know that?

You seemed quite critical of the 'true-crime circuit' in the book. The idea of consuming real crimes as entertainment is something you present as . . . bad.

Yes. I was just stating a fact – it is lucrative. And it is bad. It's disgusting, in fact.

But you just said that you took artistic licence with the story because true crime is boring. You lied to make your book more entertaining.

It's not the same. I preserved the emotional truth of the story; I didn't mean to entertain but to help people understand and empathise.

Moving on – you also apparently offered some interview subjects cash. You weren't very transparent about that.

I just said I did. But I would say that I have justified paying them, because a lot of these people did benefit from the money I gave them to speak to me, and will benefit from the fact that I have written the definitive book on the case. I think the book itself will always be mentioned when this case is discussed – it takes some heat away from the families, and directs it to me.

So you feel you've provided a sort of . . . buffer for them. Between them and the media. You've taken some of the lime-light, as it were.
Yes, you could certainly say that. The podcasters were really beginning to descend on these poor people around the time I appeared. They were able to simply direct people to the book when asked for comment. It made things easier for them in a lot of ways.

But what makes you different from those podcasters? You were using them for 'content' in more or less the same way.
There's only one of me. There are a lot of true-crime podcasters and I didn't make fun of this case at any point. A lot of true-crime podcasters seem to make it their business to make fun of the victims and the killers – and yes, I may have found some humour in the teenage oddities of the girls, but I didn't at any point mock them or denigrate them. I also didn't feel the need to make a moral judgement on them. I didn't bark about how the killers should kill themselves or judge Amanda's parenting skills. I think I treated the case with the utmost respect.

Apart from the things you fabricated.
I feel I respectfully expanded on primary source material in an emotionally truthful way.

You've referred repeatedly to 'emotional truth' – can you define that for me? What does that mean?

It means that I feel I have accurately represented the feelings – the emotional and mental states – of those involved. My prose writing was all adapted from anecdotes and from real social media posts written by the girls. As I have said, it was all very accurate information, I merely took some artistic licence in my presentation of the information.

You managed to write four perfectly accurate books prior to this. Four books with no 'artistic licence'.

And perhaps they weren't as good!

How is it that your relationship with the truth came to change around the construction of this book?

Well, the third and fourth books didn't do very well. I took that seriously. I've always been very inspired by writers like Capote and Gordon Burn and Brian Masters and I wanted to elevate the material the way they had.

Masters and Burn didn't make things up, though.

Okay, but Capote did. Granted his book was published in 1966 – it was easier to get away with it then. I think people had more respect for the authority of the writer then.

There's a lot to unpack there. Do you think your narrative authority should excuse you? Have you reflected much on the damage the book did to those who took part? Amanda Black, in particular, has expressed distress at your liberal

presentation of the facts and how much sympathy and weight you gave to the perspectives of her daughter's killers.

The thing about Amanda is – the thing I found most admirable about her – is that she also had a lot of sympathy for her daughter's killers. She's never said she wanted them in prison for life, and has always felt they were all let down by the systems around them.

Yes, but you gave so much time to her killers – there were parts of the book where her daughter – her daughter's private life – was presented in an extremely unflattering light. How could any mother, regardless of how much grace she is prepared to extend to her daughter's killers, be happy with that? You essentially made the story of her daughter's murder into an entertaining piece of fiction. It's like you saw a number of primary sources and had contact with people who knew the girls – and you proceeded to more or less write fanfiction about the case. How do you square that with this idea of emotional truth?

Shruti, you know, I really do have to question your integrity as a journalist. I was under the impression I was being interviewed here – not bollocked.

At this point Carelli told me the interview was over. He told me there were no hard feelings – he just didn't have any interest in being lectured by a journalist twenty years his junior. He told me that he refused to be shamed. And perhaps this was part of the issue for Carelli – his refusal to be shamed for the shameful. In a society which is increasingly constructed around the fear and avoidance of public humiliation – the recording and sharing and mocking of failures, mistakes and malicious behaviours – men like Carelli may be ill-suited to a public platform.

As of publication of this article Carelli is facing legal action from Simon Stirling-Stewart for defamation, and from Amanda Black for emotional distress. Carelli is also currently being investigated by the Crown Prosecution Service for his illegal acquisition of therapeutic materials from two different secure units.

As he left the café, I asked him if he had plans to write another book. He told me to fuck off.

BIBLIOGRAPHY

Works directly referenced in or were especially formative for
the writing of *Penance*:

Kamikaze Biker by Ikuya Sato, 1998, University of Chicago
Press
Man, Play and Games by Roger Caillois, 2001, University
of Illinois Press (originally published in French in 1958)
Savage Appetites by Rachel Monroe, 2020, Scribner
The Nighttime Podcast: 'The Story of Lindsay
Souvannarath', May 2021
MonsterTalk podcast, 'Episode 86: Slenderman & Tulpas' ,
30 July 2014

ACKNOWLEDGEMENTS

Thank you to my partner, George (to whom this book is dedicated), for his unrelenting support over the years I spent working on this book. I'd also like to thank him, particularly, for the stolen anecdotes which made their way into this book.

Thank you to my parents, Ken and Wendy, for their love and support – it's fine for them to read this one, if they so choose.

I'm hugely grateful to those who helped bring this novel to publication, namely my literary agent Rachel Mann at JULA, and Charlotte Colwill, who seamlessly filled Rachel's role during her maternity leave. Additionally, the team at Faber: Libby Marshall and Louisa Joyner, as well as Sara Helen Binney. I would also like to thank Marc Simonsson and MMB for all their work.

Thank you to the staff at Arvon for their friendship, kindness and accommodation during my two and a half years of employment there. The organisation's flexibility and care was invaluable to the timely completion of this book.

Thank you to David and Maria Royle (George's parents), whose support over lockdown was invaluable, and who were kind enough to take me for a day out around Scarborough for my research. Thank you also to my friends – in person and online; old and new – who kept me (relatively) sane over lockdown, listened to me complain and supplied love and laughter as we were reunited in person.

Thank you to everyone who read, reviewed or posted about *Boy Parts* – and to Influx Press for publishing it. Having a book published in 2020 was an incredibly surreal experience and I'm so grateful to those of you who reached out to me, and helped make the experience a bit less weird.

I am, as always, forever in debt to New Writing North for selecting me for their life-changing Young Writers' Talent Fund. None of the extraordinary changes in my life over the last few years would have been possible without New Writing North and I will never be able to thank them enough.